TRAGIC MAGIC

Tragic Magic

LAURA CHILDS

BERKLEY PRIME CRIME, NEW YORK

THE BERKLEY PUBLISHING GROUP
Published by the Penguin Group
Penguin Group (USA) Inc.
375 Hudson Street, New York, New York 10014, USA
Penguin Group (Canada), 90 Eglinton Avenue East, Suite 700, Toronto, Ontario M4P 2Y3, Canada
(a division of Pearson Penguin Canada Inc.)
Penguin Books Ltd., 80 Strand, London WC2R 0RL, England
Penguin Group Ireland, 25 St. Stephen's Green, Dublin 2, Ireland (a division of Penguin Books Ltd.)
Penguin Group (Australia), 250 Camberwell Road, Camberwell, Victoria 3124, Australia
(a division of Pearson Australia Group Pty. Ltd.)
Penguin Books India Pvt. Ltd., 11 Community Centre, Panchsheel Park, New Delhi—110 017, India
Penguin Group (NZ), 67 Apollo Drive, Rosedale, North Shore 0632, New Zealand
(a division of Pearson New Zealand Ltd.)
Penguin Books (South Africa) (Pty.) Ltd., 24 Sturdee Avenue, Rosebank, Johannesburg 2196,
South Africa

Penguin Books Ltd., Registered Offices: 80 Strand, London WC2R 0RL, England

This book is an original publication of The Berkley Publishing Group.

This is a work of fiction. Names, characters, places, and incidents either are the product of the author's imagination or are used fictitiously, and any resemblance to actual persons, living or dead, business establishments, events, or locales is entirely coincidental. The publisher does not have any control over and does not assume any responsibility for author or third-party websites or their content.

PUBLISHER'S NOTE: The recipes contained in this book are to be followed exactly as written. The publisher is not responsible for your specific health or allergy needs that may require medical supervision. The publisher is not responsible for any adverse reactions to the recipes contained in this book.

Copyright © 2009 by Gerry Schmitt & Associates, Inc.
Interior text design by Kristin del Rosario

FIRST EDITION: October 2009

Library of Congress Cataloging-in-Publication Data
Childs, Laura.
    Tragic magic / Laura Childs. —1st ed.
       p. cm.
    ISBN 978-0-425-22989-7
1. Murder—Investigation—Fiction. 2. New Orleans (La.)—Fiction. I. Title.
    PS3603.H56T73 2009
    813'.6—dc22   2009023622

PRINTED IN THE UNITED STATES OF AMERICA

10 9 8 7 6 5 4 3 2 1

To Jerry Langsweirdt,
my high school English teacher.

If you hadn't been there, I wouldn't be here.

Acknowledgments

Heartfelt thanks to Sam, Tom, Lance, Jennie, and Bob. And a huge thank-you to all my readers as well as the many scrapbook magazines, Web sites, reviewers, scrapbooking shops, and bookstores who have been so very kind and supportive.

TRAGIC MAGIC

Chapter 1

"THAT'S the place," said Carmela Bertrand. Clambering from her car, she pointed at the enormous three-story mansion that loomed in the darkness like some ghostly fun house tilting recklessly on its foundation. "Medusa Manor." She pushed back a tangle of caramel-colored hair and peered through naked branches with eyes that were the same shifting blue-gray color as the Gulf of Mexico. The sharp outline of turrets, finials, and gables against a faint smudge of pink in the darkening March sky made the old mansion look like it had been rubber-stamped on a piece of midnight-blue vellum from Carmela's scrapbooking shop.

Another pair of legs, these a little longer and clad in black leather, emerged from Carmela's red two-seater Mercedes. Then the rest of Ava Gruiex's shapely body followed. "Spooky," replied Ava. Gazing at the old mansion, she pulled her sweater closer around her and let loose a little shiver.

"That's the whole idea," Carmela replied. "Melody wants

Medusa Manor to be a premier attraction for all the ghost hunters, vampire wannabes, and cemetery fans who flock to New Orleans."

"And tell me again, *cher*, why we got pulled in?" asked Ava.

Carmela turned to face her friend, and this time a smile danced on her lovely oval face that had been enhanced ever so slightly with a daub of Chanel's Teint Innocence. "Because Melody's set designer quit last week and everybody else is locked up a year in advance with Mardi Gras projects."

"You mean everybody with experience," laughed Ava. Her lethal-length red fingernails pushed back a tousle of dark, curly hair, and then she carefully gathered the neckline of her red glitter skull T-shirt and adjusted it downward.

"Hey," enthused Carmela, "we've got *beaucoup* qualifications! I own Memory Mine, and you own Juju Voodoo."

"Career gals," giggled Ava. "Just put us on the cover of *Ms. Magazine*."

"Do you actually read *Ms. Magazine*?" Carmela asked.

"Only if they've got articles about movie stars and stuff," said Ava. "But mostly I get my hard news from the *Inquisitor*. I always want to know who's hiding dimples of cellulite under that red-carpet gown, who's had their tummy stitched up, and who's jabbin' Botox into their wrinkles and crinkles." Even though both women were not quite thirty and still gorgeous, they were keenly aware of the progression of time and its ensuing consequences.

"Ouch," said Carmela as she peered at her watch, then started up the walk. "We're late, better pick up the pace. Melody's gonna wonder what happened to us."

"Just tell her Boo and Poobah had veterinarian appointments and I . . ."

"Couldn't decide what to wear?" finished Carmela, who knew her friend was in a perpetual state of wardrobe flux.

Ava nodded. "Sounds reasonable to me."

"Of course it does," said Carmela. Carmela was well

aware that she had a decidedly practical, slightly conservative bent. Witness all those black and beige outfits hanging in her closet and the lack of foot-numbing four-inch heels. Carmela also tried to keep wild shopping splurges down to a minimum, and when she promised to be somewhere at seven, she morphed into a nail-nibbling clock watcher. Couldn't help herself.

Her dear friend, Ava, on the other hand, was completely laissez-faire. Bills piled up, checking accounts were overdrawn, and when Ava made a commitment, the appointed time could easily slide a half hour either way, depending on her mood. Ava even hated getting pinned down on airline reservations and always requested a flight that was "noonish."

"Cher," drawled Ava, as they tromped up the front walk to the mansion's enormous double doors, "this place is practically falling down! And I expect to see a contingent of bats circling the towers."

Ava was spot on about that. The dilapidated old mansion in the artsy Faubourg Marigny section of New Orleans was a wreck. Heat, humidity, and rain had pummeled the wooden exterior, stripping any semblance of paint and rendering it a weathered silver-gray. The front verandah had a dangerous list to it, like a Tilt-A-Whirl car that had jumped its track. A tangle of weeds, crepe myrtle, and azaleas, as well as an overgrowth of banana trees, obscured the front yard. Curls of kudzu ran rampant up one side of the mansion.

But Carmela also knew this air of abandonment would surely be part of the building's draw. This was New Orleans, after all. A city renowned for its aboveground cities of the dead, ghostly specters, voodoo queens, and haunted bayous dripping with Spanish moss. Hadn't the Travel Channel even profiled a couple of French Quarter restaurants and hotels on their *America's Most Haunted* show? Sure they had. If they'd pronounced New Orleans to be seriously haunted, to be populated by ghosts and spirits, then it must be so.

"Melody's supposed to meet us here?" asked Ava. Squinting into a lipstick-sized mirror, she was attempting to fluff her hair and apply a second coat of mascara at the same time.

"Supposed to," said Carmela, making a note of the thorny overgrowth and tumbledown wrought-iron fence. The atmosphere was definitely early Addams Family. So where the heck was Morticia? Or her trusty sidekick, Lurch?

"Place looks deserted, probably *is* deserted," said Ava. Now a slight hesitancy had crept into her voice.

"Nah," said Carmela, as they stepped onto the verandah. "Melody's here. Look, the door's open." Indeed, the large wooden door was cracked open an inch or so.

Carmela put a hand on a corroded bronze knocker, a querulous-looking raven, then pulled it back and let it drop. A hollow thud seemed to echo through the house, then boomerang back at them. It was a heckuva welcome.

"You sure Melody's in there?" asked Ava. Balancing on one leg, she slid one foot out of her four-inch-high red mules and wiggled her brightly painted toes. "New shoes," she muttered. "Kinda pinchy."

Carmela's fingertips touched the inches-open door and pressed gently. The door swung slowly inward, letting loose a hollow groan. "Great sound effect," she murmured.

Ava slid by Carmela, then suddenly stopped dead in her tracks. One hand flew to her throat; the other reached back to catch Carmela's arm in a murderous grip.

"What?" asked Carmela, wondering what had shaken her friend. *"What?"* But as her eyes slowly grew accustomed to the dark of the interior, she was able to discern the lump sitting in front of them. Long, angular, metallic, with a rounded top.

Oh," said Carmela. And for the first time, she herself felt a quick pang of nervousness about this project.

"A coffin," said Ava in a raspy voice.

"It's a . . . haunted house," said Carmela. She tried to put a little oomph in her voice, and failed miserably.

"I get that," said Ava, beginning to recover. "And I'm okay with stuff like skeletons and voodoo dolls and shrunken heads. I *deal* with that shit all day long. But actual people coffins kind of weird me out."

"But you like vampires," said Carmela.

Ava's shoulders moved up an inch. "Well . . . yeah. Sure. Doesn't everybody?"

Carmela shook her head in amusement. "You are so off the hook, Ava." Taking a few steps forward, she touched a hand to the coffin lid and drummed her fingers lightly. *Like whistling in a graveyard?* she wondered. *Yeah, maybe.* "So this shouldn't be a problem, huh?" she asked Ava.

"'Spose not," said Ava. She hesitated. "You're right, I'm getting used to the idea." She exhaled slowly. "Yeah. I'm okay now."

"Excellent," said Carmela. She lifted her eyes and gazed around the once-grand parlor that was now merely cavernous. Tattered velvet drapes that had once been mauve but were now merely drab hung in despondent swags across tall, narrow windows. A threadbare Oriental carpet covered the sagging wooden floor. An enormous ornate chandelier dangled overhead, dingy now and without any luster, but probably a magnificent piece once the crystals had been soaked in ammonia and distilled water and gently scrubbed. "This place really is Medusa Manor," Carmela marveled.

Ava glanced around, taking in the decayed splendor of the room. "Crazy," she muttered.

"Look at that enormous marble fireplace," Carmela pointed out. "And the ornate mirror over there. See how wavery our image is? How old is that mirror? What do you suppose it's seen? How old is this *place?*"

"Hundred years," Ava guessed. "Hundred and fifty?"

"I think so," said Carmela, whose interest in the project was suddenly growing by leaps and bounds. "We could work wonders with this old mansion. Transform it into a spectacular haunted house!"

Ava thought for a minute, then gestured toward one dingy, plum-colored wall. "Rows of white ceramic skulls, maybe five high, eight across, all mounted in shadow boxes. With flickering candles inside them."

"The coffin pushed up against that far window," said Carmela. "Flanked by enormous brass candlesticks."

"And buckets of roses?" said Ava.

"Maybe just long stems of thorns."

They turned in tandem, noticing the curving staircase for the first time.

"I'm seein' a dangling skeleton up there, *cher*," said Ava. "And maybe a floating head or two. Got to have a disembodied head."

"Love it," breathed Carmela. She was pleased that Ava seemed to have gotten past her coffin phobia.

"So what's the deal?" asked Ava. "Melody and her gang would lead people through here in groups of eight or ten?"

Carmela nodded. "That's Melody's plan exactly." Melody was Melody Mayfeldt. She and her husband, Garth, owned Fire and Ice Jewelers in the French Quarter. Melody was also queen bee and organizer of the newly formed Demilune Mardi Gras krewe, one of the few all-female krewes. Carmela and Ava were members of Demilune and had tossed beads from their three-tiered blue-and-gold float this past Mardi Gras.

"So . . . where's Melody?" asked Ava, frowning. "We've already got some good ideas. Now we gotta huddle with her."

"Melody," said Carmela, absently. "She knew we were coming. I just spoke with her an hour ago."

"Came and left?" said Ava.

"But the door was cracked open."

Ava walked to the foot of the staircase and called out "Melody!" at the top of her lungs.

Echoes floated back to them. But no Melody materialized.

Ava inclined her head. "Upstairs fussing around? Can't hear us?"

The two women climbed the sweeping staircase. When they reached the second-floor landing, they saw a myriad of footprints tracking across dusty floorboards, but that was all.

Ava called again. Then Carmela called. Then Ava again.

No answer came back save the hiss of the night wind rattling through fireplace flues and attic rafters.

"She's not here," said Carmela. "Darn." Now she felt a little timid about invading this slightly strange building. "We'll have to come back later."

"Maybe in the light of day," suggested Ava. "When we can see things a little better."

They descended the stairs and gave a cursory look around. Still no sign of Melody.

"Face it," said Ava, "she's not here."

"Must have been a problem at the store," said Carmela.

Ava shrugged. "Oh well."

They moved out onto the front verandah, hesitant about abandoning their meeting. Then Carmela decided there was nothing more they could do, so she pulled the front door closed behind her.

"This neighborhood is changing," Ava observed as they headed down the sidewalk toward the car.

"Getting gentrified," said Carmela. "Lots of gumbo joints, jazz bars, and sexy boutiques moving in."

"Pretty soon it'll look like Magazine Street," put in Ava. "Although that's not all—"

Carmela suddenly gripped Ava's arm.

"What?" asked Ava, pausing in her tracks to stare at her friend.

Carmela held up a single finger, shook her head to silence Ava, then glanced back at the house. She'd heard something. At least she *thought* she'd heard something. Or was she just being jumpy and imagining things?

Was she going to get spooked once they had to buckle

down and start designing sets and theatrics? When they had to put together the Chamber of Despair or the Theatre of Lost Souls? Those were ideas Melody had mentioned to her. Carmela had been noodling a half dozen more.

A low, muffled cry floated on the night air, and Carmela knew in a heartbeat this wasn't her imagination. Then the cry morphed into a scream that began slowly and built in agonizing intensity. A terrifying banshee's wail . . . or the sound of someone being . . .

Glass suddenly exploded overhead, causing Carmela and Ava to spin on their heels. Looking up, they were staggered to see a blinding flash in the third-floor tower room of Medusa Manor, as if an incendiary bomb had just been detonated! Then shards of glass rained down and, like some unholy nightmare visage, a flaming body hurtled though the broken window! Arms spread wide, flames swirling about its head, the apparition took on the appearance of an avenging angel!

Carmela watched in horror as the body tumbled downward, almost in slow motion. She let out her own cry of despair as Ava fell to her knees beside her and screamed, "Oh my Lord! Medusa Manor really *is* haunted!"

Chapter 2

BLUE and red strobes from police cruisers lit the old neighborhood. The bleat of an ambulance racked the air. Neighbors ventured tentatively out from their small, West Indies–style cottages, disrupted by the screams, the explosion, the cacophony of it all. But the damage had already been done.

A charred body, covered with a flimsy, fluttering blanket, lay sprawled on the cracked sidewalk. A sputtering gaslight overhead lent drama to the bizarre scene.

"It wasn't a haunting," Carmela told Ava as her friend sat huddled and sniffling on a cement step next to a wickedly pointed wrought-iron fence.

Carmela had spoken with the first responders immediately, attempting to give them a careful eyewitness account. Then she'd repeated her story, adding a few more remembered details when Detective Edgar Babcock arrived on the scene. His demeanor had been properly sympathetic even as he remained focused and businesslike. This was a crime

scene, after all. He was in charge. The fact that Edgar Babcock enjoyed a personal relationship with Carmela wasn't
about to interfere with his work.

"What . . . ?" began Ava. Her eyes were rimmed with
dark eye makeup that had mingled with tears, giving her
the look of a sad raccoon.

"It was more like . . . murder," Carmela whispered.

Ava's face transformed from ashen to stark white. "Oh no.
And they're sure it's . . . ?" She couldn't bear to finish her
sentence.

Carmela gave a grim nod. "I'm afraid so." She tried to
form more words, but her mouth felt like it was stuffed with
cotton. She licked her lips and cleared her throat. "They're
pretty sure, *I'm* pretty sure, it was Melody."

Ava dropped her head in her hands. "Awful," she murmured. "Simply awful."

Carmela sat down beside Ava and lifted a hand to knead
the back of her friend's neck.

Ava relaxed slightly at Carmela's touch, then raised her
head and gazed mournfully at the blanket that covered the
pathetically charred figure of Melody Mayfeldt.

"Who would do this?" she asked.

Carmela shook her head. "No idea."

"A monster," whispered Ava.

Carmela simply nodded. There seemed to be no shortage
of monsters stalking the world these days. In New Orleans,
the murder rate had skyrocketed to around two hundred
fifty per year, making New Orleans the bloodiest city in the
United States. Not so good. Especially if you called the Big
Easy home.

"Your detective friend is here," said Ava, finally noticing
Babcock. "Taking charge, I guess."

Carmela gazed over at Edgar Babcock. Tall and lanky, he
moved slowly and languidly like a big cat with a reserve of
coiled energy. As though he could pounce at any moment.
His ginger-colored hair was cropped short, his blue eyes were

pinpricks of intensity, he was clean-cut and square-jawed. Interestingly enough, Babcock was also a bit of a clothes-horse, always dressing extremely well. Tonight he wore a summer-weight wool tweed jacket, dark slacks, and elegant leather slip-on loafers that just might be from Prada.

Carmela lightly touched two fingers to her heart. "Thank goodness Babcock got the call out."

"If anybody can find Melody's killer, he can," said Ava, her voice still shaking. "Babcock's tenacious."

"A pit bull," agreed Carmela.

Carmela and Ava sat in silence watching Edgar Babcock in discussion with two African American men in navy-blue EMT uniforms. The EMTs listened to him, offered a few words back, then gave grim nods as they turned back to their rig to grab a gurney. Babcock stood there alone, letting his eyes slowly reconnoiter the crime scene, making sure his officers and the crime-scene unit were handling their assigned tasks. Then he put hands on narrow hips, bowed his head for a few moments, seemingly to compose himself, and walked slowly toward them.

Ava lifted a hand in greeting. "Hey," she said, without much enthusiasm.

Babcock stooped down to be at their level, and Carmela heard his knee joints pop. *Not so young anymore*, she thought. Then again, who was? Even though she was barely pushing thirty, she had a failed marriage to contend with, a business that was just barely profitable, and two dogs to care for. And she was part of an intrepid band of News Orleans residents whose city was *still* experiencing fallout from Hurricane Katrina, some four years later.

Carmela no longer felt the careless abandon of youth. Now she carried some baggage with her.

"If it's any consolation," Babcock said, speaking to them quietly and in confidence, "your friend was probably dead before . . . well . . . before she was thrown from that third-floor tower window and landed on the street below."

Carmela gave him a wary look. "You're positive Melody didn't burn to death?"

Edgar Babcock grimaced. "No, no, she didn't," he said, hastily. "From what I could determine, and from what the EMT guys are telling me, there appears to have been some type of gunshot or explosion—we're not sure what exactly— that resulted in a traumatic and fatal head wound."

Ava gazed at Carmela with saucer eyes. "Someone was inside Medusa Manor with us. I knew it!"

"Possibly," said Babcock. "We can't say for sure yet."

"You've searched the house?" asked Carmela. "Set up a . . ." She struggled to find the right word. "Set up a perimeter?"

"Absolutely," Babcock assured her.

"And you're positive the killer's not still in there?" asked Ava. She glanced back at the house, a little fearfully.

"Well," said Babcock, "we've conducted a fairly thorough search, even though your Medusa Manor's a very strange place. I mean, there are coffins and piles of junk everywhere, and video equipment hidden in the walls. There's also an actual hearse parked in the underground garage. If the killer is still in there, he's very well hidden."

"Melody's killer," muttered Carmela. She let her mind wander back to happier times with her friend, enjoying a fleeting memory of Melody Mayfeldt sitting atop the Demilune float this past Mardi Gras. Wearing a blue-and-silver tunic, she'd tossed armloads of beads to crazed paradegoers who were thronged twenty deep. Melody had been ecstatically happy that wild and magical night. And now here she was. Dead.

Carmela glanced at the crowd that had gathered in earnest now. Lots of curious people. Some taking photos; a woman writing furiously in a notebook; another man, a tall, thin man, kicking at things on the ground with his foot. She frowned, wondering who all these gawkers were, suddenly depressed that they'd seemingly crawled out of the woodwork. Then she pulled herself back to reality as Babcock began asking questions.

"So you two were inside the house?" Babcock asked.

Carmela and Ava both gave silent nods.

"Did you see or hear anything strange?" he asked. "Aside from the . . . coffins and such."

They both shook their heads no.

Babcock's forehead wrinkled, and he held up a hand. "Don't answer so quickly," he told them. "Take some time, give this serious consideration. What you might recall as a small detail could be important in the long run. You might think something is incidental, but when we start putting all the clues together your input could be quite helpful."

"The first thing that comes to mind," said Carmela, "is that the door was open when we arrived."

"Standing all the way open or cracked open a little bit?" Babcock asked.

Carmela held her thumb and forefinger up to show him. "An inch. Maybe two inches."

"Okay," said Babcock, nodding encouragement, "and when you went inside, what did you see?"

"Coffin," said Ava. "Big bronze honker parked front and center."

"Did you look inside?" asked Babcock. "Did you lift the lid?"

"No!" said Ava.

Carmela gave a start. "You think someone was in there? Hiding inside the coffin?"

"We don't know," said Babcock. "We have to collect the data before we can process it."

"You make it sound like you're some kind of computer analyst," said Ava, sounding huffy. "Why don't you just give us a straight answer?"

Babcock struggled a little to keep his cool. "Because we don't have any answers yet. But we will. I promise you we will." He glanced down at the spiral-bound notepad in his hand. "Did you know the victim's husband?"

"You mean *Melody's* husband?" said Ava.

"Of course we knew him," said Carmela. "Garth owns Fire and Ice Jewelers in the French Quarter." She paused. "Actually, Garth and Melody own it together. Owned it."

Babcock jotted something in his notebook.

"What?" Carmela asked sharply. "You couldn't possibly suspect Garth?"

Babcock shrugged. "He's probably not a viable suspect, unless he's unbelievably quick and was able to get back to his shop without being seen. But it appears that Garth Mayfeldt *was* at his shop when all this took place. Of course, we have to check him out anyway."

"Does Garth know about . . . um . . . Melody yet?" Carmela asked.

Babcock cocked his head and stared back at her. "He does now. I sent one of my guys over there right away."

"Have you talked to your guy yet?" asked Carmela. "How did Garth take it?"

"How do you *think* the husband took it?" asked Babcock in a slightly hoarse voice. "He completely freaked."

"Oh dear," murmured Carmela.

A squeal of brakes sounded in the street, and Babcock glanced over his shoulder. A frown passed across his face. "Jackals are here," he muttered.

"Huh?" said Ava.

"Reporters," said Babcock. He stood up and gave Carmela and Ava a cursory glance. "Don't talk to them, okay?"

"Okay," said Carmela as he stalked away.

"Hey," said Ava, suddenly recognizing a familiar face. "There's Toby LaChaise." Toby was a reporter for the *Times-Picayune* and harbored a not-so-secret crush on Ava. She raised a hand. "Say hey, Toby!"

A grin split Toby's face when he recognized her. "Ava!" he called, cutting through a crush of people and picking his way toward her.

"Don't say too much, okay?" said Carmela. She patted Ava's shoulder, stood up, and eased herself away. She pushed through the crowd of gawkers, letting her eyes search for Edgar Babcock. There was one thing she'd forgotten to ask him. The blinding flash of light she'd seen just before Melody's body came hurtling down. What had it been? Some sort of explosion or incendiary device?

And, truth be told, there was something else on Carmela's mind, too. Although she felt guilty about asking Babcock, she wondered if she'd be seeing him later tonight. If, when all this terrible business was wrapped up as best as possible, he'd come over and play snuggle partner with her. She was beginning to seriously crave the man.

If she could just get him alone for a couple of seconds . . .

A horrendously bright light suddenly shone directly in Carmela's face. She blinked hard, threw up a hand, and instinctively recognized the intrusive red eye of a KBEZ-TV video camera. There was another flurry of activity and then a woman with an enormous blond bouffant hairdo and impossibly tight red suit stepped into the spotlight, posed prettily, and held a microphone to her collagen-enhanced lips.

"Kimber Breeze," muttered Carmela. She'd had run-ins with this woman before, and they'd always ended badly. Someone, a rather wise man, had famously quoted, "never argue with people who buy ink by the gallon." That same advice could just as easily be applied to dealing with TV reporters like Kimber or any other type of paparazzi. Talk to them, say a little too much, or give the wrong impression, and your name, face, and/or sound bite would be instantly captured and transmitted to the far corners of the world where it would probably remain floating in cyberspace until the end of time.

Carmela stepped into the shadows and watched as Kimber Breeze bulldozed her way through the crowd and right up to a woman who was wrapped in an expensive-looking white trench coat and sobbing into a hanky. Kimber flashed her megawatt smile at the woman, then thrust her microphone into the woman's face. But the woman gave a terse shake of her head and turned away.

Not to be defeated, Kimber tried again. This time a uniformed police officer stepped in to intercede. Carmela could hear Kimber's angry protests all the way over here and wondered who the woman was. Maybe Melody's silent partner? The woman who'd put up all the money for Medusa Manor?

"Hey," said Ava, at Carmela's elbow now. "We should get out of here, yeah?"

Carmela agreed. "Now that the media's on the scene, it's really gonna get crazy."

"And nasty," said Ava. "That piece of blond trash is Kimber Breeze, isn't it?"

"Afraid so," said Carmela as she and Ava slipped down the sidewalk toward her car. Another TV van had just screeched to a halt, and now those people were jumping out like rabid paratroopers, shouldering lights and cameras, hoping to capture some grisly footage for the ten o'clock news.

"Turning into a circus," noted Ava, as they climbed into Carmela's car.

Carmela backed away gingerly from a white van that was tucked a little too close to her, nosed away from the curb, then negotiated a tight U-turn. As she was about to pull away, Carmela saw Edgar Babcock standing on the boulevard talking to one of the newly arrived TV reporters. Carmela noted that Babcock looked slightly harried in a tensed-up, in-the-middle-of-a-murder-investigation sort of way. He also looked as handsome as ever. Touching her brake, she eased over to the curb. "Hey," she called to him.

Babcock looked over at her and raised his eyebrows in acknowledgment. He held up a single finger to the reporter, then strode over to talk with Carmela.

"I can't stop by tonight," were his first words.

"I understand," said Carmela. She knew the job came first. Especially this job.

"Call you tomorrow," he told her.

Carmela nodded. She was just starting to pull away when she called back to him. "Hey."

Babcock stopped in his tracks.

"If Melody was already dead," said Carmela, "why would her killer set her body on fire and toss it out the window?"

Babcock looked thoughtful for a few seconds. "Don't know," he replied. "Maybe . . ." He shrugged, searching for words. "To scare you?"

Chapter 3

"YOU don't have to heat up that delicious andouille sausage gumbo just on my account," Ava told her. "But I'm glad you are." She lounged on one of the cane chairs that were bunched around the dining table in Carmela's French Quarter apartment. The charming one-bedroom unit was situated directly across the courtyard from Juju Voodoo and Ava's own apartment tucked directly above it.

"Cooking's no problem," said Carmela. "You look like you need a little fortification and I'm absolutely starving." She glanced down at Boo and Poobah. The two dogs were milling about excitedly, trying to be enticingly cute. "You two have already eaten enormous dinners," she told them. "You're done for the night. Finished. Kaput."

Boo, a red fawn Shar-Pei with an expressive, wrinkled face, stared up at Carmela with pleading eyes that said, *Please! I'm so hungry, almost on the brink of starvation!* Poobah, a shaggy black-and-white Heinz 57 dog with a ragged ear, lay down quietly, happy to let Boo carry on her hard lobbying for extra helpings.

"How about a mystery muffin?" Carmela asked. She dangled a plastic bag full of muffins for Ava to see. "They're frozen, but I can pop 'em in the microwave."

"Are they the ones made with mayonnaise?" asked Ava. "From your momma's recipe?"

"Mm-hm," said Carmela.

"Got any of your fabulous brown sugar butter to go with 'em?" asked Ava.

"Yes, I do," said Carmela. "And we're going to need some wine, too. Yes, I definitely think we need wine." She dug around in her refrigerator and grabbed the brown sugar butter and an already opened bottle of Chardonnay.

"Excellent idea," said Ava, jumping up immediately to grab a pair of crystal wineglasses. "Help calm our nerves."

"A digestif," said Carmela, pouring the wine. "That was some awful scene tonight." They clinked their glasses together, and each took a fortifying gulp.

"Never seen anything like it," declared Ava.

"Melody was such a dear person," Carmela murmured. "I can't imagine she had an enemy in the world."

Ava took another gulp of wine, let loose a tiny, genteel burp, then said, "Melody wasn't exactly Miss Popularity with some of the men's Mardi Gras krewes. Remember when she applied for the Demilune float to roll on Fat Tuesday? Lots of vigorous opposition."

Carmela thought about Ava's words for a moment. "But not enough to kill her for." She sighed. "Too bad we still haven't made it past all that male chauvinist shit."

"It's the South, honey," said Ava. "Lots of stuff folks can't get past."

Carmela ladled her sausage gumbo into red Fiestaware bowls, then added extra scoops of steaming-hot red beans. She set the bowls on yellow plates and snugged her mystery muffins into a wicker basket lined with a white cloth napkin. She pulled knives, forks, and spoons from kitchen drawers, and then Ava helped her ferry everything to the mahogany dining room table that formed a sort of demarcation line between Carmela's tidy kitchen and the slightly belle époque–style living room.

Since bidding *sayonara* to her soon-to-be-ex-husband Shamus Meechum, Carmela had made a concentrated effort to create an elegant, posh apartment for herself that was long on comfort. Countless forays through the scratch-and-dent rooms of Royal Street antique shops had yielded a brocade fainting couch, marble coffee table, squishy leather chair with ottoman, ornate gilded mirror, and a marble bust of Napoleon with a slightly chipped nose. Lengths of antique wrought iron that had once graced antebellum balconies now hung on her redbrick walls—perfect shelves for pottery, bronze dog statues, and her collection of antique children's books.

Carmela's bedroom-bathroom suite held a queen-sized bed covered with plush velvet pillows that she'd hand-stamped with romantic designs. There were also two cushy dog beds and an antique vanity table that had narrow drawers on both sides and a huge round mirror in the middle.

"Delish," proclaimed Ava, scraping her spoon against the bottom of her bowl.

"There's more beans if you want," said Carmela. "Or . . . we could have dessert. I have a cocoa loco pie."

"Homemade?" asked Ava.

Carmela smiled. "It's my home and I made it, so . . . sure."

"Let's do pie and wine," said Ava. She paused and looked at Carmela. "Gee, you're being sweet about all this. I know I wasn't much help earlier tonight. I did get slightly hysterical."

"I can't imagine what you could have done," said Carmela. "What anyone could have done. Before we could process what was happening, Melody was dead." She shook her head and muttered, "Bizarre."

"Too bad Babcock's not coming over tonight," said Ava. "You could try to pry some details out of him."

"He was playing it awfully close to the vest," said Carmela, "so I don't know what good it would be. Besides . . . even if I knew something, what could I do?"

Ava frowned slightly as she considered Carmela's question. "You're telling me you're not gonna get involved? You *always* get involved."

Carmela wrinkled her nose. "I wish you wouldn't say that."

"That was a compliment, *cher*, because you're so good at figuring stuff out. At solving actual crimes."

Carmela hunched over her glass of wine. "Oh, I wouldn't go so far as to say that."

"Well, I would," replied Ava. "Besides, Melody was our friend. And we were right there. Eyewitnesses. So it feels like our civic duty to get involved."

"Somehow," said Carmela, "I had a feeling you were going to say that." She gathered up plates and bowls, carried them to the counter, and stacked them in the dishwasher. A few minutes later she returned with slices of cocoa loco pie. "Shall we retire to the salon?" she asked.

Carmela and Ava nibbled pie and sipped wine while Boo and Poobah lay at their feet and fretted.

"You're not going to get a single bite," Carmela told Boo. "Chocolate is toxic to dogs. If I've told you once, I've told you . . ."

"Hey," said Ava. "I forgot to tell you. Thea Toliver delivered the prom dresses earlier today."

"Delivered them where?" asked Carmela. "To your shop?"

"Oh yeah," said Ava. "There's like a million dresses jammed in my office. Its like . . . frilly sardines." The food and wine were helping Ava relax.

"Oh man," said Carmela.

Several months ago, Carmela and Ava had heard about a group of women in Alabama who'd collected gently worn prom dresses and given them away, at no charge, to young women who couldn't afford dresses. They'd loved the idea so much, they'd decided this would be a fun, worthwhile thing to do. Since Hurricane Katrina, many families were still scrimping on small luxuries in order to pay for basics and fund household repairs—so prom dresses were still unaffordable for lots of young women.

Carmela and Ava had approached retail stores and bridal shops and even tapped friends to donate their daughter's gently worn dresses. Much to their surprise and delight, their idea had been met with overwhelming support. A local radio station, WNOL, had even picked up the story, doing an on-air interview with them as well as follow-up mentions. In no time at all, donated prom dresses had come pouring in, maybe even more dresses than they really needed. Two weeks from now, they were scheduled to distribute the prom dresses to young women at several area high schools.

"We're gonna have to go through those dresses one by one," said Ava. "Some are in phenomenal shape and a few are kinda ratty."

"Sort through them and toss out any bummers," said Carmela. "Sure, we can do that." She grabbed the remote control and aimed it at the flat-screen TV that hung on the wall.

Ava nodded, then turned her attention to the TV. "Think there'll be somethin' on about Melody and Medusa Manor?"

"I'm positive there will," said Carmela. "You saw Kimber Breeze flying around like the Wicked Witch of the West on her broomstick? She was practically frothing at the mouth."

"Like an ambulance chaser," said Ava.

When a picture bloomed on the screen, Carmela hit a few buttons and switched to KBEZ-TV.

"News is coming on now," said Ava. "I didn't realize it was so late."

Carmela and Ava watched as neon lights zoomed around the KBEZ-TV logo like chase lights on a movie marquee. Then Ben Bright, the ten o'clock anchor, leaned forward with his blow-combed hair and faux-serious, trust-me expression. "We lead off tonight's news with a bizarre tale of murder in our community . . ."

A graphic of Medusa Manor suddenly popped on screen.

"That's it!" yelped Ava.

Carmela fumbled for the remote again and jacked up the sound.

A head shot of Kimber Breeze filled the screen. "The scene, a haunted house," began Kimber in a hard-edged, staccato voice. "The victim, a woman with a strange attraction to the supernatural."

"Who writes this crap?" asked Ava.

"She does," said Carmela. "Kimber just opens her mouth and dreck pours out."

"Melody Mayfeldt had high hopes that Medusa Manor would become one of the premier haunted-house attractions in the country," Kimber continued. "Now, with her almost ritual murder tonight, those hopes are most surely dashed."

"I don't know if I can take this," muttered Carmela.

"Shhh," said Ava.

With breathless enthusiasm, Kimber Breeze went on to weave a greatly embellished story about Medusa Manor and share with her audience the brutal details of Melody's murder.

"She's making half of it up!" exclaimed Ava.

"She sure is," agreed Carmela. "Most of what she's saying is pure conjecture." She snorted. "Typical."

"Uh-oh," said Ava. "Here's someone who's not conjecture. Sidney St. Cyr. The guy who does the ghost walks in the French Quarter."

Now there were two people on screen: Kimber Breeze

grasping the arm of Sidney St. Cyr, trying to pull him closer into frame.

"Sidney St. Cyr was a good friend of Melody Mayfeldt," said Kimber Breeze. "Our viewers may remember Sidney as the founder of Ghost Walks Inc., the rather unique company that guides visitors on ghost walks through the more haunted parts of the French Quarter as well as our rather infamous cemeteries."

Sidney smiled nervously into the camera. He was tall, thin, and stoop-shouldered, with a slightly beaked nose. Though Sidney was in his midthirties, he projected the air of an older, wearier person.

"He doesn't look happy," said Carmela.

"Looks like Kimber's got him under her thumb," said Ava.

"Tell us, Sidney," said Kimber. "What was your opinion of Melody Mayfeldt's Medusa Manor project?"

Sidney blinked and cleared his throat. "Well, Melody was a great fan of the paranormal. And I think Medusa Manor would have been a terrific attraction."

"Because of the keen interest in haunted houses today," prompted Kimber.

"Yes," said Sidney, who looked even more frozen and stiff now.

"Sidney looks like a Popsicle," remarked Ava.

"Do you actually *know* Sidney?" asked Carmela. She'd seen him a million times, bumping around the French Quarter at night, wearing a flapping black cape and leading a group of camera-toting tourists. But she'd never actually met Sidney face to face.

"I know him a little," said Ava. "Sometimes Sidney brings his tour groups into Juju Voodoo. You know, it's all set up beforehand. We do a tarot reading or toss the *I Ching*, and then his group shops for souvenirs." Ava's shop wares consisted mainly of plastic skulls, small silk bags filled with herbal love charms, saint candles, miniature voodoo dolls, funky jewelry, and various voodoo doodads. All very harmless, but highly appealing to tourists who'd convinced themselves they were getting "the real thing."

"That's nice of him," remarked Carmela.

"Sidney's not that altruistic, honey," said Ava. "He always asks for twenty percent."

"A kickback," said Carmela.

"Sidney prefers to call it a finder's fee," laughed Ava.

"Okay," said Carmela. She nodded toward the TV. Sidney's interview had concluded, and the TV station was running random footage of the crime scene. "Who's the woman in the white trench coat? I saw her earlier tonight, being accosted by Kimber Breeze."

"Don't know," said Ava.

"As we were leaving she was talking to the police and crying," said Carmela.

Kimber Breeze's continued narration conveniently filled in the blanks. "I tried to speak with Olivia Wainwright, the silent partner in Medusa Manor," said Kimber. "But she was unavailable for comment." There was another quick close-up of Olivia Wainwright looking distraught, then she turned her back on the camera.

"So that's Melody's partner," said Carmela. "Melody mentioned a partner, but never told me her name. Of course, I really only had one quick meeting with Melody about decorating Medusa Manor."

"You can bet that project's on ice now," said Ava. "Which means we're out of a job."

"And it would have been fun," said Carmela.

"It would have been good *money*," said Ava. As small-business owners, both women were still slogging along the road to recovery, struggling to return business back to the level where it had been before Hurricane Katrina.

Kimber Breeze's face fairly glowed on the screen now. "Local scrapbook shop owner Carmela Bertrand, wife of Shamus Meechum of the Crescent City Bank chain, was first on the scene to discover the murdered woman," said Kimber. "It's interesting to note that Ms. Bertrand was also involved in a previous murder this past Halloween."

"Oh, that's gonna be helpful for your business," muttered Ava.

"Why did Kimber have to put *that* little factoid in her report?" asked a dumbfounded Carmela.

"Kimber's just yapping away and trying to score as much face time as possible," said Ava. "She adores being on camera."

"But why did she have to mention my name?" fretted Carmela.

"Maybe . . . maybe Kimber's got an ax to grind," said Ava.

Carmela thought for a minute. "That's what scares me."

Chapter 4

"WHEN I heard your name mentioned on the news last night," said Gabby, "I couldn't believe it. I mean, you were really there? You found the actual *dead* body?"

Gabby Mercer-Morris, Carmela's assistant and the wife of Stuart Mercer-Morris, the Toyota King of New Orleans, gaped at Carmela as she fidgeted nervously with the cashmere sweater knotted about her elegant neck. With flowing dark hair and luminous dark eyes, she was a beauty, though even more conservative in taste than Carmela. They'd both just arrived at Memory Mine to open the scrapbooking shop for the day. Of course, Carmela had been hoping to slip in without a huge amount of fanfare, while Gabby was suddenly demanding to hear every single detail.

"I didn't exactly *find* Melody," explained Carmela, biting her lower lip. "It was more a case of her finding *us*."

"They said she fell three stories," said Gabby, in a hushed tone. "From that creepy tower room?"

"Uh, yeah," said Carmela. "Except she was dead first."

Gabby covered her mouth with her hand and let loose a muffled "Oh my." Then her next question was, "Who do you . . . ?"

Carmela shook her head. "No idea."

"You didn't see anyone?" asked Gabby.

"No."

"Hear anything?"

Carmela didn't really want to tell Gabby about the ungodly scream that still seemed to ring in her ears. Instead she said, "Not really."

Gabby slid into a high-backed wooden chair at the large table in the back of the shop, the one they'd dubbed "Craft Central." She flattened both hands on the battered tabletop until they went white and said, "Wow."

"Yeah," agreed Carmela. "I feel the same way."

"You must have really been shaken up," said Gabby. "Probably still are."

"It's been pretty awful," admitted Carmela. "If there's an upside to last night, it was that Edgar Babcock got the call."

"So your sweetie's in charge of the homicide investigation," said Gabby. "That's good. Babcock's really smart. Really tough." Gabby loved the fact that Carmela seemed to have found romance again.

The front door suddenly crashed open, and the silver bell hanging above it *da-dinged* in rapid succession.

"We want details," demanded Tandy Bliss as she flew toward them, carrying her craft bag slung across one shoulder like a pack animal. Tandy was skinny and hyperthyroidal, with a mop of curly red hair and a pair of red half-glasses perpetually dangling around her neck on a silver chain.

Baby Fontaine was right behind her, drumming rapid clack-clacks on the wooden floor with her stiletto heels. "Carmela!" she cried. "Are you okay?" Baby was Garden District society, a blond fifty-something beauty who was a big-bucks donor to the arts and a consummate party giver.

In fact, Baby was notorious for her over-the-top Halloween and Mardi Gras parties. Her husband, Del, was a prominent New Orleans attorney.

The dynamic duo of Tandy and Baby were regulars at Memory Mine. Both were dedicated scrapbookers and crafters who loved nothing more than spending an entire day huddled over a project. If Carmela gave a rubber-stamping class, they were there. When a make-and-take project was on the docket, they were first to arrive. And whenever new paper or ribbon or decals arrived at the shop, Tandy and Baby were offered first dibs.

"Carmela doesn't know all that much about the murder," said Gabby, heading them off.

Tandy and Baby slid to a stop and peered inquisitively at Carmela.

"Sure she does," said Tandy. "She's just not at liberty to talk."

Gabby shifted her gaze to Carmela. "Is that true? Is it because Detective Babcock swore you to secrecy?"

"Your new boyfriend's working the case?" asked Baby. Elegant brows arched over inquiring blue eyes.

"That means Carmela's *really* involved," said Tandy. She put on her half-glasses, let them slide down her nose, and peered expectantly. "Right?"

"Not necessarily," said Baby, answering the question for Carmela. "Carmela's a very smart lady. She doesn't need any conflict in her relationship. She's happy leaving things with Detective Babcock just the way they are, right? Status quo."

Carmela nodded at Baby, not quite answering the question. "Babcock would probably kill me if I got involved."

"Of course he would," grinned Tandy. "But that's not gonna stop you, is it?"

Carmela bent over the table to straighten a stack of vellum. She wasn't saying a word. As far as she was concerned, everything was still very much up in the air.

Twenty minutes later the atmosphere within Memory Mine was considerably more calm. Tandy and Baby were seated at the big table in back working on scrapbook pages. Gabby was up front helping two customers pick through small bags filled with grommets and charms. And Carmela was restocking and straightening shelves.

This was the part of the business Carmela loved, of course. Straightening the colored pens and glue sticks, arranging small packages of embellishments, adding new rubber stamps to their huge wall display, and displaying all the new albums, spools of ribbon, special scissors, and card stock. Because Memory Mine was located in the French Quarter on Governor Nicholls Street, the shop itself boasted tons of charm. Longer than it was wide, the shop featured high ceilings, wide-planked wooden floors, lovely arched front windows, and brick walls.

It was along the longest wall that Carmela had placed the wire paper racks that held thousands of sheets of paper that brought her so much joy. Because Carmela, no secret here, was a bit of a paper addict. She love, love, loved mulberry paper with its infusion of fibers. Then there was Egyptian papyrus, which was always so lineny and gorgeous, and got her creative juices flowing about creating dimensional bags and boxes. Of course, the botanical vellums embedded with real flower petals and the fibery Nepal lokta paper were fabulous, too.

Recently, Carmela had received a small shipment of Indian batik paper. With its rich, dark colors and slightly puckered, accordion affect, she could hardly wait to use it in one of her many projects.

"Carmela," called Tandy. "Do you have any die cuts of military insignia?"

"Army, Navy, Marine, Air Force, or Coast Guard?" asked Carmela.

"Army," said Tandy. "I'm making a scrapbook page to honor my nephew, Dennis, who's over in Iraq right now."

Carmela grabbed a metal dog tag that was stamped *ARMY* and an Army heritage emblem and showed them to Tandy. "Will these work?" she asked.

Tandy grinned. "Will they ever. I've got this great khaki paper and a heart decorated with stars and stripes, but I need a couple more fun elements."

"Glad to be of help," said Carmela. She studied Tandy's layout. The headline read, *All give some, but some give all.* Underneath was a grouping of three photographs, all obviously taken in Iraq. Though Carmela thought the layout was shaping up to be terrific, her heart went out to the men and women who smiled out from those photos. They looked dusty and tired. And a little wary, too. She shook her head to clear it, then turned to study Baby's scrapbook page. "What are you working on?" she asked.

"I'm finally getting around to scrapping my Valentine's Day party," said Baby. "We had the whole family together, so I'm doing a double page."

Baby had started with two twelve-by-twelve sheets of pink-and-white-striped paper and added bits of white lace at the top and bottom. Die-cut hearts framed her photographs, and she'd used a gold pen to form a fanciful, loopy script that read, *Let me call you Sweetheart.*

"What I'm thinking," said Baby, "is maybe gluing candy hearts at the bottom of the page. You know, those hearts with the fun sayings?"

"I like your idea," said Carmela, suddenly aware that the front bell was dinging like crazy and the phone was jangling. "But you might want to give them a coat of Mod Podge."

"Carmela," Gabby called from behind the front counter. "Phone call." She held up the phone, waggling the receiver in her hand.

Carmela hurried to the front and grabbed the phone. She figured it was Babcock. "Yes?"

"Carmela?" said a subdued male voice. "It's Garth."

"Garth!" exclaimed Carmela, spinning around to face a

floor-to-ceiling display of albums. "Oh my gosh, are you okay? Where are you? I was going to call you!"

"I'm at the police station right now," said Garth. And this time the strain was evident in his voice.

"What's going on?" asked Carmela. They weren't trying to beat a confession out of an innocent man, were they?

Garth gave a weak chuckle that turned into a sob. "I'm trying to answer as many questions as possible so the police can get on with the sad business of catching Melody's killer."

"Do you want me to come over there?" Carmela asked. "Can I help you in any way?"

"No, no," said Garth. "I just called to see how you were doing. When Detective Babcock told me you and your friend were there last night, I was completely stunned. Must have been awful for you. Of course, it's awful for all of us, but . . ." Garth Mayfeldt seemed to run out of words.

Carmela grimaced. "You sure you don't want me to run over there?" She knew Babcock would probably hate it, would resent her presence deeply. But if she could be a comfort to Garth, that's what really mattered.

"No," said Garth. "We'll be finished here soon. Olivia is here, too, of course."

"Olivia . . ." said Carmela.

"Olivia Wainwright," said Garth. "Melody's partner. Well, silent partner, really. Olivia was the one putting up the money. I don't exactly . . . uh . . . know what Olivia has in mind. I suppose it's possible she might want to continue with Medusa Manor."

"You think so?" said Carmela. Somehow, it didn't sound like such a good idea. When something had veered that much off course, sometimes it was better to just let it go. Give the bad karma some time to dissipate.

"But I don't know anything for sure," muttered Garth. He seemed to be running out of steam. "Who knows what'll happen? Anyway, I just wanted to see how you were doing. Thank you for being there."

"I didn't do anything," said Carmela. "I wish I—"

"I have to go now," said Garth. "The detectives are back."

"Sure," said Carmela as he hung up. "Good luck with everything."

When Carmela mentioned her conversation with Garth to Tandy and Baby, they nodded sympathetically. When she told them that Garth thought Olivia Wainwright might even want to push ahead with Medusa Manor, they displayed a surprising amount of enthusiasm.

"Oh sure," said Baby. "This is New Orleans, after all. The most haunted city in America."

"Everybody pretty much knows about Sultan's Palace and Père Antoine's Alley," said Tandy, naming a couple of famously haunted places. "Some folks have even seen actual *apparitions*!"

"Don't forget St. Roch Cemetery and Marie Laveau's tomb," added Baby. "Very spooky."

"I think the idea of continuing with Medusa Manor is a little creepy," put in Gabby. The customer hubbub had died down and she'd come back to join them. "After all, Melody was *murdered* there."

"It's creepy, but it's also authentically New Orleans," responded Tandy. "Think about it. A mysterious murder might just add to the mystique of the place."

Gabby fidgeted with a couple of spools of pink gauze ribbon and some miniature silk flowers. "I never thought of it that way."

"Oh, sure," said Tandy. "Medusa Manor might prove to be a very popular place."

Seeing the uncertain looks on Carmela's and Gabby's faces, Baby asked, "Are we still going to work on collage disks today?" It was a project Carmela had mentioned to them last week.

Carmela smiled at Baby, grateful to change the subject. "Sure, if you want to."

"We'll understand if you don't feel like it," said Baby, gracefully giving Carmela an out.

"No," said Carmela, "let's do it. Help take my mind off Melody."

"So," said Gabby, always at the ready to grab supplies. "What do we need?"

"Grab that big box of scrap paper," said Carmela, "and those new angel stickers. And some of the rubber stamps that have smaller images. Oh, and why don't we just bring that entire rack of charms and jewelry findings over here." She reached behind her and grabbed a box from the top of the large flat file, then dumped it on the table. Out spilled a couple of dozen disks that had been punched from white card stock, each about two inches across.

"Okay," said Tandy. "I get that we're going to create miniature collages on these disks. But *then* what do we do with them?"

"That's the fun part," Carmela told her. She held up two collaged disks that she'd made earlier, and the three women breathed a collective "Oh."

Carmela had covered both discs with floral paper and added a tiny snippet of sheet music, a floral sticker, and a portion of a flower-themed postage stamp. Then she'd gilded the edges, inserted eyelets, and connected the two disks with small gold jump rings. The bottom disk also had a series of jump rings that held a few green and gold beads and a tiny brass leaf.

"Wow," said Gabby, clearly impressed. "When did you do that?"

"In between customers," said Carmela. Then she added, "Once you've got your disks collaged the way you want them, you can string them together to make bookmarks, tags for packages, or just fun embellishments for gift boxes."

"I think," said Tandy, perusing the rubber stamps and digging into the box of scrap paper, "that I want to do something with a Parisian theme."

Gabby held up a rubber stamp. "Got an Eiffel Tower stamp here."

"Excellent," said Tandy.

"And here's a sticker of a champagne label," said Gabby. "Though you'll have to trim it some."

"That's okay," said Tandy. "I'm gonna make at least a dozen of these things."

Baby reached for one of the packages of charms. "Think I could use this miniature picture frame?" she asked. "Slip a tiny photo in and attach it to the bottom of a disk?"

"I think that would be adorable," said Carmela.

As the women worked away on their projects, talk turned to the Galleries and Gourmets celebration that was being held in the French Quarter this Saturday and Sunday. Galleries and Gourmets was a promotion dreamed up by the local gallery owners to draw people into the French Quarter, and hopefully into their art galleries and antique shops. To sweeten the pot, almost fifty different sidewalk food booths would be offering tempting treats including fried oysters, shrimp gumbo, and muffuletta sandwiches, and there would be outdoor performances by jazz, rock, and zydeco groups.

"Sweet Caroline is going to be doing a crawfish boil," said Baby, naming one of her favorite restaurants.

"And I hear that Porta Via will be doing their famous eggs Hussarde," said Gabby. Eggs Hussarde was New Orleans's own version of eggs Benedict that featured *marchand de vin*, a wine sauce, instead of hollandaise. Gabby glanced toward Carmela. "Is your friend Quigg having a booth, too?"

"Yes he is," said Carmela. Fact was, she had been talked into designing a flyer for his French Quarter restaurant, Mumbo Gumbo. But so far, Quigg's flyers had been relegated to the back burner.

"And they're going to do televised art and antiques appraisals, too," exclaimed Baby. "It's going to be New Orleans's version of *Antiques Roadshow*."

"I only care about the food," said Tandy, putting hands on skinny hips. "Speaking of which, should we call Pirate's Alley Deli and order lunch?"

Chapter 5

CARMELA was arranging a display of leather-bound albums when Olivia Wainwright came sailing into her shop. She immediately recognized the woman's white trench coat—maybe something from Burberry?—and Olivia's long, dark hair. Olivia also seemed to have a distinct air of determination about her, a far cry from her tearful grieving last night.

Carmela watched as Olivia hesitated briefly at the front counter, speaking quietly with Gabby. Then Gabby made a slight hand gesture, pointing back toward Carmela, and Olivia spun around to face her.

Carmela started for the front of the store and met Olivia halfway.

"I'm Olivia Wainwright," said the woman, extending her hand.

"Carmela Bertrand," said Carmela, taking her hand, noting that she wore no less than five hefty gold-link bracelets. "And I'm so sorry about your partner. About Melody."

"Thank you," murmured Olivia, appraising Carmela with dark, intelligent eyes. "As you can imagine, the last twenty hours or so have been quite a shock. I've been talking to the police nonstop and I . . ." She sighed heavily and seemed to run out of words.

"Are you okay?" asked Carmela. "Can I get you a cup of coffee? Glass of water?"

Olivia shook her head. "No, thank you." Then she peered sharply at Carmela. "Excuse me, but you said your name was Bertrand? I thought you'd married into the Meechum family."

"I did," Carmela told her, "but never changed my name. Now, I'm slowly . . . what would you call it? . . . extricating myself from that part of my life."

"An independent woman," said Olivia. A slight smile of approval hovered on her elegant oval face.

"Hopefully," said Carmela. She was oddly fascinated by this woman who spoke with a Southern drawl that seemed to mask a slightly East Coast accent. And now that Olivia Wainwright knew about her failed marriage to Shamus, Carmela decided to ask a couple of questions of her own. "You're originally from New Orleans?"

Olivia shook her head. "Oh no. I grew up outside Wooster, Massachusetts. Went to school up there, too. In fact, that's where I met my husband, Stanford. We were at Boston University together. Although he was three years ahead of me."

Carmela knew that Stanford Wainwright was a doctor, a dermatologist. He had been named one of the top docs in New Orleans by *NOLA Today*, one of the local city magazines.

"So," continued Olivia, "Garth told me you were there last night. At Medusa Manor." Now her face sagged again and sadness crept into her eyes. "Such a bizarre tragedy." She bit her lip to keep from crying, but her eyes welled with tears anyway.

"Let's go back to my office," suggested Carmela. "Where

we can have some privacy." Carmela led Olivia past rows of stamp pads, markers, and tote bags and into her small office. She grabbed a stack of scrapbook-supply catalogs off her side chair, plopped them atop her messy desk, and gestured for Olivia to take a seat.

Olivia eased herself down into a red leather director's chair, pulled a hanky from her pocket, and dabbed gingerly at her nose.

"I'm sorry about Medusa Manor," Carmela told Olivia. "It would have been a fun thing to work on."

"That's why I'm here," said Olivia, taking another deep breath and obviously trying to pull herself together. "I'd like you to remain on the project. You and your associate."

"Oh, man," said Carmela, wrinkling her nose. She really hadn't anticipated this. She'd figured Olivia's dropping in today was just a pro forma visit. Garth had mentioned her name to Olivia, so Olivia had felt some small obligation.

"Last I spoke with Melody," said Olivia, "she was very enthusiastic about you and Avon."

"Ava," said Carmela.

"Ava," repeated Olivia. "Melody said you two had lots of experience with float building and that you did a masterful job last year of turning Moda Chadron into a haunted boutique." She looked around, surveying the sketches, photos, printed design pieces, and scrapbook pages that hung on the walls of Carmela's office. "And of course you're a designer and scrapbook maven and your friend owns the voodoo shop." Olivia managed a wan smile. "Seems like a good fit."

"I'm not so sure," said Carmela. "After what happened last night and . . . well, wouldn't you be happier with *real* set designers? We're kind of pretend set designers."

Olivia stared at her. "I'd prefer the two of you stay on."

"But what about the fire in the tower room?" asked Carmela. "Isn't there a lot of damage?"

"I'm told there was no real structural damage," said Olivia. "Nothing that can't be repaired."

"It's not really our cup of tea," Carmela protested weakly.

"Frankly, I think you're absolutely perfect," said Olivia. She leaned forward in her chair. "I know what you're thinking, Carmela. Bad luck, bad timing, bad karma, the whole ball of wax. The thing of it is, Medusa Manor is really half done, but it needs a couple of smart, organized people who have a slight sense of the absurd to pull it all together."

Carmela was about to launch another protest when Olivia raised a hand.

"Hear me out. Please. There's a major horror convention happening in New Orleans next month. DiscordaCon. No doubt you've heard of it?"

Carmela nodded. She had.

"I wanted the grand opening of Medusa Manor to coincide with DiscordaCon. Still want it to. Which means I'm willing to pay you and your friend a considerable sum of money to make this happen."

"Money," repeated Carmela.

"Thirty thousand dollars," said Olivia. "That's double what you were offered before. Plus you'd have almost a carte blanche budget to purchase props and theatricals."

"Thirty thousand," said Carmela.

"Fifteen thousand for each of you," said Olivia.

Carmela nodded. That was quite a chunk of change Olivia had just dangled in front of her. Enough money to pay off all her suppliers, pay the rent on Memory Mine for three months, and still have money left over for a shopping spree at The Latest Wrinkle, her favorite consignment shop on Magazine Street. Maybe even get that tweed Chanel jacket she'd had her eye on. Nothing like the cult of Chanel to get a girl's heart beating faster.

"I'd have to run this by Ava," said Carmela. She knew she was weakening. Like a wet noodle being stretched to the breaking point.

"Of course you would," said Olivia. She dug inside her oversized Gucci bag. "And please . . ." She pulled out a stack of papers. "Take a look at these, too." She handed them to Carmela. "When you see how much has been done already, it might make your decision a little easier."

"What exactly are . . . ?"

"Floor plans," said Olivia. "Along with an outline of proposed design and decorating ideas, and technical specs for the special effects that have already been installed." She smiled. "You have to know what's already in place in case you . . . *when* you start working on Medusa Manor."

Carmela quickly flipped through the top pages and found that a lot of the decorating and design work had been done or at least started, just as Olivia said.

"Melody purchased quite a few props," said Olivia. "So there's already a collection of antiques, furniture, paintings, and old carpets stashed inside the old house. Nothing particularly valuable, of course, but fun items to add to its haunted persona."

"Okay," said Carmela. She was still hesitant to take on the project, but the money beckoned.

"And finally," said Olivia, "you're going to need this." She pressed a large brass key into Carmela's hand. "The key to Medusa Manor."

Carmela gave a slight frown as she stared at the shiny key that seemed to wink enticingly in the low light of her office. "Who else has one of these keys?" she asked. "Besides you?"

Olivia gazed at her, a little startled. "Well . . . nobody. You and I have the only keys."

"What about Melody's key?"

"I suppose the police have that." Olivia stood up, ready to leave, her errand completed.

Carmela leaned back in her chair and thought about the front door standing open last night. About someone creeping around inside Medusa Manor, stalking Melody, then finally getting the best of her.

Somehow, Carmela wasn't entirely sure she and Olivia possessed the only keys.

*   *   *

Just as Carmela was about to dash out the back door, the phone on her desk buzzed loudly.

"What?" she called to Gabby, who was at the counter up front.

Gabby made a rapid series of hand signals that looked like untranslatable hieroglyphics, so Carmela ducked back into her office and snatched the receiver off the hook.

"Carmela Bertrand, how may I help you?"

"Were you on TV again?" an indignant male voice demanded.

Carmela sighed deeply, instantly recognizing the voice as that of her rat-fink, used-to-be-charming, soon-to-be ex. She could picture his lazy grin, languid pose, and handsome face. Then she was jerked back to reality remembering his stupid, boyish ways.

"I don't know, Shamus, why would you think I was on TV?" Carmela responded.

"Hell, I don't know," snorted Shamus. "But Glory said she saw you on the news last night." Glory was Shamus's older sister, a parsimonious sourpuss who'd always detested Carmela and was now bizarrely gleeful that they were in the final, gasping throes of divorce.

"Glory said it was the TV station that's got that really smokin' hot babe reporter," chuckled Shamus. "Well, she didn't phrase it *quite* like that. I'm editorializing here."

"Kimber Breeze," Carmela muttered under her breath.

But Shamus instantly heard her. "That's the one! The sexy babe from KBEZ."

"It probably wasn't me that Glory saw," said Carmela, trying to ward off any potential trouble. "Just someone who looked like me. You know, choppy blond hair, really cute." She glanced up, saw Gabby hovering in the doorway, accepted the large manila envelope Gabby held out to her. Carmela mouthed *Shamus* to Gabby, who nodded back.

"Glory was pretty sure it was you," Shamus continued.

Now he paused to gather himself into a nice, tight ball of indignation. "Please don't tell me you're involved in some wacky murder investigation again!"

"Shamus, sweetie," Carmela purred into the phone. "You don't get to tell me what to do anymore. In fact, you're not even allowed to drop so much as a lousy suggestion. You, my friend, have been dumped, discarded, and practically divorced. You are no longer necessary to my survival or my happiness. In other words, Shamus, you're obsolete."

Gabby grinned at her. "Don't sugarcoat it," she said in a stage whisper. "Just tell Shamus how you really feel."

But Shamus had already assumed the personality of a whipped puppy. "Jeez, Carmela," he whimpered. "You don't have to be so snarky. I don't deserve *that*!"

"Snarky's my new middle name," said Carmela. "So getting back to the gestalt of our conversation, kindly tell your sister, Glory, to stuff it."

"Don't try that shit with me, Carmela," sneered Shamus. "I went to college; I can toss big words around, too."

"Shamus," said Carmela, beginning to feel slightly worn down, "what do you want? Why did you call me, really?" She was pretty sure she knew why Shamus was gibbering away like a crazed chimpanzee. The envelope in her hand carried the return address of Willis B. Mortimer, Esquire, Shamus's divorce lawyer.

"Oh," said Shamus. "Yeah. I wanted to tell you my attorney is messengering over a new offer to you. For the divorce settlement."

"Is that so?"

"It's so," said Shamus.

"But is it what I asked for?" said Carmela.

Shamus snapped right back at her. "You'll just have to read it and see, Carmela."

Carmela slammed the phone down and gazed at Gabby. "Ewww," she said.

Gabby gave her a sympathetic look. "Don't let him drive you bonkers."

"Believe me, I won't," said Carmela. "Not when I'm so close to a clean getaway."

"Things have calmed down in the shop," said Gabby. "Are you still thinking about running out to buy flowers? To drop off at Fire and Ice?"

"Uh-huh. That's where I was headed just as Shamus called."

Gabby tapped a finger on the manila envelope. "Are you going to open this?"

Carmela shook her head and sighed. "Not right now. Why let Shamus spoil my entire afternoon?"

Chapter 6

"LILIES, asters, iris, cosmos," murmured Carmela as she eased her way through the walk-in cooler at French Bouquet Florals. Shaggy heads on delicate stems bobbed gracefully at her while some tightly curled buds seemed to huddle in the chill air. The aroma was a symphony of heady and sweet, mingled with grasses and moist earth, a veritable flower buffet that appealed to the eyes as well as the nose.

"See anything you like?" asked Cora Lou Connor, one of the owners. She was a tidy, middle-aged woman who wore a long denim apron over her clothes and green Wellington boots, the clumpy rubber ones favored by English gardeners.

"Still working on it," said Carmela, wondering how she could peruse thousands of paper designs and make smart inventory decisions, and then not be able to pick out a few flowers?

After a few false starts, Carmela finally settled on a bouquet of asters, dahlias, and irises. As Cora Lou rang up her purchase and carefully wrapped the flowers in purple tissue, then again in purple plastic, Carmela jotted a short condolence note, signing her name and Gabby's. Then she added Ava's name, too.

"You want these delivered?" Cora Lou asked.

"Thanks, but I'm gonna take 'em myself," said Carmela.

With flowers in hand, she dashed to her car, which was double-parked out front on Ursuline Street, thanked the merciful heavens above that the parking Nazis who haunted the French Quarter hadn't ticketed or towed her, then whipped around the corner and down the alley to Fire and Ice Jewelers.

Luckily, Fire and Ice had three reserved customer parking spaces in the rear of the building, and one of those spaces stood empty. Carmela offered another whispered prayer to the heavens, because parking spaces were a precious commodity in the French Quarter.

Pressing the buzzer at the back door, Carmela shifted from one foot to the other, hoping one of Garth's employees was there today, holding down the fort. Luck was with her, because the electronic door suddenly rasped then clicked loudly, gaining her admittance. But when Carmela pushed her way into the elegant little jewelry shop, she was stunned to find none other than Garth Mayfeldt himself!

"Garth!" exclaimed Carmela, crossing a whisper of dove-gray carpeting to greet him. "I had no idea you'd be here." She leaned forward and they gently exchanged double air kisses.

"Neither did I," said Garth, "but here I am anyway." He smiled faintly, brushing the back of his hand against the five o'clock shadow that shaded his cheeks. Garth was five feet ten with the slight, somewhat underfed build of a long distance runner, which he was, and possessed a crooked smile and slightly egg-shaped head with sparse bits of blond hair. He also had kind gray eyes that corresponded to a gentle personality. When you were a customer in his shop, Garth had the ability to focus his attention completely on you, as though you were the only one who mattered.

"Well . . . here," said Carmela, thrusting the bouquet of flowers into his hands. "These are for you."

Garth looked genuinely touched. "You are such a sweetheart," he cooed. "Thank you!" He peeled back the purple wrappings, saw the note, and took a few seconds to read it. "You're just too dear, all of you," he told her, and now his voice was heavy with emotion.

Carmela walked slowly to the main counter with Garth as he cradled the flowers. "I really didn't expect to see you," she told him, repeating herself.

Garth sighed deeply. "Ginny Hunsucker, my regular manager, is moving to a new house this week. Had the move planned for the last three months. So . . ." He shrugged.

"When it rains it pours," offered Carmela.

"Something like that." Garth laid the flowers down on the counter and fixed her with a wan smile. "I want to thank you again for being at Medusa Manor last night."

Carmela frowned and shook her head. "I wish I could have done something. But it was just . . . too late."

"I know that," said Garth. He reached over and patted her hand. "But you did do something. You were *there*."

Carmela tried to give an encouraging smile, but the effort felt frozen on her face.

"I understand from Olivia that you and Ava are going to continue working on Medusa Manor," said Garth.

"That's still up for discussion," said Carmela, deciding the two must have talked together within the last half hour. And judging from the gold bangles that had glittered on Olivia's wrists, the woman must be an awfully good customer, too.

"Melody would have appreciated your hanging in there," said Garth, tears forming in his eyes.

"Uh . . . thank you," said Carmela, suddenly feeling more than a gentle amount of pressure being exerted.

"Of course," said Garth, "dear, dear Olivia has been an absolute rock through all of this. While I've turned into an emotional wet rag."

"You have good reason to be upset," said Carmela.

Garth shrugged. "Look at me, standing here like a lump when these lovely flowers probably need water." He sniffled loudly then said, "I'll go grab a vase."

Garth disappeared into the small office at the back of the shop. Then Carmela heard a door snick open, a metallic clink, and a water faucet being turned on. *Okay, good,* she decided. *He's sad, he's morose, but he's still functioning. That's important. He's not frozen with grief.*

Carmela glanced around the shop. Fire and Ice was small, tasteful, exquisitely done. The gray carpeting neatly complemented the sand-blasted beige brick walls and whitewashed wooden ceiling. Track lighting arranged in two languid S-curves focused pinpoint spotlights on the gleaming glass cases. A flat-screen TV, mounted on one wall, the sound low, played languid footage of an Italian jewelry fashion show.

As Carmela waited for Garth to return, she wandered about, peering into the various jewelry cases, and was struck by the number of really gorgeous pieces that Fire and Ice carried.

One glass case was stuffed with estate jewelry resting on puffy black velvet pillows. An old mine-cut diamond in a quatrefoil-pronged platinum setting caught her eye, as did a pair of square, deco-style earrings encrusted with diamonds and rubies.

The next case over contained ultracontemporary pieces. Carmela quickly became entranced with a large square silver pin inset with a single ruby, as well as a brushed-gold charm bracelet adorned with teardrop-shaped aquamarines and citrines.

It had been a while since she'd been inside Fire and Ice. A while, really, since she could afford to buy fine jewelry for herself. But some of these pieces were quite spectacular.

Maybe, if she and Ava really did decide to move ahead on Medusa Manor, she'd be able to afford one of these pieces. What a treat!

Carmela edged toward a circular, stand-alone glass case. A large, black gleaming stone had caught her eye, and she was suddenly curious. But when she peered into the case for a closer look, she was surprised to see that the black stone capped a pendant that featured a miniature painting of two children surrounded by puffs of clouds.

"Victorian mourning jewelry," Garth murmured from behind her.

Carmela jumped. She hadn't heard him approach. His voice, low and gravelly, had startled her.

"That large black stone is jet," Garth pointed out. "And the pendant is edged with seed pearls. In Victorian times, seed pearls were supposed to represent tears."

"Mourning jewelry seems like a strange thing to carry," said Carmela. "I can't imagine there's much demand for it." She was staring at another pendant that portrayed a young girl cradling a lamb.

"Oh," said Garth, setting the vase of flowers onto one of the glass counters, "Melody was a big fan of mourning jewelry. And I'm an *enormous* fan. You'd be surprised how many collectors there are who are always on the hunt for a new piece of this stuff."

"Strange what people collect," murmured Carmela. "What trips their fancy."

"Mmm," said Garth. He pulled a keychain from his pocket, stuck a small key in the side of the case, and swung open a glass door. "Take a look at this." He reached into the case, selected a small gold heart pendant, and dangled it in front of her.

"Pretty," said Carmela. Suspended from a twenty-inch gold box chain was a rounded, dimensional heart. A puffy heart, really. Probably a locket.

Garth handed the necklace to Carmela.

"Does it open?" she asked.

"Of course," said Garth, in an almost encouraging tone. "In fact, it's our most popular piece of cremation jewelry."

Time stood still for a few moments as Carmela stared at him. "Excuse me?"

"Cremation jewelry," repeated Garth. He nodded toward the case. "Fire and Ice has always carried a rather extensive selection. Hearts, crosses, angels, bells, stars, and dolphins. We've even special-ordered cats and dogs."

"So they're really . . ." began Carmela. She'd just noticed the small, hand-lettered sign that rested inside the case. The one that read *Cremation Jewelry*.

"They're tiny urns," said Garth. "Designed to hold a pinch of ashes. Some are even urn shaped."

"Interesting," responded Carmela. It was the only neutral word she could dredge up at the moment.

Garth reached back into the case and removed a necklace from a white satin pillow. "This one's from the eighteen hundreds," he told Carmela. It was a silver urn inlaid with miniature turquoise tiles and dark seed pearls. "Besides her crypt in Lafayette Cemetery, this will be the final resting place for a tiny bit of Melody's ashes."

"Lovely," said Carmela. Truth was, she didn't find the piece particularly lovely at all. In fact, the whole concept of cremation or funeral jewelry seemed a bit unsettling. A trifle morbid. But she wasn't about to call out Garth concerning his taste. To each his own.

"Amazing, isn't it?" said Garth. With the silver urn dangling between his fingers, he seemed almost mesmerized. "There are even hollow bangles that can hold ashes, a lock of hair, whatever."

Carmela managed a smile, although she was finding this all quite strange. Between Melody, with her Medusa Manor, and Garth, with his collection of cremation jewelry, they seemed to have been a couple strangely obsessed with death.

When the front door suddenly whooshed open and a security buzzer sounded, Carmela felt almost relieved. Until she glanced around and saw who'd just entered the shop.

Kimber Breeze, tricked out in a cobalt-blue jacket, matching blue mini skirt, and black Gucci heels, was advancing on them like General George Patton headed for the Ardennes.

"Oh no," Carmela muttered to Garth. "You do not want to talk to this woman."

But Kimber's intrepid cameraman, Harvey, was already rolling tape as he jammed his video camera in Garth's face.

Kimber, always a quick study, took one look at the jewelry and the hand-lettered calligraphy that read *Cremation Jewelry* and grinned the grin of a hungry great white shark. She knew a good story when she saw one. And this one had been dropped neatly into her lap.

Carmela sat behind the wheel of her car, massaging her throbbing temples. Headache. A whopper of a Kimber Breeze headache. Even though she had managed to escape, Carmela hadn't completely eluded her tormentor. As she'd backed out of Fire and Ice, shaking her head and refusing to make any sort of comment, she'd still been stalked, harassed, and harangued.

Oh jeez. What a day.

She wiggled her shoulders and drummed her fingertips against the steering wheel. What now? Stop by Juju Voodoo and talk to Ava? Present Olivia Wainwright's offer to her? No, she'd already invited Ava over for dinner tonight. They could discuss it then.

Besides, Carmela was pretty sure what Ava was going to say. Ava would mull it over for a millisecond, then agree they should continue working on Medusa Manor. Fifteen grand each was just too much money to pass up. Especially when most of the broad strokes at Medusa Manor had already been done. When all they really had to do was add a few finishing flourishes. Set-decorating touches. And when they put their heads together, as designers and BFFs, they were wickedly good at what they did.

So . . . what now?

Carmela started her car, cruised down the alley, and hooked a right on Burgundy Street.

It was just a few minutes past four, so the smart thing to do would be to head over to Medusa Manor and, in the cold, clear, rational light of day, see what needed to be done. Scout the place so she and Ava could draw up their battle plans.

Black-and-yellow *POLICE LINE DO NOT CROSS* tape fluttered from the doorjamb. Carmela waved a hand and shooed it away, then stuck the brass key into the lock. And, like stepping inside Pandora's box, she suddenly found herself enveloped by the cool dimness that was Medusa Manor.

Oddly enough, she wasn't scared. Or even nervous. *Well, good*, she thought to herself. *That's one hurdle crossed.* She pulled a pen and notebook from her bag, determined to remain businesslike and focused.

The first floor would be a snap, she decided. If they moved the coffin over to the window like they'd talked about last night, that would open up a ton of space to serve as a staging area for the groups that came through. There was even room for a counter where Olivia could handle ticket sales and maybe even sell T-shirts and souvenirs. Or make a DVD of the tour and sell that. She jotted a note to herself. Good idea.

To really set the scene and get customers in the mood, maybe they could place a pair of wing chairs near the fireplace. Occupied by grinning zombies, of course. Carmela made another notation, then glanced around. Ava's wall of skulls would work beautifully. Probably add some spray-on cobwebs. They'd help diffuse the light and make the place look even more atmospheric.

Carmela studied the fireplace. It was a large carved marble piece and the perfect spot to have a motorized head peer out. And above the fireplace, like hunters' trophies, possibly hang mounted heads of a werewolf, a gargoyle, and maybe a dragon? No, wait a minute. This was Medusa Manor, so a giant Medusa head framed with wriggling snakes should go above the fireplace. Save the werewolf and other critters for . . . she grinned to herself . . . the Haunted Library? What else?

Satisfied with the main room, Carmela headed for the stairs. But as she glanced back over her shoulder, Carmela decided that the coffin shouldn't just be a static entity. Maybe it should open to reveal an animated female vampire? Sure, why not?

The second floor needed a lot more work. There were four bedrooms and, upon touring them, Carmela found that archways had been cut between each room. Smart. That way guides could lead visitors from room to room, unimpeded, without having to return to the main hallway each time.

One of the front bedrooms already had a four-poster bed, so that needed to be swagged with black net fabric and have some dangling spiders added. Or, since there were going to be actors in each room, portraying spooky characters, maybe they could do a sort of *Exorcist* theme. Rig the bed so it vibrated, pipe in organ music and scary voices.

Carmela crossed under the archway to the next room, aware of the creaking floor beneath her feet. This room was empty, except for what looked like a pile of rags.

Except the rags turned out to be green and blue rubber heads, all very witchy and warty looking, with hooked noses and long, matted hair. Okay, this was an excellent start. Call this room the Witches' Lair. Suspend the heads, maybe install some fun-house mirrors on the walls, and . . . what?

Carmela glanced around and noticed a thin white scrim hanging on the far wall.

What's this for?

She peered over her shoulder at the opposite wall and saw

projection equipment. Aha. These were some of the special effects that had already been installed. She strolled toward the screen, reached out and grazed it with the tips of her fingers, and . . . suddenly . . . *snap*!

Like a runaway window shade, the scrim rolled up with such ferocity it nearly scared her to death!

"Yipes!" she cried out loud. Then she put a hand to her heart, felt the extra pitter-patter, and laughed nervously.

So, okay, she was a little jumpy after all. Who wouldn't be? But if she wanted to complete this project for Olivia Wainwright, if she wanted to earn her fifteen grand, she was going to have to get it together.

Could she do that?

Sure she could.

Carmela slid a foot out and touched a pair of drab paintings and a framed needlepoint that leaned against the wall where the scrim had been. Of course she could pull it together. She'd been married to Shamus, endured a hurricane, and lived to tell the tale of both. Doing set decorations for this place should be child's play.

Carmela turned her attention to the larger painting, which was nested in a puddle of dust balls. It was a dark, rather hideous landscape painting that, if one wanted to display it, would need serious cleaning. Probably require at least half a dozen art restoration people on the project. For Medusa Manor, however, it was perfect.

The second painting wasn't quite as bad. A smaller painting, a landscape of a village that had a small signature in the lower right-hand corner. *Ivern.* She racked her brain, trying to recall the name from her art history class. Nope. Didn't ring a bell.

The needlepoint was simply a dusty little piece with the grim words, *Death may be the greatest of all human blessings.*

These were obviously items that Melody had purchased, along with the witch heads, furniture, and other junk. Probably relegate them to the Haunted Library to take their place among the mounted gargoyle heads. Yeah, she decided, that would be pretty cool.

Carmela took another ten minutes to walk through the rest of the second floor. She scanned two more bedrooms, headed down the back staircase, meandered into the library, and then went down into the basement. Much to her surprise, the basement was crammed full of junk. She could see another coffin, a pair of French console tables, a purple brocade fainting couch, large silver candelabra, book shelves galore, and boxes that contained heaven knows what.

Okay. This was going to require some serious sorting. There was a lot of stuff here, obviously purchased by Melody at tag sales and from local galleries. There might even be enough stuff down here to furnish the whole of Medusa Manor.

She tapped her pen against her notebook. Actually, that was pretty much what Olivia had told her. The concept was in place, now someone had to sort through Melody's purchases, pull it together thematically, and add enough scary stuff to turn Medusa Manor into a haunted house.

For the first time that afternoon, Carmela smiled to herself. This project might not be as overwhelming as she first thought it was. Maybe she and Ava could study the design plans, do a quick inventory, then commando in here and pull the rooms together with a minimum of work.

Maybe.

Chapter 7

"A SENSE of the absurd?" said Ava. "Olivia Wainwright really said that?" She lounged against the refrigerator door, dressed in a faded denim skirt and black turtleneck, sipping a glass of wine.

"Oh yeah," said Carmela as she pulled open the oven door, added Parmesan cheese to her shrimp bake, then shut the door so her dish could bubble and brown for another couple of minutes.

Ava, tilting her head to one side, looked a little pleased. "It's like she really *knows* us."

Carmela grinned. "I'm not sure whether we should be flattered or insulted."

"And the money," said Ava, a little breathless. "Olivia really said fifteen thousand each?"

"That's what she dangled," said Carmela.

"Then I think we should go ahead and grab it," said Ava. "Before Olivia changes her mind, anyway. Lord knows, we can both use the extra bucks. I know I could. Business has been okay, but no way has it been gangbusters."

"I hear you," said Carmela.

"What's this Olivia really like?" asked Ava. "Besides rich."

"She seemed nice," said Carmela. "Maybe a trifle distant. But I think she was just feeling overwhelmed, since she was the silent partner in Medusa Manor, the person putting up all the money. Melody had been honchoing the actual day-to-day stuff. Handling real estate details, set design, buying trips, and decorating. Like that."

"That's why Olivia wants us," said Ava. "Rich people always think they can fix a problem by throwing money at it."

Carmela thought about the divorce settlement she'd quickly read through, the papers sitting on the table over there like some kind of hot potato. "Sometimes they can," she told Ava.

"Your shrimp bake is delicious," raved Ava. They were at the dining table, still discussing the pros and cons of working on Medusa Manor—though most of the cons had pretty much been sloughed aside. "It was either come over here and stuff my fat face or go out for pizza with Tommy Drummond."

"Isn't he the guy who does odd jobs at Hooligan's Bar?" asked Carmela. "The one who always looks like he's on a work release program from prison?"

Ava nodded. "He's a sweet guy, but constantly on a tight budget." She grimaced. "I don't want to sound like a complete gold digger, *cher*, but I'm not a big fan of men on a budget."

"That's because you're a champagne-and-caviar lady," Carmela pointed out. "You've developed a taste for the finer things in life."

"I try to," said Ava. "Of course, when the occasion is right,

I'm also willing to settle for a glass of Big Easy Beer and a plate of Louisiana oysters."

"Nothin' wrong with that," said Carmela.

"Hey," said Ava. "Let's turn on the news, see if they're any closer to catching Melody's killer."

"Let's hope so," said Carmela, aiming the remote control at the TV set. "Let's hope something is happening." She hadn't heard a word from Edgar Babcock yet today, even though he'd promised to call.

"Look at this," said Ava, as the six o'clock news flickered on. "Kimber Breeze is doing her thing. Big whoop."

"Uh-oh," said Carmela. "Forgot to tell you. Kimber came steamrolling into Fire and Ice this afternoon when I was delivering flowers to Garth. I have a feeling her report this evening isn't exactly going to be flattering to him."

"Kimber's like the proverbial bad penny," observed Ava. "Always turns up."

"And when she does, she's trouble," added Carmela.

"What's she holding in her hand there?" mumbled Ava, squinting at the TV set.

"Cremation jewelry," Kimber answered from the screen. "A rather bizarre and strangely morbid collection found right here at Fire and Ice Jewelers in the French Quarter."

"What!" said Ava.

"See," said Carmela, "I told you it wouldn't be flattering."

They watched as Kimber Breeze did what she termed a "follow-up report" on the murder of Melody Mayfeldt, but what really turned into a commentary on the curiosities found at Garth Mayfeldt's jewelry shop.

"She's makin' him look bad," commented Ava. "Manipulating her words to make it look like he's obsessed with death and funerals. Like some sort of ghoul."

"Which he's not," said Carmela.

"At least you don't *think* he is," said Ava. She thought for a moment. "You don't think Garth could have . . . ?"

"See," said Carmela, shaking her head. "Now Kimber Breeze even has *you* thinking Garth might have been involved in his own wife's murder."

Ava frowned. "I suppose he could have been."

"No," said Carmela, "Melody and Garth were in love. And I can tell you he's extremely torn up."

"You can bet your Detective Babcock will check him out," said Ava.

"I'm sure he will," said Carmela. "It's doubtful Babcock will leave any stone unturned. But Garth as the killer? I just don't see it."

As Kimber Breeze wrapped up her report, Ava said, "Do you think Kimber had her nose done? It looks a little upturned to me. Kind of piggy." She studied the screen intently. "Or maybe a brow lift? There's something different about her."

"If you ask me," said Carmela, getting up to clear plates, "I'd say she gained weight." Obviously, Carmela harbored no love for Kimber Breeze.

"That's it," laughed Ava, as Kimber signed off. "Kimber's packed on a few pounds. Her face looks fuller and I'll bet her caboose is, too."

"Maybe more than a few pounds," Carmela called from the kitchen, really getting into it now.

"She's probably got those jiggly little dingleberry things under her arms," giggled Ava. "She better get in gear and start lifting dumbbells."

"Better lifting one than marrying one," said Carmela. Returning to the table, she plopped down a heavy manila envelope.

"What's this?" asked Ava. "You got a pen pal?"

"Lawyer stuff," said Carmela. "Shamus's attorney sent over what he termed a generous and thoughtful offer."

"Uh-oh," said Ava. "In other words, they're tryin' to weasel out."

"Bingo," said Carmela. "That would definitely be my soon-to-be-ex's pedigree. Clan of the weasel."

"That boy's got more money than some of those Shreveport oil men who drive gas-guzzling Hummers," said Ava. "And Shamus *still* won't play fair with you!"

"It's mostly Glory's doing," said Carmela. "Since she controls the family purse strings."

"If you ask me," said Ava, "I'd say Shamus is tied to big sister's *apron* strings."

"Strangling him," added Carmela.

Once the table was cleared, Carmela and Ava laid out the plans for Medusa Manor.

"When you said *plans*," said Ava, "I thought you meant ideas and stuff. Concepts. But these are real roll-'em-out blueprints."

Carmela nodded, then dug into her bag for the rest of the papers Olivia had given her. "I've got the concept and creative plans, too," she told Ava, fanning out a thick stack of papers.

Ava took a sip of wine, then began sifting through the loose papers. "Oh, hey. A memo regarding set decoration ideas for the Haunted Library and the Morgue of Madness. Yup, we're gonna need that."

Carmela shuffled through papers, too. "Here's a list of stuff Melody bought at an auction over in Jeanerette. Two tufted leather chairs, a baroque mirror, two oil paintings, a library table. Sounds like some of the stuff I saw today."

"You went over there?" asked Ava.

"Took a quick tour and jotted down a few notes," said Carmela. "I wanted to have some idea of what we had to work with."

"Coffins, for one thing," said Ava.

"Plus witches' masks, a canopy bed like we talked about . . . listen, that basement's absolutely *stuffed* with props."

"Really," murmured Ava. "So it is mostly decorating, just like you said. Move some furniture around, figure out themes for the different rooms, add the haunted touches."

"Except," said Carmela, "we have to do it all rather quickly. That horror convention I told you about . . ."

"DiscordaCon."

"Yeah," said Carmela. "That takes place in three weeks."

Ava let loose a low whistle. "So we gotta hustle. Get the fun-house mirrors and flickering skulls in perfect working order."

"That's right," said Carmela. "And we have to figure out special effects and get cracking on that, too. Then plan to move furniture starting next week. Maybe hire a couple of professional furniture movers so we don't break our backs. I know Jekyl can give us some names."

"Sounds good," said Ava.

"You know," said Carmela, tapping her pen against a blueprint, "this place is controlled by a computer program. There are apparently lights, sound effects, and special-effects projections. I noticed some of the equipment today in one of the upstairs bedrooms."

Ava groaned loudly and touched the back of her hand to her forehead. "Just shoot me now, *cher*. Because I am totally phobic when it comes to computers. Computers, iPods, BlackBerrys, those things all *hate* me."

"No way," said Carmela. "Besides, how could you be phobic about computers? You have your entire store inventory on computer."

"Lot of help that is," grumped Ava. "It's all I can do to turn on that vile machine and figure out if I've got one shrunken head or an entire case of saint candles."

Carmela patted Ava's hand. "You'll be fine. In fact, I'll talk to whoever installed the stuff and put them in charge of getting everything else online."

"I did see something about computers," said Ava. She shuffled through a stack of papers and pulled out a couple of loose pages. "Here it is. Company called Byte Head."

"Is there a person's name, too?"

"Tate," said Ava. "Tate Mackie."

"So he's the guy," said Carmela. "Excellent. Another problem almost solved."

"So what now?" asked Ava.

"Before we do anything," said Carmela, "we should go back over there. Like I said, I made notes today. But we should put our heads together and figure out what we have to work with, finalize our major room themes, and make a list of what props we need to buy."

"You mean go over to Medusa Manor," said Ava. She suddenly didn't look too sure of herself. "When?"

Carmela glanced at her watch. "Well, you have to work all day tomorrow. And I have to work tomorrow. So . . ." She raised her eyebrows.

Ava finished her sentence. "So we should drive over there right now. Even though it's very, very dark outside."

"There are lights in the house," said Carmela.

Ava grimaced. "Let's just hope they're in good working order."

Chapter 8

"THIS place looks like the Addams Family lived here, let the place sink into utter disrepair, then skipped out on the rent," said Ava. They stood on the cracked sidewalk, gazing up at the old mansion that seemed to loom over them like the hulk of a wrecked ship. A flat silver moon, not quite full, shone down upon them, icing the house in a cool glow.

"Medusa Manor's supposed to look that way," said Carmela as she stuck her key into the lock. "It's a haunted house." She jiggled the key, but for some reason it seemed to be stuck. She jiggled some more.

"What's wrong?" asked Ava.

"Don't know," said Carmela. "The lock worked fine earlier."

"Maybe it's an omen," said Ava.

"Maybe it's a bad lock," said Carmela.

"Gotta hit it with a shot of WD-40," said Ava, when the lock finally clicked open. "Do the hinges, too."

"Then you give up the cool sound effect," whispered Carmela, as the door creaked open.

"Oh crap," said Ava, snapping the light switch by the front door. "It's not exactly megawatts, is it?" Two dim lights over the fireplace glowed a sickly yellow, giving the room an ominous feel.

Carmela dug in her bag and pulled out a Maglite. "I brought along a flashlight."

"Good," said Ava. She edged a little to her right. "Wait a minute, there's another panel here. Push buttons."

"Give 'em a try," urged Carmela.

Ava punched the top button, immediately triggering a deafening cascade of wild organ music. "Yipes," she cried. "Hit something."

"Try again," said Carmela.

As Ava fumbled with the buttons, the overhead chandelier began to glow. First a low pearly white light, then subtly changing to ghostly green. And, much like the Wizard of Oz himself, who'd appeared as a terrifying, disembodied head, a woman's face suddenly materialized in the center of the chandelier.

"What's *that*?" Ava shrieked, as the eyes in the ghost woman's head suddenly rolled back, her mouth gaped open, and a long tongue lolled out. "That's hideous!"

"Projected image," said Carmela. She'd already spotted the equipment behind her and was now standing beneath the chandelier, peering up. "Look," she said, "we thought this fixture was just dingy and dirty when we first saw it, but that's because there's really fine gauze fabric covering it. Works like a kind of movie screen." She searched for a more appropriate word and remembered the window shade screen upstairs. "A scrim, really."

"Clever," said Ava, rapidly recovering from her initial shock. "Hey, you think they used Glory's face as the model for that little sweetheart?"

"Wouldn't be surprised," said Carmela. She clapped her hands over her ears. "Think you can turn that music off?"

Ava fumbled with the switch again, and the music as well as the ghastly face faded away.

"Thank you," said Carmela. "So, volume needs to be adjusted. That's just way too loud." She made a note. "But I like the chandelier effect."

"You said something about a vampire inside the coffin?" asked Ava.

"What do you think?" asked Carmela. "Good idea? Bad idea?"

"Works for me," said Ava. "But we'll need to huddle with that special-effects guy. What was his name? McKenzie?"

Carmela thought for a minute. "Mackie. Tate Mackie."

"Yeah, let's see if he can rig that up."

They did a fast walk-through of the second floor. Ava adored the witches' heads and even suggested using a witch's cauldron filled with dry ice, adding pinpoint spotlights, and, of course, having a costumed witch (and maybe even a warlock) to meet and greet guests.

They decided the *Exorcist* bedroom would pretty much decorate itself.

That left two more bedrooms.

"What about a Werewolf's Lair?" suggested Ava. "We could add a bunch of fake trees, lay green Astroturf on the floor, and arrange some marble tombstones. Have a werewolf hopping around, snarling and jumping at people."

"Excellent," said Carmela. "And for the last bedroom?"

Ava pursed her lips and thought for a minute. "You say there's lots of junk in the basement?"

Carmela nodded. "Tons of stuff."

"Then let's hold off on theming this last room until we see what we have to work with."

"Sure," said Carmela. "Plus we have to figure out the third floor, too." She consulted her notes. "The working title so far is Ballroom of the Red Death."

"It's the ballroom of death, all right," said Ava. She shifted from one foot to the other.

"I take it you'd rather not venture up there?"

Ava shrugged. "It's where Melody was killed. It's where we saw that blinding flash of light."

"If we're going to decorate Medusa Manor, we have to go up there sooner or later," said Carmela, though she, too, was a little hesitant.

"Okay," said Ava, making a sweeping gesture toward the staircase. "But you have the honor of proceeding first."

The ballroom was enormous, pretty much covering the entire third floor. Luckily, it was lit, though very dimly, like the rest of the mansion.

"Cold up here," said Ava, buttoning her denim jacket. "A cold spot."

Carmela rolled her eyes at her friend. "This place isn't *really* haunted, you know. There's no *real* cold spot." Then her eyes slid over toward the small tower room at the front of the house. "It's cold because . . . because the window's broken out." Her voice sounded small and hollow in the cavernous space.

Ava nodded. "Have to get that fixed." She glanced around. "I can still smell . . . what?"

"Sulfur?" said Carmela. "Weird."

They both glanced toward the tower room again, but made no motion to go that way. Seconds ticked by, then Ava said, "Let's go downstairs and paw through that junk in the basement."

Carmela couldn't leave fast enough.

"*Cher*, this is a treasure trove," chortled Ava. She seemed to have gotten past her nervousness of the ballroom and was digging through the mound of basement furniture. "Look, here are candlesticks to arrange at either end of the vampire coffin." She pulled out an enormous brass candlestick, then proceeded to unearth a second one from under a rolled-up Oriental rug. "A pair. Must have come from a church or something."

"That carpet will work in the *Exorcist* bedroom," said Carmela, stooping down and flipping part of it open. "Oh yeah."

"And, look, here are some smaller candelabras, an old clock, and a pair of weird metal urns."

"Funeral urns?" asked Carmela.

Ava grabbed one and held it up. Gunmetal gray on its way to a corrosive green, the urn was incised with floral designs. Elaborate handles stuck out from either side. "Heavy," grunted Ava.

"Looks enough like a funeral urn for our purposes," said Carmela.

Ava tipped it upside down, and a stream of dust trickled out. "Oops," she giggled. "There goes somebody."

"Ah," said Carmela, "they were probably used as flowerpots."

"Look at all this crap," marveled Ava, pointing at the mound they'd barely begun to explore. "There's a library table over there, a spinning wheel, and three or four bookcases."

"We could drape some of those fake cobwebs around the spinning wheel," suggested Carmela. "Make it look like someone spun them."

"Then we're gonna need big furry spiders."

"And the library table?" Carmela stood with her hands on her hips, thinking. "Probably put it in the Haunted Library."

"I haven't even been in there yet," said Ava, edging her way farther into the stacks of junk. "You think that's where these bookshelves were slated to go?"

"I'd imagine so," said Carmela.

Ava had all but disappeared now. "But I don't see any books," she called back.

"Books we can get," said Carmela. Wren West, who owned Biblios Booksellers in the French Quarter, had boxes of books piled in her basement. Many had been donated;

most were falling apart and unusable, except to make altered books.

"You know there's a car back here?" called Ava.

"Black Cadillac?" asked Carmela.

"Yeah," came Ava's hollow voice. "It's a . . . holy shit, it's a doggone hearse!"

Carmela chuckled to herself. For someone who owned a voodoo shop and professed to like spooky things, Ava was sure acting hinky. "It was on the list," Carmela told her. She glanced around the low-ceilinged basement. "The thing is, this place is a basement *and* a garage."

Ava suddenly reappeared, dusting her hands on the front of her denim skirt. "What do you mean?"

"It's an underground garage," said Carmela. "There's like a ramp that goes up to the alley."

"Oh," said Ava. "I get it." She gestured with her thumb over her right shoulder. "So somewhere beyond that junk and old black hearse, there's a garage door?"

"Yup," said Carmela. "At least it was there on the blueprints."

"Probably still there," said Ava. "I doubt they drove a hearse down the basement stairs."

"So this is supposed to be . . ." said Carmela, turning around in a slow circle.

"The Morgue of Madness?" said Ava.

"Not sure," said Carmela. "Did you see an old autopsy table when you were back there?"

"Eek!" shrilled Ava.

"Now what's wrong?" asked Carmela.

"I'm just *eek*in' on general principle," said Ava. "Like when you get your legs waxed and they rip those little strips off."

"Gotcha," said Carmela.

"Man, Melody was really planning to do this place up right, wasn't she?" said Ava. "She had a real knack for spooky stuff."

"A true calling," Carmela agreed.

"But a calling that somehow did her in," Ava added.

The two of them stood for a few seconds, thinking about the words that hung in the air between them.

"Okay," said Carmela. "Time to get going."

"We accomplished a lot," agreed Ava. "Figured almost everything out."

They climbed the stairs, snapped off the lights, and emerged into the long first-floor hallway.

"That's the library over there," said Carmela, pointing. "The Haunted Library."

Ava opened the door, and Carmela shone her light in. The room was empty except for another fireplace and a ratty-looking leather couch.

"Bookcases will go perfectly in here," said Ava.

Carmela told her about her idea for stuffed werewolf and gargoyle heads.

"Love it," enthused Ava as she backed out, crossed the hall, and pushed open another door. "In fact, I know a taxidermy shop over in Gretna that could probably dummy up some . . . whoa!"

"What?" asked Carmela.

"Uh . . . this would be your Morgue of Madness right here," said Ava.

Carmela stared into the room that had once been a kitchen. What had probably been a homey place with curtains and wood cabinets now had a row of steel morgue drawers against one wall. An old autopsy table stood directly in front of them, looking like some kind of weird human colander. Behind that was a huge metal door.

"Holy cripes," exclaimed Ava. "I think that's supposed to be the crematorium!"

"Is the door just for show or does it actually open?" asked Carmela.

"Only one way to find out," mumbled Ava, as both women stepped past the autopsy table. Ava grasped the door handle and pulled. The door swung open slowly and the two of them peered in.

"Wow," said Ava. All four walls and the ceiling of the claustrophobic six-by-eight-foot room were lined with angry-looking red-painted metal grates. A metal slab hunkered in the middle like a monolith from Stonehenge.

"I'm convinced," said Carmela.

"I wouldn't want to get locked in there," said Ava.

Carmela stepped in and touched a hand to the metal grating. "There's a scrim on this stuff, too," she told Ava. "For more special effects."

"Take a look at that switch," said Ava. One wall had a giant electrical switch, the kind Dr. Frankenstein might have used to send electrical current into his monster.

"To activate the special effects, probably," said Carmela.

Ava shuddered as they shuffled out to the main parlor.

"Kind of a crazy setup," said Carmela. "Made you nervous, huh?"

"Not me," said Ava, her hand on the doorknob. "I'm cool with everything." She smiled, and then the smile froze on her face and her eyes went cross-eyed.

"What's wrong now?" asked Carmela.

"Door's locked," hissed Ava.

"No, it's not," said Carmela. "And don't kid around, because I'm pretty sure we left it unlocked."

"Then the knob's stuck," said Ava, tugging. "Either way, nothing's happening." Her voice seemed to rise an octave and quiver.

"Let me try," said Carmela. She grasped the doorknob with both hands, tugged hard. Nothing.

"Try your key," suggested Ava.

"It doesn't work that way," said Carmela. "The key works from the outside only. When you're inside you turn the deadbolt to lock or unlock the door."

"Duh," said Ava. "So I should have been . . ." She reached

up and turned the latch. There was a loud click, then Ava tugged at the door. "Nope, still stuck."

"Doesn't make sense," said Carmela.

"A lock malfunction," said Ava. "Or maybe somebody . . . jammed it?"

"Who would do that?" asked Carmela. It wasn't an idea she particularly wanted to entertain.

The two women stared at each other for a few seconds. The notion that some unseen entity wanted them trapped inside was too frightening to contemplate.

"So we should . . . what?" asked Carmela.

"I think I . . ." began Ava. Then she stopped abruptly.

"What?" asked Carmela.

Ava stared at her with bright eyes. "Heard something."

"There's nothing in here that . . ." said Carmela. And then she heard it, too. A soft click-tick against one of the front windows. Like branches blowing against the glass. Or skittering fingernails? *No*, Carmela told herself. *Don't go there.*

Silence hung over them like black crepe.

"The garage door," said Ava, snapping her fingers. "Let's go back downstairs, push our way through all that junk, and raise the door. We'll call a locksmith first thing tomorrow to come and fix all this shit. It's not our fault some of this stuff needs fine-tuning."

"Sure," said Carmela, feeling a flood of sudden relief. "That should work."

But negotiating their way to the garage door was easier said than done.

"This stuff is a complete tangle," complained Carmela. "We're gonna have to move this box in order to get to this bookcase, then that's gonna have to slide over to . . ." She sighed deeply. It was beginning to feel like a tricky Chinese puzzle.

"I've got an idea," said Ava. "'Cept you might not like it."

"Try me," said Carmela. She was ready to do just about

anything to get out of there. The whole Medusa Manor project was starting to wear a little thin.

"We move the rug and the library table, which allows us to open the front door of the hearse. Then we climb through and crawl out the back. One hit on that garage door opener and we're outa here."

Carmela stared at her.

"See?" said Ava. "I knew it would creep you out."

"This place seems to creep us out more than usual," observed Carmela. "But, basically, I like your idea. And it should work."

Clearing a pathway to the driver's-side door took only a few minutes.

"See, *cher?*" said Ava. "Easy as sweet potato pie." She wrenched the door open, then slid into the front seat. "Yowza, this is a very weird feeling. I feel like I'm in a movie or something. *Phantasm* or one of those other creepy cemetery flicks."

"Slide over, darlin'," said Carmela. "Let me in there, too."

Ava slid over to the passenger seat, then said, "Oh, what the heck, I'm just gonna go for it." She flipped around onto her knees, then suddenly dove into the back.

Thump.

"You okay?" asked Carmela. She glanced worriedly into the rearview mirror but could see nothing. Too dark.

"There's a coffin back here," murmured Ava.

"Another one?" said Carmela.

"You don't think this place is like that creepy house in *Poltergeist*, do you? Where all those coffins pushed their way up out of the ground?"

"No," said Carmela. "I think there are the two coffins, probably bought at closeout from some going-out-of-business funeral home, and that's it. Nothing haunted, nothing strange."

"Maybe they were water damaged during Hurricane Katrina."

"Or maybe they're just last year's models," said Carmela. "Whatever their sad tale, they're props for us to use. Got that? Just props."

"Got it." Ava's voice floated back to her.

Carmela scooted across the seat and turned around. "Can you edge past it?"

"If I make like an inchworm without hips," said Ava. "Jeez, I didn't know I was so fat."

"You're not fat," said Carmela. "You're lithe. Skinny and lithe like a cat. Like Isis." Isis was a furry black cat that Ava had adopted.

"Okay, I'm up against the back door now," said Ava.

"Got it open?" asked Carmela.

"You're not gonna believe this," said Ava. "But it's, heh heh, stuck."

"Stuck?"

"I'm gonna twist around and give it a good kick," said Ava.

"You got room?"

"Sure. If I pull myself into a ball and pretend I don't have any lower ribs." There was a clunk and a soft grunt, and then Ava said, "Here goes."

Her boot heels hit the back door of the hearse. Once, twice, and then . . . *boiiiing!*

"Success!" exclaimed Carmela.

"Open sesame," Ava puffed, scrambling out the far end.

Carmela heard footsteps scuffing cement, then the metallic rattle-clink-rattle of the garage door going up.

"Your turn," called Ava.

"Good work," said Carmela, as she eased herself over the backseat, gripped the side handle of the casket, and pulled herself along. In no time at all, she'd ducked under the garage door to join Ava outside. Carmela inhaled fresh, cool air and decided it had never felt better.

"How we gonna close the door behind us, *cher?*" asked Ava.

Carmela leaned into the doorway, hammered the inside button with the flat of her hand, then pulled her arm back fast.

Another rattle-clink-rattle and the garage door slowly descended.

"Okay," said Ava, as they turned in unison and started up the patchy cement ramp. "No more haunted . . ."

They both caught a hint of movement at the same time, then saw the caped man emerge from the darkness above them.

And lifted their voices together in a shrill scream!

"Eeeeiiiiy!"

Chapter 9

"WHO are you?" screamed Ava.

"Back away!" yelled Carmela, trying to put some grit into her voice. "Or I'll hit you with a dose of pepper spray!" She didn't actually have a canister of pepper spray with her, but she hoped her threat would scare him off.

The man wearing the cape threw up his hands in an anxious gesture and took a step back. "It's me! It's only me!"

"Who's *me*?" demanded Carmela.

"Sidney," came his voice. He sounded nervous. Like he was the one afraid of being attacked.

Carmela and Ava relaxed slightly as they gazed at each other. Ava raised her eyebrows in surprise. "Sidney St. Cyr?" she called out.

Sidney stepped forward into a puddle of light. "Ava?" he said. "Hey there." Now he sounded cautiously friendly.

But Ava wasn't having it. "What the heck are you *doing* out here, Sidney?" she demanded. "You scared the living crap out of us!"

"I live down that way," said Sidney. He flapped a hand to indicate a spot somewhere down the dark alley, looking as meek and hunched up as he'd appeared on TV the other night. "On Frenchmen Street. This is my neighborhood."

"Oh yeah?" said Ava. She sounded as though she didn't believe him.

"I just finished guiding one of my ghost walks," Sidney explained. "The History and Mystery Walk. And I was on my way home."

"You just happened to be passing Medusa Manor?" Carmela demanded. Sidney's story sounded fishy to her.

"Hey," said St. Cyr, petulance creeping into his voice. "Melody was a *friend* of mine. I feel awful about her murder. The only reason I was lingering back here was I was kind of paying my respects."

"In the alley behind Medusa Manor," said Carmela. His explanation still sounded wonky.

Sidney bobbed his head. "Sure. Why not? Medusa Manor was one of Melody's big passions. She had high hopes for this place and shared a lot of her ideas with me."

Emboldened now, Carmela stepped forward, forcibly invading Sidney's personal space. "Speaking of ideas," she said, "do you have any idea who might have wanted Melody dead?"

St. Cyr looked at her sharply. "No! Of course not! Melody was a terrific person. Everyone simply adored her."

"Clearly someone didn't," Ava murmured.

"You say the two of you were friends?" said Carmela, vowing to check Sidney's story with Garth. "Compadres? Then maybe you know what Melody had been involved in recently."

"Like what?" Sidney asked, sounding puzzled. "What are you talking about?"

"Anything besides Medusa Manor?" asked Ava.

Sidney thought for a minute. "Certainly this was Melody's pet project. I mean, she was the one who found this property and went through the whole bidding process with the city to obtain it. Then she drew up a very credible business plan and convinced Olivia Wainwright to become her silent partner."

"I'm looking for something that might have been a bit more unusual," said Carmela.

Sidney gazed at Carmela for a long moment. "Well . . . I suppose there were a few things. Melody did have a slightly dark side."

"After prowling through Medusa Manor, we're beginning to understand that," said Ava.

"I don't mean that in a *bad* way," said Sidney, a hint of indignation creeping into his voice. "Melody was just extremely . . . what would you call it? . . . *knowledgeable* about the supernatural. She was a tremendous resource in helping me put together my ghost walks. Selecting routes and points of interest, helping me script my narration. Melody was especially good with the cemetery crawls. She was very much into New Orleans hauntings and history and had amassed tons of research."

"Melody did this for you gratis?" asked Carmela. It sounded like a lot of work to her.

Sidney St. Cyr bristled slightly. "Melody's research dovetailed with what I do and with a lot of her other interests."

"Like what?" asked Ava.

Sidney thought for a moment. "She was a member of the Hellfire League and the Restless Spirit Society."

"Ha ha," said Ava, taking a step back. "You're trying to scare us. Nice try."

"I've heard about the Hellfire League," said Carmela. It was a private club that was more society than spooky. "But the Restless Spirit Society? That's a new one."

"Probably because they're a relatively new group," said St. Cyr.

"Restless spirits," said Carmela, wrestling with the notion.

Sidney gave a shrug. "The group's really a bunch of ghost hunters and paranormal freaks with a few quasi researchers thrown in for good measure."

"And they do . . . what?" asked Ava.

"Investigate supernatural phenomena," said Sidney.

"New Orleans has been experiencing a lot of supernatural phenomena lately?" Carmela asked in a clearly skeptical tone.

"Well . . . actually, yes," said Sidney. "You undoubtedly know the same stories I do. About the ghosts, vampires, and even saints that are supposedly prowling our city."

"Okay," said Carmela. "I suppose so." He had her there.

"Actually," said Sidney, "the Restless Spirit guys are a fairly cool crew that gets together to creepy-crawl old buildings, looking for signs of haunting or supernatural phenomena. They take readings using infrared cameras and magnetometers. That sort of thing."

"You're telling me they crawl through old, deserted buildings?" asked Ava. "With spiders and rats and stuff." She touched her fingertips to her hair, as though she could feel crawly things bothering her.

St. Cyr nodded. "Sometimes. RSS, Restless Spirit Society, is basically urban explorers with a paranormal bent. They've explored several old factories and abandoned buildings. And Melody once told me they went through an old mortuary and a salt cave. She was really into that stuff."

Ava shook her head. "You're kidding, right?"

"No," said Sidney. "I'm absolutely serious."

As they were driving home, Ava asked, "Do you trust Sidney St. Cyr?"

"Not sure," Carmela replied. "I don't know him well enough to make any sort of pronouncement."

"What did you think about this Restless Spirit Society?"

Pausing at a stop sign, Carmela stared up at spidery

branches etched against the silvered, almost-full moon. "I think they sound very strange."

"You think we should check 'em out?" asked Ava.

Carmela thought about Medusa Manor, the Hellfire League, and the Restless Spirit Society. Three keen interests of Melody's. Almost a . . . what? A triple witching?

"What do you think?" pressed Ava.

"I think . . . yes," said Carmela.

Back in the French Quarter, Carmela dropped Ava off outside the front door of Juju Voodoo, then circled around the block, bumped down a cobblestone alley, and pulled her car into one of the long, low garages that backed up against her apartment building.

Hurrying across the dark courtyard to her apartment, Carmela was thinking how nice it would be to ease into her cozy bed and curl up with a good book—until she saw her door standing ajar. Two inches ajar, to be exact.

She paused beneath the canopy of the spreading live oak tree, listening to the patter of the fountain. This was bad, she decided. This was very bad. Had someone broken into her apartment? And if so, where exactly were the dogs? Her so-called *guard* dogs?

Lifting her chin and squaring her shoulders, Carmela went to the door and called out in her gruffest voice, "Is someone in there?" Then, as if they'd really answer her, she called, "Boo? Poobah? You guys okay?"

Easing the door open with her toe, moving with extreme stealth, Carmela tiptoed in.

"I was wondering when you'd show up," said a man's voice.

"What!" exclaimed Carmela.

There was a long, low chuckle, and then a light snapped on. Edgar Babcock was stretched out in her leather easy chair with Boo and Poobah curled up next to him.

"What do you think you're doing!" exclaimed Carmela.

"Waiting for you," replied Babcock.

"Excuse me," said Carmela, "but I'm talking to Boo and Poobah." She planted her hands on her hips and stared directly at her two dogs. "You guys are supposed to be on red alert. On guard duty. Not asleep at your post. Ten demerits for each of you!"

Boo raised her head daintily and gave a delicate snort. Poobah kept his head between his outstretched paws and rolled his eyes nervously.

"A likely story," sniffed Carmela. She turned her attention back to Babcock. "And how exactly did *you* get in here?"

Babcock favored her with a lazy grin, then an affable shrug. "Picked your lock."

"What!" she cried. What was it with locks tonight? "You didn't really."

He cocked his head and reached out an arm to grab her, but Carmela danced away from his fingertips. "Sure I did," he told her. "It's a piece of crap. You oughta invest in a Schlage or a Medeco. Something substantial that the creeps in this city can't pop like a grape. Something that will protect you, keep you safe."

"I thought that's what you were here for."

Babcock stretched farther and grabbed her hand, then finally pulled her down next to him. "Mmm," he said. "That's how you think of me? As your own personal Rottweiler?"

Carmela finally broke down and gave him a teasing smile. "It's *one* of the things."

Kisses were in order then. Long, slow kisses that went beyond mere greetings.

"Where were you?" Babcock asked, when they finally pulled apart. He sounded more than a little breathless.

Carmela gave him what she hoped was a totally innocent smile. "Out with Ava."

"*Out* can be a pretty big area," Babcock said in an agreeable tone. "*Out* could be shopping on Magazine Street or having gumbo over at Mumbo Gumbo and flirting with that oily-looking owner who's always asking you for a date. Or *out* could be sticking your nose where it doesn't belong."

"You're wrong on all counts," Carmela told him. "We just popped over to Medusa Manor."

Babcock reacted as if an electric wire had been run up his leg. "What?" he cried, then leaned forward in his chair. "Are you crazy! After what just happened, why in heaven's name would you venture back there?"

"Olivia Wainwright asked us to continue with the decorating."

"And you said yes," said Babcock, incredulous.

Carmela gave him a look of pure innocence. "Well . . . yes."

"Bad idea," snapped Babcock. "Wait a minute, did you cross the police line? I'm pretty sure our crime-scene tape was still strung up."

"Oh, that," said Carmela, feeling a twinge of guilt. "I think it all blew down."

"Yeah, right," said Babcock, gripping her hand tightly. "I have to say, it's particularly disheartening when the public, you in particular, has little or no regard for police authority."

"Sorry," said Carmela, with faux contriteness.

"And I really hate the idea of you going back to that place."

After their terrifying little lockdown experience tonight, Carmela might have agreed that Medusa Manor wasn't exactly a user-friendly place, but she wasn't about to give Babcock the satisfaction. And she sure as heck wasn't going to tell him about how she'd shimmied through a hearse to escape!

"Ava and I are pretty pumped up that we're going to continue working on the place," Carmela told him.

"Who hired you to do this?" Babcock asked.

"Olivia Wainwright, the silent partner." She stared at

him, thinking. "But you already know about Olivia, right? You must have talked to her."

"You might say that," he said, rubbing his hand up her arm.

"Olivia's not a suspect or anything like that, is she?" asked Carmela. "She's on the up-and-up?"

"I'm really not at liberty to say." He cocked his head and gave Carmela a half smile. "You don't by any chance have something to eat around here, do you?"

"Since you already invaded my home, I assume you checked the refrigerator."

"Guilty as charged," said Babcock, "but I didn't see much."

Carmela sighed. "What are you in the mood for?"

"I don't know. I missed dinner, so anything is good. Even a doughnut if you've got it."

"A cop who likes doughnuts," said Carmela. "How original."

"Or, rather, a beignet," said Babcock, referring to the tasty deep-fried pastries served at Café du Monde in the French Market. "Far better than any garden-variety cake doughnut."

Carmela walked over to her refrigerator and peered inside. "How about some monkey bread?" she asked him.

"What?" he called out.

Carmela grabbed two cans of refrigerated biscuits, a stick of butter, a bag of pecans, and a jar of maple syrup. "It's this quick-bread thing I sometimes make. Not from scratch, but still good."

"Honey," he said, "if you make it I know it's gonna be wonderful."

Thirty minutes later Babcock was singing the praises of Carmela's monkey bread. "This is *so* good," he told her. "And you seriously made this from refrigerated biscuits?"

Carmela nodded.

"Tastes like it's from scratch."

"That's the general idea," she told him. "Want another piece?"

He nodded.

Carmela cut him another hunk of monkey bread, slathered it with butter, and put it on his plate.

"Thanks."

"Got a question," she said.

Chewing contentedly, Babcock smiled at her. "Shoot."

"About the fire up in the tower room . . ."

"Wasn't really a fire," said Babcock.

"But the walls looked all charred."

Babcock nodded, still chewing. "Best-guess scenario we have right now is an incendiary device."

"Explain please," said Carmela.

He tore off a bite of monkey bread and swirled it in the butter that had slid onto the plate. "Bomb, grenade, that type of thing."

"So it suggests someone with military training?" Offhand, Carmela couldn't think of anyone with that type of background.

"Or just access to that kind of stuff," said Babcock. "These days, you can buy that shit everywhere. Get it on the Internet or from crazies who sell it out of the backs of their trucks or set up gun garage sales at public storage lockers."

"Gun garage sales?" said Carmela. It was interesting what you learned hanging around with a cop.

When Babcock finally claimed to be stuffed, Carmela cleaned up, slid the dirty dishes into the dishwasher, and wandered back to the leather chair, where Babcock was leafing through one of her fashion magazines.

"Ladies really like this stuff, huh?" he asked.

She nodded and sat down beside him. He dropped the magazine. She snuggled in next to him and he tipped his head down and kissed her on the eyebrow.

"Tickles," she told him.

"I saw a packet from a lawyer sitting over there," he told her. "Everything okay?"

She nodded. "Just settlement papers."

"The ex files," said Babcock.

"Hah," said Carmela. "Good one."

Finally they started to kiss and neck a little more seriously. Which, of course, meant a move into the bedroom and lighting the candles in the silver candelabra that Carmela had pinched from Shamus's house.

Boo and Poobah, respecting Carmela and Babcock's privacy, remained in the living room.

As they were drifting off to sleep, Carmela finally asked the question she'd been dying to ask all night. "Any suspects?"

"Mmm," said Babcock, rolling over onto his side and snuggling in contentedly. "One or two."

Carmela's ears perked up, but she let a couple of beats go by. Then she asked, "Who?"

When nothing was forthcoming from the other side of the bed, she asked "Who?" once again. But for all the good it did her, she may as well have been a barred owl, hunkered in a tree, solitary in the night, listening hard for the scuffle of unsuspecting mice.

Chapter 10

GARTH Mayfeldt came sailing into Memory Mine just as Gabby was turning on lights and Carmela was trying to coax their ailing coffee maker into spitting out a few turgid cups of chicory coffee.

"Now I'm a suspect!" were the first words out of Garth's mouth.

"What?" said Gabby, whirling about, looking suddenly stricken. "Are you serious?"

Doggone, thought Carmela. Why hadn't Babcock shared this with her last night when he was sharing her bed? She let that notion rumble through her brain for a few seconds. Probably, she decided, because if he'd told her that he was looking hard at Garth, he wouldn't have gotten an ounce of shut-eye. Or any monkey bread, either.

Gabby led Garth to the back table, then sat down beside him in a commiserating gesture. She was a frequent customer at Fire and Ice and pretty much thought the world of Garth. Especially since he'd helped persuade her husband to buy a glamour-girl three-carat marquise-cut diamond ring for her last anniversary.

After their coffee maker finally oozed forth a single cup, Carmela carried a red ceramic mug to the table and slid it toward Garth. "Okay," she said. "What's up? Why have the police suddenly turned their beady little eyes on you?"

Garth took a quick sip of coffee and shook his head angrily. Color flared in his cheeks and his sparse hair stuck up slightly, as though even his scalp were outraged. "A couple of things," he told them. "One, because Melody and I had taken out fairly substantial insurance policies on each other."

"A lot of couples do that," said Gabby. She turned wide, questioning eyes on Carmela. "Don't they?"

Garth cleared his throat nervously. "Yes, they do. But I can see where it might *appear* suspicious."

Carmela took a deep breath. "What else?" she asked Garth.

Garth pursed his lips and assumed an unhappy face. "That story Kimber Breeze did last night on funeral jewelry made me look like some kind of death cult creep. Nasty calls started pouring in and, this morning, when I arrived at Fire and Ice, two detectives were waiting for me." He sighed. "They asked lots more questions. Nothing new about that, except for the fact that their attitude has suddenly gone from deep concern to all-out interrogation."

"Any other reason you think you've been added to the suspect list?" asked Carmela.

Garth rubbed his hands across his face and gave them a baleful look. "Probably because they don't seem to have anyone else!"

"That's absolutely unfair!" declared Gabby.

"Shameful," sniffed Garth.

Carmela thought for a few moments. "You were alone at Fire and Ice on Monday evening." It was a statement, not a question.

"Yes," said Garth. "So, of course, in the minds of the police the timing works perfectly."

"Timing?" said Gabby.

Carmela filled in the blanks. "The police think Garth might have had adequate time to drive to Medusa Manor, kill Melody, then run back to the shop."

"But he wouldn't do that!" exclaimed Gabby. She was gung-ho for Garth's innocence. So was Carmela. Sort of.

The three of them sat staring at each other for a minute, and then Garth swallowed hard a couple of times. "Listen," he said, gazing directly at Carmela. "I understand you're kind of an amateur investigator."

Carmela raised her eyebrows.

Garth continued. "In fact, I hear you're remarkably adept at solving mysteries."

"Who told you that?" asked Carmela.

Garth gave a tentative smile. "Jekyl Hardy."

"Aiii," said Carmela. Jekyl Hardy was a dear friend who spent one crazed month each year designing and building spectacular Mardi Gras floats. The other eleven months he focused on art consulting and antiques appraisals.

Buoyed by Jekyl's words regarding Carmela, Gabby added, "Carmela's not just good at solving mysteries, she's almost a pro."

"I wouldn't say that," protested Carmela.

"No," said Gabby, "you have a very good head for tracking down clues and figuring stuff out. Remember when Shamus's Uncle Henry was murdered? When Shamus was kidnapped? You were the one with the smarts to follow the trail."

"Carmela," said Garth. He swallowed, grimaced, then stared at her plaintively. "Would you help?"

Would she help? There it was. Carmela supposed she'd been on a collision course with this request ever since she'd witnessed poor Melody tumbling from that tower window. However, if the police were now looking hard at Garth, should she be doing the same? Was he . . . could he be . . . a suspect? A killer?

"Carmela," said Gabby. "Will you help him?"

Carmela shook her head, realizing she'd drifted off for a few moments.

"Will you?" Garth asked again. "Please?"

Carmela stared at him, still thinking.

"The thing of it is," said Garth, "you've agreed to continue decorating Medusa Manor. So you're already in the thick of things."

"He's right," said Gabby, as the bell over the front door dinged and two customers pushed their way in. "So what have you got to lose?" She stood, gave Carmela a pleading look, then headed for the front counter.

Carmela drummed her fingers on the battered wooden table. "I'm not sure where I'd start," she told Garth.

He gazed back at her with a hopeful, encouraging smile.

"Okay," said Carmela, gesturing with her fingers. "Talk to me. Tell me what Melody had been up to lately."

"Mostly Medusa Manor," said Garth.

"Any problems with that business?"

"None that I know of," said Garth.

"Let's start from the beginning, then," said Carmela. "Melody was the one who located the property?"

"Oh sure," said Garth. "The place had been in foreclosure. When Melody heard about it and took a quick tour, she thought it'd work perfectly for her haunted-house concept."

"And then Melody talked Olivia Wainwright into putting up the money?"

"Something like that," said Garth. "I know there were a couple of other groups interested in the building, but in the end it came down to sealed bids. Melody and Olivia emerged as high bidders."

"Do you know who the other bidders were?" asked Carmela.

Garth started to shake his head, then said, "Wait a minute. Melody did mention something about Sawyer Barnes trying to get his hands on the property."

"And he is . . . ?" asked Carmela. The name sounded familiar, but she couldn't attach it to anything concrete.

"Sawyer Barnes is a developer," said Garth. "A guy that Melody was pretty scornful of. Apparently he buys historic old homes, cuts them up, and turns them into overpriced, overdesigned condos."

"Just what New Orleans needs right now," said Carmela. "Another real estate developer bent on eradicating history."

"I hear you," said Garth.

"Do you think there might have been bad blood between Melody and this Sawyer Barnes?"

Garth's front teeth nibbled his bottom lip. "Don't know. But from what I hear, he's a carpetbagger type. From not here." *From not here* was how folks in New Orleans described people who hadn't been born and bred in the area.

"Just a minute," said Carmela. She slipped into her office, grabbed a spiral notebook and a squishy black pen, then returned to the table. Flipping open to a fresh page, she jotted down the name *Sawyer Barnes*.

"Are you going to check him out?" asked Garth.

"Maybe," said Carmela. "We'll see." She tapped her pen against the notebook. "How close was Melody to Sidney St. Cyr?"

Garth peered at her sharply. "Why do you ask?"

"Just wondering," said Carmela. "My friend and I ran into him last night outside Medusa Manor."

"Well," said Garth, "they were friends, certainly."

"Melody never mentioned any professional rivalry between the two of them?"

Garth shook his head. "Not that I can recall. Why? You think Sidney had something to do with her death?" He looked fairly stunned.

"Doubtful," said Carmela. "I'm just trying to look at all the angles."

Garth put a hand over his heart. "You scared me there."

"Sorry," said Carmela.

"No," said Garth, "now I see what Jekyl was talking about. And Gabby, too. You have a real knack for this stuff."

"I haven't done anything yet," said Carmela. She tapped her pen again. "Do you have a claim on Medusa Manor? Are you part owner now?"

"Not really," said Garth. "Olivia was bankrolling it, so she's the real owner. Melody did quite a bit of antiques scouting, so reimbursements will have to be made. But I doubt it'll amount to all that much."

"How much did Melody buy?" asked Carmela, even though she pretty much knew the answer to that question.

Garth cocked his head, thinking. "I know she picked up a pine highboy to house the sound system, some gigantic brass candlesticks from a church, and a metal slab from a funeral home." He shook his head. "Sounds a little crazy, doesn't it?"

"What else?" asked Carmela. She was well aware of the hearse and the huge pile of stuff in the basement.

"I know Melody poked through the scratch-and-dent rooms of quite a few Royal Street antiques shops," said Garth.

"Do you know which ones?"

"Mmm . . . probably Dulcimer's Antiques, Metcalf and Meador, and maybe Peacock Alley. There were probably more, but those are the only ones I remember her mentioning." Garth looked puzzled. "You think there's a connection there?"

Carmela didn't think so, but she dutifully wrote down the names anyway. "The designer who quit," said Carmela. "Know anything about him?" Carmela didn't know his name.

Garth squeezed his eyes shut, thinking. Then they popped open suddenly and he said, "Henry Tynes."

"That's his name?" asked Carmela. She thought it sounded

like the name of a prep school. Or an English shoe manufacturer. "Any idea why Tynes quit?"

Garth shrugged. "Melody said it was because he had other commitments."

Carmela knew that could be code for a better job, a desire to jet off for a spring vacation, or just loss of interest.

"Actually," said Garth, "the police asked quite a few questions about him."

"What, specifically, did they want to know?"

"How long Tynes had worked for Melody, what he was tasked with, why he quit. Basic stuff."

"But they didn't give any indication that this Henry Tynes was a suspect?"

"I figure if they asked about him, he was on their short list," said Garth.

"Good point," said Carmela. "How about the fellow who set up some of the special effects?"

"Tate Mackie," said Garth.

"What do you know about him?" Carmela asked.

"He's a good guy. Runs that shop, Byte Head, a couple of blocks from here. He called me yesterday to offer his condolences. I think he and Melody got along pretty well."

"Okay," said Carmela. She was scribbling in her notebook, but it didn't feel like any of her notes were worth much. Just filling pages. "Tell me about Melody's extracurricular activities."

Garth looked puzzled. "Huh?"

"The Hellfire League and the Restless Spirit Society."

"Oh," said Garth, thinking now. "The Hellfire League, not so much. She kind of lost interest in that a year or so ago. Her folks were big society hoo-has, but Melody was bored by that stuff."

"But Melody was into the other one?" asked Carmela. "The Restless Spirit Society?"

"She was," said Garth, "although she never talked much about it. Melody would toddle off to her creepy-crawl, then come back late at night, all dusty and dirty and babbling about cold spots and glowing orbs." He looked at Carmela with bright eyes. "Who knows, maybe they really did detect the occasional ghostly presence."

"Sure," said Carmela. "Maybe." Although she'd heard countless tales about the ghosts of New Orleans—in Pirate's Alley, at Le Petit Theatre du Vieux Carré, at Le Pavilion Hotel, and many other French Quarter places—she'd never had the privilege of coming face to face with an actual card-carrying member of the spirit world. And seeing was believing, right? "Anything else?" Carmela asked Garth.

His face sagged. "Just one more thing. Melody's memorial service will be tomorrow. Eleven o'clock at Lafayette Cemetery."

"Oh my," said Carmela, feeling a deep sadness well up within her.

Tearing up suddenly, Garth said, "You will come, won't you? To help us memorialize Melody and keep a watchful eye. Just in case . . . well, you know."

Carmela nodded. She didn't think Melody's killer would have the audacity to show up at the cemetery. Then again, you never know.

Once Garth departed Memory Mine, Carmela flew into high gear. She called a local glazier and arranged to have the glass repaired in Medusa Manor's garage and upstairs windows, then put in a call to a locksmith to deal with that sticky front door lock.

Finally, Carmela joined the living. She helped Cindy, one of her regular customers, select a series of floral and tea-themed rubber stamps so she could create personal, distinctive invitations for a tea party she was hosting.

Another customer wanted to create a special scrapbook page for her daughter, who'd starred in a high school production of Verdi's *La Traviata*. Because one of the photos of the daughter singing on stage was so striking, Carmela suggested she mount the photo on foam core, then cut out the costumed figure of her daughter. Carmela then advised the woman on how to create a background using a page of sheet music from *La Traviata*, glue a sheet of bronze-colored tissue paper on top of it, then add peach, pink, and gold translucent paint highlights using a sponge and colored ink pads. When the background assumed the look of a sun-dappled Tuscan wall, the foam core figure would be mounted and the edges of the sheet music finished off with strips of embossed metallic paper.

When there was finally a break in the action, Carmela sat down at her iMac and Googled the Restless Spirit Society.

Amazingly, the group had a fairly decent Web site. The splash page was a collage of gritty black-and-white photos, all taken from unusual angles. There were photos of low, rounded tunnels with dark openings; crazy angles of Gothic-inspired buildings; a grainy shot of the interior of an old shoe factory. All very eerie and Hitchcock looking. The accompanying text was purposely coy about the group's activities and what buildings they'd specifically explored. Carmela decided this was par for the course when it came to urban explorers and ghost hunters. Some groups, she'd heard, roamed abandoned industrial sites and trekked through tunnels, churches, old hotels, and cemeteries. Most of the time they entered with great stealth under cover of darkness. And entered illegally, too.

As Carmela clicked through the various pages, she stumbled upon a small Events section. And, lo and behold, one of their forays was scheduled for tonight. At, of all bizarre places, something called the abandoned Mendelssohn Insane Asylum.

Should I? Carmela wondered. Her right hand twitched on her computer mouse, and then she clicked the e-mail button. Fully realizing this was a shot in the dark, she quickly typed a message—*My friend and I would like to join your group tonight*—then hit Send.

Hopefully, she'd get an answer back in time. Hopefully,

the Restless Spirit Society had an open-door policy regarding new members.

Since she was still on the Internet, Carmela ran a quick Google search on Sawyer Barnes. There were dozens of hits, mostly short newspaper blurbs about his efforts to buy rundown properties and rehab them. One blurb had a photo of Barnes. He was curly-haired, square-faced, an attractive forty-something.

Looks the part of a real estate developer, she decided.

Then, because Carmela still felt a little jazzed about the Restless Spirit Society, she grabbed her phone and hit speed dial. She had to talk to Ava at Juju Voodoo right away.

When a busy signal buzzed in her ear, Carmela decided to slip out the back door and run down the alley to pitch Ava on the idea of another night of impromptu exploring.

"Ava?" Carmela called out as she pushed her way through the red wooden door of Juju Voodoo. Overhead, a dancing skeleton clicked and clacked his bony welcome, while a display of flickering red votive candles greeted her in the dark interior that smelled mildly of sandalwood and patchouli oil. All around were counters stacked with voodoo dolls, tarot cards, saint candles, incense, shrunken heads, life-sized hanging skeletons, and necklaces hung with carved teeth and bones.

"That you, *cher*?" Ava's head suddenly popped up between two colorful Haitian masks, and then a smile spread across her lovely face. "If it isn't Little Orphan Annie," she exclaimed. "What're *you* doin' here?"

"Came to invite you on a snipe hunt," said Carmela.

"Mmm . . ." Ava rolled her eyes expressively and pushed back a mass of dark curly hair. "I haven't been on a snipe hunt since I was fifteen years old and went to Bible camp. And then it wasn't exactly snipe I was after, if you catch my drift." She grinned a wicked grin and flicked a bloodred nail against a hunk of white frizzy goat hair that stuck out from the sides of one of the masks.

"Okay, how's this," said Carmela. "What would you think about exploring an old insane asylum tonight?"

Ava put a hand to the side of her face as though she were pondering mightily. "Now there's something to consider. So far, my plans include staying home, parking my butt in front of the TV, and watching a bunch of desperate women who are from either the OC, Wisteria Lane, or New York City. Which I suppose makes *me* look slightly desperate. Or I suppose I could toddle off with you on what sounds like another, dare I say it, hair-raising adventure."

"I knew you'd say yes," said Carmela.

"I didn't say yes!"

"I know you," said Carmela. "You can't resist this stuff." She gazed around Juju Voodoo, taking in the array of very strange merchandise. Was that really a goat head over there in the corner?

Ava grabbed a curved plastic dagger whose handle was decorated with colorful feathers and pretended to plunge it into her heart. "You've got me there, *cher*. I'm a pushover for the macabre."

"Of course you are."

Ava held up an index finger. "One question."

"Ask away."

"Why would we do this?"

So Carmela told Ava about Garth's visit, his fears that the police had him squarely in their sights, how she'd promised to help him (sort of), and how Melody had been very involved in the Restless Spirit Society.

"Now you've really been pulled into the soup," said Ava, grabbing a deck of tarot cards off the counter. "Helping Garth, having pillow talk with the chief investigator, and making deals with Olivia Wainwright."

"Not really," said Carmela. "Not so much."

"Oh, come on," insisted Ava. "You're *mired*. And this isn't the good kind of soup, like shrimp gumbo. It's crummy old cream of mushroom."

"I so love how your mind works," said Carmela.

"Me, too," said Ava, giving her best pussycat grin as she shuffled her tarot cards from one hand to the other. Cards flashed by. The Knight, the Empress, the Lovers.

"So you'll come along?" Carmela asked. "If I get a response from them, that is?"

"Why not?" said Ava. Then she crooked her little finger and guided Carmela back toward her office. She paused in front of the closed door, then flung it open wide. "Ta-da!" she announced with great fanfare.

Jammed on rolling racks, suspended from wires in the ceiling, were dozens of pink, white, mint-green, eggshell-blue, and mauve prom dresses. Some were long, others short and perky, still others a demure tea length. Many sported scooped necks and capped sleeves and were decorated with floral appliqués and bows. A few were slightly over the top with bustles, riots of ruffles, and streaming ribbons.

"Holy cats!" exclaimed Carmela, "it looks like a fabric mill exploded in here."

"Aren't they cute?" asked Ava, fingering the sash of one.

"I'm not sure they're exactly our style," said Carmela. "But if you're a high school girl dying to go to your spring prom and can't afford a dress, they'll probably do just fine. Better than fine."

"Yeah," said Ava. "What I'm gonna do is go through 'em and weed out the bummers. Then have 'em delivered to the Hay School auditorium." She flopped down in the large purple swivel chair that was parked behind her cluttered desk and sat cross-legged. Then she idly flipped a few of the tarot cards onto her desk, facedown.

"What are those things telling you?" Carmela asked. She wasn't a believer in tarot, *I Ching*, numerology, or anything else that purported to predict the future. On the other hand, it didn't hurt to take a peek. For amusement purposes only, as they say in the fine print.

Ava flipped one of the cards over. It was a wizened old man wearing a dark purple cloak. The Magician.

"What's that one supposed to mean?" Carmela asked.

A frown insinuated itself between Ava's perfectly waxed brows, and she shook her head slowly. "I'm no expert at reading these things," she said, "but I'd guess it means somebody lurking in the background."

"Doing what?" asked Carmela.

Ava gazed up at her. "Pulling the strings?"

Chapter 11

GLISANDE'S Courtyard Restaurant, directly across Governor Nicholls Street from Carmela's scrapbooking shop, was one of Carmela's favorite bistros. The dining room was decorated in an elegant French palette of eggshell, pale blue, and yellow. White linen tablecloths graced the tables, and diners sat on plushly upholstered high-backed chairs. Windows were swagged with linen draperies, and fresh sunflowers were artfully arranged in old French crocks. Very Old World.

The courtyard garden out back, where Carmela sat waiting at a table, was equally elegant. Bougainvilleas tumbled from Romanesque-looking pots as a three-tiered fountain pattered away. Antique bird houses and wrought-iron carriage lights hung from a loosely latticed ceiling woven with tendrils of curling ivy that allowed just the right amount of sunlight to filter through.

Carmela normally adored sitting back here for a leisurely lunch, but today she was on pins and needles. Today she was meeting Shamus for lunch. The ex. Or rather, her soon-to-be-ex. So she fidgeted, twitched, ordered a glass of Chardonnay, changed her order to iced tea, then switched it back to wine again.

Typical of Shamus, he was a good twenty minutes late. Finally, Carmela spotted him, cutting a handsome swath through the dining room, heading back toward the sunny outdoor courtyard. Along the way, Shamus glad-handed a number of acquaintances while surreptitiously sneaking peeks at the occasional good-looking woman. *No surprises here*, thought Carmela. *A leopard never changes its spots.*

When he reached Carmela's table, Shamus offered her a dazzling smile, then bent down to kiss her. At the last moment, Carmela turned her face, so Shamus's lips just grazed her cheek. It ended up being a quick and chaste kiss. One that said, *We're so over.*

"Lookin' good, babe," said Shamus as he sat down across from her. That was Shamus's standard greeting, and it hadn't changed from the time they'd been dating until now. Carmela didn't let it bother her, because Shamus pretty much greeted all women that way. Though his words were obnoxious, he considered them charming.

Peering at Carmela's empty wineglass, Shamus said, "You're drinking. I guess I better order one, too." He crooked a finger, brought a waitress scurrying over, and then spent the next five minutes specifying exactly what kind of bourbon he wanted, what type of water, and how he wanted his drink precisely mixed. Then he glanced over at Carmela. "You want another . . . what? Glass of wine?"

"Please," Carmela told the waitress directly. If she let Shamus do the ordering, it would take forever. And she had business to conduct.

"So," said Shamus, settling back in his wicker chair and crossing his long legs, "you *are* involved in a murder."

"Not really," said Carmela. She'd set up this lunch for the sole purpose of discussing the divorce settlement. No way did she want to get sidetracked.

"Yes, you are," Shamus insisted. "I hear things. In fact, I have my finger on the pulse of this city."

"No, you don't, Shamus," said Carmela in a calm, slightly bored tone. "You live in a completely insular world that's dictated by your family and a relatively small stratum of New Orleans society. Which means you all eat at the same restaurants and attend the same parties. And you, I know for a fact, still hang out with your old frat-rat buddies. The only difference is that now you're all ten years older and have moved up a notch from toga parties to the Pluvius krewe." The Pluvius krewe was the bad-boy Mardi Gras krewe that Shamus belonged to.

Anger flashed in Shamus's eyes. "You think you've got me all figured out, don't you?"

"Yes and no," said Carmela. "I pretty much know how you're going to react to most things, but once in a while you change things up and really surprise the crap out of me."

Shamus brightened. "I do? That's good, huh?"

Carmela reached over and patted his hand. "Of course it is, Shamus."

Their drinks arrived and they perused menus. One of the best things about lunch at Glisande's Restaurant was their grilled pompano. The fish always arrived steaming at the table, tender and succulent, drizzled with buttery caper sauce and accompanied by a golden mound of sweet potato French fries.

Carmela snapped her menu shut. "Grilled pompano for me."

"Me, too," said Shamus. He motioned the waitress back over, managed to communicate their order without too much extraneous direction, then smiled lazily at Carmela.

Carmela narrowed her eyes and decided to parlay Shamus's considerable banking connections into cadging a few bits of information. "Have you ever heard of a real estate developer by the name of Sawyer Barnes?"

Shamus studied her. "Is that who you're dating now?"

"No!"

"Then who is it?"

"None of your business."

"Sure it is," said Shamus. "You're still my wife." He smiled to himself. "My little wifey."

"Not for much longer," said Carmela. She hoped the amendment she wanted to tack on to Shamus's proposed divorce settlement wouldn't bring their already slow progress to a screeching halt. "Sawyer Barnes?" Carmela tried again.

Shamus scooped a croissant from the bread basket and slathered on an inch of cheese butter. "He's a real estate guy. A real player."

"How so?" asked Carmela.

Shamus took an enormous bite of his croissant. "Mmm, good."

"And so heart healthy," said Carmela.

Shamus ignored her remark. "Crescent City Bank did a little business with Barnes. From what I understand, he started out developing small apartment buildings over in Kenner. You know, like four-plexes, maybe an eight-plex. Shitty little deals. Recently, however, Barnes made the leap to dabbling in upscale condos. Sawyer Barnes buys . . . what would you call them? . . . *unusual* properties and converts them into very designer-type condos. In fact, he just did some really gorgeous two-story condos in an old cotton warehouse on the edge of the CBD." CBD was the Central Business District.

"Okay," said Carmela, "what else do you know about Barnes?"

"I just told you," said Shamus. "He's a developer. Oh, and he had that hot decorator chick, Suzi Wanamacher, do up the models in a super contemporary style." He paused. "S-curved sectionals and digital art, what more do you want? Go over and take a look at the places yourself if you're so darned interested." Shamus smirked. "But watch out for Barnes. He's a good-looking guy, lots of dark, curly hair. And, from what I hear, quite the hound dog."

"Duly noted," said Carmela.

The waitress brought their drinks, and they each took a couple of long gulps. A cooling-off period, Carmela decided. Or maybe they were fortifying themselves, working up to the big discussion.

"Hey, guess what," said Shamus.

"I don't know, Shamus," said Carmela. "What?"

"Something really cool happened. Take a wild guess."

"Glory finally went into spin-dry," said Carmela. Glory Meechum, Shamus's crazy big sis, always seemed in desperate need of an alcohol detox program.

"Don't be silly," scoffed Shamus. "The big news is that I'm gonna have some of my photos on display at the Click! Gallery this Saturday night during Galleries and Gourmets."

"That's wonderful," said Carmela. "It only took you . . . what? Four years to get a show together?"

Shamus frowned. "Photography's hard, babe. You of all people should know that. You deal with that shit at your scrapbook shop."

"Yeah," said Carmela, "that's how we refer to it, too."

Shamus rolled his eyes. "You know what I mean."

"So these are your bayou photos?" Carmela forced herself to be polite. After all, she wanted Shamus in a good mood, a *receptive* mood.

Shamus nodded. "Mostly photos I shot at the camp house." Shamus's family had a camp house in the Baritaria Bayou, a creaking, sagging cabin with a spacious front porch and tin roof that was an utter delight when rain pattered down.

"I'm happy for you, Shamus," said Carmela, in a half-hearted manner.

"You gotta stop by Click! and see 'em," said Shamus proudly. "I've got great photos of sunsets on the bayou, flocks of ibises, and even some wild nutria."

"Will your photos just be on display?" asked Carmela, "or will they be for sale, too? Is this a real gallery show?"

"For sale, for sure," said Shamus. "Hey, I see this as a lifetime calling. So I sure as heck want to make *money* at it."

"Mmm," said Carmela, as the waitress and another server arrived at their table with their luncheon entrées. The two servers stood poised for a moment, then set the entrées down in front of them in one choreographed movement.

"Excellent," said Shamus, grinning at the cuter of the two women.

Carmela took a bite of her pompano. Crispy on the outside, tender and moist on the inside.

Shamus dug in, too. "So good," he marveled.

"Shamus," said Carmela. "I read through the settlement offer you sent over."

"Mnnuhh," said Shamus with his mouth full. "I knew you'd be amenable to everything. Sounds like we're finally making progress."

"No," said Carmela. "Not really."

Shamus's eyes went wide, and his fork clattered noisily to the table. "What?"

Carmela gazed across the table at him. "I want the house, too. The Garden District house."

Now Shamus's shocked look turned to puzzlement. "The house? What house? You mean Glory's house? Or the one Uncle Henry lived in?"

Carmela shook her head. "Neither."

Understanding suddenly dawned in Shamus's eyes. "You mean *my* house?" His voice was an outraged screech.

"Technically, it was *our* house," said Carmela.

"You didn't live there that long!" said Shamus.

Carmela fired back immediately. "Neither did you, Shamus. In fact, you were the one who slipped into his boogie shoes at the first sign of trouble and left me all by myself."

"You had Boo," said Shamus, looking sheepish.

"And she was the only one I could count on," Carmela pointed out. "Because when you made no effort to come back, Glory took devilish delight in kicking me out!"

"Glory's always been a little high-strung," muttered Shamus. "She was just worried about me."

"Worried about you," said Carmela. "What a terrific family you've got there. You're like the Medicis, building your own nasty little empire, always trying to thwart outsiders."

Shamus had abandoned his pompano and was chewing his fingernails furiously now. Chewing, then spitting them out. Chewing. Spitting. Carmela tried not to watch. It had never been one of his more endearing qualities. Then again, what had?

Finally, Shamus said, "If I agree to deed the house to you, then we'd be done with it? A onetime deal, no alimony?"

Carmela nodded. "I could live with that."

"We'd be finished?"

"Kaput," promised Carmela.

Shamus grimaced. "I'd have to *move*."

"You're right about that," said Carmela. "Because if you didn't, then we'd be roommates again. Really lousy roommates. Even worse than before."

"Hmm," said Shamus, thoughtfully. "Not so good."

"No kidding," said Carmela.

But Shamus wasn't through squirming and moaning. "What would I do?" he wondered. "Where would I live?"

"I don't know," said Carmela. "Figure it out. You've got plenty of money; you're the scion to a big-assed banking family."

He peered at her.

"And there are excellent opportunities open to you," Carmela told him in a very pep-talk tone of voice. "Glory's always foreclosing on somebody. That's how she gets her kicks. Maybe you could move into one of her repo places. Someplace closer to downtown, closer to the action."

Shamus suddenly brightened. "You know, that's a very real possibility."

*   *   *

Instead of dashing back across the street to Memory Mine, Carmela swung down Governor Nicholls Street, hung a left at Burgundy Street, and in about three minutes found herself standing outside Byte Head, Tate Mackie's computer repair shop. It had once been a souvenir shop, and its large front windows had dripped with purple, gold, and green Mardi Gras beads, oversized beer mugs, pimp cups, boxes of pralines, and T-shirts that proclaimed *The Big Easy* or *Got Beads?* or *Laissez Les Bon Temps Rouler*. Now the front windows had *Byte Head* painted in jagged red letters, and the display area was stuffed with used computers, keyboards, and boxes of software.

Inside, Carmela found herself surrounded by even more computer equipment as well as several used computer desks and workstations.

A woman with a notebook computer wrapped in a pink afghan stood at the counter.

"It just crashed," she lamented to the young man who was waiting on her. "Now all I get is a speckled screen." She sniffed loudly. "My whole life's swirling around in there somewhere."

The young man, who Carmela assumed was Tate Mackie, asked a few technical questions as he wrote up her order ticket. "Leave it here," he told her, "and we'll see what we can do."

"You think you can fix it?" asked the woman, almost in tears now.

"If we can't fix it, then we'll at least try to recover your data," he assured her in a soothing voice.

"My data," she crooned. "My poor data. Yes, that would be good."

As the bereft computer user handed over her computer and slipped away, Carmela moved up to the counter. "Tate Mackie?" she asked.

The young man nodded. He was dressed in black jeans and a red T-shirt with a white, oval NOLA logo.

"I'm Carmela Bertrand," said Carmela, introducing herself.

Tate Mackie stared at her for a few seconds, and then a smile lit his face and he snapped his fingers. "Hey . . . yeah. Olivia Wainwright said you'd be getting in touch."

"Right," said Carmela. "My friend Ava and I are going to be finishing up the decorating on Medusa Manor."

A shadow fell across Tate Mackie's face. "Melody," he said. "She . . . she was a very cool lady."

"Yes, she was," said Carmela.

"Have you heard anything?" Tate asked eagerly. "Are the police any closer to catching her killer?" He pursed his lips and frowned. "If I could get my hands on the monster who murdered her, I'd . . ." His hands opened and closed spasmodically. Tate Mackie was visibly upset.

"The police are still chasing down leads," Carmela told him.

"But nobody's in custody," said Tate, sounding both angry and frustrated.

"No, not yet."

"Bummer," said Tate. Then he gazed at Carmela with a mixture of wonder and horror on his face. "And you were there when it happened. I saw the report on TV."

"Unfortunately . . . yes," said Carmela.

Tate shook his head vigorously, like a dog shaking off water, then said, "Must've been awful."

"It was pretty upsetting," said Carmela. "Which is why I agreed to finish the decorating. Help finish out Melody's pet project."

"For her memory," said Tate, nodding. "Kind of a testament to her. Yeah, I get it. It's . . . it's what I want to do, too. Melody came up with some really great ideas for Medusa Manor."

"And you already implemented some of the computer gadgetry," said Carmela, digging into her bag. "I've got the plans Olivia gave me."

Tate shoved the silver laptop off to the side so Carmela could roll out the plans. Then, for the next ten minutes, Tate recounted what he'd already installed in Medusa Manor and what he had planned.

"That all sounds good," said Carmela. She'd been furiously jotting notes, asking questions, nodding at his answers. Finally, she straightened up and looked around Tate Mackie's shop. "You repair computers," she said, "but you also do special effects."

"I gotta earn a living," he told her. "But I'm really a frustrated special-effects guy. My dream is to someday work on feature films. But . . ." He glanced about his shop. "This is what I do for the time being. Pick up the pieces when people drop-kick their laptop or their Dell goes into deep freeze." He grinned. "What kind of computer do you use?"

"An iMac."

"Do you back up?"

"Sure," said Carmela.

"You'd be surprised how many people don't," said Tate. "Then they come crying to me and expect magic." He glanced about his shop. "Anyway, it's all pretty much the same thing, isn't it? Magically repairing hard drives, creating special effects and doing CGI?"

"CGI," said Carmela. "I keep hearing that term. What exactly does it mean?"

"It's short for computer-generated imagery," explained Tate, grabbing a silver Toshiba from the table behind him and setting it on the counter. "Pioneered years ago at Industrial Light and Magic on the coast, perfected by some of the best and wackiest minds. There's lots of ways of using it. To bring dinosaurs to life, simulate outer space, whatever. I've already created several special-effects images for Medusa Manor—a howling banshee and a ghostly face, on computer."

"Okay," said Carmela.

"Then I project the image, larger than life-size, using

video equipment." He pushed a couple of buttons and a crone's face appeared, the eyes glowing like red coals, the tongue waggling like a serpent. "It's pretty cool. What I was thinking, for the Morgue of Madness, was taking the crematorium thing to the max, creating some very realistic effects with licking flames." He pushed a couple more buttons, and the image on the screen flickered from the crone's face to a wall of dancing flames.

"Wow," said Carmela, amazed and a little in awe, too. "You can really bring that to life? Make it look like it's really happening?"

Tate nodded. "If you want . . . I can make it crackle and leap like the fires of Hades."

Chapter 12

"THEY brought keys for you," said Gabby, dropping a miniature stack of shiny brass keys into the palm of Carmela's hand. It was midafternoon and she'd finally made it back to Memory Mine. "Apparently someone jammed the lock with superglue."

"Yeah?" said Carmela, wondering briefly if Sidney St. Cyr had been the culprit. "So . . . the door's fixed? Already?"

Gabby raised her eyebrows and glanced at her watch. "You've been gone for hours."

Carmela felt an instant pang of guilt. "Oh no, I have, haven't I? Was the shop terribly busy? Did I heap everything onto your capable shoulders once again?"

Gabby shook her head and waved a hand. "Nothing I couldn't handle. Gee, I didn't mean to lay such a heavy guilt trip on you."

"Well, I didn't mean to be gadding all over the French Quarter, either," said Carmela.

"You've got a lot on your plate right now," said Gabby. "I know how close you were to Melody. Garth, too."

Carmela glanced around the scrapbooking shop. Two customers were in back, perusing the display of rubber stamps. Another was halfway down the center aisle, picking out various sheets of paper. "Gabby," said Carmela, "when Garth came in this morning, you didn't get any sort of, uh, *feeling* about him, did you?"

Gabby, smart girl that she was, cocked her head. "What exactly are you asking, Carmela?"

"I think you probably know."

Gabby crossed her arms in front of her in an almost protective gesture. "Okay, yes, I suppose I do. And my answer would have to be no. My impression of Garth is that he's genuinely bereft. He and Melody had a loving and caring marriage and a really good business partnership. He would never . . ." She stopped abruptly, then said, "He would never," with great finality.

"Okay," said Carmela. "I was just trying to get a read on things. See if you picked up any weird vibes."

"It's your friend Babcock who's cornered the market on bad vibes," said Gabby. "If I were you, I'd give him a call and tell him not so politely to back off. Poor Garth has enough to deal with right now without being browbeaten by the NOPD."

"I think you may be right," said Carmela. She'd been planning to call Babcock anyway. Not to tell him to back off, but to ask him why he hadn't bothered mentioning to her last night that Garth had suddenly morphed into a suspect.

She headed back to her office, chatting with customers along the way, then digging out sheets of marbleized paper for one woman. Finally, Carmela sat down at her desk and dialed the phone.

"Hey," Babcock said to her. "I was wondering if I'd hear from you today."

Carmela didn't pull any punches. "How come you didn't tell me Garth Mayfeldt was suddenly your prime suspect?"

There was a pause, and then Babcock said, "I was wondering how long it would take you to find that out and jump on my case. And the answer is, not very long. You must have a heck of a network, lady."

"You haven't answered my question."

"I didn't tell you because you're my girlfriend, not the police commissioner. And because it really isn't any of your business."

Carmela was taken aback for a moment. By his abruptness and his choice of words. "Your girlfriend? Is that what I am?"

"I guess so," said Babcock. He let loose a warm, throaty chuckle, then added, "Face it, we weren't exactly playing tiddlywinks last night."

"Well, no," said Carmela. "But *girlfriend* just sounds so formal."

"*Friend?*" suggested Babcock.

"No, no," said Carmela. "I really do prefer the former."

"Okay," said Babcock. "So no hard feelings about what has to remain my professional responsibility?"

Carmela thought for a minute. "Since I'm more than a little involved in Melody's murder . . . since I was a peripheral witness to . . ."

"Is that what you are?" needled Babcock. "A peripheral witness?"

Carmela ignored him and plunged ahead. "Because Melody was my friend and *you* are my friend, I thought I might be allowed on the inside, so to speak."

Babcock's voice was kind when he spoke to her. "You know, Carmela, I don't just close my eyes and toss darts at a board. And I sure don't sit cross-legged and consult with mystics or swamis when I put together a solid list of suspects. There *is* a strict methodology."

"What are you talking about?"

"Suspects are questioned for any number of reasons."

"Sure, but what possible reason could you have for questioning Garth?"

Babcock exhaled loudly. Carmela was keeping the pressure on. "The money for one thing."

"You're talking about the insurance," said Carmela. "Big deal. Lots of couples take out insurance policies on each other."

"Let's just say there were extenuating circumstances," said Babcock.

Carmela was beginning to feel a tinge of frustration. Arguing with Babcock was like watching Beckett's play *Waiting for Godot*. The plot was slightly glacial, and there never seemed to be a clear resolution. "What are you talking about?" she demanded.

"For your information," said Babcock, "and I trust this will go no further, Fire and Ice is perilously close to bankruptcy."

"What!" said Carmela. Clearly this was news to her.

"The shop is insolvent," said Babcock.

"No way!" said Carmela, her words coming out as a surprised gasp. And all along she'd figured Garth and Melody were doing so well, thought they'd recovered from Hurricane Katrina and all of the ensuing nonsense with a minimum of pain.

"From what we've determined so far," said Babcock, "unpaid creditors are circling like hungry vultures. So it's only a matter of time before the shop goes under."

"But there's the insurance money," said Carmela.

"Ah," said Babcock. "Now we get to the crux of the matter."

"Garth would never be that desperate," said Carmela.

"That remains to be seen," said Babcock.

"Innocent until proven guilty," said Carmela, trying to

sound tough, but feeling discombobulated by the news that Fire and Ice had been . . . was in . . . dire financial straits.

"So now you know," said Babcock. He paused. "Happy?"

"Not really," said Carmela.

"See?" said Babcock. "There's a lesson there. Be careful what you—"

"Wish for," murmured Carmela. "I know, I know, I've heard it all before. Talk to ya later." She unceremoniously dumped the receiver onto its cradle.

Feeling out of sorts, tapping her foot nervously against the base of her chair, Carmela checked her e-mail and was rewarded with an answer from the Restless Spirit Society. She and her friend were indeed welcome to participate in their foray at the abandoned Mendelssohn Insane Asylum tonight. The group would meet at their chosen destination at nine. For her convenience, a map was attached.

Carmela snatched up the phone and hit speed dial.

"Juju Voodoo," came Ava's voice. "Two-for-one saint candles and seven ninety-nine for our special Cajun love potion that comes with a one hundred percent guarantee."

"I think I might need some of that love potion," Carmela told her friend.

Ava recognized her voice instantly. "Not to keep *your* cutie coming back. It's obvious Edgar Babcock is head over heels for you."

"Maybe so, but there seems to be a new wrinkle in Melody's murder investigation," said Carmela. And even though she'd told Babcock she'd keep quiet about it, she quickly related to Ava how Fire and Ice was close to bankruptcy.

"I had no idea!" exclaimed Ava. "That's awful."

"No," said Carmela, "we haven't gotten to the awful part yet. Now the police think Garth might have killed Melody out of desperation for the insurance money."

Carmela expected Ava to say, "No way." Instead, she just gave a long, drawn out "Hmmm."

"You think Garth could have been that desperate?" Carmela asked. She hated to even voice the words.

"Possible," said Ava. "But not probable."

"Now it sounds like you're sitting on the fence," said Carmela.

"I'm a fence-sitter from way back," said Ava.

"No, you're not. You're a lady who's rarely afraid to take a stand."

"Honey," said Ava. "What we saw Monday night, Melody's poor body cartwheelin' through the air . . . I'm *still* having scary, jittery nightmares over it. So here's the thing: if Babcock's got issues with Garth's innocence, then I'm willing to reserve judgment. I say let the police have a go at him."

"Strange how things have unraveled since this morning," said Carmela. "When I kind of promised Garth I'd look into things for him." She paused. "He was so anxious to see if I could shake any suspects loose. Does that sound like the kind of request that would come from a guilty man?"

"Don't know," said Ava. "But, honey, we live in Louisiana. Down here lots of folks still believe in Napoleonic law."

"Guilty until proven innocent," said Carmela.

"Bingo," said Ava.

Feeling more than a little unsettled, Carmela turned her attention to the flyer she'd been working on for Quigg Brevard, her friend and a local restaurateur. The flyer was supposed to promote the food booth that his restaurant, Mumbo Gumbo, was setting up on Bourbon Street for Galleries and Gourmets. Unfortunately, she'd been late starting the project and now was feeling bad. In fact, the one-page handout should have been finished last week. But then the scrapbook gods had smiled benevolently and Memory Mine had enjoyed a welcome flurry of business. And then, of course, the Medusa Manor job had come up. And so, like a lot of other things, the flyer had been temporarily forgotten.

Carmela frowned and stared at her 8½-by-11-inch layout.

She'd started with a screened-back photo of a French Quarter brick building; superimposed smaller shots of candlesticks, an old painting, and a Tiffany lamp; then added fanciful drawings of Tabasco sauce, an oyster on the half shell, and a bowl of gumbo. Quigg's flyer for Galleries and Gourmets was looking good, but it needed to be pulled together more. Carmela thought for a minute, then grabbed a handful of oil crayons. Working swiftly for ten minutes, she generously hand-tinted everything, giving it a unified look and theme.

Pleased with her efforts, all she had to do now was decide between plain Helvetica type or the bouncy . . .

Carmela straightened up, suddenly aware of a flurry of activity at the front of her store. And Gabby's voice saying a friendly "Well, hello there."

Then, before Carmela could pull herself out of her own personal design marathon, someone was standing behind her. She blinked, turned her head, and found herself staring into the intense dark eyes of Quigg Brevard.

The owner of both Bon Tiempe Restaurant and Mumbo Gumbo, Quigg Brevard was handsome, a shameless flirt, and a bit of a bachelor bon vivant. Tall, olive skinned, and broad shouldered, Quigg had the innate ability to set women's hearts to racing—and knew it.

"Hey," said Quigg, his voice almost a chuckle, "you didn't color inside the lines."

"No," said Carmela, "it looks better all squiggly like that."

He cocked an appraising eye. "At least you're working on it. I wondered where that thing was."

A hundred excuses suddenly bubbled up inside Carmela's head. But instead of plucking one out and trying to run with it, she simply said, "I'm sorry, Quigg. I know I'm really late on this."

Quigg's brows knit together. "Galleries and Gourmets *is* just three days away."

Carmela bit her lower lip. "Yes, and I feel awful. But . . .

your flyer's almost finished and I promise there'll be no charge."

Quigg's big hand reached past her, and his index finger hovered at the top of the page where the headline read, *Goody, Goody, Gumbo*. "Cute," he said. Then he quietly studied the rest of the copy, which pretty much listed all of his food items.

Carmela rolled her chair back, forcing Quigg to take a step backward. Then she stood up to face him. "I really am sorry." She smiled up at him, aware of his presence so close to her.

"You already said that." Quigg smiled as though he knew he made her slightly nervous.

"I'm just . . . flustered," she told him. "I figured I could get this flyer done in a snap and then . . . I don't know . . . things came up. As government bureaucrats are wont to say—mistakes were made."

"But you do take responsibility," he said, moving a half step closer to her. "And I appreciate that, seeing as how I came all the way over here to see what the heck was up with my flyers."

Now Carmela was backed up against her desk. She could feel the edge of it pressing against her hip. "Which is good," she told him. "Because now you can proof it."

"Sure." His eyes never left hers. "Actually, I just did. Looks great."

"Then give me a little room and let me finish the design at the bottom." Carmela grabbed a rubber stamp of a jalapeño pepper, rubbed it against a red ink pad, then made a series of impressions at the bottom of the page. "There," she told him. "Done."

He looked at the flyer, a little mystified. "Terrific, but that's only one."

"This is the original," she told him. "Now I'm going to scan it into my computer and print out a few hundred on white linen paper."

"That's how it works, huh?" he asked.

"It's one way," she told him.

"Hey," he said, grinning. "I saw you on TV the other night."

Carmela waved a hand. "It was nothing."

"You look good on camera. Very photogenic."

"I was backing out of a store. Trying not to be interviewed. How good could I look?"

"You impressed me," said Quigg. He cocked his head and gave her a lazy smile. "Say . . . your divorce final yet?"

Carmela shook her head. "Nope. But counting the days."

"Mmm," murmured Quigg. "Not soon enough." He started to lean in.

Putting a palm flat against his chest, Carmela exerted a fair amount of pressure. "Whoa, there. Kindly back off."

He did. But not by much.

"We had some good times together, didn't we?" Quigg asked.

Carmela had to admit they had. Back when Shamus had left her the first time and she'd finally decided to get back into the swing of things, she'd attended a fancy Garden District dinner party with Quigg. It had been pleasant, but he hadn't seemed eager to give up his bachelor ways. Since then, they'd had dinner together a couple times at Bon Tiempe, his upscale restaurant over in the Bywater part of town. There'd been sparks between them, but none that had seriously ignited. Still, Quigg did appear to be simmering a bit now. Now that she was . . . otherwise occupied?

"If you can wait five minutes," Carmela told him, "I'll have these flyers ready for you."

Quigg fixed his laser-beam brown eyes on her. "What about distribution?"

Carmela smiled back. "That's up to you."

Now Quigg screwed his face into a worried look. "See, that's where I've got a problem. I'm supposed to check out this property on Magazine Street that I might be signing a lease on. Then I have to drive all the way down to Theriot to pick up eighty pounds of alligator steak. To cook for Saturday night."

"So you're saying . . . what?" asked Carmela.

"The flyers should really be distributed today," he told her.

"So run your errands tomorrow," she told him.

"That alligator meat is thawing even as we speak. Do you have any idea what eighty pounds of alligator can do to a BMW?"

She grinned. It didn't sound good. "So you're . . . what? Asking me to distribute your flyers?"

"Only as a practicality," said Quigg. "And then only to local galleries. The ones up and down your street here. And, um, maybe over on Royal and Bourbon Streets, too."

She gazed at him, then finally said, "I suppose it's the least I can do, considering I caused the delay."

"You're a peach," he told her.

While Quigg's flyers were spitting out of her printer, Carmela quickly ran to help Aysia Burgoyne, a woman who was fast becoming one of their regular scrappers.

Aysia, at forty, had cascades of reddish-blond curls, a peaches-and-cream complexion, and a romantic wardrobe of ruffled blouses and silk pencil skirts, and was married to Thompson Burgoyne, a private financier.

"I just discovered the most wonderful photos of my grandmother," cooed Aysia, "and decided to make some kind of commemorative album. But . . . I'm not sure where to start."

"How many photos?" asked Carmela.

"Six really nice sepia-tone photos," Aysia told her. "But all fairly small. None more than four by six inches."

"What if you put them into a booklet?" suggested Carmela, pulling out a small, ready-made chipboard album that consisted of eight pages. She studied it quickly, then handed it to Aysia. "This one will give you three double spreads on the inside."

"Okay," said Aysia, turning the album over in her hands. The stiff white paper didn't seem to impress her.

"What you'd do is cover each spread with fabric," Carmela hurriedly explained. "Pick something luxurious, like a brocade floral, to serve as your background. Then cover a piece of card stock with a contrasting piece of brocade and mount one of the photos onto it. Maybe add some bits of old lace around the edges, then flourishes like gold tassels, an old-fashioned beaded pin, gauzy ribbon, or pressed silk flowers."

"I adore that idea," declared Aysia.

"The real trick," said Carmela, grabbing a snippet of plum-colored ribbon as well as a bronzed angel charm, "is to build up layers. Maybe keep the colors in the plum–magenta–Persian red family, and try for three or even four overlapping fabrics. And don't worry if your album looks a little messy; you *want* it to look aged and atmospheric."

"And you've got tassels and beaded pins?" asked Aysia.

"At the front counter," directed Carmela.

Once Quigg's flyers were all printed, Carmela tamped them into a nice thick stack, then decided there was probably time left to deliver some of them. She could hit a few antique shops and kill two birds with one stone. That is, deliver the flyers and ask the shop owners if Melody had been in buying antiques lately. Carmela was looking for some sort of thread or connection, though she knew it would probably be quite tenuous.

Devon Dowling, the owner of Dulcimer's Antiques, was a short, fat, balding man with a scrawny pigtail down his back and a fat pug snuggled in his arms. He happily accepted a handful of Quigg's flyers, but told Carmela he hadn't seen Melody in his store.

"You're sure she came in here?" Dowling asked. "Mimi are I are generally here every day, but I don't recall seeing Melody." He kissed the pug Mimi on top of her furry little head, then assumed a pensive expression. "Terrible thing, that poor lady."

Peacock Alley Antiques was pretty much the same story. They were happy to take some of the flyers to pass along, looking forward to the upcoming Galleries and Gourmets festival, but didn't recall seeing Melody in their shop.

In the third gallery, Metcalf and Meador Fine Arts and Antiquities, Carmela had better luck. But mentioning Melody's name brought a wave of sadness to Jack Meador, the proprietor.

"Oh my gosh," he said, "can you believe what happened?" Meador was a tall, thin man, slightly ethereal with a long, hangdog face. He wore a tweed jacket with bagged-out pockets, as though he perpetually overstuffed them with keys, change, cell phone, whatever. In recalling Melody's death, he looked even more hangdog.

Carmela wanted to tell him she surely could believe what happened to Melody, because she had been right there, Johnny-on-the-unfortunate-spot. Instead, she commiserated with Meador for a few minutes. But when he pulled out a white hanky, honked loudly into it, then finally said, "You know, Melody was in here not so long ago," Carmela's ears perked up.

"Shopping for antiques?" Carmela asked.

Meador's narrow shoulders gave a slightly affirmative shrug. "I wouldn't exactly call them antiques. The items Melody bought were mostly just old."

"So not from your sales floor," said Carmela. She glanced around and her eyes fell upon Sung dynasty vases, elegant oil paintings, a mahogany secretary with brass fittings, antique lamps, a pair of Chippendale chairs, and hundreds more tasty pieces. Underfoot were fine Oriental carpets, and at least a dozen glittering chandeliers hung from the high ceiling.

"Melody was shopping for that Medusa Manor place of hers," said Meador. "So she was more interested in character than quality. She pretty much confined her shopping to the back room and the basement."

"You probably don't know this," said Carmela, "but I'm taking over that project for Melody."

Meador brightened slightly. "You are? Say, she put a few things on hold. Think you might still be interested in them?"

"They're here?" asked Carmela.

Meador nodded. "Back room."

"Let's take a look."

They wove their way past dining room sets, highboys, and a pair of towering brass vases, then pushed through a Chinese red velvet curtain into the back room. Meador pointed out the items Melody had perused.

"That dining table over there, those two paintings. Not great pieces, but not terrible, either."

"We could still use those things," Carmela told him. "It's a big place to fill."

"Yeah?" said Meador. "I have some other stuff Melody looked at. An old round-top trunk, a lamp, more paintings. Fact is, I purchased a rather large lot of things at auction up in Baton Rouge. I did okay, cherry-picked the best stuff for the front of my shop. But there was an awful lot of junk, too. Not the antique quality I've built my reputation on, and certainly not the kind of items knowledgeable collectors would want in their homes."

They tromped down narrow wooden stairs into a musty basement that was lit by four bare bulbs.

"See what I mean?" said Meador.

Staring at a high, round-topped trunk, Carmela could visualize a ghoulish body popping out of it. "That trunk would work really well," she told Meador. "So would that twisty-looking lamp."

"Tell you what," said Meador, "I'll give you a good price on the lot. The stuff we looked at upstairs plus these two pieces." He pulled a calculator from his baggy jacket pocket, poked in a few numbers, and showed it to Carmela.

She ran the numbers in her head, then nodded. "Okay."

"I'll even be happy to deliver everything. Just let me know when I can get in there."

They trooped back upstairs and exchanged business cards.

Meador picked up one of the flyers Carmela had given him earlier and studied it. "This event Saturday and Sunday is a good thing, you know? It's been tough sledding these past few years. We need something like this to give a boost to the galleries and restaurants. Sure, there's been music and jazz festivals, but mostly those just benefit the bars."

"It's going to be a good time," said Carmela.

Jack Meador crinkled his eyes at her. "I think you're right."

Chapter 13

"HOLY cats!" exclaimed Ava, as she lifted her smoked sunglasses to stare at the four-story, redbrick monstrosity that loomed in front of them on the hill. "You didn't tell me we were going to visit Dracula's castle."

"It's an old insane asylum," said Carmela, turning her car into the overgrown drive. "I told you that."

Ava didn't look particularly happy about their destination. "Isn't that a rather politically incorrect term these days?"

"It wasn't back then," said Carmela, "when this old place was still in business." She slowed her car, gazing at the Gothic letters that spelled out *Mendelssohn Asylum* in the twisted, wrought-iron archway.

"Place doesn't exactly look welcoming," said Ava as they bumped up the drive. "Look . . . the windows are either broken or boarded up, and rusted chains are stretched across all the doors."

"This is the kind of place the Restless Spirit Society lives for," said Carmela. "An abandoned building that might be haunted." And it really was abandoned, Carmela noted. Located some ten miles out of town, right on the edge of a vast bayou. As for the haunted part, well, that remained to be seen.

Ava pulled a tube of bright red lipstick from her bag and applied it to her generous lips. "When you told me it was a tour, *cher*, I was imagining something a little more refined. With refreshments included. Champagne, perhaps, and some nice cheese and crackers." She flipped the visor mirror down and smiled at herself. "Last art studio tour I went on, that's what they had."

"We'll be lucky to find a chunk of stale bread," Carmela chuckled. Then she crunched across gravel and pulled in next to the half-dozen cars that were already parked there.

"Oh man," said Ava, "this place makes Medusa Manor look like a cute little storybook cottage."

Gigantic columns paraded across the front of the building that had once housed the psychotics, alcoholics, and eccentrics of New Orleans. Two balconies, one on top of another, protruded over the front yard. Carmela could imagine administrators lining up there in past days, scrutinizing visitors as they arrived, wondering which ones would stay, which ones would attempt a daring escape.

"At least we're not the only ones here," grumped Ava as they climbed from the car. The evening's cool air and the bayou's humidity immediately wrapped around them like a wet blanket as streaks of lightning flashed in the sky. "Hopefully that thunderstorm won't hit until we're back home."

"I wouldn't want to get caught here without lights," agreed Carmela.

Ava frowned. "Lights. They do have lights in there, don't they?"

"Probably not, but I brought my trusty flashlight," said Carmela, hoisting her Fendi tote bag. "Even remembered to put in fresh batteries. I didn't want to come unprepared."

"Carmela, you're such a little Girl Scout. What's the motto? Be prepared?"

"I think that's the Boy Scout motto."

"Huh," laughed Ava. "In my experience, boys and men are always prepared." She reached a hand down the front of her red silk blouse and pulled out a thin chain with a silver medal. "See. I *knew* there was a reason I wore my Michael the Archangel medal! Guaranteed to protect us from negativity and evil spirits!"

"Car-a-mello?" A perky blond cheerleader type suddenly popped up in front of them.

"Carmela," said Carmela. She tapped an index finger to her chest. "I'm Carmela. And this is my friend, Ava."

"Mindy Deerfield," said the woman in a thick Southern drawl as she shook hands eagerly. "Membership secretary for the Restless Spirit Society. Glad you gals could join us tonight."

"Thanks for letting us participate," said Carmela.

"Consider us thrilled," said Ava, deadpan.

"Love to hear that," giggled Mindy. "You gals got much experience with urban exploring?"

"Mostly in boutiques and bars," said Ava. "And the occasional upscale hotel." She put a hand on one shapely hip. "So . . . you look like you know your way around this place. You gonna be our guide?"

Mindy favored them with a gleaming, toothy smile. "There's actually going to be three guides tonight for the asylum tour." Mindy turned quickly and started up the front steps, fluttering a hand for them to follow. "So come on along and meet our group."

"Okay," said Carmela, thinking, *That's why we're here*.

Inside, Mendelssohn Asylum was cool, dark, and creepy. High ceilings lent a cathedral look to the reception area. Chipped marble floors, institutional green paint peeling from the walls, and bars on the front windows and across the far end of the reception area gave a distinctly prisonlike feel.

"So nice and homey," remarked Ava, looking around with curiosity. "But without that overdone decorator look."

"Love the grayish-green paint," whispered Carmela. "What would you call that color? I mean, if you went to Home Depot and were asking for a paint swatch?"

"Mouse poop?" said Ava, as they joined the group of two dozen or so would-be explorers.

"Okay, everyone listen up," said a tall, rangy man with shoulder-length blond hair. "We're going to go over all the preliminaries for tonight."

"That's Elmer Coltrane," Mindy told them in a stage whisper. "He's club president."

"We've got a couple of newbies joining us tonight . . ." Elmer Coltrane glanced at Carmela and Ava and nodded politely. "So we're going to talk a little bit about safety, equipment, and who'll be functioning as guides."

Feet shifted, shoulders hunched forward expectantly, and an excited hum rose from the group gathered there. Most of the explorers wore black mesh multipocketed vests, khaki slacks, boots, and helmets, so it was hard to distinguish men from women and what the age spread might be. But Carmela had the impression that most of the group was in their twenties and thirties, with far more men than women. Two men who were diligently fiddling with strange-looking equipment looked to be in their forties.

"As we move through the asylum," said Coltrane, "remember that apparitions don't necessarily assume a human form. And that all your senses can be used to detect the ectoplasmic residue left behind by a spirit."

"Huh?" said Ava.

"What I mean," said Coltrane, "is that even clairambience, your ability to taste a spirit's message, could come into play."

"Yuck," whispered Ava.

"Most of you already know Mindy Deerfield and Jimmy Fletcher," continued Coltrane. "The three of us will guide you in separate groups to hopefully maximize your personal urban adventure experience. In a few minutes we'll pass out safety helmets for those of you who don't have your own, as well as helmet cams for those who are interested and electromagnetic field detectors and infrared motion sensors for those who want to focus on spirit auras. Of course, safety is always our number one concern. We've secured permission to explore most of Mendelssohn Asylum, but as you might imagine, a few areas are off-limits because of structural damage. Other areas may be contaminated with spores or bird droppings, so wearing a mask is going to be critical."

Mindy, ever helpful, held up a green surgical mask, the type that was commonplace in most hospitals.

"Spores," muttered Ava. "What kind of spores?"

"I'm not sure we want to know," said Carmela, accepting a mask and safety helmet from Mindy.

"You want to wear one of the helmet cams?" Mindy asked Ava.

Ava nodded eagerly, suddenly won over. "Really? Sure!" Then she turned to Carmela. "I get to wear a helmet cam, how cool is that?"

"See?" said Carmela. "This tour might redeem itself after all."

"I think you might be right," said Ava, buckling the safety strap under her chin.

"Oh, you're gonna love it," Mindy assured them, giving an excited shudder. "I mean, it's all so exciting. Can't you just feel the energy and vibrations? Even in this old reception area where poor tortured souls were turned over to the care of professionals."

"I think Mindy grew up here, don't you?" said Ava in a whispered aside to Carmela. Carmela nodded, barely holding in her laughter.

Once the helmets, cameras, flashlights, electromagnetic detectors, and recording devices had been distributed, turned on, and tested, Elmer Coltrane led them down a long hallway and into an old chapel. Pews and kneelers had long since been stripped out, but medieval-looking light fixtures, obviously nonfunctioning, dangled overhead, and a rough wooden crucifix tilted on one wall.

The club president cleared his throat. "Before we go any farther, I'd like you all to gather in a circle." Everyone slowly complied as Mindy scurried about, handing out tiny white vigil lights. "As you all know," continued Coltrane, "Melody Mayfeldt was a dearly loved member of the Restless Spirit Society. She was a true believer in the great beyond, and we honor her now, with the firm belief that Melody has gone on before us to pierce that veil of mystery we can only hope to fleetingly glimpse." He bowed his head. "She is our fallen comrade."

Boots grated on cement as throats were cleared and candles lit.

He continued. "For those of you who would like to attend Melody's funeral, it will be held tomorrow morning in Lafayette Cemetery. I can't think of a more fitting or beautiful place to be laid to rest. And now . . . a moment of silence."

Everyone bowed their head.

Carmela, finding the bobbing of the headlamps and the tiny white candles slightly disconcerting, peered out from beneath her helmet at the Restless Spirit membership. Melody may have been a beloved member, she decided, but was there someone in this group who hadn't found her quite so beloved? Someone who'd been jealous of Melody's role in the organization? Someone who'd made a pass at Melody and been angered at her rebuff? Someone who was young, reckless, and disreputable and found out Melody had owned a fancy French Quarter jewelry store?

Carmela knew there were as many possibilities as there were people here. The thing she had to do was watch, listen, and maybe ask a few questions. Just like any good investigator would.

After a few minutes, candles were snuffed out and a ripple of excitement ran through the ghost hunters.

"Whose group do you want to be in?" Carmela whispered to Ava.

Ava rolled her eyes. "I'd rather not pair up with the cheerleader."

"So maybe . . . Jimmy Fletcher's group?" said Carmela. She grabbed Ava by the elbow and edged over toward him.

"He looks like a college professor," said Ava. "So maybe we'll learn something."

Fletcher *did* look like a professor, Carmela decided, even with the gray T-shirt that proclaimed *Ghost Hunter*. He was in his midforties and slightly balding, but he possessed sparkling eyes and a pleasant smile.

"I guess we're with you," Ava told Fletcher, batting her eyelashes in a not-so-subtle manner.

Fletcher just smiled knowingly and handed her a small digital voice recorder with a directional microphone, which she promptly passed on to Carmela.

And then they were off, their group heading down a long, dark corridor with just flashes of light from their helmets to show the way.

Fletcher wasn't a bad guide. He'd obviously read up on the history of Mendelssohn Asylum and was able to talk knowingly and with authority. He led them into small, shabby rooms and individual monastic cells that inmates had once called home. A few remnants of padded mattresses still clung to these walls and exuded a pungent, unpleasant smell. The occasional skittering of mice made Carmela wish she'd worn boots so she could tuck in her jeans.

"Here we find the stone staircase that takes us down to the basement hydrotherapy rooms," said Fletcher. "The individual treatment rooms, which are also located down here, will probably look more like torture chambers to today's more sympathetic eye."

Rough stone steps spiraled down into the ground. Even though the building was cool, dampness clung to their bodies and seemed to soak into their clothing.

"As you can see," said Fletcher, "two different pools were located down here. Water therapy was often used in an attempt to shock patients back into their right mind. Obviously, images of Chinese water torture or witch dunking at Salem come to mind, since most poor souls were unable to complain or refuse treatment."

Carmela and Ava edged their way past a long-empty pool and down a hallway, then followed the group into one of the private treatment rooms. A metal table stood in the center. Four-inch straps of rotting leather were bolted to the top, middle, and bottom. These were straps used to hold the head, arms, and legs of the patient. In the eerie white light from the helmets, the table looked cold and violent. A pile of rotting sheets lay at one end.

"Anyone want to try out the table?" Fletcher asked.

The group took a collective step back.

He chuckled. "I thought not."

Carmela glanced around. Dripping water seemed to add to the atmosphere of dread and helplessness. A heavy pressure seemed to surround them. Maybe . . . maybe there really was something to this restless spirit thing?

"It's been said," began Fletcher, "that many people feel like they're being buried alive as they walk these halls. Some say it's departed souls who are trying to warn visitors to flee."

"I'm ready to cut and run to the nearest bar," said Ava in a stage whisper.

There were a few nervous giggles, and then Jimmy Fletcher held up an index finger. "At this juncture, might I suggest we split into groups of two and utilize our various devices and electromagnetic detectors? This is the time and probably the place to try to determine if any spirits are present."

Carmela raised a hand. "What exactly is an electromagnetic detector?"

"Exactly what its name implies," said Fletcher. "It detects magnetic fields. And if it registers strong, erratic pulses, we know there's definite activity."

"What kind of activity?" asked Ava.

"Ghostly," said Fletcher in a slightly ominous tone.

Chapter 14

"THIS is just awful," said Carmela. Her flashlight played across the walls of several more treatment chambers. Some had bars on the doors, while others had small sliding windows that had allowed staff to surreptitiously peek inside. Each door looked to be almost five inches thick. They definitely meant business down here.

"I keep expecting to see shackles and chains hanging from the walls," whispered Ava.

"They probably had those at one time," said Carmela. "Then modernized . . . to this."

"From the Tower of London all the way up to the Spanish Inquisition," said Ava. "Imagine that." She slapped her hand against the side of her helmet, startling Carmela.

"What?" said Carmela.

"Just making sure my helmet cam's on," said Ava. "You got your recorder on?"

Carmela gazed at the tiny green screen on her handheld unit. "It's on. In fact, it's been on for the last ten minutes. Probably the only thing I'm gonna pick up is station WRNO. Or my irregular heartbeat."

"Maybe," said Ava, "we need to descend into the bowels of this place to discover its true psychic source."

"You make it sound so enticing," said Carmela.

"You know what I mean," said Ava, pointing down a dark corridor. "Down in the boiler room or maybe even the morgue. Since this place is . . . was . . . a hospital, there has to be a morgue."

Carmela frowned. The whole notion made her jumpy. "I *suppose* it should be down here somewhere."

Together, shoulders touching, the two women edged down the passageway. Dirt and glass crunched underfoot, and water oozed from zigzag cracks in the walls.

"This remind you of anything?" asked Ava.

"You mean like Medusa Manor?" asked Carmela. "Maybe a little, but Medusa Manor is Disneyland compared to this place."

"This place is definitely hardcore," agreed Ava.

"I was reading on the Restless Spirit Society's Web site," said Carmela, "that buildings can take on and retain a sort of physical imprint of violence that occurred there."

"Like psychic footprints," said Ava.

"Something like that," said Carmela.

"And the air, too," said Ava, sniffling. "It's like mold and bleach with a faint smell of blood and urine. Like hopelessness and desperation all melded together." Ava stopped abruptly and clutched Carmela's arm. "Oh my Lord!"

"What?" said Carmela, turning toward Ava and momentarily blinding her with her light.

"I'm almost positive I stepped on a dead body!"

Carmela took a deep breath, then aimed her beam of light at the floor. A dirty, lifeless doll lay in a crumpled heap beneath Ava's feet. "Take it easy, it's just a doll," Carmela told her.

Ava let loose a sigh as she glanced quickly down at it, then kicked it out of her way. "Gettin' jumpy."

Gazing back at the rag doll, Carmela wondered how it got there, who it had belonged to. Dropped, perhaps, by some little girl on her way to treatment? The black eyes of the doll stared, vacant and accusing. Carmela shuddered.

"Cold?" asked Ava. "Want to turn back?"

"Maybe we—" began Carmela, but the rest of her words died instantly. The green screen of her directional microphone had suddenly come alive, crackling and jumping like mad. "Ava, I'm picking something up!"

"On your recorder? You mean like voices?"

"Something," said Carmela. She focused on the eerie green light and watched, fascinated, as it spiked and peaked.

"Maybe voices of former inmates," Ava said in a hushed voice.

"Or maybe nothing at all," said Carmela, "because it just stopped." She looked around. "Maybe just mice . . . or bats?"

"I know you think this ghost-hunting equipment is pretty much pseudoscience," said Ava. "But if we really found something, I could do a video recording with my helmet cam."

"You sure that thing's turned on?" asked Carmela.

Ava ran her hand up the back of her black Kevlar helmet and felt for the tiny cam. "You see a red light?" she asked Carmela, leaning forward.

The red button burned steadily. "Yup," said Carmela.

"Then let's keep going," said Ava, clutching Carmela even tighter.

They tiptoed down the corridor until it ended in a T.

"Now what?" asked Ava.

"Mmm, maybe . . . right?" said Carmela.

After only a few tentative steps down the new corridor, Ava hissed, "This floor is disgusting." She stopped and balanced on one leg, trying to check the bottom of her shoe while aiming her light at it. "I think I stepped in a pile of pigeon droppings. Can you believe it? These are Coach shoes

I got on sale at Saks. I *love* these shoes! I had to fight off two other snarling size nines to get them."

Tilting her head again, Carmela focused her helmet light on Ava's shoes. "You stepped in something, all right, but I don't think there are any pigeons hanging around down here."

"Then what . . . ?" But Ava didn't have time to finish. Something swooped past her face, brushing gently against her head. Then its leathery wings flapped and the creature circled again.

Ava let loose a horrific shriek. "A bat!"

As if on cue, more bats came hurtling down the corridor, swooping and flapping around them.

"No," cried Carmela, "it's a whole battalion!" They grabbed each other and crouched low. Ten seconds later, there was only the echo of pulsing wings.

"Whew!" said Ava.

"Did you get *that* on camera?" asked Carmela.

"I was too busy cowering," said Ava. "And worrying about getting rabies. What about you? Did those little eeps and beeps register on your meter?"

"No," Carmela responded, "but now I'm picking something up again."

"So not bats," said Ava.

"Unless it's the echo of their dead forebears," said Carmela.

"Or maybe mice," suggested Ava.

"Did you know," said Carmela, deadpan, "that mice think bats are angels?"

Ava stared at her friend for a few seconds, then smacked her on the arm. "Oh, *you*!"

Together they eased forward again. Ten feet down, they came to a decrepit metal door.

"Dead end," said Ava. "And I do hate the way that sounds."

Carmela aimed her helmet light at a faded sign. Faint red

letters spelled *Boiler Room*. She touched her hand to the door handle. "What do you think?"

Ava licked her lips nervously. "I suppose we could take a quick look."

Together they put their shoulders against the heavy metal door and pushed. Reluctantly, the door swung open on rusted hinges. Then they were standing in the doorway, their lights focused on the massive boiler that dominated the cramped, low space. Cobwebs hung down from ductwork like shrouds.

"Still picking something up?" asked Ava.

Carmela shook her head. "No. Nothing."

They eased their way toward the boiler. When they were barely five feet away, a click-tick sounded from within and a red glow appeared behind a thick metal grate. Ava nudged Carmela.

Carmela adjusted her light. "Not coming from me," she said.

Ava shook her head from side to side. "Me, either."

"That thing didn't just turn on," said Carmela. "This place's been vacant for years!"

"Then wha . . . ?" began Ava. She hushed as there was a loud scrape against cement, then another click.

"Someone else is in this room," Carmela told her in a low voice.

"Oh, Lordy," moaned Ava. "Who? The ghostly remains of some poor tortured soul?"

"Now you sound like Mindy," hissed Carmela.

"Then smack me with a wet noodle," said Ava, "because I've gone over to the dark side."

"Somebody there?" called a man's voice. Not a ghostly voice, but a rich, resonant baritone.

"Just us ghosts," Ava called back a little shakily. Together, she and Carmela took a giant step backward as a man emerged from the shadows behind the boiler.

"You're with the group," said Carmela, homing in on his khaki vest and safety helmet.

"No, I live here," said the man in a slightly mocking tone, miffed at being interrupted by them. "Of course, I'm with the group."

"We thought you might be a poor tortured soul," said Ava, bristling at his sarcasm. "Turns out, we were right."

"Ladies," said the man, a little more cordial now. "I'm just doing a little harmless exploring."

Carmela tilted her head up, aiming her light directly in the man's eyes.

"You want to get that light out of my face?" he asked.

"Sure," said Carmela. She shifted her head slightly. "You know," she told him, "you look kind of familiar."

He waved a hand. "People are always telling me that. Separated at birth, that kind of thing." He gave a false-hearty laugh.

"What have you got there?" Carmela asked, gesturing at the device he held in his hand. It was black, about the size of a BlackBerry, with a small screen that flashed several lines of LED readouts.

"Oh," said the man, slightly startled. "It's an XMap, a kind of GPS device."

"I don't remember Mindy handing those out," said Ava.

"She didn't," said Carmela. "It belongs to him." She gestured toward the man, who took a half step backward. "So what's it do?"

The man shrugged, trying to retain his casual air. "It uses GPS to map and measure property."

"And how does that help detect spirits?" asked Ava.

"It doesn't," said Carmela, suddenly getting a feeling for who this might be. Taking a step toward the man, she backed him up against the old boiler. "You're not interested in spirits, are you? Your primary interest is in real estate."

"Huh?" said Ava.

"If you ladies will excuse me . . ." The man stepped deftly past them, ducked through the doorway, and took off down the corridor.

"What was *that* about?" asked Ava.

"You know who he is?" asked Carmela.

Ava shook her head.

"I'll bet a hundred bucks that was Sawyer Barnes . . . the developer who bid against Melody for the Medusa Manor property. I looked him up on the Web this morning."

"No shit," said Ava. "So . . . what? You think he wants to buy *this* property, too?"

"Maybe," said Carmela. But the real question spinning wildly in her head was, had Sawyer Barnes desperately wanted to own Medusa Manor? And if so, had he been willing to kill for it?

Chapter 15

LAFAYETTE Cemetery, established in 1833, was once part and parcel of Madame Livaudais's fine plantation. It served as a city of the dead for more than a century, fell into a terrible state of disrepair, and, more recently, was refurbished to become the resting place for the crème de la crème of New Orleans. As a must-see on a de rigueur Garden District tour, Lafayette Cemetery stands as a somber, picturesque, and unique monument.

However, Lafayette Cemetery contains more than a few secrets. It's where Marie Laveau, the voodoo priestess, is buried and where the "secret garden"—a square of four tombs built by four friends—is located. It's also the supposed lair of zombies and ghosts, the place where scenes from *Interview with the Vampire* were filmed, and where the vampire Lestat supposedly resides.

This Thursday morning, Carmela and Ava strolled along the cemetery's narrow gravel pathways, past towering obelisks, vaults, and decaying statues, heading for the site of

Melody Mayfeldt's memorial service. After last night's rain, the sun now shone down brightly, bouncing off bleached, whitewashed tombs and tilting gravestones, making them look like shiny, uneven teeth.

"I'm impressed," said Ava. "Melody is being laid to rest in a family crypt in a very prestigious cemetery."

"Her folks were longtime residents here in the Garden District," explained Carmela. "Hence, a family crypt."

"Which I think is right over there," said Ava, narrowing her eyes and pointing with a black-gloved hand. "At least that's where everyone seems to be congregating. Behind that wrought-iron gate."

"Then that must be the place," said Carmela.

As the two of them drew closer, they could see a mahogany coffin resting atop a wooden bier, a string quartet just beginning to set up, and a rather large group of mourners milling about. In fact, far more mourners than they'd expected to see.

Carmela bit her lip as they approached. It was one thing to know her friend was dead. It was another thing to come face-to-face with her coffin.

"This has turned into quite the social gathering," whispered Ava. "Look, there's Baby over there. And aren't those some of the people from last night? From the Restless Spirit Society?"

Carmela nodded. "And I see a few restaurateurs and shop owners from the French Quarter." Feeling slightly heartened, she gave a faint smile. "Nice that they came to pay their respects."

"And some Demilune krewe ladies, too," said Ava, suddenly dabbing at her eyes. "Sweet of them to show up."

They edged through the crowd, nodding to people they knew, then tucked in next to Baby.

Carmela put a hand on Baby's arm. "Thanks for coming." Baby nodded knowingly as she gave a sad smile.

"You're looking quite glamorous," Ava whispered to Baby. "All decked out in your Dior suit."

"And you're looking unusually sedate," replied Baby. Indeed, Ava had forgone her usual tight jeans and low-cut T-shirt to pour herself into a severely tailored black suit.

In her simple black sleeveless dress and string of pearls, Carmela suddenly wished she'd worn a veil or even a scarf to cover her bare shoulders. Something to make her look a little more funereal and less cocktail-partyish. Oh well, nothing ever turned out as planned, did it? Not her marriage, not her business expectations, not even her relationship with Edgar Babcock. Because who knew where *that* was going?

On that slightly downbeat note, Carmela let loose a deep sigh and surveyed the crowd. Everyone was suddenly scrambling for the dozen or so wobbly black metal folding chairs that had just been set up by a bored-looking funeral director. But because there were far more mourners than chairs, the activity looked more like a children's game of musical chairs. Grab one or you lose.

"That's weird," said Ava, observing the scramble. "You'd think they'd set out more chairs."

"Maybe Garth didn't expect this many people to show up," said Baby.

Garth, thought Carmela. Where was Garth anyway? Her eyes scanned the assembled group. Ah, there he was. Standing next to the casket, talking to Reverend Robertson, a gray-haired, round-faced minister Carmela remembered slightly from another service she'd attended. Her eyes continued to rove the crowd, finally settling on the man she and Ava had encountered last night in the boiler room.

"Baby," Carmela whispered, touching her friend's shoulder. "Do you know . . . is that Sawyer Barnes over there?"

A tiny line insinuated itself between Baby's elegant blond brows as she studied the man across the way. "Yes," she finally whispered back.

"You're sure?" asked Carmela. "You've met him before?"

Baby nodded. "At a NOMA benefit." NOMA was the New Orleans Museum of Art.

"Sawyer Barnes?" Ava inquired in a low voice. She'd overheard their exchange.

This time both of them nodded.

"What's he doing here?" Ava wondered out loud. A few moments of pregnant silence hung in the air, and then she added, "Think he's got something to feel guilty about?"

"I don't know," said Carmela. "Good question."

And then the funeral began. The string quartet played Grieg's *Notturno*, Opus 54, No. 4, making the piece sound lyrical and soulful at the same time. As the final strains drifted away on the wind, Reverend Robertson opened his black book of prayers and stepped in front of the flower-banked coffin.

"Dear friends," he began, "we are gathered today to celebrate the life of Melody Mayfeldt, a soul tragically taken from us far too soon."

Carmela hunched her shoulders forward, listening to Reverend Robertson's words, thinking about Melody, wondering if Edgar Babcock was any closer to solving her murder.

Babcock. Could he be here?

Carmela's head rose like a periscope, scanning the crowd, the perimeter, the few tourists who had gathered to gawk.

Nope. Don't see him.

But she did see someone interesting. Sidney St. Cyr. Leaning against a slate-gray tomb, Sidney managed to look even more hunched and pinched than usual.

Sidney, Carmela thought to herself. *I wonder how his ghost walk business is going? I wonder what's he's been up to lately?*

"Let us listen and heed," said Reverend Robertson, "the comforting words of the Twenty-third Psalm. The Lord is my shepherd, I shall not want . . ."

As the service continued, Carmela watched as Sawyer Barnes eased his way slowly through the crowd—behind the musicians, through a small group of mourners—then ducked behind a small monument, finally ending up right next to Olivia Wainwright. Barnes's shoulder touched Olivia's ever so slightly, as if in greeting, and when she turned to acknowledge him, she favored him with a faint smile.

Interesting, thought Carmela. Or was it? They probably did know each other, since it was Olivia's money that had been used to outbid Barnes for Medusa Manor. Carmela decided she was probably jumping at shadows and, instead, focused her attention on Garth Mayfeldt.

Hunched next to his wife's coffin, Garth looked like a broken man. His complexion was pale as a ghost, dark circles engulfed his eyes, and his clothes seemed to hang on him like a scarecrow's. Carmela's heart went out to Garth, and she wondered how on earth he'd make it through the rest of the service.

As if in answer, Reverend Robertson closed his book and told the crowd, "And now, Garth would like to say a few words." The reverend reached a hand out to steady Garth, then Garth took a tentative step forward.

Pulling a piece of paper from his jacket pocket, Garth stared at the crowd blankly, then said in a shaky voice, "I'd like to read a final poem for Melody." He paused, cleared his throat, then continued. "It was written more than a hundred years ago by Edgar Allan Poe and serves to sum up our . . ." Garth's voice cracked and faltered, and then he bowed his head. Reverend Robertson put a hand on Garth's shoulder and said a few whispered words to him, but Garth shook his head. He wanted to continue. After taking several deep breaths, he licked his lips and began his reading:

> *I saw thee on thy bridal day—*
> *When a burning blush came o'er thee.*
> *Though happiness around thee lay,*
> *The world all love before thee.*
> *And in thine eye a kindling light*
> *(Whatever it may be)*
> *Was all on Earth my aching sight*
> *Of Loveliness could see.*

"What the heck?" Ava muttered to Carmela as Garth continued his reading. Her eyes met Carmela's and they gazed at each other, both slightly confused. "Isn't that kind of a weird poem?" she whispered.

"Weird for a funeral," Carmela murmured under her breath.

"And what's with all the fire images?" Ava whispered back. "Kind of creepy, if you ask me."

Carmela just nodded.

Once Garth finished the final stanza of his poem, the string quartet broke into Beethoven's *Für Elise*. That was the signal for the pallbearers to gather around Melody's casket. Once assembled, they grabbed the brass handles, bent down, then grunted in unison as they hoisted their heavy burden to their shoulders. Then it was a short, stiff-legged march to the gaping doorway of the family crypt. The coffin was carried in and slid onto a small stone slab, and then the pallbearers shuffled back out, looking slightly red-faced and flushed from their grim task. As the funeral director shoved the heavy door closed, a final, dull thud sounded.

Raising a hand in a comforting gesture, Reverend Robertson murmured, "May our Heavenly Father receive thee into his loving arms for all eternity."

Bowing their heads en masse, the crowd responded with a gravelly "Amen."

The funeral service was concluded.

But Carmela's curiosity was more than piqued. Watching Sawyer Barnes and Olivia Wainwright engage in a more animated conversation now, she wished desperately that she could be a little mouse behind the tombstone and eavesdrop on them. And just as she toyed with the idea of actually going over there, of butting in on their private confab, the two shook hands and parted. Well . . . so much for that notion.

Ava tapped Carmela on the shoulder. "What do you think

is the protocol? Should we go express our condolences to Garth?"

"It's probably the right thing to do," said Carmela.

"You go," urged Ava. "You know him better than I do. I'm gonna go talk to Sidney over there. See what that little twerp has been up to."

Carmela walked over to where Garth was standing and waited in a sort of cemetery receiving line for a few moments. "It was a lovely service," she told Garth when she finally arrived at the head of the line. "I'm so very sorry about Melody."

Garth Mayfeldt clasped Carmela's hands in a rough but trembling grip. "I can't believe she's really gone." His red-rimmed eyes looked sunken and hollow.

"If there's anything I can do to help, please let me know," said Carmela.

"Please," Garth implored her, "just keep your eyes and ears open as promised. The police are still completely hung up on the insurance money and don't seem to be building a case against anyone but me!"

"I promised to help and I will," Carmela assured him. "But what I'm most concerned with right now is you. You look utterly exhausted."

"I'll be fine," Garth responded in a hoarse voice, but he didn't sound very convincing.

"Can you take some time off from the shop?" Carmela asked.

Garth shook his head. "Better not to. Now there'll be twice as much work to do."

"But not twice as much business," said Carmela.

Garth suddenly looked even more glum. "No. Unfortunately not."

"I've heard talk . . ." Carmela began. She wasn't quite sure how to phrase her concern.

"About how Fire and Ice may be insolvent?" rasped Garth.

Now he looked both grief-stricken and angry. "Yes, I'm sure you have. But I'll manage. I always do."

"You certainly wouldn't be the first French Quarter business to restructure or even throw in the towel," Carmela told him gently. "And you won't be the last." She knew first-hand the difficulties that small shop owners faced.

"Please," said Garth, "my only thought right now is finding justice for Melody." He reached out and gripped her hands again. "And if you can help in any way . . ."

"My dear, dear Garth," said Olivia Wainwright in somber, mellow tones. She'd cut directly to the head of the line and now stood firmly ensconced at Garth's left elbow. Her cultured face wore a look of utmost concern.

"Olivia . . ." Garth responded. He seemed pleased to see her.

Olivia placed a hand on Garth's shoulder and caressed it gently. "It's all right," she cooed, trying to comfort him.

Carmela watched Olivia's hand move up until her entire arm encircled Garth's neck in a gentle hug. Carmela couldn't help noticing the wide gold band and enormous pear-shaped citrine ring wrapped around Olivia's middle finger. A matching pair of citrine earrings dangled from her ears. Carmela couldn't resist a peek at Olivia's necklace. Yup. More citrines. Gorgeous gems. Real killer pieces. The kind of serious gold and gem pieces that . . . and now something clicked in the back of Carmela's head . . . that she'd seen in the glass cases at Fire and Ice?

Okay, Carmela decided, *Olivia must be one of Garth's premier customers. Nice to have people of that ilk supporting your store.* And then, as Olivia's hand continued to make small circles on Garth's shoulder, Carmela wondered for the first time if there was something going on between Garth Mayfeldt and Olivia Wainwright. Was this hug just a little bit beyond the verge of mere friendship?

When Olivia finally tore herself free, she turned to face

Carmela. "Our boy is going to be just fine," she said in grand-pronouncement style.

"Of course he is," responded Carmela.

"He simply needs lots of support," continued Olivia.

Carmela wondered if Olivia meant emotional support or financial support.

Reverend Robertson cut in then, wishing Garth well as he took his leave.

"Olivia," said Carmela, seizing this small opportunity to speak to her. "I hate to bring up business, but Ava and I have made real strides with Medusa Manor."

"Oh?" said Olivia. Her eyes followed Garth as he shook hands with several other mourners.

"In fact," Carmela continued, "it's probably good that we grab a quick meeting so I can give you a progress report." *And maybe ask a few questions*, she thought to herself.

"Hmm," said Olivia, glancing at her watch, acting even more distracted. "I suppose I could find some time today."

"That'd be great," said Carmela. "Say your home . . . three o'clock?"

"Fine, fine," said Olivia, turning her attention back to Garth.

"Ready to head back?" asked Ava, digging in her purse for her sunglasses.

"I suppose so," said Carmela. There were still two dozen or so people milling about, but that probably wouldn't last long. They'd begin scattering any moment. "What were you grilling Sidney about? I saw you two with your heads together."

"He's such a strange duck," said Ava. "I was telling him a little bit about the Mendelssohn Asylum and now he's all hot to put it on his tour."

"I noticed that Mindy showed up with some of the Restless Spirit Society folks; maybe you could hook those two up."

"The cheerleader and Sidney," chuckled Ava. "Now that'd

be a combo. Like Jennifer Aniston hooking up with Marilyn Manson!"

"Did you notice how cozy Olivia was with Garth?" asked Carmela.

"She did seem awfully affectionate, now that you mention it."

"I hate to say this," said Carmela, "but it seemed like Olivia was a little sweet on Garth."

"That would throw a twist into things," said Ava. "You sure she's not just a really good customer?"

"I'm not sure of anything," said Carmela.

They walked in silence for a few moments, past a large tomb with a sculpture of a kneeling angel on top. Then Carmela said, "Just for *what if* purposes . . . what if the two of them had wanted Melody out of the picture?"

"Seriously?" said Ava, her eyes widening. She shook her head. "I don't know. Garth seems awfully upset."

"I'm sure remorse can assume the appearance of mourning," said Carmela.

"Okay," said Ava. "If you're headed in that direction. Then what if Garth doesn't figure into the equation at all? What if Melody and Olivia got into some sort of horrible argument? One thing led to another and . . . *kapow*! It wouldn't be the first time business partners feuded."

"It *was* an unequal partnership," murmured Carmela. "Olivia put up the money, while Melody did all the grunt work."

"Which *we're* doing now," Ava pointed out.

"It never occurred to me," said Carmela, "that Olivia might have gotten rid of Melody on her own."

Ava squinted into the sun. "Do you think Olivia knows how to rig an incendiary device?"

"Don't know," said Carmela.

"If you ask me," said Ava, "she seems like one of those entitled shopaholic babes who's barely able to work a toaster."

"I hear you," said Carmela. "Okay, then what are we to

think of the dynamic duo of Olivia Wainwright and Sawyer Barnes? They were whispering like crazy, thick as thieves."

"And here I thought they were rivals," said Ava. "Sort of."

"Maybe somewhere along the way, they joined forces," said Carmela. She wasn't sure why they would, but it felt like *something* was going on.

"*Cher*," said Ava, "you've got a real tangle of suspects and motives. Probably more complicated than Babcock's real list. You two should get together and—"

"I would if he'd return my calls," snapped Carmela. "Or stop by my place."

Ava gazed at Carmela with deep concern. "Trouble in paradise? Oh, *cher*, say it ain't so."

"It's not exactly trouble, it's just . . ."

Ava threw her arms around Carmela and gave her a hug. "There, dear heart, a python squeeze *pour vous*. Now . . ." She stepped back and delicately shook her index finger in Carmela's face. "I want you to remember how dedicated Edgar Babcock is. He's your own little Dudley Do-Right action figure, always fighting on the side of good. You wouldn't want it any other way, would you?"

Carmela shook her head. "No," she said slowly. "It's just that his job demands more of him than I'm willing to share."

"Look at it this way," said Ava. "You were married to that puke Shamus, and he was unwilling to share *anything*."

"Except the dogs," said Carmela. "He didn't mind taking care of the dogs."

"You can't base a marriage on dogs," said Ava. "Heck, your marriage didn't even last a single dog year!"

Carmela giggled. Ava had a point.

"Now you've got this terrific guy who thinks the sun shines out of your . . . well, you know what I'm saying," laughed Ava. "So my advice is—hang in there, baby."

Ava held Carmela's hand as they passed a row of long, low

tombs decorated with fanciful wrought-iron crosses. Thirty years ago, before the city supervisors and cemetery historians had made a concerted effort to protect and care for these cemeteries, some of these tombs had actually cracked open and the bones of the hapless inhabitants spilled out for all to see. Now, thankfully, all cemeteries were accorded continual care and maintenance and regarded as historic properties and major tourist attractions.

"Of all the New Orleans cemeteries, I've always loved this one best," said Ava. She stepped briskly off the white gravel path and over to a low, rounded tomb. "Looky here. This is the grave they filmed for the *Interview with the Vampire* movie. Tom Cruise and Brad Pitt stood right here." She hugged herself and gave a sexy little jiggle. "Can't you just feel their vibes?"

"Maybe they should put up a plaque," said Carmela.

"No way," said Ava. "This place needs to be protected. We've already got Sidney and his ghost walks parading through here. All we need are more frenzied vampire groupies making sacred pilgrimages."

They walked a little farther, noting some of the more interesting carvings. Angel heads, a lamb with a cross, a man's head on a lion's body, a large head with a sorrowful, upturned gaze.

"That head would be perfect for one of our floating heads," said Ava.

"Looks good to me," said Carmela. "Can you take a mold?"

"Sure," said Ava, "but maybe there's even a better one. No need to settle for the first thing we see."

As they circled around a white marble crypt, Carmela suddenly squealed with delight, "Oh my gosh!" She gestured frantically to Ava. "Come here and tell me what you see!"

Ava stood next to her and peered at the tomb. "Um . . . that one's good, too. A woman's face."

"But what else do you see?" prompted Carmela. "What kind of woman?"

Ava squinted. "Medusa!" she suddenly shouted. Smiling, she reached out a hand and traced the carved head with the tips of her fingers. It was indeed a woman's head ringed with a wreath of snakes that dominated one side of the tomb. The fearful Medusa of Greek mythology.

"This is exactly what we need over the fireplace at Medusa Manor," said Carmela. "What do you think? Can you do it? Can you lift a mold from this tomb and create a Medusa head?"

"Child's play," said Ava. "Of course I can." One of Ava's hobbies was mask making. She was a real pro at making plaster casts, then turning them into leather masks that could be painted, pinched, and embellished with beads, feathers, and fabric. At one time Ava had even considered becoming a full-time mask maker. She'd since decided that running Juju Voodoo was far more profitable. Masks were better left as a sideline. And there was always a demand, especially around Halloween and Mardi Gras.

"Let's come back tonight and take molds," suggested Carmela. "Hop right on it."

"Sure," agreed Ava.

A sudden crunch of gravel from the far side of the crypt caused both women to freeze. Was someone creeping around over there?

"Someone's been listening to us," whispered Carmela.

Ava gestured frantically, indicating for Carmela to go one way, she'd go the other.

But when they met on the other side of the crypt, no one was there.

Carmela looked puzzled. "I thought I heard someone."

Ava shrugged. "False alarm. Nobody here now but us 'fraidy cats. Oh well, gotta take off. I've got a huge box of skulls stashed in my car that I want to drop off at Medusa Manor."

"Then you're gonna need a key." Carmela fished in her bag and pulled out one of the newly cut brass keys.

"This is gonna work?" asked Ava. "No problema?"

"Shouldn't be a problem," said Carmela.

"Excellent. I can't wait to see how my skulls work out."

Carmela frowned. "You sure you don't want me to go with you?"

Ava shook her head. "Honey, I'm on a ditch-and-drive mission. I'll drop the boxes of skulls and bones and be out of there like a bat outa you-know-where. I doubt my car will even touch the driveway."

"Okay," said Carmela, "but . . . be careful."

Chapter 16

"OH, you're back, too!" exclaimed Gabby. "How was the service?"

"Sad," said Carmela, slumping over and resting her elbows on the front counter.

Gabby gave a knowing nod. "As are all funerals, I suppose. Did lots of people show up?"

"It was a very good turnout," Carmela told her. "I think Garth was very touched."

"That's good," said Gabby.

"How has it been here?" asked Carmela.

"Steady, but not exactly a breakneck pace. Your friend Aysia came back to pick up some die cuts and templates. And Tandy and Baby are waiting in back. You were going to do a demonstration today?"

Carmela touched a palm to her forehead. "Completely slipped my mind. And Baby never mentioned it at the service."

Gabby looked concerned. "Well, they're here. And you

wouldn't have to twist any arms to get those other two ladies to join in." She nodded toward two women who were rummaging through a box of discounted stickers. "They were asking about classes before."

"Then let's round 'em up," said Carmela.

"You know what you're going to do?" asked Gabby, looking slightly apprehensive. "You have a project in mind?"

"I never know *exactly* how things will turn out," responded Carmela. "But, yes, there's always a germ of an idea. Thank goodness I have a vivid imagination."

"Things just pop into your head, don't they?" said Gabby.

"You might say that . . . yes," said Carmela, hurrying back to her office, grabbing for essentials on the way. In fact, she decided, sometimes her head popped with too many ideas.

"I thought what we'd do today," began Carmela, once everyone was settled at the back table, "was work on a craft project that dovetails with all the different elements of scrapbooking. I'm talking about exotic papers, rubber stamping, collages, embellishments, fabrics, ephemera, and even incorporating small collectibles." She hesitated, to see how her audience was reacting so far. Big smiles greeted her.

Carmela reached behind her and grabbed a wooden shadow box off a wire shelf, then held it up for everyone to see. Roughly eight by ten inches, the shadow box was approximately two inches deep and had a solid back wall. "I'd like to show you how to create a votive box," she told her audience.

"Just stop right there," said Tandy, adjusting her red-framed glasses. "Do you have more of those things?" She gestured at the shadow box.

Carmela nodded. "A dozen or so in different sizes."

"Because I'm going to want to make a couple," said Tandy.

"Maybe," Baby put in tactfully, "we should let Carmela demonstrate how to make one first?" She reached into her tote, pulled out a tin of her famous Southern coffee cookies, and placed it on the table.

Tandy gave an imperceptible nod as her hand snaked out to grab a cookie. "Of course."

It didn't take Carmela long to explain her votive box. In fact, the instructions were so simple, she worked as she talked.

First, Carmela lined the back of the shadow box with a sheet of purple brocade floral paper. Then, she finished the four edges with a contrasting sheet. A small piece of antiqued sheet music and a sprig of pink-and-mauve dried flowers were arranged and tacked against the back wall. Some cream-colored vintage lace was snugged at the bottom of the shadow box to form a ruffly floor. Then Carmela added a small antique statue of an angel, along with a cream-colored candle, a gold key, a small locket, and a crucifix.

"Amazing," said Baby. Since she'd also just come from Melody's service, she pretty much understood Carmela's mindset. "A lovely tribute," she added.

Tandy narrowed her eyes. "But what if I want to make a votive box to celebrate . . . say . . . my baby granddaughter's birthday?"

"Easily done," Carmela told her. "You could start with a more playful background or even a color photocopy of her birth certificate, then add some baby-inspired items. Think old-fashioned wooden building blocks, a small angel statue, a knit bootie, dried flowers, paper dolls, bits of lace and ribbon, some brass butterfly embellishments . . . whatever *you* think personalizes it."

"Neat," said Gabby, who had come back to watch and grab a cookie.

"You could even make a votive box filled with wedding keepsakes, couldn't you?" asked one of the other women at the table. She laughed. "My daughter's getting married next month."

"I think that would be lovely," said Carmela.

While Gabby pulled out more selections of romance-inspired paper, Carmela grabbed some embellishments—gilded leaves, buttons, charms, unique fibers, silk flowers, bunches of plastic grapes, even some antique labels she'd had lying around.

"This is a great idea," Gabby whispered to Carmela. "Are you going to add it to your class schedule?"

Tandy overheard. "Class schedule? Come on, Carmela, tell us what's cooking in that clever brain of yours."

"Still noodling things around," Carmela told them. "But right now it looks like I'll be doing classes on graffito and memory boxes, as well as a class I'm tentatively calling 'artifacts.'"

Tandy wrinkled her nose with interest. "Artifacts. What's that?"

"Scrapbook pages, collages, and altered books that look aged and antique," said Carmela. "Think medieval-looking triptychs or Parisian-inspired notebooks or even Egyptian-type collages."

"Sounds very decorator-y," said Baby. "Where do I sign up?"

Carmela worked with the group for another fifteen minutes or so. Then, when they were all well on the way to completing their personal masterpieces, she scuttled up front to arrange new packets of beads and brass brads. When the phone shrilled at the front desk, she almost welcomed the interruption. "Hello?"

"Carmela?" purred a familiar male voice.

"Babcock," she said, pleased that he'd finally called. "We missed you this morning. At Melody's funeral."

"Think of me as being there in spirit," he told her.

"What? Because you've narrowed down your suspects? You're ready to crack this case wide open?"

Babcock sighed. "Investigations don't usually unfold that dramatically, Carmela."

"What a shame," she replied.

"What I really called about was to see if you had time for a late lunch," said Babcock. "Unless, of course, you've already eaten."

"No, no," said Carmela, "I'd love to meet you. That would be a real treat; we never have lunch together." She hesitated. "You don't want me to meet you in some dingy police cafeteria, do you?"

"Not at all," said Babcock. "What I thought was . . . I'd pick up a sack of doughnuts and we'd eat at my desk."

Carmela made a gagging sound.

"Not keen on doughnuts, huh?" said Babcock. "Then how about going to Bistro Rouge? It's a warm day; we can sit outside."

"Perfect," said Carmela. "See you there in twenty minutes?"

"Better make it thirty."

Carmela popped back to check on her crafters. Tandy was well on her way to creating an angel votive box. She'd lined her shadow box with a cream-colored vellum and added some gold embossed paper and a filmy pair of angel wings. All that was needed now was to add a photograph of her angelic granddaughter.

Baby was working a sort of gilded-gold Venetian theme.

"We have some miniature Venetian masks," Gabby told her. "If you're interested."

"I think I am," said Baby.

"Hey," said Tandy, "have you girls heard about that new crafter's retreat over in New Iberia? The lady who owns it is really into jewelry making, so she calls it a *bead and breakfast*."

"Cute," said Gabby.

Carmela bent down and whispered in Baby's ear. "Is there any way you can find out more about Sawyer Barnes?"

Baby nodded. "I could call Del. He has a fairly wide range of acquaintances and resources. I'm sure he could pull up something for you." She reached in her bag for her cell phone.

"Much appreciated," said Carmela as the bell over the front door tinkled. She turned, a ready smile on her face. And was dismayed to see the glowering face of Glory Meechum, Shamus's perpetually argumentative sister, as she stomped her way into the shop. *Now what could have brought Glory to Memory Mine?* Carmela wondered. As if she didn't know.

"Glory," said Carmela, speeding toward the front of her shop. "I had no idea you were going to drop by."

"No," spat Glory, "I doubt you would, Carmela."

Carmela grimaced. She really didn't want her personal issues paraded in front of everyone.

"What's wrong, Glory? How can I help?" Carmela figured if she came across a little more friendly, a little more appeasing, she might be able to lessen Glory's impact.

But Glory was a large, helmet-haired woman in a splotchy gray housedress masquerading as a neutron bomb.

"Car-*mela!*" she brayed. "I thought we had a *deal!*"

Rats, Carmela thought to herself. *Now I'm never gonna get my divorce settlement.*

"Nothing's poured in concrete yet, Glory," said Carmela, struggling to keep her tone neutral. "But Shamus has been very amenable to my request."

"Oh, bull-jabbers!" snorted Glory. "First you want one thing, then you want another." She stared down at Carmela, her whole body fairly quivering, one baleful eye twitching and blinking like mad.

Carmela took a step back. Glory was two hundred fifty pounds of angry banker on a pair of run-down orthopedic heels. She didn't fancy a knock-down, drag-out fight with her.

"We talked about you receiving alimony," spat Glory. "Now you're asking for the house."

"Things changed," said Carmela.

"That's a load of crap," said Glory.

"No," countered Carmela, "New Orleans changed. The economy's still dicey . . . so I need to know I'll be secure."

"But you're asking for an entire house!" wailed Glory. "Shamus's house."

"It was my house, too," said Carmela. "Until Shamus bailed on me. And then you went ballistic and drove me out." She shook her head. "No, Glory, I'm standing firm. In fact, I've already gone over this with Shamus. He's definitely come around to the deal." Carmela tried to breathe slowly, but her head was spinning. Glory Meechum's negative energy could pack a real psychic wallop. Carmela put a hand on the counter to steady herself. Somewhere, in all the background noise, she heard high heels approaching fast, like castanets.

"You don't deserve to live in the Garden District," Glory spat out, the whites of her eyes looking like two boiled eggs. "You're not good enough. You're . . ." This time Glory's voice dropped to a mean hiss. "You're . . . trash!"

Baby was suddenly at Carmela's side. "Glory," she said in her coolest society lady manner. "Is there something I can help with? Because I couldn't help but overhear your mentioning the Garden District. And since I'm on the Neighborhood Watch Board and the Historic Homes Committee, I was wondering if I could lend my influence in some way? That is, if you had some sort of problem."

"No," said a sullen Glory. "Carmela and I are finished here."

"Thank goodness," Carmela muttered under her breath.

"Got your back, darlin'," said Baby, as Glory spun about and stomped out the door.

"You're an angel," said Carmela. For some reason Carmela was feeling decidedly fragile.

Baby swept an arm around her. "Glory's nothin' but a mean old snake! Don't pay attention to anything she says. It's all bile and venom."

"But it can sting," said Carmela.

"I know that, honey," said Baby. "So all you can do is hold your head high and let her words roll right off your back. She's genuinely crazy, you know."

"I know," said Carmela. Boy, did she know.

"So," continued Baby, "I called Del and gleaned a little bit more information for you."

Carmela suddenly perked up. "About Sawyer Barnes?"

"Right," said Baby. "Del said pretty much the same thing you mentioned earlier. That Sawyer Barnes is a real estate developer with a penchant for turning grand old mansions and unique properties into condos."

"Okay," said Carmela.

"Del also mentioned that Barnes is a member of the Pluvius krewe."

"Shamus's krewe," said Carmela. That was an interesting factoid.

Baby nodded. "And that Barnes was in the military at one time and probably served in the Gulf War."

"Thanks," said Carmela. She thought for a few moments. "Not a huge amount to go on."

"No, it's not," said Baby, patting Carmela's shoulder, "but it's what we've got. And since you're a very smart lady, I assume you'll figure out how to put it all together."

Chapter 17

EDGAR Babcock lounged at a table in the back courtyard of Bistro Rouge. Potted palms encircled the brick-studded patio, a corrugated tin roof lent partial shade, and across the way a large stone pizza oven glowed with red-hot embers. Two tall glasses of sweet tea, coated with beads of condensation, sat on the small wrought-iron table in front of him.

"You read my mind," said Carmela, slipping into a green wooden chair across from him.

"Lunch will be served shortly," Babcock told her with a lazy smile. "I hope you don't mind, but I took the liberty of ordering for you. For us." He glanced at his watch, a heavy-looking Tag Heuer replete with multiple dials. "I don't have a whole lot of time."

"I hope you realize I'm counting carbs," sang Carmela. She grabbed her sweet tea and took a long sip, appreciating its cool deliciousness.

"Then you'll probably be adding up triple digits today," Babcock told her mildly.

Carmela set her glass down and smiled sweetly at him. "Nice to see you. Nice change from the day I've had so far."

"You're talking about Melody's funeral?" He gazed at her, then reached across the table and took her hand. "I would have been there if I could."

"What kept you . . . ?" Her voice trailed off as the waitress arrived at their table, a large silver tray propped against one hip. Babcock relinquished her hand as Carmela's eyes surveyed the offerings. There was a plate of cornmeal-crusted oysters for her. Perfect and golden, dusted with ancho powder, and perched atop a salad of mixed greens and sliced avocado, then drizzled with Creole mustard dressing.

Babcock's lunch was an oyster po'boy. More fried oysters artfully arranged on grilled French bread along with the requisite toppings of shredded lettuce and sliced tomatoes dripping with spicy rémoulade. Side dishes of red beans and dirty rice were placed between them.

"Just what I had in mind," Carmela giggled, "a nice light lunch."

"But I can tell you like it," said Babcock, grinning and trying to wiggle his eyebrows comically.

"No," said Carmela, unfurling her napkin into her lap and digging in, "I *love* it."

"So," said Babcock, "you going to share details about this morning?" He dug his spoon into the red beans.

"Depends," said Carmela.

"On what?"

"On how much you're willing to share with me."

Babcock set his spoon down. "Come on, Carmela. You know I can't make you privy to police matters. Besides, the last thing I want is for you to get involved."

She shrugged. "I'm already involved."

"You know what I mean," Babcock sighed.

"Okay, okay," Carmela muttered under her breath. "As you might imagine, there was a good-sized crowd at Melody's service."

"Uh-huh. Keep going."

"Maybe I should have just videotaped the whole thing."

"Maybe you should take it easy. You're as spicy as this food."

"Mmm," said Carmela, taking a large gulp of sweet tea. Dang, those oysters delivered a kick! "All right, there were quite a few shopkeepers from the French Quarter and a lot of women from the Demilune krewe."

"To be expected," said Babcock, in an encouraging tone.

"Basically a lot of friends and acquaintances of Melody's."

"So no real surprises?" said Babcock. "Nothing out of the ordinary?"

"Not unless you count the poem Garth read," said Carmela, reaching for a scoop of dirty rice.

"Something he wrote himself?" asked Babcock.

Carmela pushed away a few strands of hair that had slipped into her eyes. "No, it was your basic creepy poem by Edgar Allan Poe."

"Poe?" Babcock paused. "That seems like an unusual choice for a memorial service."

"Trust me," said Carmela. "It was. The poem Garth read spoke about fire as well as a burning blush."

"So?" said Babcock.

Carmela frowned. "It just seemed like bad taste, considering how Melody died."

"You're saying there was some sort of subtext?"

"Probably not," Carmela said slowly. "At least I don't think so." She gazed at Babcock, who seemed to be genuinely weighing her words. "I shouldn't have said anything. Now Garth is going to shoot straight to the top of your suspect list again."

"No, he won't," said Babcock. "Because he's already there."

"Because of the insurance money," said Carmela.

Babcock nodded. "That and a few other things I can't go into."

"Did you ever consider," said Carmela, "that you're not digging deep enough? That the real murderer is walking around out there, chortling to himself, assuming he got away scot-free?"

Babcock favored her with a tired smile. "If you can think of anyone like that, feel free to pass his name along."

Carmela stared at him. Actually there *was* someone who partially filled the bill. Should she mention him to Babcock? Well, why on earth not? "Okay, smart guy," she said. "What about Sawyer Barnes?"

Babcock's right hand jerked spasmodically, sending his glass of sweet tea crashing into his water glass and spilling both glasses across the white linen tablecloth. A sudden silence engulfed them as diners all around turned to stare. Brandishing a towel, their waitress clucked and scurried over.

When order had finally been restored, Carmela said, "Looks like I touched a nerve."

"How did you know Sawyer Barnes was on our suspect list?"

"Excuse me?" said Carmela. "Maybe because Barnes bid against Melody for the Medusa Manor property? Because he comes across like a sore loser?"

"Do you think Sawyer Barnes is still interested in that property?"

"It's possible," said Carmela, remembering Barnes's whispered chitchat with Olivia Wainwright this morning. "He was at the service this morning and ended up having a rather cozy conversation with Olivia Wainwright. I suppose Barnes could have been asking her if she was interested in selling."

"Is she?" asked Babcock.

"Doubtful," said Carmela, "since she was so hot to have Ava and me finish the project. But I can certainly ask Olivia. I'm supposed to meet her later today."

"You know," said Babcock, "Garth Mayfeldt has been trying his darnedest to nudge me in the direction of Sawyer Barnes."

"So he has his suspicions, too," said Carmela.

"But then," said Babcock, "Garth *would* want to deflect suspicion from himself."

"Who wouldn't?" said Carmela, giving him a pussycat smile. "You're a formidable investigator. You've probably got lots of people running scared."

Babcock fixed his gaze on her. "You know, Carmela, I'm not always sure when you're kidding or not."

"Neither am I," said Carmela. She stared across the patio, where two pizzas were being pulled from the wood-fired oven. "You know who else sort of freaks me out?"

"Who?" asked Babcock.

"Sidney St. Cyr."

"That ghost walk guy?" said Babcock.

"Do you realize," said Carmela, "that Sidney practically has a license to creep around the French Quarter? He's leading ghost tours at all hours of the day and night, scurrying up and down every back alley and through every courtyard and byway. I know he looks mild-mannered, but you never know about people."

"I hear you," said Babcock. Which Carmela knew, in Babcock-ese, translated to *I haven't the foggiest idea what you're talking about.*

"The French Quarter's always been a hotbed of crime," said Carmela. "What if Sidney's ghost walks are really a cover-up for something else?"

Babcock shrugged. "Petty crime's a way of life here. Tourists are forever reporting pickpockets and muggers, while residents file theft and peeping Tom reports on a daily basis."

"Maybe you should stay on Sidney's butt," suggested Carmela. "He was hanging around Medusa Manor the night after Melody was killed."

"An investigator always has to look for serious motive," Babcock told her. "If you think Sidney St. Cyr was involved in Melody's death, what was his motive?"

Carmela thought for a few moments. "Maybe Sidney was jealous of Melody? Maybe he thought the opening of Medusa Manor would siphon business away from his ghost walks?"

"That's a pretty big stretch," said Babcock.

"Still," said Carmela. "Could you keep an eye on him?"

"I thought you were already doing that."

"Well, yeah, I am. Kind of," said Carmela. "Someone has to do your job," she teased. "But, face it, you're the one with an entire police force at your disposal."

"Hardly," sniffed Babcock. "I've got maybe six detectives. And two of them aren't even that good."

"All the more reason to deputize me," said Carmela.

Babcock looked askance at her. "Sweetheart, I've got enough problems without tossing you into the mix."

Carmela was showing a customer how to sponge-paint onto cardstock, then use a screen to create an additional pattern, when Jekyl Hardy walked through her door. Because Mardi Gras was still many months away, Jekyl was busily dealing and appraising antiques, while making plans to lead an art tour to New York City.

Jekyl was also one of Carmela's dearest friends. They both volunteered with the Children's Art Association and hung out at French Quarter clubs like Dr. Boogie's and Moon Glow.

"You see where I'm going with this?" Carmela asked her customer. "Sponge the yellow paint first, add a tinge of pink for contrast, then oh-so-carefully place the screen on top of your paint job and daub on your mauve-colored paint to create a sort of beehive effect." When she saw that her customer had mastered the technique, Carmela pulled herself away to greet Jekyl.

"What brings you into my territory?" she asked him. Jekyl Hardy was rail thin, with long dark hair pulled into a sleek ponytail, and even darker eyes. He had a penchant for dressing in black from head to toe and was always pleased when people likened him to Lestat, the vampire in Anne Rice's novel.

Jekyl made a big show of administering double air kisses to Carmela, then grinned impishly. "It's *my* territory this weekend, darling," he told her. "NOMA has jumped on the Galleries and Gourmets bandwagon with a vengeance, which turns out to be fortuitous for me. They've decided to set up an appraisal booth in Jackson Square and staff it with yours truly as chief appraiser, arbiter of good taste, and art critic par excellence."

"So . . . an appraisal booth like *Antiques Roadshow,*" said Carmela.

"Hopefully, something of that ilk," said Jekyl, rolling his eyes. "And hopefully people will actually bring their objets d'art to me for careful consideration."

"That should be a great addition to the event," said Carmela. "And lots of fun, too."

Jekyl's gaze turned serious. "KBEZ-TV is even going to cover some of the appraisals. So hopefully, I'll make the ten o'clock news."

"It should be wonderful publicity for your business," said Carmela, knowing Jekyl's business hadn't exactly been gangbusters lately.

"Only if people don't lug in junky fruit jars and nineteen fifties tobacco tins, expecting them to be worth a fortune!" said Jekyl.

Carmela grinned and shook her head. "You're such a snob, Jekyl."

Jekyl held an index finger to his lips. "Shh. Kindly don't tell anyone."

Back in her office, Carmela hit speed dial.

Ava answered on the first ring. "Juju Voodoo. If it's haunted, you want it."

"Ava?" said Carmela. "It's me."

"*Cher!* I was just thinking about you. We received the most marvelous shipment today of love potions in funky little blue pharmaceutical bottles. They look like the *Drink Me* bottles in *Alice in Wonderland*."

"You think it could help me work a spell?" asked Carmela.

"Couldn't hurt," said Ava. "Plus I got a new shipment of jewelry. Earrings, to be exact. Really cool, dangly black crow earrings and green luna moth earrings."

"Luna moths," said Carmela. "Nice."

"So," said Ava. "What's up?"

"I just had lunch with Babcock, and guess who's *not* on his list?"

"Uh, the redheaded guy in the zoot suit who does sketches of tourists down in the French Market?"

"You're close," said Carmela. "Babcock pretty much snickered when I brought up Sidney St. Cyr's name."

"You're telling me Babcock is still stuck on Melody's husband as the prime suspect?" said Ava.

"Yup. On the plus side, he acted a little hinky when I brought up Sawyer Barnes's name."

"The slum landlord."

"Barnes may have started out with rat-infested buildings," said Carmela, "but he's turned them into fancy condos."

"Same thing," said Ava. "But, *cher*, I gotta tell you, Sidney's the one who's starting to send shivers up my spine."

"Why do you say that?" asked Carmela. She wasn't crazy about Sidney, either, and tended to put faith in Ava's gut instincts.

"Sidney just feels . . . involved," said Ava. "I know we don't have any evidence against the guy, but he creeps me out."

"A lot of guys creep you out," said Carmela.

"Not so much anymore," said Ava. "The older I get, the more I've lowered my standards."

"Just don't go too low," laughed Carmela.

"I wish we could think of some way to trap Sidney," said Ava.

"What do you mean? How?"

"I don't know, let my brain centrifuge it for a little while, okay?"

"Sure," said Carmela, giggling at the image of Ava's brain as a spinning centrifuge. "So . . . we're still on for tonight?"

"Of course," said Ava. "What better time to visit a cemetery than a night with a full moon?"

Chapter 18

"LUNA moths," said Carmela, wandering up to the front counter. "Do we have any luna moths?"

Gabby looked up from the product catalog she was studying and fixed Carmela with an inquisitive look. "You mean the genuine fluttering variety or the paper variety?"

"Paper," smiled Carmela.

"In that case, you're probably in luck," responded Gabby. "Some exquisite tissue paper butterflies and moths were shipped to us along with the Flora and Fauna Sticker Collection. We didn't actually order the moths; they were just kind of an add-on from the vendor."

"Can you lay your hands on them?" asked Carmela. "The moths, I mean?"

Gabby drummed her fingers on the counter, looking thoughtful. "Maybe I put them with the collage images?" She came around the counter, pulled out a drawer from their large flat file, and rummaged around. "No, not here," she muttered. "Okay, let me try the art file that has all the bird die cuts and stickers." She slipped past Carmela and slid open another drawer. "Yes, you're in luck. Here they are." Gabby pulled out a plastic envelope and handed it to Carmela. "You're going to make something moth oriented, are you?"

"Just an idea I had," said Carmela. "Ava mentioned luna moths and I suddenly had a brainstorm."

Thirty minutes later, Carmela had a good start on her luna moth votive box. She'd started with dark-blue mulberry paper, crumpled it slightly to add texture, then adhered the paper to the back of her box. A sweep of dried Australian fern had been added, then, on top of that, a branch of silvery willow eucalyptus. A drape of pearls was positioned along the back, and then Carmela added a large brass moon charm and silver embossed stars. Finally, the pale-green tissue paper luna moth was carefully positioned on the branch of eucalyptus.

"I really like it," said Gabby, peering over Carmela's shoulder. "It's very . . . what would you say? . . . evocative. You should put it on display in our front window."

"Along with a poster to advertise our new votive box classes," said Carmela.

"What?" said Gabby, surprised. "I didn't know you were planning actual classes on this stuff."

"I am now," said Carmela.

"Well, great," enthused Gabby. She watched as Carmela stamped individual letters onto a piece of silver tissue paper, tore around the edges, then positioned the paper in the votive box. The paper carried the message *Like a Moth to the Flame*.

"Perfect," said Gabby. She gazed at the votive box, then shook her head and said, "Say, don't you have a meeting this afternoon?"

"I'm out of here in two shakes," said Carmela, placing a final snip of pale-green ribbon inside her votive box.

*   *   *

The Garden District was aptly named, Carmela decided, as she maneuvered her car into a parking spot on Chestnut Street. Because this entire neighborhood really was a garden of earthly delights. Live oaks reigned supreme, of course, forming leafy green bowers over the quaint streets. And then there were the azaleas, jasmine, sweet olives, and gardenias, abundantly elegant, setting off block after wondrous block of Southern belle époque mansions in perfect style.

Olivia Wainwright's magnificent home was done in the Italianate style. A lovely yellow stucco villa-type home surrounded by an elaborate wrought-iron fence of intertwined morning glories and hollyhocks.

"You have a lovely home," Carmela told Olivia when she was greeted at the front door.

Olivia, looking very lady-of-the-manor in a peach silk tunic and matching slacks, feigned surprise. "Do you really think so?" She waved a hand, as if to deflect Carmela's praise. "But this old place needs *so* much work," she sighed. "You know what these houses are like . . . patch, patch, patch. It never ends."

Carmela did know a thing or two about old houses. In fact, if her divorce agreement with Shamus sailed through, no thanks to his sister Glory, she'd be the new owner of a rather large house that sat just two blocks away from Olivia's home. No need to tell that to Olivia, though.

"Come on back to the solarium," called Olivia, speeding ahead of her.

Carmela followed, glancing at walls adorned with contemporary oil paintings, a living room that featured a pair of Mies van der Rohe Barcelona chairs, a Noguchi coffee table, and . . . could that be? . . . a real Henry Moore sculpture?

"I see your taste runs to contemporary," observed Carmela.

Olivia wrinkled her nose as she led Carmela into the glass-walled solarium and flopped down on a white wicker chaise longue, then indicated for Carmela to take the adjacent chair. "You can thank my husband for that. And all the women who flock to him for their pricey little Botox and Restylane injections." She snickered slightly. "But if I had my way, I'd do this whole place up right with Sheraton and Hepplewhite furniture. Decorate in a way that pays homage to tradition as well as this grand old architecture." She sighed. "But Dr. Wainwright does prefer mo*derne*." Her petulant pronunciation put all the emphasis on the second syllable.

"The thing about these old homes," said Carmela, ever the optimist, "is that you can furnish them almost any way you want and they still come out looking terrific."

"You think?" said Olivia.

"There's a house just a block from here," said Carmela. "The Baldwin Mansion?"

Olivia nodded slightly.

"The woman who owns it now, Sally Fischer, furnished it in Country French. Lots of tapestries, distressed ceiling beams, and Provençal print fabrics. And the thing is, the place looks spectacular."

"Really," said Olivia, sounding slightly bored now. She reached for a small silver bell sitting on a side table and gave it a jingle. A few moments later, a housekeeper appeared. "We'd like some tea, please," said Olivia. She glanced at Carmela. "You like oolong?" Carmela nodded. "Then oolong it is, please," she told her housekeeper.

"It was a lovely service this morning, don't you think?" Carmela asked.

Olivia nodded curtly. "Lovely. Garth did a fine job in planning it."

Carmela took a few moments to study Olivia's jewelry. This afternoon, Olivia wore completely different pieces to complement her outfit. A silver cuff adorned with a large amethyst. Matching silver-and-amethyst earrings.

"You know," said Carmela, "I meant to tell you this morning, you have the most exquisite jewelry. In fact, you seem to have amassed quite an amazing collection."

Olivia smiled. "I have a generous husband."

Carmela was not to be deterred. "Some of your pieces look slightly familiar to me. Perhaps I saw them at Fire and Ice?"

"Perhaps," said Olivia. Then she pulled herself upright in her chair. "Shall we get started?"

That was obviously Carmela's cue to pull out her notes.

"We've made great progress on Medusa Manor," Carmela told Olivia as she sifted through pages. "All of the upstairs bedrooms have been themed and are in the process of being decorated. Same with the downstairs parlor and library."

Carmela proceeded to take Olivia Wainwright on a virtual tour of Medusa Manor, giving exact details on each room, elaborating on what had been accomplished so far, as well as explaining work they still planned to carry out.

"I've met with Tate Mackie at Byte Head," Carmela told her, "and he's installing some truly spectacular special effects. We're talking banshee images and ghostly specters, as well as what's going to look like actual crackling flames in the crematorium."

"Excellent," said Olivia as their tea arrived, and Carmela wasn't sure whether she was referring to the work she and Ava had done on Medusa Manor or the oolong tea.

"Ava and I have pretty much thrown ourselves into this wholeheartedly," Carmela continued, "and we're trying our best to add some unique twists."

"Is that so?" Olivia managed to look politely inquisitive as she poured a cup of tea and handed it to Carmela.

"For example," said Carmela, "we're going back to Lafayette Cemetery tonight to make molds of some of the more interesting tomb decorations. From those molds we'll be able to create various masks that we'll mount on walls or illuminate for floating heads."

"And you're staying on budget?" Olivia asked.

"I'd say so, yes," said Carmela. "I had a nice piece of luck when I found some paintings and tables at Metcalf and Meador. Jack Meador gave us a really great price on everything."

"Mmm," said Olivia, taking a sip of tea.

Carmela flattened out the papers she had balanced on her lap. Olivia was sending out vibes that confused her. A few days ago Olivia had wanted to go full steam ahead on Medusa Manor, and now she barely seemed interested. What had happened? Was Olivia thinking about backing out of the project? Or had Sawyer Barnes made her an offer she couldn't refuse?

"As far as timing goes," Carmela continued, "most of the major installations are slated to go in next week. Then we'll have another two weeks for fine-tuning. For instance, we still have to figure out what's going on in the ballroom as well as down in the basement."

"Maybe," said Olivia, frowning slightly, "you should just complete the first and second floors. As agreed upon."

"Absolutely we'll do that," said Carmela, "but I was under the impression that the entire building had to be decorated and ready for the big unveiling during DiscordaCon."

Olivia took another sip of tea, then set her teacup down with a clink. "Let's not worry about all that right now." She glanced at her watch and frowned again. "The thing is, I need to go out of town on a short business trip."

"Oh," said Carmela.

"I don't want to mire you down with details," said Olivia in a no-nonsense, please-don't-ask-questions tone of voice, "but I have a lot of plates spinning in the air right now. So I think it's best you carry on with the decoration of the first two floors."

"Sure," said Carmela. "We can do that."

"Don't think I don't appreciate your efforts," Olivia said hastily, "but things are in motion right now that could affect your project."

"Look," said Carmela. "If you want us to put everything on hold right now, we can do that. I can prepare a progress billing for you immediately." *And you can pay us immediately, too*, she thought to herself.

Olivia waved a hand. "No, no, please just push ahead as planned. But do be aware, things could change."

"Sure," said Carmela. "No problem." Even though, to her, it felt like a rather large problem indeed.

Heading down Chestnut Street, Carmela thought about her somewhat unsettling meeting with Olivia. Decided the woman either was a poor decision maker, was planning to sell Medusa Manor to Sawyer Barnes, or was going to abandon the project altogether. Or maybe Olivia was just plain schizo. Or a dud when it came to business. Or maybe . . . something else was going on. Something Carmela couldn't quite figure out.

Carmela hung a left and slowed her car as she pulled in front of Shamus's house. The house that had also been her house for a while. That might be her house again if Glory didn't toss a wrench into everything.

It was a wonderful house, really. Not quite as large as Olivia Wainwright's place, but with more personality. A Greek revival style, painted slate gray with white trim, and capped with an octagonal turret.

Carmela stared up at that third-floor turret. She and Shamus had never really done anything with that small third-floor room. Her suggestion of a library had been countered by Shamus's suggestion of a place to exhibit his photographs. They'd never been able to compromise on what to do with the space. A metaphor, probably, for their failed marriage and failed reconciliations.

Now the turret room just reminded Carmela of the turret room at Medusa Manor. Where Melody had plunged to her death.

Why, Carmela wondered, were there never clear answers for any of the important things in life?

Chapter 19

"**R**EADY to take off, chickie poo?" Ava called as she stood in the doorway of Carmela's apartment. With those words, Boo and Poobah came hurtling toward her. Tails wagged, fur flew, and two wriggling critters danced about, administering wet, sloppy kisses to their Aunt Ava. Ava shrieked with laughter as she bent down to accept their heartfelt greetings. "Smooches from pooches!" she exclaimed.

Carmela appeared a few seconds later. "Don't encourage them. They think they're coming with us."

"Aren't they?" asked Ava. She knelt down and grabbed Boo's fat little face. "Are you going to guard us tonight? Are you, darlin'?" Boo's tightly curled tail wagged like an overtaxed metronome.

"You look cute," said Carmela, eyeing Ava's outfit. She was wearing tight blue jeans that conformed to her curvaceous hips and a slinky long-sleeved dark-green T-shirt that proclaimed, *I'm not really lost, I'm just exploring.*

"Cool shirt," said Carmela. "Where'd you get it?"

Ava fluffed out her voluminous dark hair. "Don't know. I think some guy left it in my store."

Carmela stared at her. "Some man left his T-shirt in your store?"

Ava shrugged. "Sure."

"Let me get this straight," said Carmela. "A man came into your store, removed his shirt, and left bare chested?"

Ava gave a coy smile. "Yeah. I guess so."

"Some people have all the luck," declared Carmela. "People come to my shop, all they forget are their rubber stamps or a couple pages of scrapbook paper. Then, if we manage to track down the rightful owner, they're generally sour about having to make an extra trip back."

"You run a conservative, family-type business," said Ava. "While I run a . . ." She searched for the appropriate words.

"Wacky, offbeat shop," filled in Carmela.

"But fun," said Ava. "We always have fun."

"I can see that," grinned Carmela. "So, you brought your mold-making kit?"

Ava held up a large black nylon bag. "Check."

"Okay then," said Carmela, stepping outside and attempting to close the door behind her, while trying to pry furry, protesting paws from the doorjamb.

"Hey," cackled Ava, "you're all gussied up, too." She was referring to Carmela's turtleneck and baggy jeans covered with colorful squiggles and splotches of paint. "You wore your Jackson Pollock jeans! How perfectly artsy."

"Zip it," instructed Carmela.

Ten minutes later they were scurrying through the side gate of Lafayette Cemetery.

"Place looks deserted," remarked Ava. "Tourists have all gone home. Snapped their last photos and gone in search of more exotic locales. Sipping Hurricanes at Brennan's or hitting the clubs on Bourbon Street."

Glancing up at the full moon that shone like a silver

beacon through twisted branches, Carmela asked, "Did you bring your wooden stake and garlic? Or your magic charms, just in case?"

Ava waggled a wrist to show off a half-dozen jingling, shiny bracelets. "My silver bracelets are guaranteed by the manufacturer to ward off werewolves. But the instructions, which I think were printed in archaic Romanian, strangely didn't mention anything about vampires." She cocked her head at Carmela. "Why? You feeling spooked tonight?"

"To tell you the truth," said Carmela, "I've had this weird feeling all day that someone was following me."

"You were pretty jumpy this morning, when you thought someone was listening in on us after the service," Ava pointed out.

"But no one was there," said Carmela.

"Or at least we didn't *see* anyone," said Ava. "On the other hand, I firmly respect your hunches. If you think somebody's dogging your footsteps, maybe they really are. And now that you mention it, is it possible Sidney St. Cyr could be creeping around behind your back?"

"Hah," said Carmela, "when I told Babcock I had a bad feeling about Sidney, he pretty much laughed in my face."

"That's not very nice," said Ava. "You're entitled to your suspicions and intuitions; it's your God-given right as a female."

"But you think there's something off about Sidney, too," said Carmela.

Ava nodded slowly. "I do. Maybe Sidney had something to do with Melody's death, or maybe he's just one of those guys who creep you out. You know what I'm talking about? It can even be a little thing, like hairy hands or floppy lips, or just the odd look a guy gives you. But it spooks you, deep down inside."

"You said this morning that you wished there were some way we could trap Sidney. What did you mean by that?"

"Maybe . . . trap him with words?" said Ava. "See if we could trap him in a lie?"

"A lie about Melody?"

"I suppose that would be the general idea," said Ava.

"I'm impressed by your twisted, suspicious mind," said Carmela, "but do you have any idea how to make that happen?"

Ava thought for a few moments. "What if we persuaded Sidney to drop by Juju Voodoo tomorrow night?" asked Ava. "Tell him we need his expertise or advice on some kind of séance? What would you think of that?"

"Then we'd ask him a few leading questions," said Carmela, warming up to the idea.

"Sure," said Ava. "We'd see if we could trip him up. Or, better yet, we could do a tarot reading that reveals a specific card dealing with murder."

"I like the way you think," said Carmela. "The way you stack the deck."

They crept through the cemetery, gravel crunching underfoot. No light shone anywhere, except for moonlight glimmering off whitewashed graves.

"Are we going the right way?" asked Ava.

"Dunno," said Carmela. "In the dark everything seems all twisted around."

Ava sighed. "I think we passed that same obelisk five minutes ago."

"Well, shit," said Carmela. "Then we *are* lost. Going in circles."

Ava tapped her chest. "No, we're not. Like my shirt says, we're just exploring."

Carmela pulled her Maglite from her handbag and flipped it on. The thin beam landed on the glass window of a large crypt.

"Jeez," said Ava, startled. "Why do they put windows in those things anyway? You ever wonder about that?"

"No," said Carmela. "I'd rather not."

"And then bars over the windows," continued Ava. "Like if you got locked inside by mistake you could *see* out, but you couldn't *get* out."

"Are you trying to totally creep me out?" asked Carmela. "Because you're succeeding quite nicely."

"Sorry," said Ava, pointing. "Hey, flash your light over there."

Carmela turned her beam on a row of low, rounded tombs.

"There it is," said Ava. "Just past the Lestat tomb. Our Medusa head."

"Whew," said Carmela. "Good catch. Let's get this done and get out of here."

"No problem," said Ava. Dropping her nylon bag, she rummaged inside. Finally, she pulled out a roll of plastic wrap and several ziplock bags.

"You brought sandwiches?" Carmela asked.

"Baloney," said Ava. "Actually, I'm trying to be a respectful little art conservator. I don't want to damage or stain the tombs any more than they already are, so I'm going to use plastic wrap to protect Miss Medusa's face." Ava knelt down and tore off a sheet, then carefully placed the plastic across the face. Using the tips of her fingers, she gently pushed and kneaded the plastic into place. "Now pop open that baggie," Ava instructed Carmela.

"Got it," said Carmela. "Oh, it's clay."

"A special polymer clay that sets up in just a few minutes." Ava worked the clay into a ball, flattened it out into a large disk, then placed the disk over the plastic-protected face. "Now we press this clay into each little crack and crevice, okay?"

Quickly, the two women worked together, pressing and poking the clay so as to capture each and every feature. When they were finished, Carmela asked, "How long before it sets up?"

"Five minutes," said Ava.

"So," said Carmela, leaning against a tomb, "I met with Olivia this afternoon."

"Yeah," said Ava. "How'd that meeting go? Was she happy with your progress report? Are we gonna get a bonus?"

"Not exactly," said Carmela. "In fact, she was jumpy and distracted. Told me to please carry on with the decorating of Medusa Manor, but be prepared for a change of plans."

"What's that supposed to mean?" asked Ava. "Oh man, does that mean we're not gonna get paid?"

"We'll get paid, all right," said Carmela, "but I'm thinking Olivia might sell the property to Sawyer Barnes after all."

"What?" said Ava. "You mean she's going to flip it? She's going to flip a haunted house?"

"I never thought of it that way," said Carmela. "It does seem a little strange."

Ava touched a finger to her clay and determined that it was hardening nicely. "So you're telling me this is an exercise in futility? Olivia might not even want the masks we're making?"

"She said to keep working on Medusa Manor, so that's what we'll do," said Carmela. "And we'll keep a running tally of all our time and expenses, just in case she does pull the plug."

"Hmph," said Ava. "Just when I was all revved up over these masks."

"If the Medusa Manor project gets canned, maybe you could use them for something else?" said Carmela.

Ava nodded. "I suppose. For Halloween or Mardi Gras. That's when I get requests for unusual masks." She touched the polymer again. "This is hard."

"So now what?" asked Carmela.

"Now comes the tricky part," said Ava. She plucked carefully at a corner of the plastic wrap and began to slowly peel the wrap-and-clay image away.

"Easy," cautioned Carmela. But Ava was both proficient and patient. In no time at all she had her polymer cast peeled off. Turning it over gently, she showed it to Carmela.

"Perfect," murmured Carmela. All the details of the face had been captured—in reverse.

"All we have to do now," said Ava, "is fill the mold with plaster. That gives us a positive image. Then stretch some wet, pliable leather over that and—"

"What?" said Carmela.

"I said stretch—"

Carmela held up a hand. "No, I heard something," she whispered.

"Something or someone?" Ava whispered back.

Carmela shook her head. "Probably jumping at shadows." She glanced about nervously. This morning, this piece of cemetery had been sunny and bright. Now the rows of tombs and crypts seemed to hold only secrets and shadows. Blue and black danced about like desperate souls seeking the living.

"Let me pack this up," said Ava, hurrying now.

Carmela agreed. "Better that we—"

A loud grating sound, like flint against stone, suddenly echoed down the row of tombs.

"What?" said Ava, her voice rising a half-dozen octaves.

Huddling together, the two women peered into the dark. And were rocked to the core when a sudden flash of light exploded before their eyes! This was followed by a low whump, like a huge Fourth of July rocket being launched. Then an enormous bright blue flame erupted from the top of a neighboring tomb!

"Holy crapola!" screamed Ava.

The blue flame danced and shimmered and shot straight up into the air, like a gusher of light. Red and gold flames swirled and twirled within it, accompanied by a deafening whoosh!

"What the . . . ?" said Carmela, raising a hand to shield her eyes from the brilliant, sparkling light.

And then, just as fast as it had appeared, the flame flickered and was gone, spewing foul-smelling smoke in its wake.

"What was that?" gasped Ava. "Some kind of electrical fluke? A downed power line?"

"I don't think so," said a still-stunned Carmela. "It seemed too . . . uh, *purposeful* for that."

"Maybe a natural gas leak?"

"Maybe somebody trying to scare us?" said Carmela.

Ava stared at her. "Then their little ploy worked like a charm. I think we oughta scram from here!"

Carmela's front teeth closed down over her lower lip. "Wait a minute, not so fast."

"Are you crazy?" gibbered Ava. "The Prince of Darkness just tried to cast a spell on us."

"I doubt it was anything that ominous," said Carmela. She held up a hand again, and the two of them stood there, listening. "You hear anything?"

Ava shook her head. No.

"Whoever orchestrated that little display probably took off," said Carmela.

"Which is exactly what we should do."

"We should really . . . check it out," muttered Carmela.

"Let's not," said Ava. But she grabbed Carmela's sleeve and followed in her footsteps anyway.

Slowly, quietly, they tiptoed over to the once-flaming tomb.

"Nothing here," marveled Ava, batting away residual smoke. "It was like . . . magic."

"More like a magic trick," said Carmela, staring at a black scorch mark across the top of the tomb. She reached out, poked a finger at bits of black and gray ash, and found they were still warm. "Do you have any more of those ziplock bags?" she asked Ava.

Ava nodded.

"Grab a couple."

"You gonna play *CSI*?" asked Ava.

"I'm going to try," said Carmela. "That is, if Babcock co-operates. If he'll agree to send this . . . this residue . . . to a testing lab."

Ava brought her bags and a small putty knife. Together they scraped at the soot and residue that coated the tomb. Small black and gray flakes of ash fell into the bag.

"Got enough?" asked Ava.

Carmela pinched the bag closed and held it up for inspection. "Looks okay."

"Then let's get out of here," said Ava. "Before something else happens!"

Chapter 20

AVA reclined in the leather chair in Carmela's apartment, staring at her painted-pink toenails. Boo sat on the floor, her shiny brown eyes studiously watching Ava's every move. "What happened out there, anyway?" asked Ava. "A couple of good-looking gals go for an innocent nighttime stroll in a historic cemetery and end up runnin' for their lives."

Carmela handed Ava a steaming mug of cocoa. "We didn't run for our lives. We may have been scared out of our undies, but we held fast."

"Still," said Ava, "the big question remains. Who set that fire? Who's the loony who was trying to scare us?"

"Seems to me we have our choice of loonies these days," said Carmela, sitting down to face her. "Which roughly translates to suspects in Melody's murder."

"There's Garth," said Ava. "Melody's strange-and-gettin'-stranger husband. And Sidney St. Cyr, who, as we all know, adores tromping around cemeteries at night."

"And Sawyer Barnes," said Carmela. "The developer who still seems to be on the hunt for Medusa Manor." She blew on her own cocoa and took a sip. "And, bizarre as this sounds, I can't stop thinking about Olivia Wainwright. She was pretty much the only one who knew we were going out there tonight to take molds."

"But even if Olivia murdered Melody," said Ava, "why would she come after us? Wouldn't she figure an incident like a flaming tomb would just goad us into digging deeper? Into going to the police?"

"You'd think so," said Carmela.

"And we *are* going to the police, aren't we?" asked Ava.

Carmela reached out and stroked Boo's furry head. Her little dog was still staring at Ava as if mesmerized. "I'll talk to Babcock," Carmela promised. "See if he can have the contents of our baggie analyzed."

"Run it through the trusty police-o-matic clue analyzer," said Ava.

"If it were only that easy," said Carmela.

"You know Babcock's gonna be all grumpy and crabby about this," said Ava.

"Like his service revolver, he's on a hair trigger," said Carmela. "He upsets easily. There's a reason I've laid in a good supply of Tums, Rolaids, and various antacids."

"Ah," said Ava, "the touchy tummy syndrome."

"What I'm thinking," said Carmela, "is that the residue from tonight's fiery tomb may possibly match up with the residue from the fire at Medusa Manor."

"Whoa," breathed Ava. "I never thought of that. So that would mean . . . uh . . . what exactly?"

"It would mean that whoever murdered Melody was right there in the cemetery with us tonight, sending a rather firm warning."

"That scares the bejeebers out of me," said Ava.

"Me, too," said Carmela. She stood up, grabbed a book of matches off the fireplace mantel, then leaned down and lit the six rose-colored pillar candles that were arranged on a wrought-iron rack inside her fireplace.

"That's nice," said Ava. "Cozy."

"Mmm," said Carmela.

They watched the miniature flames leap and dance, each thinking about their earlier scare. Finally Carmela said, "You want something to eat?"

"I thought you'd never ask," said Ava.

Padding barefoot into the kitchen, Carmela pulled open the refrigerator door and rummaged around. "I've got cheese and crackers. Actually some really ripe Brie cheese."

"Perfect," called Ava.

"Okay, give me a minute," said Carmela.

"Say," said Ava, "if I owe you, like, a bazillion dollars for food, just let me know, will you? I don't want to be known as a freeloader."

"You're not," said Ava. "You're more like an appreciative snacker."

"You think?" said Ava, pleased.

"Believe me," said Carmela, "it's not an issue."

Ava continued to stare into the fireplace. "This is gonna sound like a real wild card, *cher*, but do you think that special-effects guy had anything to do with this?"

Carmela came in carrying the snacks on a tray. "Tate Mackie?"

"Yeah."

"Why would he try to scare us? What would be his motivation?"

Ava shrugged. "Maybe trying to impress us? Impress you?" She grabbed a small silver knife and spread the creamy Brie on her cracker.

"No," said Carmela. "I don't think so."

Ava took a big bite. "So whoya um realuh shushpec?"

"Huh?"

Ava chewed faster, then swallowed hard. "Who do you really suspect?"

"At this point," said Carmela, "I don't have a clue. But I have to say, Garth is not looking pristine any more."

"Do tell," said Ava.

"At lunch today, Babcock said something about Garth being at the top of his list because of the insurance money as well as a few other things he couldn't go into."

"Really?" said Ava. "Then you gotta grill him. Find out what those other things are."

"I think you're right."

They dropped the subject then, finished their cheese and crackers, and chatted about Medusa Manor. Although, with Olivia's warning that the project could be put on ice, their hearts weren't completely in it anymore.

"I've been sorting through those prom dresses at my office," said Ava, "and there are a couple dozen that are truly ghastly. All torn and dirty, really the dregs."

"Then we should just toss them," said Carmela.

"I had another idea," said Ava. "What if we hauled 'em over to Medusa Manor and used them in some creepy display? You know, do a *Bride of Frankenstein* or *Bride of Chucky* thing in that fourth upstairs bedroom?"

"That's a wonderful idea," enthused Carmela. "We'll fix some veils to float above the tattered dresses and arrange bouquets of dead flowers. I love it!"

"I thought you might," said Ava. "I thought, considering your divorce and all, dead brides would really cheer you up!"

After Ava took off, Carmela decided to call Edgar Babcock. She slipped into a terry cloth robe, lay down on her bed, and dialed his cell phone.

Nada. He wasn't answering. Which meant he wasn't at home.

Okay, she decided, *next best thing. Call the precinct station.* She called, but they weren't exactly cordial about rousing him on his car radio and putting a message through, but finally they did.

Ten minutes later Edgar Babcock called back.

"You called." There was the faint sound of police chatter in the background.

"I was wondering if you could stop over here."

"Man," he said, yawning, "I'm really—"

"It's important," said Carmela, a slight urgency in her voice.

That was enough to trip his cop's instinct and make him immediately suspicious. "What?" he asked. "Did something happen?"

"You could say that," said Carmela.

"What now?"

Carmela drew a deep breath. "Here's the thing," she told him. "Ava and I went to Lafayette Cemetery tonight—"

"You what!" screeched Babcock.

"We went to—"

"I don't believe you!"

"Do we have a bad connection or something?" asked Carmela. "Because I can hear you just fine, but you seem to be having trouble."

"Just tell me what happened," demanded Babcock. Carmela could hear faint clicking sounds and was pretty sure it was Babcock grinding his teeth.

"As I was saying, Ava and I went back to Lafayette Cemetery to take some tomb molds."

"Some what?"

"Are you going to let me tell this or not?" she asked.

"Sorry. Just spit it out and try to talk a little faster, okay?"

"I'm trying," said Carmela. "Anyway, just as we removed a large piece of plastic from a perfectly lovely Medusa head, there was this enormous burst of fire, and flames shot up from the top of a tomb."

Now Carmela seemed to detect a strange gurgling sound coming through her phone.

Finally, Babcock said, "A flaming *tomb*?" His voice was just this side of disbelief.

"You know what?" said Carmela. "I think you should just come over here and let me tell this in person. Otherwise I'd hate to think you were slouched over in your car somewhere having a heart attack."

"Ten minutes," he told her through clenched teeth.

Babcock made it in nine.

"Hello," Carmela said, holding open the door.

"You're crazy, you know that?" he huffed.

"Nice to see you, too." Carmela grabbed the sleeve of his jacket and pulled him into her apartment. Across the courtyard, she saw a curtain move in the upstairs window. Ava. Carmela grinned to herself as she pressed against Babcock and gently nuzzled him.

But after getting his welcome kiss, Babcock quickly grasped Carmela's shoulders and held her at arm's length. "Tell me the whole story," he said, peering at her with burning curiosity, "and don't leave anything out."

"Better sit down, then," Carmela told him. "And let me get you something to drink." She shooed the dogs off the chaise longue so Babcock could flop down there, then went into the kitchen and whipped up yet another cup of cocoa. Just as she was about to slide the steaming black mug onto a small silver tray, Carmela snicked open a cupboard door and grabbed a bottle of peppermint schnapps that she'd had forever. Uncapping the bottle, she poured a hefty shot into Babcock's cocoa, and stirred it around.

"Here you go." She handed the cocoa to Babcock, sat down at his feet, and proceeded to tell her story. Babcock sipped, listened, and sipped some more. Ten minutes later he seemed considerably more relaxed.

"So," he said, "you and Ava stirred up a hornet's nest. You've got someone very worried."

"That's what I think, too," said Carmela, "but I have no

idea who." She frowned and stared at him, as if hoping he could shed some light.

Babcock remained thoughtful. "And you took scrapings of this mysterious fire residue?"

Carmela reached into her pocket, then presented him with the little baggie of soot. "Could you have it analyzed?"

Accepting the bag, he held it up to eye level and shook it. "Probably."

Carmela smiled. "You seem much more relaxed now."

Babcock tilted his empty mug toward her. "Must be your delicious cocoa. Chocolate with a minty flavor. Kind of tastes like Girl Scout cookies."

"Something like that," said Carmela. She took the empty mug from his hand and set it on the floor. "At lunch today, you mentioned something about Garth being your number one suspect because of the insurance money as well as a couple of things you couldn't go into. Can you go into them now?"

Babcock focused on her as he shifted in his chair. He seemed to be pondering something. "There's a witness," he finally said. "We have a witness, a woman who works in the business across the alley from Fire and Ice, who thinks she saw Garth get into his car around the time of the murder."

"Oh no!" said Carmela. "Really?"

Babcock nodded.

"Did you confront Garth about this?"

"Not a confrontation per se," said Babcock, "but we put it to him a number of different ways."

"And did he have an explanation?"

"He had a rather convenient alibi that's almost impossible to check," said Babcock. "Garth told us he went out to his car to grab a package. Said that's probably what she saw."

"So the witness could have been mistaken?" said Carmela.

"Possibly," said Babcock. "Or she could be helping us build a case against him."

Carmela slumped in her chair. "I was hoping it wasn't Garth."

Babcock stared at her patiently. "I didn't say it was."

"But you just said—"

"There's more," said Babcock. "But you've really got to keep this quiet."

Carmela nodded vigorously.

"I mean *really*."

"Yes," she said. "Of course, I will."

"We've been digging in city records and it turns out your buddy Sawyer Barnes . . . ?"

Carmela peered at Babcock sharply.

"It seems Mr. Barnes owned a property, a somewhat dilapidated triplex over in Algiers that he wasn't able to unload when the real estate market flattened out and then took a nosedive. And somehow, magically, that property met with a fiery demise. So, of course, he was able to collect on the insurance."

"Are you serious?" said Carmela. Now he had her undivided attention.

"There's more," said Babcock, pausing for effect.

She stared at him.

"Sawyer Barnes served in the military."

"I heard that," said Carmela. It was one of the little factoids Baby's husband had uncovered for her.

"He was a Navy SEAL."

Carmela stared at Babcock for a long minute. "Wait a minute," she finally said. "Aren't those the guys who are trained in demolition? The guys who deal with explosives and incendiary devices?"

Both pairs of eyes were suddenly focused on the little baggie that lay limply on the chaise.

Babcock gave the briefest of nods. "You got that right."

Chapter 21

"WHAT did you think about the new settlement offer we put on the table?"

"Hmm?" said Carmela. She'd just arrived at Memory Mine five minutes earlier, and Shamus's call was the first phone call of the morning. "There's a new offer?" Shaking her head to clear away the cobwebs, Carmela took another sip of coffee from the cup she'd just purchased at Pirate's Alley Deli.

"Hell, yes," snarled Shamus. "The darned papers should have been messengered to you first thing this morning. You didn't get them?"

"I don't know," said Carmela. And now she could hear him yelling in the background at some poor woman named Maxine. "Your envelope probably got mixed in with the morning mail. I haven't sorted through everything yet. I just got here." It wouldn't pay to tell him that Edgar Babcock, police lieutenant extraordinaire, had kept her up well past her usual bedtime last night.

"Go look, will you?" Shamus was cranky, crankier than usual.

"Call you back," said Carmela, dropping the receiver abruptly. "Hey, Gabby," she called to her assistant, who was in the back of the store restocking racks of paper, "did I get a delivery this morning? Like a really large envelope?"

"Um . . . yeah," said Gabby, balancing stacks of paper. "Quicksilver Messenger Service dropped something off. I figured it was probably photos or something."

"Okay, thanks," said Carmela. She took another sip of coffee, decided she should have ordered a *grande* instead of a regular, and began pawing through the stack of envelopes, flyers, and bills on the front counter. When her fingertips touched a large manila envelope, she pulled it out and glanced at the return address. Willis B. Mortimer, Esquire. Yup, this was it. Ripping open the envelope, Carmela quickly scanned the ten-page document. When she was finished, she set the stapled pages down, touched a hand to her heart, and exhaled slowly. Because Carmela suddenly felt like the weight of the world had been lifted from her shoulders. Glory had somehow, crazily, miraculously, agreed to a modest cash settlement as well as the deed to Shamus's Garden District home. Hallelujah!

Carmela wasted no time in calling Shamus back. "Obviously, I need to run this by my lawyer, but I'd say we have a deal."

"Fine," said Shamus. "Good." He'd blown off his steam and sounded reasonable now.

"And I think we should sign this agreement right away," added Carmela. "Immediately, in fact."

"What's the all-fired hurry?" grumped Shamus. "It's taken us three years to get to this point."

"You are so right," said Carmela. "There's been delay after delay, which I know has been exasperating for both of us. So now that we finally have an agreement we can live with, I think we should bring things to a rapid conclusion. Also, the last thing I want is for your big sister Glory to suddenly pop a pill and change her mind. So . . . when can we meet?" pressed Carmela. "And where?"

"Jeez Louise," sniffed Shamus, "you sure are hot to get rid of me."

You have no idea, Carmela wanted to say, but she held her tongue and didn't. Instead, she crossed her fingers and told a little white lie: "Shamus, we gave it a good shot. We were very much in love, but couldn't make it work. Why not sign the papers right now while we still have fond memories of each other?"

There was a long pause, and then Shamus said, "You have fond memories of me?"

"Of course I do," said Carmela, lavishly stroking his ego.

"Hey, babe," laughed Shamus, "do you remember the time we stayed in that little B&B in Bogalusa? It had that really creaky bed and the heart-shaped—"

"Shamus," said Carmela, cutting him off, "let's really try to meet tomorrow."

"Tomorrow?" said Shamus, his voice rising in a squeak. "That soon?" Now he sounded hurt.

"I think it's best."

Several deep sighs were followed by, "I suppose we could meet at the Crescent City Bank offices . . ."

"Perfect," said Carmela. "What time?"

"Uh . . . nine?" said Shamus.

"See you then," said Carmela, giving him the proverbial bum's rush.

"Hey, babe," came Shamus's plaintive voice, just before she hung up. "Bring the dogs, will you?"

"You finally have an agreement?" asked Gabby. She waved her hands in the air in front of her, as if to clear away any impropriety. "Sorry, but I couldn't help but overhear you."

"It's looking good," said Carmela, "as long as Glory doesn't stick her fat nose in at the last minute."

"I'm happy for you, Carmela," said Gabby, giving her a little hug. Ever the romantic, Gabby had burned candles and prayed to St. Valentine in hopes that Carmela and Shamus would eventually reunite. But now, after all their bitter wranglings and Shamus's infidelities, she'd pretty much accepted the divorce. And, of course, Edgar Babcock had recently come on the scene. So Gabby was thrilled beyond words that Carmela was romantically involved again. The fact that Babcock was tall, handsome, well mannered, and a terrific dresser didn't hurt, either.

"You know what?" said Carmela, "I feel fantastic. I haven't felt this good in . . . in years."

"Some women are meant to be married," said Gabby, "some women are meant to be free."

Carmela studied Gabby for a moment. "You really believe that?"

Gabby nodded. "I do."

"Does that mean I'm not cut out for marriage?"

Gabby's face fell. "Oh no, I didn't mean it like that! I just meant that . . . well, you've been on and off with Shamus for so long and now that the situation is resolved, it's time for you to focus on *you.*"

"Nicely put," grinned Carmela. "You talked your way out of that one."

"I hope I did," said Gabby. "Because I sure don't mean to be a busybody or even a cynic."

"You're not," said Carmela. "Believe me."

Gabby picked up a stack of metallic paper, looking more than a little relieved. "Oh, you know what? We received a shipment of that deckle-edged paper you like and some of those tiny manila envelopes with the tie and button closures."

"Perfect," said Carmela. "I had someone ask about those envelopes just the other day."

They got busy then as the clock cranked toward ten and

customers, regulars as well as French Quarter visitors, began to trickle in.

One woman wanted to make personalized wine labels, so Carmela showed her how to create a Tuscan background using watercolors on beige card stock. With a little careful placement, a rubber stamp of an old monastery yielded a winery visual, helped along with some overstamping of grape and leaf designs. All that was needed was hand lettering on the label and a bit of raffia to tie around the neck of the bottle.

Another customer wanted to make seating cards for a fancy dinner with an opera theme. Carmela showed her how to create small black one-fold cards with manila library pockets on the inside. Carmela then suggested creating collaged and stamped tags to go inside those pockets. Some of the papers she chose for the woman included themes of musical notes, fancy scripts, and florals. Suggested rubber-stamping ideas included portraits of Italian Renaissance ladies, musical notes, and sketches of European-style villas.

"This morning is completely flying by," remarked Gabby when there was a slight break in the action.

"Business is *good*," breathed Carmela. She reached out and rapped her knuckles on one of the flat files, a little knock on wood for insurance purposes.

Gabby jerked her head toward the front counter. "I think that lady might need a little help selecting fibers and tassels to embellish her album."

"You want me to make some suggestions?" asked Carmela.

Gabby nodded. "Would you? You always have such innovative ideas."

But when Carmela offered to help, she was waved away.

"I'm taking my time and having fun," the woman told her. "I just want to look at everything you have before I make my decision."

"No problem," said Carmela. "And if you want larger tassels or beaded tassels, just ask. We have some stashed in back."

Carmela turned to her shelf of albums and began straightening them. She put the old-fashioned black albums on the left; tucked a trio of larger red leather albums next to them; and was about to add two suede-covered albums, when a hand dropped softly on her shoulder. She whirled, expecting Gabby. Instead, she found herself gazing into the dark, limpid eyes of Sidney St. Cyr.

"Sidney!" she cried. "What are you doing here?" He'd surprised as well as flustered her.

Sidney arranged his long face into a smile. "I came by to see you, Carmela."

She placed the suede albums on the shelf and pulled herself together. "What's up?"

Sidney dropped his head, gazed at his black high-top tennis shoes for a few moments, then glanced back up at Carmela. "I . . . I came by to offer my help."

"Help?" Carmela wasn't sure what Sidney was talking about. Did he want to help with Medusa Manor?

Sidney plunged on ahead. "I understand you've been making a few inquiries about . . . well, about Melody's murder."

Carmela's nod was almost imperceptible.

"And I thought," continued Sidney, "that perhaps I could help."

Carmela gave a slow reptilian blink and then said, sweet as pie, to Sidney, "Why don't you come back to my office, where we can talk?"

Sidney followed docilely and, once they were settled, told her in a rush of what appeared to be heartfelt sentiment, "Melody was my friend, too. A *good* friend."

"I know she was," said Carmela. She was seated in her swivel task chair with Sidney across from her in a director's chair, his long legs splayed out.

"The police don't seem to be getting anywhere," said Sidney, gazing at her rather intently.

"No, they don't," agreed Carmela. She gulped, took a deep breath, and plunged ahead. "In fact, last night Ava and I were just remarking on that rather sad state of affairs. About how Melody's death is so . . . so unresolved."

Sidney nodded emphatically, punctuated with a slight sniffle.

"I know this might sound somewhat unusual," said Carmela, "given the circumstances, but Ava and I were actually thinking of conducting a séance."

Sidney's eyes widened. "To try to get in touch with Melody? To try to talk to her?" This clearly intrigued him.

"Um . . . yes," said Carmela. "That would be the general idea."

"I think it's a wonderful idea!" cried Sidney.

"You do?" She leaned back in her chair, pleased that he'd jumped at the idea. The bait.

"Absolutely," said Sidney. "When did you want to do this?"

"Ava actually mentioned something about having a séance tonight at her place," said Carmela.

A frown flitted across Sidney's face. "It would have to be later. I have a ghost walk tonight. Going to hit a couple old hotels, Pirate's Alley, a voodoo temple, like that."

"So maybe ten or ten thirty would work for you?"

"Ten thirty," said Sidney, "would be perfect."

"Good," said Carmela. "I'll call Ava and tell her you're eager to participate."

"Wouldn't it be something," said Sidney, "if we really made contact?"

"Yes, it would," agreed Carmela.

Sidney's big hands slapped his knees, then he rose from his chair. "See you tonight. And thank you!"

"You're not going to believe this," Carmela told Ava when she picked up the phone, "but we're set for tonight."

"Tonight . . ." said Ava.

"The séance!"

"Oh my gosh, you *talked* to Sidney?"

"He came waltzing into my shop!" exclaimed Carmela. "On his own accord."

"And you just laid it on him," said Ava.

"Something like that."

"And he agreed to it?" said a still-surprised Ava.

"Are you kidding?" said Carmela. "Sidney jumped at the chance. This is an eager boy we have here."

"Hot dog!" exclaimed Ava. "Like a rat to the trap. Aren't you the clever one."

"Maybe," said Carmela. "We'll see."

"We'll set up a Ouija board in the back room," enthused Ava. "Make sure it's dark and draped, suitably spooky. Then, if we have to, we'll move on to tarot cards."

"I leave this completely in your capable hands," said Carmela. "You're the one who's the voodoo lady of New Orleans."

"Don't tell anybody," said Ava, dropping her voice to a whisper, "but I'm really the *faux* voodoo lady. Truth be told, all my love charms and gris-gris bags are really filled with herbs and spices. Good for flavoring jambalaya or baking a turkey."

"My lips are sealed," laughed Carmela.

"So what time tonight?" asked Ava.

"Ten thirty. Sidney has a ghost walk and Babcock's taking me out to dinner."

"So you'll have to ditch him," said Ava. "Easier said than done."

"Naw, he was over last night, so I pretty much wore him out."

"You wicked girl," said Ava.

"I certainly hope so," laughed Carmela.

"So . . . I culled through those prom dresses that were jamming my office and picked out the bummers. I'll probably haul them over to Medusa Manor this afternoon."

"If you're going over there," said Carmela, "I'll call Jack Meador at Metcalf and Meador and tell him to deliver the stuff I bought from him. There's a table, a couple of paintings, a trunk, and a lamp."

"Sounds like a plan," said Ava.

Chapter 22

"YOU stamp directly on the leather?" asked Byrle.

Carmela nodded. Byrle Coopersmith, one of her regulars, had dropped by with Tandy this afternoon and begged for a few ideas on embellishing small notebooks. Byrle wanted to make several, in different motifs, to give as gifts.

Carmela had mulled this over for a couple of minutes, then pulled out a number of leather scraps as well as some western-themed rubber stamps. She'd directed each woman to choose a stamp while she selected a buffalo image.

"First I'll stamp the image on leather," Carmela told them. She pressed the rubber stamp against a black ink pad, then stamped a buffalo impression on her scrap of leather. "Then I'll use a wood-burning tool to burn along the outline." She picked up a wood-burning tool she'd had heating, then leaned forward and touched the tip of the tool to the leather. There was a hiss and the distinct scent of burning leather as Carmela eased the tool around the stamped buffalo image until it resembled something a branding iron might have created.

"Cool," said Tandy. "Then what?"

"Now I'm going to make a slightly ragged cut around my buffalo image, leaving maybe an inch or so on each side. Then I mount that image on a torn, slightly oval piece of brown card stock."

"Okay," said Byrle, "but what about the album itself?"

"That we're going to cover," said Carmela. She'd already found a piece of tan paper with an aspen leaf design, so she used spray adhesive to mount it on the album cover, then wrapped the excess paper around to the inside. "Now I can adhere my buffalo piece to the front cover, then add a leather cord with some beads."

"And maybe a feather?" asked Byrle.

"Love it," said Carmela. "In fact, the more layers you can build up, the better."

"That's really the key to crafting, isn't it?" asked Tandy.

Carmela nodded. "Layers and coordinating colors. That's how you achieve a certain . . . what would you call it? A richness."

Carmela helped Tandy and Byrle for another ten minutes, then disappeared into her office for a quick lunch. Gabby had run out for po'boys, so that's what Carmela was hunched over now—a classic New Orleans French roll sandwich stacked with roast beef, tomatoes, onions, pickles, and plenty of mayonnaise.

As mayonnaise dripped on her papers and Melissa Etheridge wafted from the CD player, Carmela flipped through pages of her business planner. Early on, when she'd first conceived Memory Mine, she'd written an initial business plan. That had become the template for her one-year, five-year, and ten-year plans. Amazingly enough, she was starting to close in on that five-year plan! Of course, not everything had gone according to plan. There'd been little business hiccups along the way and then one great big hiccup known as Hurricane Katrina.

But scrapbooking was still the number one craft in America, and it had long since dovetailed into other areas, too. Business and customer satisfaction scrapbooks were huge—she had created at least six of them last year. Her favorite had been a scrapbook for Storyville Catering that had incorporated photos of their food offerings and beauty shots of their tablescapes interspersed with testimonial letters from happy customers.

The art of scrapbooking had long since extended to family journals and recipe scrapbooks, too. Then there were crafts such as card making, tag art, rubber stamping, memory boxes, votive boxes, collages, and altered books.

Carmela smiled to herself as she turned a page to study her monthly accounts. Sales were okay, but bills were coming due and it looked like her rent was going to get jacked up again. Good thing she and Ava had scored that Medusa Manor gig.

As if on cue, the phone rang.

"Carmela," came a hushed voice. "It's Garth."

Medusa Manor's been sold, she told herself. Then she said, "Hey there, how are you?"

"Okay." Garth's voice sounded hoarse and just this side of tears.

Not okay, thought Carmela. In fact, Garth sounded terrible. "I know the funeral yesterday was tough," she told him. "You were very brave to get through it as well as you did."

"Kind of you to say so," said Garth. "I was calling to see if you've . . . uh . . . made any sort of progress." His voice faltered. A few seconds passed, and then he cleared his throat and continued. "You were going to kind of snoop around, see if you came up with anything that might be . . . uh . . . relevant or even suspicious."

Like you, she wanted to say, but didn't. "There *are* a few people who, I think, warrant a closer look," she told Garth.

"Who?" he asked, pouncing on her words.

"I know you told me Sidney St. Cyr was a good friend of

Melody's," said Carmela, "but he just seems a little strange to me."

"To me, too," said Garth, eagerly.

"And Sawyer Barnes, the fellow who originally tried to buy Medusa Manor, has a slightly shadowy background."

"Why do you say that?" asked Garth.

"Turns out one of his properties mysteriously caught fire, and he has a history of slightly shady deals as well as high-pressure negotiations," said Carmela.

"The property catching fire scares the shit out of me," said Garth. "How did you find out about that?"

Carmela grimaced. "Actually, Detective Babcock mentioned it to me." Was that one of the things he'd warned her not to repeat? She couldn't quite remember.

"Do you know," said Garth, "if he's seriously looking at Barnes?"

"I'm pretty sure he is," said Carmela.

"Because if he isn't, I'm gonna call Babcock and really try to pressure him."

"No, no," said Carmela, "don't do that. I promise you, I'll talk to him and try to, you know, nudge him hard in that direction. Don't you call Babcock, though. You're just too . . . emotionally distraught right now."

Carmela heard rapid, shallow breathing, and then Garth said, "I suppose I am. You've . . . you've been a real friend in all of this. How can I ever thank you?"

By being innocent, thought Carmela. "No thanks are necessary," she said. "I'd be doing this even if you hadn't asked. Melody was a dear friend."

"You're the dear," said Garth, as he hung up quietly.

"Oh crap," muttered Carmela. "What did I get myself into?"

"Hey cupcake," called a voice behind her, "I'd say you got yourself into a big load of bat guano!"

Carmela spun in her chair to find Ava's grinning face looming over her. "Ava! What are you doing here?"

Ava waved a hand, then collapsed opposite her. "I got tired of slumming and wanted to see how the other half lived."

"Then you made a wrong turn," said Carmela. "No high life here."

Ava pulled a gold compact from her Louis Vuitton bucket bag and began powdering her nose. "I just came back from Medusa Manor," she told Carmela. "I took the really bad prom dresses over and hung 'em up. Boy, do they look phenomenal! Like an entire cotillion of ghost brides. Very creepy."

"I can't believe you went over there all by yourself."

"I didn't," admitted Ava. "I made Miguel go with me." Miguel was Ava's assistant at Juju Voodoo. "He was a huge help. Put hooks in the ceiling and everything."

"If we keep pushing like this," said Carmela, "we'll get this project finished in time for that horror convention."

"For sure," said Ava.

"Did the other stuff get delivered, too?" Carmela asked.

Ava had finished with the powdering and was now applying plum-colored lip gloss. "Yup. Jack Meador was real swell about it, too. Even hauled some of the stuff upstairs."

"Finally," said Carmela, "someone who's actually proactive and helpful."

"Ain't that a breath of fresh air?" asked Ava. She snapped the top on her lip gloss and peered at Carmela. "I meant to ask you, has anyone bothered to talk to the original designer?"

"You mean the original designer for Medusa Manor?"

Ava nodded. "Yeah, the one who quit."

"No," said Carmela, slowly. "Somehow he got lost in all of this." She thought for a few moments. "But now that you bring it up . . . maybe we should." She spun her chair a half turn and pawed through the papers on her desk, and finally found what she was looking for. "Henry Tynes," she said. "Maybe I should go talk to him."

"Do you know where to find him?"

Carmela placed an index finger on the paper again and scanned down. "Tynes is, uh, let's see, one of three partners in a design firm. Xanadu Design."

"Xanadu," said Ava. "That name sounds familiar. Wasn't that an old nightclub? Like Studio 54?"

Carmela leaned back in her chair and smiled. "'In Xanadu did Kubla Khan / A stately pleasure-dome decree.'"

"Ooh, *cher*," Ava cooed. "You are so smart!"

An hour later, sparked by her conversation with Ava, Carmela found herself standing in the reception area of Xanadu Design. Turned out it was located only a few blocks from Memory Mine, in a rehabbed brick building. A baby boutique occupied the first floor, and Xanadu Design had the second floor.

"Henry will be right out," the receptionist told her. "He's just finishing up with a client."

"Thank you," said Carmela, looking around the lobby. The design firm had retained the flavor and character of the old building, opting to keep the wood floors and yellow brick walls, and had hung an interesting mixture of contemporary oil paintings and examples of their design work on the walls.

Carmela studied some of the design work Xanadu had done. There was a package design for the St. Charles Coffee Company and a logo design for the Maison Villeroy Hotel. Not bad. Kind of reminded her of her early days before she opened Memory Mine, when she was part of the in-house design staff at a food product company named Bayou Bob's. When she'd designed labels for Catahoula Ketchup and Turtle Chili.

"Miss Bertrand?"

Carmela whirled about to find a tall, good-looking young man gazing at her. He was dressed business casual. Or, rather, design firm casual, with a graphic T-shirt and chino slacks.

"Henry Tynes?" she asked.

The man nodded. He was in his early thirties, with dark tousled hair, an olive complexion, and a serious look about him. Although, Carmela decided, that serious look might be because he was pressed for time. Maybe had a design deadline.

Carmela crossed the lobby and shook his hand. "Thanks for seeing me on such short notice."

"No problem," said Tynes. "C'mon back to my office." He spun on his heels and led her down a short corridor that had maybe six open cubicles on each side. Three were occupied, the others were piled with storyboards, computer gear, and cardboard boxes.

"We're a young company," Tynes told her, "which is why we're running a little lean right now." He led her into his cubicle at the end of the hall, indicated for her to make herself comfortable on a small leather couch, then sat down across from her in a yellow plastic bucket chair.

"Which is why you agreed to take the Medusa Manor job," said Carmela.

Tynes nodded. "That's about it. Initially, we were under the impression there was to be quite a bit of design work. Logos, print ads, a Web site . . . you understand."

"But it turned out to be more set design," said Carmela.

Tynes nodded. "Not that I dislike set design. I actually did quite a bit of it when I was in school."

"So you got about halfway through the project," said Carmela, trying to lead the conversation.

"That's right," said Tynes. "Then we were approached by a major client. A software company that had amassed some serious start-up money and wanted us to create a complete campaign for them. I'm talking from the ground up: logo design, corporate graphics, print ads, Web site, and a national print campaign."

"Sounds big-time," said Carmela.

"Believe me, it is," said Tyne. "And a dream job, the kind that can put a little company like ours on the map. Maybe even get our work recognized in *Print* or *Communication Arts* magazine."

"So you said good-bye to Medusa Manor," said Carmela.

Tynes grimaced slightly. "We did. I felt bad about it, but . . . business is business. I suppose we never should have strayed from our corporate mission in the first place."

"And then Melody was murdered," said Carmela.

Tynes's face crumpled in anguish. "A bizarre turn of events," he replied, then touched fingers to his chest. "I really thought she was a terrific person. I can't imagine anyone having it in for her."

"I imagine the police questioned you about this," said Carmela.

"Three separate times," said Tynes. "And I really racked my brain to try to remember anything that might shed a speck of light on why this might have happened."

"But you didn't come up with anything," said Carmela.

Tynes shook his head, looking sad. "Not a single thing. Neither have the police, I guess."

"You can't remember anything peculiar or out of the ordinary happening while you were working on Medusa Manor?"

"That's exactly what the police asked," said Tynes. "And believe me, if I remembered *anything*, I would have told them."

"Hmm," said Carmela. She crossed her legs, gazed at him.

"Sorry," said Tynes. And, to her, he really did appear sorry.

"So what did you come up with?" asked Carmela. "For the software account, I mean?"

Tynes scrambled to grab a half-dozen boards that lay scattered on his desk. He seemed relieved Carmela had changed the subject.

*   *   *

As Carmela wandered down Esplanade, she was pretty sure in her mind that Henry Tynes wasn't a potential suspect. He seemed genuinely upset at Melody's death, but also a little removed. After all, he'd resigned from the project two weeks before she and Ava had come on board. Of course, he and Melody could have had a falling out that no one knew about. But, somehow, that just didn't feel right. No, Carmela suspected that Henry Tynes was as puzzled by Melody's death as everyone else was. As everyone else professed to be, that is.

Taking a turn down Dauphine, Carmela decided to drop by Byte Head and check in with Tate Mackie again. He'd sent her a couple of e-mails updating her on special effects, and she wanted to see what he'd come up with. Since she and Ava were still working on Medusa Manor—at least for the time being.

"This is gonna blow your socks off," Tate Mackie told her. His fingers flew across the keyboard of his Dell computer as he conjured up his newest CGI effects.

"Yipes," cried Carmela, peering at the screen. "Are those zombies?" She watched, enthralled, as a legion of zombies lurched their way through a graveyard. And not just any graveyard . . . Carmela recognized it as being St. Louis No. 1!

"You actually filmed at St. Louis No. 1?" she asked Tate.

He grinned happily. "Yup, took my little camera there at high noon and used a filter. Ain't it great?"

"It all looks so real," she said, shivering.

Tate's fingers once again worked the keys. "You ain't seen nothin' yet," he told her, punching up another special effect. "I came up with this for your *Exorcist* bedroom. Bedcovers that turn into writhing snakes."

"Uh . . . yeah," said Carmela, averting her eyes. Snakes she didn't need. "So that's it? Those are the last two pieces?"

"Got one more," Tate told her. "The pièce de résistance for your crematorium. I fine-tuned the flames—see how they flicker and dance now? Then really grow in intensity?"

"Wow," said Carmela, watching the computer screen, feeling slightly mesmerized.

"What I'll do," said Tate, "is install this first thing tomorrow. I'll sync it to that big switch that's in there and install a couple of high-intensity heat lamps."

"You'll need a key," said Carmela, digging in her bag, hoping Tate Mackie really was on the up-and-up. That he hadn't been involved in Melody's demise.

"When these flames are projected on the wall it'll look like the gates of hell yawned open," said Tate. "Pretty terrifying stuff, huh?"

"Sure is," said Carmela, deciding the final product did seem a little too real for comfort.

Tate grinned at her and winked. "The magic of movies."

Chapter 23

"WHY isn't my hair drying?" Carmela shrilled, ripping pink Velcro rollers from her hair and tossing them about frantically. One landed behind Poobah's ear and stuck tight like a burr; another landed on Boo's tail. "Is it me or do I have humidity-challenged hair tonight?" Scampering from her bedroom to the living room, she leaped over a reclining dog and grabbed for the phone. A serious intervention was required.

"Ah-yes?" said Ava, picking up on the first ring.

"Do you have a hair dryer with, like, megawatts?"

Ava was ready to meet the challenge. "Honey, I've got a hair dryer with more turbo power than a jet engine."

"Get it over here, will you?"

"You're all whacked out 'cause you're having dinner with your cutie tonight," chuckled Ava.

"Not with sopping hair I'm not."

Two minutes later, Ava came flying through the front door brandishing a silver high-tech, high-wattage hair dryer.

"Is this gonna work?" asked a frantic Carmela, grabbing it from her.

"Are you kidding?" said Ava, following her into the bathroom. "This thing could defrost the combined cities of Minneapolis and St. Paul during a January blizzard."

Carmela plugged in the hair dryer, turned it on, and grabbed for the towel rack as she staggered under the thrust of the power. "Yowza."

"See?" said Ava. "Told ya." She lounged in the doorway, looking chic and casual in black jeans and a tight pink T-shirt that said, *You want breakfast in bed? Then sleep in the kitchen.* "Now use a fat brush and really pouf it to get some lift," encouraged Ava. "Then we'll gel you up. Nothing like a little hair gel to finish things off."

Carmela checked herself in the mirror. After only a few minutes, Ava's hair dryer had done the trick. Her blond hair had dried into a chunky, piecey 'do that was, amazingly, very high fashion.

"Now let's tackle your makeup," said Ava, eyeing her.

"I don't really use that much," said Carmela. "A little eye shadow and some mascara."

Ava held out a little square box.

"What's that?" asked Carmela.

"False eyelashes. Gotta go for that Amy Winehouse smoky eye look. Then let's arch those brows with a little brow gel."

"What are you, the local Mary Kay rep?"

Ava gazed at her placidly.

"Sorry, not a speck of brow gel in the house," Carmela told her. She reached down and snatched a pink roller from Boo's mouth.

Ava was not to be deterred. "Then we'll smoosh a dab of hair gel on a Q-tip," advised Ava. "Works like a charm."

Ava worked her magic then, helping Carmela with the false eyelashes, coaxing Carmela's brows into a lovely arch. As a finishing touch, she lined Carmela's lips with a dark cocoa lip liner, then filled in with reddish-brown lip gloss.

"I feel like I'm ready to walk the red carpet," exclaimed Carmela, appraising herself in the mirror. "Whew, what a change!"

"Change is inevitable," said Ava, "except from a vending machine."

"You are so off the hook," laughed Carmela.

"So, *darlin'*," drawled Ava. "Where's pretty boy taking you tonight?"

"That new restaurant, Yellow Bird," said Carmela.

"Mmm, fancy. What are you planning to wear?"

"Maybe my tweed jacket and a pair of cream-colored slacks?"

"Ewww." Ava grimaced.

"Not good?"

"Very good if you're attending a Junior League meeting or chairing a committee to save the spotted owl and want to look straightlaced and conservative. But if you're gonna party at Yellow Bird, the hippest, trendiest new restaurant in the French Quarter?" Ava shook her head. "No, *cher*, I think not."

"Then what?" asked Carmela, glancing at her watch. Babcock was going to be here in twenty minutes. She had to seriously shake her booty!

"Desperate times call for desperate measures," advised Ava. "I'll be right back!"

Carmela dashed back into her bathroom, spritzed on some extra hair spray, and added a little blusher for good measure. By the time she emerged, Ava was back, holding up a slinky black dress for her to admire.

"Very sexy," admitted Carmela. "But will it fit?"

"No problem," said Ava. "As long as we grease you up and use a shoehorn."

But it wasn't the squeezing into the dress that bothered Carmela. While she inhaled mightily and Ava slowly cranked the zipper up the back, she studied herself in the mirror. "One shoulder. I can't remember when I wore a one-shouldered dress."

"This is vintage Lanvin," Ava told her with pride. "Snatched from the racks of The Latest Wrinkle. And for a little added glitz . . ." Ava produced a jeweled spider pin and pinned it on carefully.

"Shoes," said Carmela, starting to panic at the late hour.

"Stiletto heels," advised Ava. "The more teetery the better."

Carmela scrounged in her closet and produced a pair of sequined black mules. "Will these work?"

"Perfect," pronounced Ava. "Have a fabulous evening, but be sure to get to my shop a little after ten. We want to get it all set up for Sidney!"

Yellow Bird was indeed hip, hot, and trendy. The line to get in jostled out the door and stretched partway down Toulouse Street. But Edgar Babcock either had greased the skids or knew someone. Because when they arrived they were immediately escorted to the main dining room and given a table at one of the prime banquettes against the wall.

"Very nice," commented Carmela. "Where we can see and be seen." She glanced around the elegant, subdued room that was dimly lit. Cream-colored walls wore a sheer glaze of yellow and gold, tablecloths were creamy linen, bountiful bouquets of fresh yellow roses were everywhere, and elegant little yellow birds hopped to and fro in gilded cages.

The other customers were all trendy restaurant- and club-goers in their twenties, thirties, and forties. Not a lot of tourists had found the place yet.

"In that dress, you undoubtedly want to be seen," said Babcock as he snuggled closer to her. "I love it. It's so . . . not quite you." He threw her a rakish grin.

"You can say that again," murmured Carmela.

"And your eye makeup is much more dramatic than usual."

"You like it?" asked Carmela. She was afraid it would start melting on her face and turn her into the Joker.

"I do," said Babcock. "Although it might take some getting used to."

"My stylist really wanted me to rock it tonight."

Babcock grinned as their waiter presented them with an oversized cardboard folio. A drink menu.

"We have a drink menu," said Carmela, keeping up her light banter. "Remember the days when a drink menu consisted of a few standard cocktails, red or white wine, and light or dark beer?"

"A lot of the guys down at the precinct think you can judge a woman's personality by the drink she orders," said Babcock, peering at her, a mischievous smile on his face.

"Is that so?" said Carmela. "Then kindly stun me with your insight."

Babcock grinned an easy grin. "Okay. How about this . . . a woman who orders a Dixie Beer is probably going to be fun-loving and fairly low maintenance."

"That's a slam dunk," said Carmela. "How about a woman who orders a martini?"

"Ooh, that would definitely be your high maintenance lady," said Babcock. "A woman with a high quotient for pearls, serious gold jewelry, and designer duds." He held up a finger. "But a woman who orders shots or maybe an upside-down margarita . . ."

"Yes?" giggled Carmela.

"She's . . . how shall I put this? . . . *easy*."

"What about wine?" asked Carmela. "What about a woman who likes a good vintage wine?"

"Like you," said Babcock.

"Like me," said Carmela.

Babcock reached over and grabbed Carmela's hand. "I'd

say a woman who prefers wine tends to be classy, creative, and smart."

"I think you're the smart one," said Carmela. "To have such a snappy answer."

Yellow Bird's menu was New Orleans contemporary and offered such delights as tuna tartare, bing cherry and blue cheese microgreens salad, white truffle tortellini, salmon with raspberry coulis, and blackened catfish with red pepper purée.

Carmela choose a strawberry and feta cheese salad as a starter and chicken piccata for her entrée. Babcock went with oysters casino and a pork chop infused with maple brine. They decided to split a bottle of Moët & Chandon White Star Champagne.

"I think you've showed remarkable restraint," said Babcock.

"What?" said Carmela. "In ordering?"

"No, in not asking about the baggie of ashes I sent to the crime lab."

Carmela raised her newly gelled brows. "Since you brought it up . . ."

"The lab found residue of potassium nitrate, aluminum powder, and shellac," Babcock told her. "Frankly, it's all pretty basic stuff you can find anywhere. A hardware store, a building supply store."

"But is it lethal?" asked Carmela.

Babcock shook his head. "No, just flammable when mixed together in the correct amounts. Which probably means that whoever followed you into that cemetery last night was trying to scare you rather than harm you."

"Good to know," said Carmela, "but the real question is, how did that particular residue compare with the residue you scraped up at Medusa Manor after Melody was murdered?"

Babcock wrinkled his nose. "It's similar, but not exactly the same."

"But the bombs or explosions or whatever they were could have been engineered by the same person?"

"Possibly," said Babcock.

"So we didn't crack the case," said Carmela. She sounded disappointed.

"We will," said Babcock, taking a sip of champagne. "In fact . . ." He looked around, as if to make sure no one was listening. "This afternoon we moved one step closer."

Carmela peered at him. "You know something. What?" she demanded. "Tell me."

"You sure you want to know?" asked Babcock. "Because this has to do with your buddy Garth Mayfeldt." He picked up the basket of dinner rolls and passed it to her.

Carmela selected a French roll. "Tell me. Please."

"We discovered that Garth Mayfeldt is a member of the New Orleans Fireworks Club."

Carmela's eyes went wide. "Holy shit. So Garth had access . . ."

"To all the components that went into making last night's fiery little surprise," said Babcock. "Because Garth Mayfeldt knows how to make his own fireworks."

Carmela suddenly felt sick to her stomach. "I'm not sure I'm going to be able to eat now," she told Babcock.

"If I thought you were going to lose your appetite, I wouldn't have told you about Garth," said Babcock. "This place is expensive!"

Carmela set her butter knife down. "No, seriously."

"Seriously," said Babcock, "I don't have the case sewn up yet. But if I had to make an educated guess, I'd say we're a day or two away."

"Hmm," said Carmela. *Garth? Really?*

"On the other hand," said Babcock, "we're still talking to Sawyer Barnes, trying to figure out how badly he wanted to get his hands on Medusa Manor."

"What about Sidney St. Cyr?" asked Carmela. She was

wondering if the setup she and Ava had planned for later tonight might just be an exercise in futility.

"What about Sidney?" asked Babcock.

"Is he on your suspect list?"

"Yes and no," said Babcock. "No, because we haven't found any real connection or evidence. And yes, he's on my *personal* suspect list because you seem to have a strong feeling about him."

"Thank you," said Carmela.

"But let's not talk about the investigation," suggested Babcock. "Let's just focus on us." He gazed deeply into her eyes. "Or, better yet, on you. How's your settlement coming? Are you even close to being extricated?"

"Closer than you think. I'm supposed to meet with Shamus and his lawyer tomorrow morning."

"Seriously?" said Babcock. "That's good news. Great news, in fact!"

"I'm just praying the meeting will go off without a hitch."

"By *hitch*, you mean his family interfering."

"Or Shamus changing his mind," said Carmela. "Lord knows, he's done it before."

"You just have to hang tough," advised Babcock. "Keep a positive attitude that it will all work out."

"I did that in my marriage and look where it got me."

"Hey," said Babcock. "That chapter is closed; you've got your whole life ahead of you."

"Minus a few years," said Carmela. She grinned at him and suddenly felt part of her false eyelash pop loose.

"Everybody has a few wasted years," said Babcock. "Or thinks they do."

"Do you?" She poked at her eyelash. Nothing doing. That sucker just kept flipping every time she blinked.

He stared at her intently. "I'll tell you about it some time. Just not tonight. Tonight I want to hear about you. Are you still plugging away on the Medusa Manor project? Still hanging bats and propping open coffins?"

"Even better," said Carmela, sliding out of her chair to go to the ladies' room. "We've got a guy creating video projections of lurching zombies and writhing snakes."

Hurrying past all the coveted tables, heading toward the back of the restaurant, Carmela passed the bar. It was loud and smoke-filled and featured a sort of stainless steel monkey-bar apparatus where couples could actually climb up and perch at various levels.

Fun, she thought to herself. Then she just happened to notice Olivia Wainwright sitting at the bar. With that double take, she also noticed Sawyer Barnes sitting next to her.

Having a drink together? Carmela skidded to a stop, backpedaled as best she could in high heels, and peered around the corner.

Yup, there they were. Acting a little cozy, too.

Carmela continued on her way to the ladies' room. What was going on? Wasn't Olivia supposed to be going out of town? Or had she changed her mind? And why?

As soon as Carmela had fixed her false eyelash, she hustled back to Babcock.

"You have to go look in the bar," she told him.

"Why?" he asked. "Is there a pole dancer or something?"

"No, I just saw Olivia Wainwright having a drink with Sawyer Barnes."

"Seriously?"

"No, I made it up. Yes, seriously. Go look. See for yourself."

But when Babcock went to look, they were gone.

"You're sure you weren't just seeing things?" he asked her as he slipped back into the booth. "Maybe you've been hanging around Medusa Manor too much. Maybe it was just a projection."

"No," said Carmela, through gritted teeth, "they were there."

Chapter 24

"AVA?" Carmela knocked at the front door of her friend's shop. The shiny red door, illuminated by a small overhead light, had fat, bouncing black letters that spelled out *Juju Voodoo*. In the multipaned front window, a neon sign glowed bright red and cool blue, illustrating a palm with its basic head, heart, and life lines. A wood shake roof, slightly reminiscent of a Hansel and Gretel cottage, dipped down in front.

Still no answer, so Carmela turned the handle and pushed the door open. She was greeted by the scent of sandalwood incense, then an immediate impression of a red glow and a cool rush of air. And Ava, hurrying to greet her wearing a long black velvet gown, cut generously low to show off her female attributes. It was the kind of slinky outfit Morticia Addams might have worn to entice Gomez, or Ava to pique the interest of Sidney St. Cyr.

"You made it," said Ava, giving Carmela a slow wink. "You have any trouble pulling yourself away from the studmuffin?"

"He was a little miffed that I had to leave early, but I let him assume it was because of tomorrow's big settlement meeting."

"You see," said Ava, leading Carmela toward the back of her store, "he's malleable. That's what you want in a man: someone who's cute and smart, but still a little bit malleable."

Carmela glanced around the shop as she followed in the whisper of Ava's footsteps. Rows of gleaming white skulls grinned at her. A shelf of crystal balls seemed to glow magically from within. Aided, no doubt, by some strategically placed lighting. "We're going to do this in your back room?"

"Sure," said Ava. "We'll light a few candles for atmosphere and play some haunting music to ratchet up the chills. And . . ." She paused at the thermostat and hastily pressed a few buttons. "I want this place icy cold to help welcome any ghostly apparitions."

"I can see you've done this before."

Ava stepped over to a shelf and grabbed a large silver candelabra. "A few times for fun, a few times for real. *Cher*, go grab eight of those tall white tapers, will you?"

Carmela went back out to the darkened shop, passing counters of sachets and charms, monkey paw key chains, and small jars of herbs. Vials filled with "blood" lined a shelf, along with jars of floating "eyes" that watched as she passed by. Carmela selected the candles and hustled past crystals and a tree of small amulets, back to Ava's "reading room."

A crystal skull sat on the table, the air was heavy with exotic smoke, music tinkled around the table from hidden speakers, and the air-conditioning had already chilled the small space.

"Say now," said Carmela, "this place is already starting to give me the creeps."

"Success then," said Ava. She set a Ouija board in the center of the table, then picked up a planchette, the Ouija board's movable indicator. It was an intricate scrolled metal triangle with three short legs covered with felt pads to allow for smooth, silent gliding across the board. Smiling, Ava placed the planchette carefully in the center of the board.

Carmela studied the Ouija board setup. The planchette seemed to hunker there by itself, waiting for eager fingers to rest atop it. Then, hopefully, it would glide across the board, spelling out words or answering yes or no. Carmela shivered in spite of herself.

Ava grinned. "Are you afraid we may actually make contact?" Before Carmela could answer, a sharp rapping echoed throughout the store.

Both women jumped, then laughed at how easily they'd been startled.

"That's gotta be Sidney," said Ava, bouncing up from her chair. "I'll go let our guest in."

A few minutes later, Sidney St. Cyr, dressed all in black and sporting a long black cape, entered the room. His perpetually stooped shoulders flexed his posture forward as he approached Carmela and extended a slender arm.

"Nice to see you again," Carmela said, as his cold, slightly moist fingers wrapped around hers.

"My pleasure," said Sidney. "I'm delighted to join you tonight."

Ava hustled in with a small silver tray that held three brandy snifters and a crystal decanter filled with amber liquid. "Spirits to get the spirits moving?" she chimed. She placed the tray on the table, uncorked the bottle, and poured a finger of brandy into each glass.

Sidney accepted a snifter and swirled the liquid around. He brought it under his beaklike nose and inhaled deeply, savoring the aroma. Then he closed his eyes and took a blissful sip. After a moment he spoke. "What kind of séance did you have in mind?"

Ava lifted a hand to casually indicate the Ouija board.

Sidney smiled and nodded. "Have you had much success with this?"

"I don't want to brag," said Ava, "but I've been very lucky in finding answers. Of course, each time the results are a little different. There's no real predicting what might happen."

"I'm always amazed at the responses Ava gets," added an enthusiastic Carmela, expecting Ava to give her a conspiratorial kick under the table.

"Then let's get started," said Sidney, rubbing his hands together. "Let's . . ." He paused, suddenly looking a little wary. "Shall we try to, uh, contact the spirit world?"

"Yes," said Ava, closing her eyes and tilting her head back. She placed her enameled fingertips lightly on the planchette. "Let's try to make contact with a spirit guide. See what we can find out about Melody."

Sidney swallowed hard and took another sip of brandy. "Sure. Why not?"

"Then let us begin," intoned Ava. "Everyone place your fingertips gently next to mine."

As Carmela and Sidney stretched their arms forward, the lights seemed to dim, as if on cue. Carmela wondered how Ava had managed that.

"Spirit guide," said Ava, "we implore your help. We ask that you guide us safely into another dimension."

All three glanced down at the board and waited.

Nothing happened.

"Let's approach this in a slightly different way," said Ava. She drew a deep breath and asked, "Is there a spirit present?" She glanced at Carmela and Sidney. "Please, everyone concentrate on that question."

The flames of the candles seemed to flicker, and shadows danced around them.

Carmela thought she felt the planchette begin to move. Helped along by Ava? Helped unconsciously by herself? She didn't know. But her eyes widened in surprise as the planchette moved slowly toward the upper left-hand corner of the Ouija board, then stopped abruptly over the word *Yes*.

The temperature seemed to take another dip.

"Welcome, spirit," said Ava. "Will you kindly tell us your name?"

The planchette jerked once and then slowly slid over to the letter *M*. Then it continued on to *E*, where it stopped.

"*M—E*," said Ava. "Is that correct?"

The planchette suddenly slid to the upper left and stopped over the word *Yes* again.

"We have made contact with the great beyond," said Ava, her voice taking on the tenor and tone of a medium from an old William Castle horror flick. "Is there something you can tell us? Is there something we should know?"

"We have to focus harder," said Carmela.

"Spirit guide," said Sidney, "is there something you want to tell us?"

The planchette stayed in place for a long time, then finally glided to the right and landed on *M*. It paused there for a second, then continued on to the *U*. It seemed to circle that letter, then moved to the left and stopped over the *R*.

Carmela's eyes widened again.

The planchette continued left to the *D*, then stopped.

Suddenly, the planchette vibrated, then shot violently from beneath their fingertips. It zoomed across the board and continued off the table, running smack dab into the wall, then clanking noisily to the floor.

The room fell silent.

Everyone bent forward to stare at the planchette now lying inert on the floor.

"Well . . ." said Sidney, looking a little shaken. "We've never had anything like *that* occur on one of my ghost walks."

"I'd venture to say Ava's never had anything like *that* happen in her shop before," said Carmela.

A cool breeze seemed to circle the table.

Then Ava spoke up. "Perhaps the tarot cards can tell us more." She picked up the Ouija board and placed it on a shelf, then grabbed the deck of tarot cards that was conveniently stacked there. Making a big show of shuffling the cards, she was careful not to mix up the card order she'd rigged earlier.

"This is a little more my style," said Sidney, giving a slightly nervous laugh. "I'm a big fan of tarot cards."

"So you believe in them," said Carmela. "You use them for guidance."

"Once in a while," said Sidney. He glanced at Ava. "I prefer to use a six-card layout."

"Then that's what we'll do," said Ava. She peeled off the first card and laid it on the table. It was an angel with golden hair wearing a long white robe. "This is Temperance," said Ava. "As you can see, she's pouring water from one goblet into the other, which is supposed to signify harmony and balance."

Carmela peered at the card. "She looks a little like Melody."

Sidney's eyebrows shot up and he sat back in his seat. He nodded his head in agreement.

"The problem," said Ava, tapping the card with her fingertip, "is that this card is upside down, so it has the reverse meaning of discord and chaos."

"You mean like . . . murder?" Carmela prompted.

Ava gave a tight nod, then ran her fingers over the rest of the deck. "Kind spirits, what can you tell us about this poor woman?" Ava's fingers peeled off the next card, then flipped it onto the table. "The Tower," she said.

The card showed a castle turret on fire. Lightning bolts and roiling clouds formed the background; a man and a woman seemed to have leaped from the tower and were plunging to their death.

"What does *this* mean?" asked Carmela.

This time Sidney answered. "Sudden change, release . . . downfall."

"Or death?" Carmela asked.

"Perhaps," said Sidney. He no longer seemed to be enjoying himself.

Ava continued. "The next card tells of . . ." Her hand turned over the Judgment card. It showed an angel blowing a horn, gazing down at three people who seemed to be standing inside their own coffins.

"That looks ominous," said Carmela.

"This card foretells judgment day, rebirth, and absolution," said Ava. "The angel is calling the faithful to heaven, while the unbelievers . . . well, let's just say their fate isn't quite so rosy."

"This is a very strange tarot reading," said Sidney in a whispery voice.

Ava didn't waste any time. She flipped over the next card. It depicted a man walking toward the edge of a cliff, completely unaware of any danger. "The Fool," she announced harshly. "Which means . . ."

"Accepting your own folly," finished Sidney.

"Look at his hand!" exclaimed Carmela. "He's pointing at something." Her gaze followed the Fool's fingertip. "He's pointing at you, Sidney!"

Sidney seemed to shrink back in his chair.

Ava glowered at him. "Did you kill Melody?" Her voice was rough, caustic.

"Is that what this is all about?" Sidney yelled, his voice rising in a squawk. "No, of course not! I had nothing to do with Melody's death!" He scrambled to his feet and glowered at them, then seemed to recover slightly. "This was a setup!" he yelled, his face turning a blotchy red. "You're both trying to accuse me of something I didn't do!" He turned sharply, threw his cape over his shoulder, and staggered away. Hitting the doorjamb with one shoulder, he stumbled slightly, then strode through the shop and out the front door. Both women heard the door slam behind him.

"Mother of pearl!" exclaimed Ava. Shock and surprise were written across her face. "What do you think?"

"I think Sidney's really ticked off," said Carmela. "I think you can probably kiss his ghost walk business good-bye."

Ava shrugged. "But was this enough to send him scurrying to the police? Will it prompt a confession from him?"

"Only if he's guilty," said Carmela. "And even then we have no guarantees. But, seriously, you had me going with all your spectral incantations and spooky effects. I was ready to jump up and confess myself."

"It was good, wasn't it?" Ava mused, pleased with herself.

"That was some cool trick," said Carmela, "sending that planchette zooming across the table."

Ava stared at her friend in amazement. "I thought *you* did that!"

Chapter 25

"**Y**OU brought *dogs?*" screamed Glory. She screwed her doughy face into a look of horror and disbelief. "This is an underhanded ploy, Carmela. You know I *despise* those filthy, mangy creatures!"

Glory stood hunkered in the doorway, blocking Carmela's access into the second-floor conference room at the downtown office of Crescent City Bank.

"Shamus asked me to bring them," Carmela responded, fighting to maintain her cool and restrain a growling Boo from nipping Glory. Boo was a good girl, but when provoked she could definitely make her displeasure known. With sharp little teeth.

"Out!" Glory shrilled, her arms flailing about her body, her face going red, and her fleshy upper arms quivering.

Carmela gritted her teeth, tightened up on the leashes, and waited for Shamus. She knew she had to remain especially centered and grounded this morning. Dealing with Shamus, Glory, and the lawyers was not going to be a walk in the park.

But Glory continued to glower, ordering Carmela, once again, "Take those dogs outside!"

"Hey!" Shamus called from down the hallway. "You brought the dogs! Cool!" He loped down the carpeted hallway, a silly grin on his handsome face. When he reached Carmela and her furry charges, he dropped to his knees and pulled Boo and Poobah into his arms. They greeted him with soft snorts and wet kisses.

"Shamus," said Glory, in a still-thunderous tone, "you are *not* bringing those creatures into my conference room."

"C'mon, Glory," wheedled Shamus, "Boo and Poobah are part of the family."

"They carry disease," argued Glory.

Carmela, glancing from Glory to Shamus, was beginning to enjoy this bizarre sideshow. "She's right," she finally chimed in. "They could be carrying fleas or ticks. And you know what that means . . ." Carmela favored Glory with a bright smile. "Lyme disease." That, she decided, would add insult to injury.

Glory shrank back like a vampire confronted with holy water and a crucifix.

"I'll keep 'em at one end of the room," Shamus assured his sister, while frowning at Carmela.

"We'll surely have to fumigate," muttered Glory as she skittered on ahead to take her place at the conference table.

Even though Shamus had formally agreed to Carmela's divorce settlement, today was no slam dunk. Shamus's lawyer, Willis B. Mortimer, Esquire, sniped at Carmela's attorney, Shawna Hardwick. Hardwick shook it off and struck back, a petite African American woman in a red power suit who wasn't about to take any shit. As the attorneys argued back and forth, Shamus seemed to settle into a blue funk. And Glory played her role as the hysterical wild card or the eight-hundred-pound gorilla in the corner, depending on how you looked at things.

Carmela decided the entire meeting was like the bad third act of a really bad soap opera. Only (sigh!) this was real life.

"Just make her sign the papers," Shamus said, morosely. "Make it all go away."

"Thanks so much, Shamus," said Carmela. "And do you think you could have possibly been a little more considerate early on? Maybe you shouldn't have left me, argued so melodramatically to get back together again, then cheated on me again!"

"You're not exactly lily white," snarled Shamus.

"I never cheated on you," said Carmela.

"But you started seeing other men," grumped Shamus.

"Only after we were officially separated," Carmela pointed out. "And because you were the one who encouraged me. You told me to get out there and look around."

"Maybe I was wrong," said Shamus. "Maybe we were both wrong."

The two lawyers exchanged worried glances.

"Shall we continue with this?" asked Shamus's lawyer.

Shamus nodded faintly.

"Please do," said Carmela.

"Fine," said Mortimer. "As it stands now, what Mr. Meechum and Ms. Bertrand will be agreeing to today is as follows . . ." He picked up the typed agreement, adjusted his glasses, studied it for a moment, then said, "Ms. Bertrand will now forgo the previously agreed-upon alimony and will instead receive the deed to Mr. Meechum's Garden District property as well as a cash settlement in the amount of ten thousand dollars."

Glory's fist suddenly slammed down onto the table. "The house," she muttered.

Mortimer lifted furry eyebrows and gazed at her. As personal as well as corporate counsel, he seemed used to Glory's frequent outbursts. "It's what has been agreed upon by both parties," he intoned.

"But it's not *fair*," seethed Glory.

"Are we going to get this done or not?" asked Carmela's lawyer. "Because if we have to come back in here . . ." Shawna Hardwick's tone was just this side of threatening.

"Let's get it done," said Shamus, slumping in his chair. "Let's get it over."

Glory's face turned a darker shade of red, and she twitched her nose. "That house has been in our family for decades. This arrangement simply isn't acceptable!" She pulled a plain white hanky from her sturdy black bag and sneezed into it. "The house should never have entered into this negotiation!" She sneezed again, then looked accusingly at Carmela with red-rimmed eyes. "See what you've done! You dragged those hideous beasts into my conference room just to trigger my allergies!" She turned to confront attorney Mortimer. "It's a ploy!" she cried, sneezing again and causing him to duck.

"Could we please move this along?" asked Shawna Hardwick.

Shamus popped up from his chair and grabbed Glory's arm. "Let me walk you to your office. You can sit down, relax, get some fresh air."

Glory dabbed at her nose while allowing herself to be half-dragged, half-carried from the conference room. A couple minutes later, Shamus came back, red-faced and sweating bullets.

"*Now* can we proceed?" asked Hardwick.

"Wait," said Shamus, holding up a hand. "We haven't discussed custody of the dogs."

"What!" exclaimed Carmela and the two attorneys in unison.

"I'm their daddy," said Shamus. "I need to have at least partial custody."

"You get no custody of Boo," said Carmela. "She was my dog before we got married."

"What about Poobah?" Shamus whined. "I love Poobah."

At hearing his name, Poobah lifted his head and gave an

eager doggy grin. His torn ear flopped and a string of drool dropped slowly to the carpet.

Mortimer regarded the dog. "You're *sure* you want custody?" he asked Shamus.

"Poobah was a stray that you found and I took in," Carmela told Shamus. "So the way I see it, we probably have . . . uh . . . joint custody."

That prompted a whispered conference between Shamus and his lawyer. And some exuberant yips and tail wagging on the part of Boo and Poobah.

Mortimer listened, nodded, made a few jottings, then gazed at Carmela over horn-rimmed spectacles. "Saturday walks and once-every-other-week sleepovers?" he droned, as though it were the most reasonable request in the world. "The dates to be mutually agreed upon by the two parties."

Carmela nodded. It sounded fair to her.

"Looks like we have a deal," said Shawna Hardwick.

While the documents were being retyped, Shamus bored them all with chatter about his photographs that were on display at the Click! Gallery tonight. "Plus, I don't know how many of you know this," said Shamus, "but tomorrow's Glory's birthday, so we're going to celebrate by having a cake at the gallery." He smiled at Carmela. "You should drop by for cake and ice cream."

Carmela shrugged. "Yeah. Right." Like she cared.

"And the Pluvius krewe is going to roll a float tonight," Shamus added. "In honor of Galleries and Gourmets, we got it all gussied up with a Chinese art theme."

"Terrific," said Carmela, with even less enthusiasm.

Ten minutes later, a secretary who'd been shanghaied to work this Saturday morning came running back with the revised documents.

Carmela signed first, then Shamus.

When it was all over, Shamus smiled gamely and tried to give Carmela a kiss. But at the last minute, she did her little trick and turned her head so his lips just grazed her ear.

"I'm glad we got this wrapped up," Shamus told her, his brown eyes slightly misty.

"No shit," replied Carmela.

Carmela dropped off the dogs at her apartment, kissed their respective furry noses, then headed to Memory Mine. Not surprisingly, the French Quarter was jammed with people and work crews jostling to set up for Galleries and Gourmets. Which meant Carmela had to forcibly push her way through the crowds.

The food booths were the big hot thing, of course. Come five o'clock tonight there would be booths selling boiled crawfish, jambalaya, stuffed mirliton, po'boys, hush puppies, homemade pralines, kettle corn, turtle soup, muffuletta sandwiches, frozen daiquiris, and Dixie Beer.

But as Carmela made her way down Royal Street, she saw that many of the antique shops were also busily setting up. Dulcimer's Antiques already had two large library tables angled in front of their shop, and Devon Dowling, the owner, was slowly arranging some of his smaller tabletop items: candelabras, colored glass, antique pitchers, a few small paintings, some leather-bound books, and what looked to be a Tiffany lamp. Mimi, his chubby little pug, stood under the table, watching the proceedings. When Mimi saw Carmela, she gave a desultory tail wag.

"Mimi looks nervous," said Carmela, coming up behind him, noticing that his pigtail hung halfway down his back.

Dowling whirled around, looked uncertain for a moment, then crinkled his eyes when he recognized Carmela. "Mimi's a little hothouse flower just like me," Dowling said airily. "Prefers to stay inside."

"So you're not looking forward to tonight's festivities?"

Dowling wrinkled his nose. "Oh, I suppose it's all well and good," he told her in a slightly petulant tone. "I don't anticipate selling any more pieces than I normally would. And I'm certainly not convinced that displaying antiques like you would baskets and pinch pots at an art fair is the smartest strategy in the world."

"If it's any consolation," said Carmela, "you've got a great-looking display." She turned her attention to his table, which really did hold a number of tasty treasures. "I can't imagine people won't stop and take notice."

"But will they buy?" asked Dowling. "Or are they just coming down here for the food and music?" He reached down, scooped up Mimi, and snuggled her in his arms. She grinned happily and stared at Carmela with shiny, dark eyes.

"Have to wait and see," said Carmela. She reached out and touched the rosebud lid of a pink-and-cream-colored teapot. "Is this from Meissen, by any chance?" she asked.

Dowling suddenly looked a lot less bored. "As a matter of fact, it is. Are you in the market for a collectible teapot?"

"What's it like out there?" asked Gabby. She was standing in the front of the shop, sorting through various packets of brads, buttons, and beads. "It's been quiet in here, but I see hordes of people streaming by."

Carmela smiled as she dusted her hands together. "Getting very crowded. There's a ton of people, and excitement seems to be building."

"Now tell me the real news," said Gabby. "How did your meeting go? Did you settle? Did you finally close the deal?"

Carmela's grin stretched across her face. "I'm a free woman," she told Gabby. She was just getting used to that notion and it thrilled her. Free at last; no more Shamus sticking his big, fat, meddling nose in her business. The only contact she'd have with him was arranging doggy sleepovers. And he'd probably tire of that soon enough.

Gabby peered inquisitively at Carmela. "You're a free woman who now owns a great big Garden District home?"

Carmela bobbed her head. "Even though Glory put up a last-ditch effort to squash it, the house is mine. Although, truth be told, I'm not sure how long I'm going to keep it."

"What!" exclaimed Gabby. "After all you went through? That house is yours. It's the spoils of war."

"That house is also humongous," said Carmela. "The smart thing would be to sell it. Buy a smaller property and invest the rest of the money."

"That's the kind of thing that financial lady on CNN would tell you to do," said Gabby. "You know the one I mean, Suze Orman."

Carmela nodded. She was a big proponent of carefully calculated plans. Well, most of the time she was.

Gabby came around the counter and gave Carmela a hug. "You're a good businesswoman, Carmela."

"I'm not so sure about that," said Carmela, hugging her back. "But I know Shamus's house . . . *my* house now . . . could turn into a money pit. Just the monthly upkeep is murderous."

"Shamus will have a fit if you turn around and sell it," giggled Gabby.

"You're right," said Carmela. "So there really is an upside to all of this."

Fifteen minutes later, Ava called, looking for her own update.

"Well . . . ?" she said.

"It's over," said Carmela. "Absolutely, formally, signed-sealed-and-witnessed-by-two-attorneys-and-a-notary over."

"Glory didn't make trouble?"

"I said it was over," Carmela told her. "Not that it was over easy."

"But you got the house!" chortled Ava. "Which, I have to believe, is worth well over two million buckaroos in today's real estate market. So you're a multimillionaire, *cher*! Which means we gotta celebrate tonight at Galleries and Gourmets."

Carmela gave a slight groan.

"I don't want to hear it!" cautioned Ava. "You know we've been planning to go to this for weeks. I'm even gonna wear my fat jeans so we can really pig out."

"Your fat jeans are, like, a size four," laughed Carmela. "While mine are . . . well, never mind."

"We *gotta* go," said Ava. "I'll wheedle and whimper until you plead for mercy!"

"Okay, okay," said Carmela. "I'll do a turn around Jackson Square with you." Jackson Square, adjacent to St. Louis Cathedral, was where most of the music and food concessions would be concentrated.

"But we gotta check out the galleries, too," said Ava. "And Jekyl's gonna be doing his appraisal thing, so we gotta go bug his skinny ass."

"Forgot about that," said Carmela. Yeah, it sounded like they were probably going to make a night of it.

"Then maybe we can all mosey over to Dr. Boogie's afterward," suggested Ava. "You, me, Jekyl . . . maybe have Babcock meet us there, too. If he's not too busy whaling on somebody with a rubber hose."

"Would we be going to Dr. Boogie's to check out that cute bartender you've had your eye on?"

"Uh . . . yeah," said Ava. "Friends with benefits, as in free drinks."

"Okay," said Carmela. "Sounds like a plan."

"Oh, *cher*, Miguel and I were at Medusa Manor this morning doing some decorating and arranging the downstairs coffin. Tate Mackie dropped by, too, to program in the final special effects, so don't push any buttons or anything or you'll find yourself being chased by zombies. Personally, I think everything looks spectacular, but I'm dying to hear high praise from you."

Carmela glanced at her watch. It was after one o'clock. The settlement meeting this morning had chewed up a good part of her day.

"I'll take a run over there right now," said Carmela.

"That's assuming we still have the contract," said Ava. She hesitated. "Do we?"

"Ask me again tonight," said Carmela. She hung up the phone, peeked at her watch, and frowned. Then, because Ava's question was still ringing in her ears and she still hadn't gotten last night's image of Olivia and Sawyer Barnes out of her head, she grabbed the phone and dialed Olivia's number.

The housekeeper answered and, finally, after a five-minute wait, Olivia came on the line. "Hello?" she said, a slightly imperious tone to her voice.

"Hello, Olivia, it's Carmela."

"Yes?" The imperious tone was still there.

"Correct me if I'm wrong, but I was under the impression you were going out of town."

A silence spun out, and then Olivia said, "I was, but something came up." More silence. Then, "Why are you asking? What business is it of yours?"

"I'm curious," said Carmela. "About the status of Medusa Manor and your relationship with Sawyer Barnes." Before the words were out of her mouth, Carmela could almost hear Olivia bristling.

"You are prying, Miss Bertrand." Imperious had merged with haughty.

"Probably . . . yes," continued Carmela. "But with an unsolved murder hanging over all our heads and an unresolved situation with Medusa Manor . . . well, I just think it's better to be open about everything."

"Really," said Olivia, her tone icy.

"Is Sawyer Barnes trying to buy Medusa Manor?" pressed Carmela.

Olivia let loose a long sigh, then said, "Honestly, yes. He is. And I believe I could make more money by selling the place."

"I see," said Carmela. "It's your decision, of course, but I just want you to know that we've continued working on

Medusa Manor and that most of the video effects are now in place."

"Fine, fine," said Olivia. And now she sounded distracted. "We'll see what happens. You'll still get paid for all your work, of course."

"Of course," said Carmela. "That goes without saying."

Chapter 26

FOR some reason, Carmela couldn't get out the door of Memory Mine. First, there was a sudden influx of customers and she didn't dare leave Gabby to fend for herself. Then Devon Dowling called to say he just realized he had some matching teacups and would she be interested in buying a set? And then, just as Carmela was wolfing down a carton of yogurt, making plans to slip out the back way, Garth Mayfeldt called.

"Carmela," he said, "I really need to talk to you." He sounded anxious and depressed. Then again, why wouldn't he? The police had elevated him to suspect numero uno in his wife's murder.

"Garth," said Carmela, sincerely wishing he hadn't called. "What's wrong?"

"Everything!" wailed Garth. "Now the police are asking me to submit to a lie detector test!"

Carmela wasn't sure what to say. "Did you agree?" Deep in her heart, Carmela thought this request might be for the best. Strap a lie detector on Garth, ask the hard questions. Of course, some people had the innate ability to fool lie detectors. Sociopaths and psychopaths. The type of people who also profiled as cold-blooded killers.

"My lawyer says no way," said Garth, "but I'm thinking I should do it. To clear my name." He hesitated. "What do you think?"

Carmela was floored. "I . . . I really can't tell you what to do, Garth. That a decision only you can make."

"I know," said Garth. "It's just that . . . well . . . there aren't a lot of people whose opinion I completely trust."

Oh dear, thought Carmela.

"But I trust you," continued Garth. "You've stood by me from the very beginning. You were Melody's *friend*, for goodness' sake. You took on her Medusa Manor project. That counts for a lot!"

"I don't know what to say, Garth." Now Carmela was in turmoil herself.

"I'm in agony!" wailed Garth. "I go from being practically catatonic to this highly charged state where huge waves of grief wash over me."

"You may need some professional counseling," Carmela said, gently. Clearly, this was way out of her realm of expertise.

"I just need a friend," whispered Garth.

Carmela thought about Olivia Wainwright, thought about how friendly and solicitous she'd been at the funeral. Wasn't she Garth's friend? Wouldn't she make a better counsel? Carmela pondered this for a moment, then was jolted by another thought. *Have I been earmarked as confessor? Is Garth in such a state of high anxiety that he's ready to confess that he murdered Melody?*

"Carmela," said Garth. "Are you still there?"

"I'm here, Garth."

"I . . . I just need someone to talk to." Now his voice had dropped to a whisper.

"Where are you, Garth? At Fire and Ice?"

"Yes, we're getting the shop ready for Galleries and Gourmets."

"You're going to be open tonight?" asked Carmela.

"Afraid so."

"Tell you what," said Carmela. "I'm planning to catch the festivities this evening, so I promise to drop by. Okay?"

"Will you really?" asked Garth. "You promise?"

"Absolutely," said Carmela. "I'll be there." She decided that if Garth had a guilty conscience and might be aching to spill his guts, she'd be safe going to his store tonight. After all, there was safety in numbers, right?

Carmela pulled up in front of Medusa Manor and glanced up at the third-floor tower room, steeply pitched roof, and arched windows. And she decided that even in benign daylight, the place looked slightly menacing. Which was mind-blowing if you were a dyed-in-the-wool haunted-house fan, but not so good if your friend had been murdered here.

Sticking her key in the lock—the new, improved lock—Carmela pushed open the door. And was quite literally thrilled at what her eyes beheld. Because Ava and her assistant, Miguel, had clearly done some unique decorating. Rows of gleaming white skulls grinned eerily from their perches on the wall. Black netting and a myriad of huge, furry spiders hung over a reception desk that Ava had magically unearthed from somewhere—the basement, perhaps?

The large bronze coffin had been arranged against the far window and was now flanked with brass candlesticks and stuffed with a life-sized tuxedo-clad dummy that Carmela supposed would, at the push of a button, sit up and shriek a welcome to guests.

Carmela grinned as a shiver ran through her body. Medusa Manor was magical and maniacal at the same time.

Upstairs, Carmela was delighted with the *Exorcist*-style

bedroom. The headboard and footboard of the old bed had been padded with rags, just like in the movie. The walls were painted Williamsburg blue. A Bible sat on the nightstand. All the set needed now were actors to portray the possessed person as well as the exorcist himself.

The next bedroom contained the ghost brides. Well, they weren't really ghost brides, she told herself. Just dinged-up prom dresses that weren't usable—except for this. Ava had gone so far as to rip and slash some of the skirts so the shredded remains caught the air currents and fluttered eerily. White, feathery masks had been hung to approximate heads, and the upper torsos had been stuffed with bubble wrap to appear more lifelike.

Ava had been hard at work in the Witches' Lair, too. Now the rubber witch heads were mounted on poles, and a larger scrim had been installed to accommodate the special-effects projection. Still, a lot of props were still missing. The cauldrons, dry ice, maybe even a few black cats. This clearly needed work.

Carmela walked around the room, acutely aware of her footfalls on the creaking wooden floors. There'd been other stuff in this room, too, hadn't there? She crossed her arms, frowned, then stepped over to the closet and pulled it open. Two paintings and a framed needlepoint leaned against the back of the closet wall.

Grabbing the needlepoint and the smaller of the two paintings, Carmela decided they'd probably work well in the downstairs Haunted Library. That place would look its spooky best crammed full of paintings, leather books, candles, stuffed crows, and stuffed animal heads. Maybe even install a harpsichord and a candelabra with twisted candles.

Carmela climbed the stairs to the third-floor ballroom. Up here the air felt warm and close and a little suffocating. Dust motes twirled in shafts of light that managed to penetrate grime-smeared windows. Rustling sounds in dark corners of the vast room told her there might be bats.

Carmela felt frustrated that she still hadn't come up with a workable theme for this place. Maybe because the attic was so enormous, maybe because it also felt . . . empty. Of course, if Olivia decided to sell Medusa Manor, then all their rush-rush decorating would be for naught. Their work would just be trashed.

A sad thought, Carmela decided. But the future of Medusa Manor wasn't in her control, so there was no point fretting over it.

So . . . now what? she wondered. *Just keep working on this place while keeping things in perspective? Go out with Ava tonight and have a good time?*

But not that good. Because Melody's killer was still walking free.

Tucking the artwork securely under one arm, Carmela turned, walked a few steps, and stopped dead in her tracks.

Because she'd heard a noise. Downstairs, on the second floor. And it was a real noise made by a real person, not an intruding bat.

Carmela slipped out of her shoes and cautiously, silently, descended the stairs to the second floor. And heard the same noise again. Feet shuffling across floorboards, the creak of a wire.

Someone walking among the ghost brides? Had to be.

Creeping forward, Carmela put a hand on the doorjamb, peered in . . . and saw real-life feet and legs moving among the ghost brides!

"Who are you?" she yelled. "What do you want? I've got pepper spray, so you watch out!"

"I was looking for you," said a familiar voice.

Carmela put a hand to her heart and caught her breath. *Babcock?*

At that same moment, Edgar Babcock silently exited the swaying forest of ghost brides.

"What are you doing here?" she screamed, still caught in a paroxysm of fear. She took a couple of deep breaths, hiccupped, and tried to calm down. "How did you even know I was here?"

Edgar Babcock smiled at her, as though they'd simply met during a casual stroll through a garden. "I called Memory Mine. Gabby said you were over here."

"Oh."

His brown eyes flashed, and he gave a low chortle. "That's all you've got to say?" He grinned and stretched his arms wide. "How did it go this morning? Is it over? Are you free?"

"Free as the wind," she told him, dropping the paintings and shoes, stepping into his embrace.

"Hallelujah!" exclaimed Babcock, planting a big smacker on her cheek. "Of course, now I'm going to have to move my checking account."

She pulled back. "Shamus wouldn't . . ."

"I'm kidding," said Babcock. "Kidding." He leaned down, kissed her again, full on the lips, then circled his arms around her waist. "You know, I really wish you weren't working on this."

She pressed her cheek against his shoulder. "By *this*, you're referring to Medusa Manor?"

He nodded as his hands moved in small circles on her back.

"After today I may not be," Carmela told him. "I talked to Olivia Wainwright earlier, and she told me . . . confessed, really . . . that she may be selling this place to Sawyer Barnes."

He released Carmela and held her at arm's length. "She told you that?" He seemed puzzled.

"Yes," said Carmela. "And now I just told you."

"People like to tell you things, don't they?" said Babcock.

Carmela nodded.

"You can get in trouble that way. I'd hate to see you get into any more trouble."

Carmela shifted from one foot to the other. "You think I'm in trouble?" she asked, finally.

"Someone clearly tried to frighten you in the cemetery the other night. And last night . . ."

"What about last night?" asked Carmela.

"You were up to something," said Babcock.

"Why would you say that?" Was this man psychic? Carmela kept a tight smile on her face.

"You had that look," said Babcock. "And your body language projected a certain . . . what would you call it? . . . contained energy. Like something was coiled inside, just waiting to break free."

"Well, I'm not going anywhere now," she told him.

He lifted an eyebrow. "No?"

"Maybe a quick trip through Galleries and Gourmets tonight." She smiled prettily. "Will I see you there?"

He nodded. "Sure. Probably." He paused, then asked, "Did Garth Mayfeldt happen to call?"

Carmela decided Babcock *had* to be psychic. Or else he was just a very skilled detective. "Why do you ask?"

"Probably because you seemed so tight with him."

"Maybe not so much anymore," said Carmela, dodging the question.

But her answer was enough for Babcock. "Good girl," he told her, pulling her close again. "Better to leave the detecting to the professionals."

Carmela continued to smile at him, feeling the warmth of his hands on her back, the strength of his body pressed against hers.

Should she tell Babcock that she planned to see Garth tonight? No. Somehow that might be better left unsaid.

Just let events play out. See where they led.

Chapter 27

"WILL you look at that?" purred Ava. "Deep-fried strawberries!"

Carmela and Ava were right in the fray of Galleries and Gourmets, strolling through Jackson Square, ogling the food booths, heading for Royal Street, the part of the French Quarter where the finest art and antique galleries were located. People jostled all around them, while street artists did sketches, musicians played for coins and dollar bills, and horse-drawn carriages laden with tourists clip-clopped by.

"This is my idea of health food!" said Ava, stepping up to the counter and jamming a hand in her pocket to extract a few dollars. "These jeans are so tight I can barely get my money out," she giggled.

"I think I see a couple quarters in your back pocket," Carmela told her.

"Thanks," said Ava, digging around. "Hey, you want fried strawberries, too?"

Carmela held up a hand. "Pass."

"You're gonna eat, aren't you?" asked Ava. "I don't want to be the only oinker here tonight."

"Not to worry," said Carmela. "I think I see a skewer of fried oysters that has my name on it."

"Ooh," squealed Ava, "get one for me, too!"

They nibbled as they walked and talked.

"I'm so thrilled you liked my ghost brides," said Ava.

"I loved everything you did," said Carmela. "It was above and beyond what I could have imagined. You're a very skilled designer."

"Be a pity if Olivia sells the place," said Ava, alternately munching fried oysters and popping fried strawberries into her mouth. "I'd kind of like to finish staging the rooms, enjoy a sense of accomplishment."

Carmela nodded. "I hear you."

"If Medusa Manor *does* sell," said Ava, "we ought to think about setting up our own haunted house."

Carmela gave a genteel snort.

"No, I'm perfectly serious," said Ava. "We could . . . um . . . set it up in your new Garden District home!"

This time Carmela laughed out loud. "I love it!" she cried. "Shamus would go bonkers and Glory would . . ."

"Have a shit fit!" cried Ava.

Two people turned to stare at Ava.

"Oops, sorry, naughty word," laughed Ava, sticking a hand out and making a wiping motion in the air, as if to erase her words.

"Even if we just *tell* Shamus that's our plan, we'll drive him nuts," said Carmela. "So that's what we're going to do."

"Ooh ooh," said Ava, pointing at a frozen daiquiri stand. "We for sure need a couple of those. A little hickory dickory daiquiri therapy."

So that's what they did—finished their food, bought two frozen daiquiris in plastic *geaux* cups, and strolled past more food booths as well as a wooden stage that featured the zydeco rhythms of Lady Bee and the Evangelines.

When they hit Royal Street, they heard their names being shouted.

Ava's head spun around, searching the crowd. "Who's callin' us, *cher*?"

But Carmela had already spotted Quigg Brevard, manning his Mumbo Gumbo booth. "It's Quigg," she told Ava.

Ava wrinkled her nose and wiggled a couple of fingers at Quigg. "I always thought you'd be dating him," she told Carmela in a low voice.

"I did date him once," said Carmela, as they strolled toward him. "After Shamus and I separated the first time."

"No sparks?"

"It wasn't that," said Carmela. "He just seemed . . . I don't know . . . a little obtuse."

"He doesn't look obtuse now," commented Ava. "He looks *gooood*."

Carmela had to agree. With his dark hair and olive skin, Quigg was the picture of a handsome restaurateur, glad-handing the crowd.

"Hey there," said Ava.

Quigg immediately pushed a small bowl filled with steaming gumbo at her. "Here, beautiful, have some alligator gumbo." Then, with a slightly leering look, he handed another bowl to Carmela. "You, too, gorgeous."

"We're beautiful *and* gorgeous," said Ava. "Imagine that."

"That's what Quigg calls you when he can't remember your name," Carmela said, as she dipped a plastic spoon into the gumbo.

Quigg kept his eyes riveted on Carmela. "I'd never forget *your* name," he told her, then winked. "That gumbo spicy enough for you ladies?"

"Maybe not," said Ava, flirting. "We're pretty spicy ladies."

"Hey," Quigg said to Carmela, "I heard your divorce is final."

"How would you know that?" asked Carmela.

Quigg gave a wink. "Chalk it up to French Quarter chatter. Not much escapes us down here."

"You should date him again," said Ava as they strolled along. "Or else I will."

Carmela paused to look at a brass dog statue that was on display. It was a King Charles Cavalier, possibly old. "Not me, since I'm pretty happy with Babcock. But you, you should go for it."

"Maybe," said Ava. She nudged Carmela with her shoulder. "You and Babcock really got it goin' on, huh?"

"I think so," said Carmela. "I hope so."

"You two planning to hook up later?"

Carmela set the dog statue down and nodded. "I'm supposed to give him a call." They walked along, shouldering their way through the crowd, stopping occasionally to look at a painting or knickknack.

"Oh my gosh!" said Carmela.

"What?" asked Ava.

Carmela pointed an index finger at a sign over Ava's head. "The Click! Gallery. Shamus's photographs are on display there."

Ava looked skeptical. "Now? Tonight?"

"That's what he said."

"Shamus actually got it together and snapped real photographs?" asked Ava. Because she'd always regarded Shamus as being positively indolent, she was having trouble wrapping her brain around this concept.

"I think he took the photos a couple of years ago," Carmela told her. "He just now got around to printing and matting them. And . . . exhibiting them, I suppose."

"This I gotta see," said Ava, heading for the entrance.

"No," said Carmela. "I don't think—"

"C'mon, *cher*, it'll be fun," urged Ava.

"No it won't," said Carmela under her breath.

Shamus's photos weren't a total bummer. There were lots of rather competently done shots of misty bayous, swirling water, bayou landscapes, flying birds, and sunsets over water.

"Carmela!" exclaimed a stunned Shamus. "You actually came!"

"We just happened to be walking by," murmured Carmela. "Ava kind of pulled me in." She nudged Ava with her shoulder.

"We wouldn't miss this for the world!" sang Ava. She took a step forward, whirled about, and took in the white-walled gallery with its blond wood floors and politely admiring crowd of Meechum relatives. "Very nice."

Shamus's photos lined both walls of the narrow gallery and, at the rear of the space, a large white linen-covered table was laden with bottles of expensive champagne and an enormous three-tiered cake.

"Even a fancy cake!" Ava exclaimed.

Shamus was quick to explain. "It's Glory's birthday tomorrow. So I thought we'd celebrate here . . . tonight."

"Kill two birds with one stone," said Carmela.

Shamus narrowed his eyes at her. "Something like that."

"And there's the birthday girl now," sang Ava.

They all turned to look at Glory posing stiffly beside Clark Berthume, the owner of Click!, who was grinning widely, if not a trifle uncomfortably, as he began lighting the candles. They watched as Berthume worked his way from the top tier down to the bottom tier.

"Lots of candles," commented Carmela.

"And don't they make a fine fire!" said Ava in a voice that rang through the gallery. "I haven't seen anything like it since the burning of Atlanta!"

Carmela choked, hiccupped, and burst out laughing. Glory glanced sideways, caught sight of them, and gave her trademark glower.

"Be nice," chided Shamus.

"Shamus, my dear boy," said Ava, clapping a hand solidly on his shoulder, "when are you going to get a backbone?"

"That's so not fair," protested Shamus.

"But so very true," said Carmela.

"See if you get any more invitations from the Pluvius krewe," said Shamus, sounding both hurt and petulant.

"We know plenty of krewe members," Ava told him in a breezy tone. "We can horn in on your parties any time we feel like it."

"In fact," said Carmela, "aren't you supposed to be riding a float tonight?"

Shamus glanced at his watch and grimaced. "Yeah, yeah, I am. In fact, I better get going." He looked unhappy as he put an arm around each of them. "You don't mind if I escort you girls out, do you? I'd hate to see Glory get any more upset."

"Sheesh," said Carmela.

Carmela and Ava strolled out of Click!, turned down Royal, then hooked a left on St. Philip Street. The crowds were slightly thinner here, so it was easier to enjoy the gallery windows stuffed with art objects and admire the antiques and artworks that were on display outside.

"I sure hope folks are buying tonight," said Carmela, thinking about Devon Dowling's remark about people coming out just to enjoy the food and music.

"I don't know," said Ava, "times are still tough."

"Fire and Ice is going to be open tonight," said Carmela. "I told Garth I'd drop by."

"What for?" asked Ava.

"Because he called me earlier and sounded semidesperate. Said he needed someone to talk to."

"And you're that someone?"

Carmela sighed. "Looks like."

They bought Hurricanes in plastic cups, then turned back on Bourbon and strolled along, enjoying the strains of zydeco music that floated up from Jackson Square. The strong drinks, the warmth of the soft spring evening, and the golden glow from the old-fashioned gaslights that lined the cobblestone streets had put them in a giddy mood.

"This is my favorite time in the French Quarter," Ava sighed. "When the sky's all purple and dusky and the gaslights flicker on. You can close your eyes and imagine what it was like here a hundred years ago."

"Not so different," said Carmela. "Same brick buildings, Creole cottages, and hidden patios with pattering fountains."

"Same ladies of the night, House of the Rising Sun," said Ava.

"Like I said, not so different," grinned Carmela.

They wandered along Bourbon and turned down Pirate's Alley. Because the street was fairly narrow, booths lined only one side of it.

Ava tried on a peridot ring, then a couple of silver bangles. "No, not quite right," she muttered, looking around.

Carmela found a moonstone ring, but wondered if she could find it cheaper somewhere else.

When they were almost at the end of Pirate's Alley, Ava said, "Don't look now, but I think we're being followed."

"What!" said Carmela, alarmed.

Ava gripped Carmela's arm. "No, no, don't turn around. We'll stop at this booth filled with antique glass and try to get a gander."

"Okay," said Carmela. Thoughts of Garth Mayfeldt, Sawyer Barnes, and Olivia Wainwright swirled in her head. Or was Babcock tailing her? Trying to be coy? Watching out for her? Or, worse yet, spying?

Ava was putting on a good show at the booth, acting indifferent to whoever was shadowing them. "How much is this candy dish?" she asked the sales clerk. "And do you have any pitchers?"

Carmela reached out, picked up an amber goblet of pressed

glass, then turned slowly. As she did, there was an odd flash of light, and someone ducked behind a parked truck. "You're right," she told Ava. "Someone is watching us."

They left the booth and walked another twenty feet, then stopped and whirled quickly. Nothing.

"You see that shop up ahead?" asked Ava. "Barten Antiques? Maybe if we stop in front of the window, we can catch a reflection in the glass."

"Worth a try," said Carmela.

They slowed their pace, stopped in front of Barten Antiques, and tried to focus on the reflected faces that swirled past.

"This isn't working," said Ava. "I think I'm searching the reflections and then my eyes start to unfocus. Bad depth perception, I guess."

"I'm not seeing anything," said Carmela. "Oh . . . wait a minute."

"You see somebody?" Ava whispered anxiously. "Who is it?"

"Oh shit!" exclaimed Carmela.

Chapter 28

"SIDNEY, you insane, skulking, little weasel!" cried Ava.

Sidney St. Cyr, slumped over the video camera that was cradled in his arms, shifted his dark gaze from Carmela to Ava. Even with his black clothing and trademark cape, he looked like the proverbial kid who'd been caught with his fingers in the cookie jar. Albeit a big kid. And one who should know better.

"What were you *doing?*" Carmela demanded. "Filming us?"

Sidney licked his lips rapidly and cleared his throat, but no actual words of explanation sprang forth.

"Holy crap!" said Ava, practically baring her teeth, "he was *filming* us." She grabbed for Sidney's camera, but he wrenched it away from her flailing grasp.

"I'm calling Detective Babcock," said Carmela, reaching in her shoulder bag for her mobile phone.

That finally prompted a startled response from Sidney. "No, don't!" he cried.

Carmela's eyes shot daggers at him. "Give me one good reason why I shouldn't call the police."

"Please, let me explain," begged Sidney. "I really can explain."

"This better be good," grumped Ava.

"Talk," ordered Carmela.

"Last night," began Sidney, "at Ava's shop, I realized what you were doing."

"What are you babbling about now?" demanded Ava.

"You were investigating," said Sidney. And now his words seemed to emerge with more speed, gathering momentum. "You were investigating *me*. You had *me* pegged as a suspect in Melody's murder." He cocked his head like an inquisitive magpie and stared at Carmela. "Right?"

Carmela gave a grudging nod.

"All right," said Sidney, licking his lips again. "At first I was seriously ticked off. Furious, in fact. But then I came up with what I decided was a very big idea."

"What big idea might that be?" asked Ava. "And please understand, Sidney, I'm not buying a word of this happy crap. In my book you're just a two-bit, garden-variety stalker!"

Ava's words emboldened Sidney. "When I realized you two were seriously investigating Melody's murder, I got the idea to film you."

Carmela just shook her head, puzzled. "What?"

"Huh?" said Ava.

Sidney's narrow face blossomed into a crooked grin. "I'm talking about true crime! Don't you get it? If you two were hot on the trail of the murderer—or even a suspect—I wanted to capture it on film!"

"Now I've heard everything," muttered Ava.

Sidney was rolling now. "The way I figure it, you've got it

more or less narrowed down." He focused an intense, almost maniacal gaze on Carmela. "Am I right?"

Carmela stared back. There *was* a certain bizarre logic to Sidney's argument.

"So I figured," continued Sidney, "that if I filmed you two . . . in *action* . . . it would be like a true crime story. Sort of along the lines of reality TV!"

"You are so off the hook," said Carmela.

"No way you're getting anything on TV," said Ava, dismissively.

But Sidney stood his ground. "If that doesn't work out, it might be the kind of thing I could add to my ghost walks."

Ava snorted.

"Or put on YouTube," said Sidney. "No, really, think about it." He grinned, his thin lips tilting up like a child's carved jack-o'-lantern. "It might work, right? Carmela? I might have something, huh?"

"Maybe," Carmela said without much enthusiasm. "Maybe you'd have something if *we* had something."

Sidney's face fell. "You don't? You're not hot on the trail?"

"Hardly," said Carmela.

"You're living in Never-Never Land," Ava told him.

"Well . . . heck," said Sidney. Their words had knocked the wind out of his sails.

Ava poked Sidney hard in the chest with an index finger. "I'm only gonna tell you this once, Sidney! Stop creeping around and leave us alone before I pop you in the nose!"

"Sidney St. Cyr is one of the most screwed-up people I've ever met," said Ava. "And I've had the pleasure of dealing with some real morons."

"Dealing with them or dating them?" asked Carmela.

"Both," admitted Ava.

"Still," said Carmela, "there was a certain childlike logic to his little film project."

They wandered back toward Jackson Square, heading for the NOMA art appraisal booth.

"Childlike is right," said Ava. "Hey, there's the appraisal booth. And there's Jekyl. Looks like he's being interviewed . . ."

"By Kimber Breeze," said Carmela. As they got closer to the booth, she noted that Kimber's blond hair looked even blonder under the lights.

Ava noticed, too. "Looks like Kimber frosted her hair," said Ava.

"Permafrost," snorted Carmela.

They hung back while Jekyl did his slick little patter for the camera.

"It's always amazing how many truly interesting items people have stashed away in their attics and garages," said Jekyl, smiling broadly, staring directly into the red eye of the camera, assuming a very professional broadcaster's stance. "Just the other day a woman showed me what she thought was a pair of sterling silver sugar tongs, but turned out to be George the Third asparagus tongs, hallmarked London 1810."

"Amazing," cooed Kimber.

"Earlier today," continued Jekyl, "a man brought in a Navy cutlass that had been made by the Dufilho firm right here in New Orleans. Worth at least sixty-five hundred dollars."

Kimber slid closer to Jekyl, the better for her cameraman to get his two-shot. "So you're inviting folks to bring their mysterious attic treasures down here for a professional appraisal?"

"Not so much a monetary appraisal," said Jekyl, "more like a historical and cultural perspective. Courtesy, of course, of the New Orleans Museum of Art." Jekyl gave the camera his very broadest smile. "And we'll be here until ten tonight and from twelve to six tomorrow, so there's still plenty of time."

"You looked like the Cheshire Cat," Ava told him afterward. "I kept waiting for you to disappear and just your cheesy smile to hover in the air."

Jekyl lifted a hand and smoothed dark hair that was slicked back in a tight ponytail. "Just trying to be media friendly," he told her, breezily. "Anytime you're on camera, it's excellent exposure."

"No, it's not," said Carmela. "Not in my experience."

Jekyl hastened to soothe ruffled feathers. "Darlin'," he said, throwing a skinny arm around Carmela's shoulders, "you just had a bad run-in with that nasty TV lady. But I'll bet, in the long run, it was good for business. The name Memory Mine is probably stuck like a burr in the minds of all those viewers."

"Maybe," said Carmela, still not convinced.

"And now, my dear," said Jekyl, turning toward a woman who was waiting in line, "I'm going to lend my eye to this absolutely gorgeous desk clock that this lovely lady just brought in."

"Jekyl's a charmer," said Ava.

"He probably twisted Kimber right around his little finger," said Carmela. "He does everyone else."

"That's what you get when you've got a hotshot reputation as an antiques expert *and* you're the premier float designer in New Orleans," said Ava.

"But the Pluvius krewe didn't ask Jekyl to redo their float for tonight's parade," said Carmela. "They recruited some other poor soul."

"Probably paid them a pittance, too," said Ava.

"Believe me," said Carmela, "the Pluvius krewe isn't known for their generosity."

"Just their party-hearty ways," laughed Ava.

They wandered along for a few blocks, ultimately heading for Fire and Ice, their errand unspoken between them.

But when they finally arrived at the front door of the jewelry store, Carmela hesitated. "I really don't want to do this," she told Ava.

"But you told Garth you'd stop by," Ava reminded her.

Carmela gave a little shudder. "I know I did, but now I'm regretting it. Garth is at the top of Babcock's suspect list and from the way Garth was talking earlier . . ."

"You think Garth was trying to tell you something?" asked Ava. "Maybe wanted to . . . confess?"

"The thought had crossed my mind."

"Wouldn't that be something." Ava peered nervously at her friend. "So, you gonna go in?"

"Only if you come with me."

"Sure," said Ava. "In for a penny, in for a pound. Besides, with that bad mourning jewelry publicity he got, the shop probably won't be very busy."

Boy, was she wrong.

Fire and Ice was jammed. Customers clustered around the glass cases, mingled in the aisles, and pushed up against the front windows. It took Carmela and Ava more than a few minutes to negotiate the crowd and reach the back of the store where Garth was fluttering about, pouring flutes of champagne.

"Garth!" said Carmela, waving to him.

Garth smiled at her, finished pouring a glass of champagne, then hastily greeted her. "Can you believe this crowd?" He sounded practically giddy.

"I'm shocked," Ava told him. "I thought you said business was bad. That you'd experienced a real backlash over that TV report on mourning jewelry."

"At first business was slow," said Garth. "But then folks got curious and started trickling in. And now . . ." He swept an arm to indicate the crowd. "Now we're jammed."

"Curiosity seekers?" asked Carmela, as Ava wandered off.

"Some," said Garth. "But a few honest-to-goodness buyers, too."

"You sounded so down this afternoon," said Carmela. "When you called."

"I know I did," said Garth. "And I really want to apologize for that. I had no business imposing my depression and grief on you. You've been nothing but kind and helpful, and it was shameful of me to pay you back that way."

"No problem," said Carmela. But, of course, it really was. If Garth had been ready to confess to her, and now his mood was higher than a kite because of an influx of customers, what kind of mental stability did that indicate? Manic-depressive? Of course, now the correct term was *bipolar*. Still, it meant tremendous mood swings. Which certainly must be what Garth Mayfeldt was experiencing. Right?

"Here," said Garth, pouring two more glasses of champagne. "You mingle while I show a few estate pieces to Mrs. Roget over there."

Carmela tapped Ava on the shoulder and handed her a glass of champagne.

"Mmm," said Ava. "Bubbly." She took a sip, and then they elbowed their way over to a glass case that contained a wonderful display of pearls. "You see that?" said Ava, tapping her fingers on the top of the case, "Tahitian pearls. The very best kind."

"I thought Baroque pearls were the best," said Carmela.

Ava nodded, knowingly. "The older ones are fantastic. But hard to find these days, except maybe in a few fine jewelry stores and auction houses like Christie's in New York."

"I didn't know you were such an expert on pearls," said Carmela.

"I love 'em," declared Ava. "Tahitians, Baroques, coin pearls, even mabe pearls."

"How much would that strand of Tahitian pearls run?" asked Carmela, gazing into the case, finding herself slightly fascinated by the dark luster and elusive gray-green colors of the little baubles.

"Let me put it this way," said Ava. "I have a single ranched

Tahitian on a silver chain, and that cost almost seven hundred dollars."

"Holy smokes!" said Carmela. Shamus had once bought her a strand of pearls, but they'd been freshwater pearls. Little Rice Krispie–looking things. Not so great.

Ava took another sip of champagne. "So your buddy Garth seems to be in a good mood. And this is only, let's see . . ." She put a hand to her head. "Two days after his wife's funeral service. A fast recovery, I'd say."

Carmela stared at Ava. "You think it's strange, too." It was a statement, not a question.

"I think there's a reason Garth tops Babcock's suspect list. I think there's more to him than meets the eye."

"You don't think he's just on some sort of manic high?" asked Carmela. "The grief got to him, so he's overcompensating with an upbeat, business-is-good attitude? Then he'll crash in another couple of days?"

"Hey," said Ava, "do I look like a head shrinker? I'm the one with *plastic* shrunken heads hanging on my wall."

"But so authentic looking," said Carmela.

Ava laughed as she held up her half-empty champagne glass and waggled it slightly. "Gonna get another hit, *cher.* Hold all wild and crazy thoughts till I get back."

As Ava pushed off through the crowd, Carmela gazed around Fire and Ice. The bell over the door was *da-dinging* like crazy, people continued to muscle their way in, and champagne corks continued to pop like firecrackers. Carmela sighed as she was jostled away from the counter, then turned her eyes on the large flat-screen TV that hung on the side wall.

KBEZ was broadcasting live tonight, giving lots of coverage to Galleries and Gourmets as they showed quick clips of people jostling in the French Market, in Jackson Square, and over on Royal Street in the heart of antique shop mania. There was another fast cut to Kimber Breeze, and then she was suddenly live, smiling into the camera, microphone held close to her inflated lips.

"I'm reporting directly from Bourbon Street," said Kimber. The camera pulled back to reveal Kimber sitting up high in a cherry picker and pointing toward a giant float. Kimber continued, "And I'm sitting directly above the most amazing Pluvius krewe float."

Carmela watched as the camera panned across a fluttering green-and-gold background, then pulled back again to reveal the head of an enormous Chinese dragon. The dragon's giant eyes rolled back in their sockets, the mouth suddenly gaped open, and a huge tongue of blue flame leaped out, surrounded by a twinkle of orange.

"What?" said Carmela, standing stock-still among the cluster of customers. There was something familiar about the way that flame had danced and sparkled. She backtracked through recent thoughts and images for a couple of seconds, and then deep inside her head something seemed to ping.

"Oh my Lord," she breathed. "Could it be?"

Chapter 29

ROARING and snorting, the Chinese dragon float rumbled its way down Royal Street. Eighty feet long, with a head the size of a garbage truck, the float was an amazing sight to behold. Cheering wildly, the eager crowds parted like the proverbial Red Sea.

Sprinting alongside the dragon float, Carmela tried to keep pace, all the while yelling for Shamus.

"Shamus!" She was starting to gasp, she'd run so many blocks. "Shamus, are you up there?"

Up ahead, a uniformed police officer put out a hand to stop her.

"Lady . . . you can't do that!"

Blasting past him, ignoring him completely, Carmela renewed her efforts. "Shamus! Shamus!" she cried.

A familiar face suddenly appeared from above. It was Sugar Joe, one of Shamus's friends and the heir apparent to one of western Louisiana's major sugarcane plantations.

"Sugar Joe!" Carmela called. "Stop! Please stop!"

First, Sugar Joe frowned. Then, when he finally recognized her, his face broke into a delighted grin. "That you, Carmela?"

"I have to talk to Shamus." She was puffing hard now, running out of breath as she struggled to keep pace. "It's . . . it's an emergency! Life or death!"

"Then come on up here," called Sugar Joe. He leaned down and suddenly grasped Carmela's wrist!

"Oh my Lord!" screamed Carmela as she felt herself go airborne. But as Sugar Joe lifted her, she knew there was no turning back. Kicking her feet, trying to gain purchase on the steep side of the float, Carmela was pulled ever upward.

"Got you, got you!" Sugar Joe told her, his handsome face screwed into a knot of tension. There was a final tug, and then she landed on the float's lower deck as it lumbered past a sea of screaming onlookers.

Trying to catch her breath, fighting to calm her racing heart, Carmela steadied herself against Sugar Joe.

"What's wrong, sweetheart?" he asked her. He'd always been a nice, solicitous sort.

She recovered quickly enough. "I need to talk to Shamus!"

That was enough for Sugar Joe. He grabbed Carmela by the wrist again and pulled her along to the back of the float, underneath the dragon's tail, where there was a small platform. "Just a minute, honey." He turned and yelled into a small three-by-three-foot-hole in the papier-mâché. "Georgie! Bufus! Tell Shamus to get his butt down here, will you?" He turned to Carmela and smiled. "He's comin'."

"Thank you," said Carmela, still working to catch her breath.

"You want a drink?" asked Sugar Joe. "Bourbon?"

Carmela just shook her head.

"You like our float?" asked Sugar Joe. "We retrofitted our Chinese dragon float from Mardi Gras and added some really wild pyrotechnics."

"That's what I—" began Carmela.

"Carmela!" Shamus's face suddenly appeared in the opening of the papier-mâché. "What are you doin' here?" He was surprised, yet not overly startled to see her. Obviously, Shamus had been hitting the bourbon, too.

"I was just telling Carmela about our float," said Sugar Joe. He grinned at her through what was probably a high-test alcoholic haze. "We even had to get a special permit from the city, and then that almost didn't go through."

"That's what I want to know about," said Carmela, excitedly. "About the dragon, about the fire!"

Shamus and Sugar Joe exchanged glances, and then Shamus said, "Take it easy, babe. It's not that big a deal."

Carmela was suddenly leaning forward and in Shamus's face. "Can you make your dragon breathe fire on command?" she demanded.

"Well . . . yeah, I guess," Shamus responded. He put a hand to his mouth and muffled a small burp. "Somebody's gotta hit a button or something."

"Show me," said Carmela. "Show me this instant."

Sugar Joe grinned at her. "Jeez, you're a pushy little thing." Then he turned his laughter on Shamus. "How'd you ever let her get away, anyhow?"

But Carmela was prodding Shamus like a pack animal, forcing him to pull her into the guts of the float and take her to the command center.

Shamus led her along a narrow plank, bending down, trying not to smack his head on the wooden and metal struts that formed the underlying skeleton of the float. "The fire breathing is the coolest," he told her. "This new guy in the krewe . . . we nicknamed him the Chemist . . . he's the one who set it all up. He's the one who had to goose those assholes over in city hall for the special permit."

"Chemist?" shrilled Carmela. "Who's the Chemist, Shamus?"

"Huh?" Shamus stared at her and grabbed a strut for support. He was having trouble tracking Carmela's rapid-fire questions. Having a little trouble staying on his feet, too.

"The guy you call the Chemist," said Carmela, practically screaming at him now. "Who is he? Is he a member of the Pluvius krewe?"

Shamus gave a silly smile. "Well, yeah. Duh. You don't think we'd let just *anybody* ride our float, do you?"

"Who is it, Shamus?" shrilled Carmela. "Is it Sawyer Barnes?"

Shamus stared at her. "Huh?" He looked momentarily confused. Finally he said, "No. It's . . . um . . . that antique guy. Jack Meador."

"What?" exclaimed Carmela. "Is he here? Is Jack Meador here right now?"

Shamus still looked puzzled. "I don't think so. I think with all the big doin's he's over at his gallery."

At the next corner, as the float slowed down to make its turn, Carmela heard gears grinding deep inside. She hopped off. She hit the pavement hard, shoved her way through the jabbering crowd, then huddled flat against a brick building and pulled out her mobile phone.

Got to call Ava, she told herself, frantically pushing buttons.

Ava answered right away. "That you, *cher*? Where did you run off to, anyway?"

"Gotta get over here right away!" she screamed at Ava.

"Where's *here*?" asked Ava, picking up on the fear and tension in Carmela's voice.

"Metcalf and Meador Antiques," said Carmela. She added, "Meet me outside," then quickly hung up.

Her next call was to Edgar Babcock. But all she got was voice mail.

Carmela left a short, shrill, but hopefully detailed message, then struck off down the street. As she flew past street vendors, antiques dealers, and food booths, her mind was in a tumult. Babcock had told her that the ingredients in the

cemetery flare had been potassium nitrate, aluminum powder, and shellac. What he'd characterized as "fairly simple
stuff."

*Stuff maybe an art and antiques dealer might have lying
around?*

Sure, why not? Potassium nitrate was a basic ingredient
in paint stripper. Shellac was used for all sorts of things.
Shining up wood, stuff like that.

On the sidewalk in front of Metcalf and Meador, three
trestle tables were set in a U-shaped arrangement. They
were filled with goods: paintings, jardinières, a silver teapot,
a mirror and brush set, lots of small brass statuary. A young
woman Carmela had never seen before was talking up the
merits of an antique Seth Thomas mantel clock to a well-
dressed young couple. Jack Meador was nowhere to be seen.

Carmela went flying through the front door before she
had time to check her anger or her speed. "Meador!" she
yelled. "Jack Meador!"

The interior of the shop was dark and warm and hushed. A
clock ticked quietly; French table lamps with dark, fringed
shades cast a creamy glow.

Oh crap, Carmela, she suddenly told herself. *This is so not
smart.*

Just as Carmela stopped abruptly and was ready to do
some serious backpedaling, something cold and metallic
pressed against the side of her head.

"Shut up," came Jack Meador's feral snarl. "Shut up and
let me think for a minute."

Chapter 30

"YOU'LL never get away with this!" Carmela screamed through the bandana that was pulled tightly across her mouth. Though she was trussed and bound like a turkey, stuck in the back of Jack Meador's van, her muffled screams continued as she kicked relentlessly at the side panels.

"Shut up," Meador told her again for about the hundredth time. But he sounded worn down, like a broken record. Carmela was getting to him. They'd been driving for ten minutes, weaving through nasty traffic, crawling down narrow secondary streets.

And even though Carmela was putting up an aggressive and brave front, she was terrified. She'd come to the quick realization that Jack Meador had probably killed Melody. And now she was Meador's prisoner. She wasn't sure how she was going to get free, but she knew she had to.

The van spun fast around a corner and Carmela, who'd

been kneeling, making another impassioned plea, was suddenly sent sprawling. By the time she'd righted herself, the van had rocked to a hard stop.

"What do you want?" Carmela screamed at the top of her lungs. She'd somehow managed to dislodge the bandana that was tied across her mouth.

No answer. Jack Meador no longer sat in the driver's seat.

Huh?

The back door flew open and Meador grabbed for her. Quick as a rattlesnake, Carmela struck back, kicking him hard on the chin, losing a shoe in the scuffle. Meador backhanded her hard on the side of the head, causing her to skitter away from him.

He beckoned her with his fingers and a wave of the gun. "Come here. I want to show you something."

Carmela instinctively knew she'd have a better chance if she was out of the van. Inside, she was helpless, a total prisoner.

Grudgingly, she edged toward him. "What?"

When she was within reach, Meador grabbed the rope that bound her hands and waist and pulled her rudely out the back. She landed in darkness. No streetlamps, nobody around to call for help.

Carmela glanced up, saw the outline of a familiar turret, and was stunned when she realized they were directly in front of Medusa Manor!

"I want something," Meador told her as he marched her up the dark walk. "And you're going to get it for me." He shoved her up against the front door, stuck a short pry bar in the doorjamb, and popped the door off its hinges. "Get inside," he growled.

"You're crazy!" yelled Carmela, stumbling her way into the dark building, stiff-legged and tightly bound.

"There's something here that I want," Meador repeated.

"And you're going to be a good little girl and get it for me."

"What are you talking about?" Carmela screamed as Meador pushed and shoved her to the center of the room.

Meador bent forward and, in a stage whisper, said, "I want that painting."

"What?" Carmela was momentarily stunned. *Painting? What painting?*

"Where is it?" Meador demanded.

Carmela's head snapped around, taking in the first-floor parlor. "Over on that wall," she told him, nodding at a desultory landscape, a grouping of bare willow trees.

Meador shook a finger at her angrily. "Not that piece of crap, the *real* painting. The Ivern."

Carmela gave a slow blink. *That's what this is about? A painting?*

"Ivern?" she said, genuinely perplexed.

"Emilio Ivern," snapped Meador. "As in student of Goya."

Shit, thought Carmela. *I really should have paid more attention in art history class.*

"Oh, *that* painting," she said to him, nodding slowly, as if comprehension were slowly dawning. *The one I tucked under my arm and carried downstairs to the library.*

"Where is it?" Meador demanded.

"Upstairs," Carmela told him, without hesitation.

"Go," said Meador, shoving her toward the stairs.

Carmela balked. "First untie me."

Meador shook his head. "No way."

"I can barely move like this, let alone climb those stairs."

Jack Meador seemed to consider this for a few moments, then loosened one of the ropes that ran around Carmela's hips.

"C'mon, man." She gave him a look of disgust.

Meador adjusted more ropes and loosened one arm. "That's all you get. And never forget, I have a gun!"

"I'm not going anywhere," said Carmela. She trudged slowly upstairs, feigning difficulty. "The Ivern," she said when they reached the landing. "It's worth something?"

Meador nudged her in the back. "A small fortune. Keep moving, please."

When they reached the second floor, Carmela paused.

Meador was anxious now. "Come on, come on."

"I'm all turned around in the dark," she told him in a whiny voice. "And we've moved things around so many times, trying different—"

"It's a small painting," he said, practically gnashing his teeth.

"So I think it's in . . ." She hesitated. "The bedroom."

"There are *four* bedrooms," Meador snarled. "Think hard and don't get cute."

Carmela stared down the long dark hallway, then lifted her right shoulder. "That one."

Meador nudged her in the back again. "Go."

Carmela walked stiffly into the ghost bride bedroom. "I think we hung it on the back wall . . ."

The words weren't out of her mouth when she plunged directly into the dark room with its cotillion of hanging ghost brides. Dodging left, she set an entire row in motion; zigzagging right, she ran low, feeling the stiff, frayed dresses brush against her.

"Hey!" screamed Meador, suddenly tangled by the furor she'd stirred up. As if life had been breathed into their bodies, the entire room of ghost brides swayed frantically, their dresses a whisper of rustles and sighs.

"Get back here!" Meador screamed at the top of his lungs.

But Carmela was running for her life! Dashing from the ghost bride bedroom, she ducked into the connecting closet, emerging in the *Exorcist* bedroom.

Frantic now, Meador ran back out into the hallway, listened for a few moments, then cautiously stepped into the Witches' Lair.

That was all Carmela needed. She tiptoed stealthily toward the back stairs, praying for a clean getaway.

The second step down tripped her up. A loud squeak rent the stillness, and then Jack Meador was pounding after her in the darkness!

A zombie on the lower steps went flying, hanging bats banged her in the head, and spiderwebs were filmy barriers that Carmela virtually flew through.

And still Jack Meador was hot on her trail!

Tripping on the last step, crashing painfully to her knees, Carmela scrambled to pull herself up, losing a few more of her ropes and grabbing a nearby brass candlestick in the process.

"I see you!" bellowed Meador. One hand reached out and pawed at the back of her blouse, but Carmela lunged around a corner into the Morgue of Madness. She skittered slightly, dancing around the metal table, then shoved it at Meador. Because there was no place else to run to, Carmela flung open the door and ran full-tilt into the crematorium.

Meador, hampered momentarily by the heavy table, came crashing in ten seconds later.

Carmela was ready for him. With the heavy candlestick poised high above her head, she brought it down hard on top of Meador's head. There was an ugly crunch, followed by a high-pitched scream, as it glanced off the back of his neck. Meador swore as he staggered, sank to his knees, then went facedown on the floor.

Without hesitating, Carmela lunged for the huge metal switch on the wall and pulled it down hard. Then she was slaloming out the door, slamming it closed behind her.

Inside the crematorium, the newly installed special effects jumped to life in a spectacularly frightening manner. Heat lamps glowed with full intensity, flames leaped and danced on the walls, and a motor roared like a jet engine.

And Jack Meador, stunned by the blow to his head, threw his hands over his face and screamed as though the flesh on his body were being scorched by the hellish flames of eternity.

Chapter 31

RUNNING for her life, Carmela stumbled into the front parlor, crying, hiccupping, screaming for help. A glance to the left revealed the terrifying snake-ringed face of Medusa over the fireplace. A step to the right and Carmela was suddenly flinging herself against the front door.

The door stuck for a moment, as though someone were on the other side, holding on, and then it crashed open and Carmela rushed into a pair of waiting arms.

Struggling to get free, flailing wildly, Carmela didn't realize just who had hold of her.

"Easy, easy," came Edgar Babcock's soothing words. "You're safe."

Carmela stopped her struggling and stared, wide-eyed, at Babcock. "How did you know where I was?"

"You left me a voice mail, remember?"

To Carmela that voice mail seemed like a lifetime ago.

"Jack Meador killed Melody," Carmela blurted, her words beginning to tumble out. She was aware of two police cruisers screaming up to the curb and officers running toward them. "And then he tried to kill me. There's some sort of . . . of painting . . . a really valuable painting that he was trying to get his hands on. Melody must not have known it was valuable, because Meador killed her or robbed her or . . . or . . . whatever." Carmela suddenly went limp in Babcock's arms.

"Inside," was Babcock's taut instruction to the uniformed officers.

"He's got a gun!" Carmela cried after them. "Meador's armed!"

"So are we," said Babcock, suddenly leaving her on the doorstep and dashing in after the officers.

"Wait a minute!" said Carmela, lunging after him. But Babcock's long strides had already put him twenty paces ahead of her.

Carmela finally caught up in the Morgue of Madness, where the five of them were clustered around the crematorium door, mumbling in low voices.

Babcock finally noticed her. He didn't look happy. "Why is it so hot in there?" he demanded. "Is it a real crematorium?"

Carmela shook her head. "It's all smoke and mirrors. Heat lamps and projections."

One officer gazed at Babcock and said, "Guy was screaming his head off like he was being tortured. Then we heard a loud gasp."

"Just seemed to give up the ghost," said another officer.

"Ghost," said Carmela. "Hah."

They all listened for a few moments and finally heard a low groan from inside.

"Throw the gun out," barked Babcock. "Or would you rather we toss in a nice stun grenade and let you spend the night together?"

"I'll throw it out," came the subdued voice of Jack Meador.

Out on the front verandah, handcuffed and in custody, Jack Meador seemed to regain some of his feistiness.

"I understand Ms. Mayfeldt showed up at your gallery with the Ivern painting?" Babcock was questioning Meador while Carmela clutched the painting she'd hastily retrieved.

Meador stared at them.

"And you knew exactly what it was," said Babcock.

Meador had a crazy gleam in his eye. "Yes, but she didn't," he barked. Glaring at Carmela, he curled his lip and said, "I want a lawyer."

"Easily done," said Babcock, as the officers led Meador away. He reached a hand out. "Let me see that thing."

Carmela handed him the painting she'd just pulled off the wall in the library.

He tilted it to catch the light. "Oh man," groaned Babcock.

"It's not *that* bad," said Carmela, a note of reproach in her voice.

But Babcock wasn't looking at the painting. His eyes were focused on the street, where Ava Gruiex and Jekyl Hardy had just pulled up in Jekyl's Jaguar. "Just what we don't need."

"Cher!" screamed Ava, tottering up the walk, coming full-tilt on three-inch stilettos. "I was so *scared*! Are you okay?"

"I am now," said Carmela, allowing herself to be kissed, hugged, and generally fawned over by both Ava and Jekyl. Then, of course, she had to relate her story, kidnapping, and ensuing rescue in Technicolor-type prose.

Jekyl carried the painting inside Medusa Manor, where he could study it under semidecent lighting.

"This is a phenomenal piece," he pronounced. "Emilio Ivern was a student of Goya. This painting is probably worth a fortune!"

"I'm beginning to understand that," said Carmela.

"Where did Melody get this painting?" asked Babcock.

"I'm pretty sure she bought it at auction," Carmela told them.

"Finders keepers," said Jekyl.

"Is that so?" asked Ava. "So who owns it now?"

"If Melody paid for it, Melody owns it," said Babcock. "Or at least her estate does."

"Then Garth owns it," said Carmela.

"And he has no idea of its value?" asked Ava.

"I doubt he even knows it exists," said Carmela.

"Lucky guy," said Jekyl.

"Is he?" asked Carmela. "Is he really?"

Ava found it necessary to hug Carmela a few more times. Then she said, "So . . . there was no . . . what would you call it? . . . collusion between Olivia Wainwright and Sawyer Barnes?"

"Only a possible real estate deal," said Babcock.

Carmela nodded. "And Sidney was just a . . ."

"A crackpot," finished Ava. "Who's gonna be mighty unhappy when he finds out what happened."

"Didn't get to film the nail-biting ending," said Carmela.

Ava put an arm around Carmela. "Saved by the ghost brides, huh? I knew those dresses were good for something."

"Ghost brides?" asked Jekyl.

Babcock just shook his head. "You'd have to see it to believe it."

But Ava was not to be deterred. "Something old, something new," she sang. "Something borrowed, something blue." With a mischievous gleam in her eye, she grabbed Carmela's hand and linked it with Babcock's. "Who knows, it could happen to you!"

"Ava!" shrilled Carmela. But her smile was a mile wide.

Scrapbook, Stamping, and Craft Tips from Laura Childs

Have Fun with Photo Bloopers

Everyone has a few photos that didn't turn out quite as planned. Somebody moved, somebody blinked, your son stuck out his tongue. No problem. Just create a Photo Blooper page at the back of your album. This is your chance to go wild with colors and design ideas, then add all those crazy photos. You're sure to get plenty of laughs!

3-D Objects as Background Pages

Lay a baby outfit on a color copier and make a copy to use as a background for your scrapbook page. This color-copy technique works great for all sorts of bulky objects such as badges, scarves, T-shirts, and even floral bouquets.

Storybook Fun

All kids have a favorite storybook, so why not scan or color-copy drawings from their favorite book, then add them to a scrapbook page? Have that lovable bear, goofy Muppet, or sweet little mouse capering right across your child's own scrapbook page.

Antique Your Own Paper

Turn tan, khaki, and light-brown paper into antiqued paper by scratching it up with an emery board or sandpaper. Then put a little dark brown ink on a rag and rub gently in the lines for an even more dramatic effect. Could be the perfect background for that wonderful old photo of your grandparents!

Flower Power

It's fun to add flower motifs to your scrapbook pages, especially when you're doing engagement, wedding, or even summer themes. But why settle for flat flowers when you can have something tactile? Using velveteen paper, cut petals and centers, then scrunch them up slightly and glue them together as daisies, lilies, even bluebells.

Handprints and Footprints

Pour a little acrylic paint into a dish. Then place your child's hands or feet into the ink, coat generously, then press those little fingers and toes against a piece of paper or directly against your scrapbook page. Your kids will love doing it and you'll have a wonderful, permanent memory.

Designer Ribbon on a Budget

Love the designer ribbon that fancy gift and floral shops use, but don't like to pay the price? Create your own by buying inexpensive, wide ribbon at a craft store, then stamping your own designs onto it using metallic ink.

Backward Scrapbooking

Did you know you can build your concept and select your papers and designs *before* you take your photos? Here's an example: You've found the perfect beach-themed paper, seahorse stickers, and surfboard die cut. So go ahead and scrap that page—leaving room for a photo or two. Once you've created your concept, you'll know exactly what type of photo you need to take!

The Power of the Pen

Never underestimate the personal touch of homemade captions. Take a squishy pen and write your own thoughts, remarks, or memories directly beneath your photos.

Favorite New Orleans Recipes

Andouille Sausage Gumbo

½ cup olive oil
⅔ cup flour
3 cups chicken stock
½ cup onion, chopped
½ cup celery, chopped
½ cup green bell pepper, chopped
4 Tbsp. Cajun seasoning
1 lb. andouille sausage or smoked sausage, sliced crosswise
2 bay leaves
1 Tbsp. Worcestershire sauce
1 cup okra, sliced
Hot cooked rice
Hot sauce, to taste

Heat the oil in a large stockpot, then add the flour, stirring constantly over low to medium heat. After 10 minutes, you should have a golden roux. Slowly add 1 cup of the chicken stock and stir until the stock is completely incorporated. Then add the onion, celery, and green bell pepper, cooking and stirring for 5 to 6 minutes, until the vegetables begin to get tender. Add the remaining chicken stock and the Cajun seasoning, sausage, bay leaves, Worcestershire sauce, and okra. Bring to a gentle simmer and allow to cook, uncovered, for 1 hour. To serve, remove the bay leaves, spoon the gumbo over rice, and add hot sauce to taste.

Mystery Muffins

2 cups flour, sifted
1 Tbsp. baking powder
1 tsp. salt
¼ cup mayonnaise
1 cup milk
1 Tbsp. sugar

Preheat the oven to 375°. Sift together the flour, baking powder, and salt. Add the mayonnaise, milk, and sugar and mix until smooth. Scoop a small amount of batter into each of 12 greased muffin tins, filling them about ½ to ⅔ full. Bake for 18 to 20 minutes.

Brown Sugar and Sour Cream Butter

¼ cup sour cream
½ cup butter, softened
1 Tbsp. brown sugar

Pulse the sour cream, butter, and brown sugar together in a food processor until smooth. Slather on top of hot Mystery Muffins!

Carmela's Cocoa Loco Pie

2 eggs
1½ cups sugar
3 Tbsp. unsweetened cocoa powder
1 can (5 fl. oz.) evaporated milk
½ cup butter, melted
1 tsp. vanilla extract
9" unbaked pie shell

Preheat the oven to 250°. Beat the eggs well, then add the sugar and cocoa powder and beat to incorporate. Beat in the evaporated milk, melted butter, and vanilla. Pour the mixture into the 9" unbaked pie shell and bake for 45 minutes. Let the pie cool before serving.

Parmesan Shrimp Bake

¼ cup olive oil
½ cup onion, finely chopped
¼ tsp. red pepper flakes
1½ lbs. uncooked shrimp, fresh or frozen, peeled
½ cup diced tomatoes
Salt, to taste
⅔ cup grated Parmesan cheese

Preheat the oven to 350°. Heat the oil in a large skillet, then sauté the onion for 4 minutes. Add the red pepper flakes and sizzle for 30 seconds. Add the shrimp and sauté for 2 minutes. Stir in the diced tomatoes and salt to taste and cook the mixture for another 2 minutes. Transfer the shrimp mixture to a baking dish and bake for 10 minutes. Sprinkle the grated Parmesan on top of the shrimp and bake for an additional 2 to 3 minutes until golden and bubbly.

Monkey Bread

2 cans (7.5 oz. each) refrigerated buttermilk biscuits
1 cup brown sugar, packed
1 tsp. cinnamon
1 tsp. nutmeg
½ cup butter or margarine, melted
½ cup finely chopped walnuts or pecans
½ cup maple syrup

Preheat the oven to 350°. Cut each biscuit into quarters. In a small bowl, combine the brown sugar, cinnamon, and nutmeg. Now dip each biscuit piece in melted butter and roll it in the sugar mixture. Layer half the pieces in a 10-inch fluted tube pan and sprinkle with half of the nuts. Repeat to form a second layer on top. Pour maple syrup over the entire top. Bake for 25 to 30 minutes or until golden brown. Immediately invert the Monkey Bread onto a serving plate.

Southern Coffee Cookies

1 cup sugar
½ cup butter or margarine
1 egg, well beaten
2 cups flour
½ tsp. baking soda
¼ tsp. salt
1 tsp. baking powder
½ tsp. cinnamon
¾ cup cold coffee
½ cup raisins, chopped
½ cup walnuts or pecans, chopped
1 tsp. vanilla

Preheat the oven to 400°. Mix the sugar and butter together until creamy, then add the beaten egg and mix well. In a separate bowl, combine the flour, baking soda, salt, baking powder, and cinnamon. Stir together, then add to the creamed mixture. Mix well, adding in the coffee, a little at a time. Combine the raisins, nuts, and vanilla, then fold into the batter. Drop cookies onto a greased baking sheet. Bake for 12 to 15 minutes.

Chicken Piccata

¼ cup milk or cream
¼ cup flour
2 Tbsp. grated Parmesan cheese
Salt and pepper
2 chicken breasts, halved or butterflied
4 Tbsp. olive oil
4 Tbsp. butter

⅓ cup chicken stock
3 Tbsp. lemon juice
¼ cup chopped fresh parsley

Pour the milk into one bowl, and mix the flour, grated Parmesan, and salt and pepper to taste in another bowl. Dip the chicken breasts in the milk, then dredge them in the flour-and-cheese mixture. Heat the olive oil and 2 Tbsp. of the butter in a skillet and fry the chicken breasts over medium heat until golden brown, 3 to 4 minutes per side. Remove the chicken and keep warm. Add the chicken stock and lemon juice to the skillet and heat over medium heat, stirring and reducing the liquid by half. Whisk in the remaining butter, then add the chicken and reheat for 1 minute. Place the chicken breasts on a plate, pour the sauce over them, and sprinkle with the parsley.

New Orleans Roast Beef Po'Boy

2 small French loaves, split lengthwise
Mayonnaise
1 cup shredded lettuce
10 oz. thinly sliced roast beef
4 slices cheese
1 tomato, thinly sliced   ·
Hot beef gravy (optional)

Split the French loaves and toast them lightly under the broiler. Spread the bottom halves with mayonnaise, then layer with the shredded lettuce, roast beef, cheese, tomato, and gravy. Add the top half of the loaves and serve. Serves 2 to 4, depending on how hungry you are!

Deep-Fried Strawberries

½ cup flour
2 tsp. sugar
1 egg, beaten
¼ cup dry white wine
1 Tbsp. cooking oil
2 cups fresh strawberries
Oil for deep frying
Powdered or granulated sugar for rolling

In a mixing bowl, combine the flour and sugar. In a separate bowl, combine the egg, wine, and cooking oil. Add the egg mixture to the flour mixture and beat until smooth. Dip the strawberries in the batter and deep-fry, a small batch at a time, in 2 inches of hot oil for approximately 2 minutes. Remove and drain on paper towels. While still warm, roll the strawberries in powdered or granulated sugar.

Frozen Daiquiri

1½ fl. oz. light or dark rum
1 Tbsp. Triple Sec
1½ fl. oz. lime juice
1 tsp. sugar
1 cup ice

Mix the ingredients together in a blender at high speed until firm. Pour into a frosty stemmed glass and enjoy!

IT might have been Kindred Spirit Days in Elmwood Park, but Suzanne Dietz wasn't exactly feeling the spirit. Shifting from one moccasined foot to the other, stuck behind a table selling slices of soggy pineapple cake, hard-as-a-rock fudge, and gooped-up cherry pies for the Library Committee's fund-raiser, Suzanne would have much preferred to be back at her own place, the Cackleberry Club.

Closing her eyes against the intrusion of laughing clowns, frenetic jugglers, and accordion music, she imagined herself bustling about in her own cozy café this Sunday afternoon. If brunch ran late, as it often did, she'd be juggling plates of eggs Florentine, huevos rancheros, Slumbering Volcanoes, and towering omelets stuffed with gooey, molten Gruyère cheese.

Eggs, of course, were the morning specialty at the Cackleberry Club. But lunch was delectably creative, too, with specials like drunken pecan chicken, brown sugar meatloaf, and frozen lemonade pie. And Suzanne also laid out a pretty snappy afternoon tea that could probably tempt even the most proper English lady.

"We ought to be selling our own cakes and muffins and scones," Petra murmured, as if reading Suzanne's mind. Petra was the second partner and principal baker and chef at the Cackleberry Club. "I don't know how we got roped into this. Trying to be do-gooders, I suppose. I thought we'd be selling books!"

"Me, too," said Suzanne as she brushed back shoulder-length silver blond hair and gazed with keen blue eyes at the morose selection of baked goods. "Ours would certainly be better quality. Unfortunately, this stuff is . . ." She glanced around to make sure one of the pie makers, a glum-looking little woman named Agnes, wasn't in earshot. " . . . beyond pathetic."

"I'm terrified folks will think these baked goods are from the Cackleberry Club," Petra murmured in hushed tones. Brown-eyed and square-jawed, Petra was big-boned and bighearted. She was known to show up at the front door of a new neighbor with casserole in hand, owned an overweight Russian Blue cat named Rasputin, and had mastered the art of trout fishing.

"Heaven forbid," said Suzanne, pushing up the sleeves of her denim shirt and letting loose a slight shudder. The Cackleberry Club was her baby and she considered herself a stickler for quality control.

"Just look at us," said Petra with a giggle, "we're two volunteers who are really curmudgeons at heart." In fact, they weren't curmudgeons at all. Suzanne, Petra, and their friend, Toni—the third partner in the troika that ran the Cackleberry Club—were just mature women who didn't give a rat's backside about what people thought or said about them. Now that they were on the high side of forty, careening toward fifty, they spoke their minds and lived their lives with grace and fortitude, without dwelling on past actions or feelings of remorse. For some reason, this somewhat pragmatic midlife philosophy led to better mental health and left them all feeling strangely liberated.

"We're on our own now," Suzanne had told Petra some six months ago. "Free to blaze our own trail; free to make our own mistakes." Suzanne's husband had just passed away and, a few months earlier, Petra's husband, Donny, had gone into the Center City nursing home. But even as Alzheimer's had robbed Donny's mind, it had ignited Petra's spunk and determination.

As a final coup de grâce, Toni's slightly younger juvenile delinquent husband, Junior, had up and left her for a bar waitress with a head full of hot pink extensions.

That's when a merciful God had smiled down, taken pity, aligned the planets, and helped set gentle plans in motion for the Cackleberry Club to be—excuse the pun—hatched.

The Cackleberry Club, a whitewashed, rehabbed Spur station out on Highway 65, was a kitschy, quirky place. With a decent kitchen installed, battered wooden tables and chairs put in place, and legions of antique salt and pepper shakers and ceramic chickens arranged on shelves, a delightful little café with a tangle of wild roses out front had emerged.

Because there were a couple of extra rooms for sprawling, it became readily apparent that a Book Nook might bring in extra business. So cases of books, mostly mysteries, romances, and children's books, had been ordered and neatly arranged on shelves. Petra, who was a knitting and quilting freak, decreed there was also room for a Knitting Nest in an adjacent room. Colorful skeins of yarn and hundreds of knitting needles were carefully displayed, along with towering stacks of quilt squares. And once rump-sprung armchairs were liberated from attics, draped with woolly afghans, and arranged in a cozy semicircle, customers felt more than welcome to sit and stay awhile.

In a relatively short time, a few months to be exact, the Cackleberry Club had emerged as the crazy quilt apex for food, books, knitting, quilting, and good old-fashioned female bonding that drew fans not just from Kindred but from all over the tri-county area.

Petra nudged Suzanne with an elbow. "Look. Mayor Mobley's squeezed in a little campaigning."

Suzanne gazed past the face-painting booth and the funnel-cake wagon to watch their pudgy mayor swagger along, glad-handing folks and slapping oversized campaign buttons into their palms. "What a slimeball," she muttered to herself. Though Kindred was a picture-postcard little town with historic brick buildings and well-kept homes skirted by towering bluffs and remnants of a hardwood forest, their mayor, as top elected official, left something to be desired. Suzanne always had the niggling feeling that Mayor Mobley was just this side of legitimate. And that various permits, licenses, and easements could be more easily obtained by greasing his sticky palms.

"Ozzie never came back for his pie," observed Petra, looking at the paltry few that had been reserved. Ozzie Driesden was the local funeral director as well as a civic booster. Of course, what funeral director wasn't a civic booster? They all wanted to win friends and influence people for that final trip to the great beyond.

"Hmm?" murmured Suzanne, still keeping a watchful eye on the swaggering Mayor Mobley.

"Ozzie bought a cherry pie earlier, but hasn't been back to pick it up."

"Tell you what," said Suzanne, frantic to ditch out. "I'll run the pie over to Ozzie, and you pull out your squishy black magic marker and slash prices on all this stuff. Hopefully, it'll magically fly off the table so we can boogie on out of here."

"Deal," said Petra, as Suzanne snatched up Ozzie's pie. "But I think I'm going to slip a few ginger-spice cupcakes to that poor fellow sitting by the picnic tables. He looks like he hasn't had anything to eat in a week."

"Better taste them first," warned Suzanne. "You wouldn't want to kill him."

Delighted to be done with the bake sale, Suzanne set off down Front Street, finally able to relax and enjoy the afternoon. What little was left of it, anyway.

An orange September sun hung low in the sky, but the faint rays were still warm and relaxing on her back. A lingering lazy-day feeling before the crispness of autumn took hold.

In fact, Suzanne was casting admiring glances at fire maples and daydreaming about riding her horse across a sunny hillside of blazing sumac when she pushed open the front door of the Driesden and Draper Funeral Home.

That's when the day's warmth and Suzanne's good humor suddenly came to a crashing halt.

The mingled aromas of overripe flowers, chill air, and . . . what else? . . . chemicals? . . . jarred her mind and assaulted her sensibilities.

Suzanne wrinkled her nose and set her jaw firmly. Well, of course it's going to smell funny, she told herself, taking a few tentative steps into the entryway. It's a funeral home. There's always going to be . . . chemicals.

She shook her head as a shiver oozed its way down her spine. When Walter had died, they'd held his visitation right here, in this very funeral place.

Squaring her shoulders, Suzanne crossed the whisper-soft celadon green carpet and called out, "Ozzie?" in what she hoped was a confident and slightly authoritative voice.

She waited a few moments, keeping company with a grandfather clock, a wooden podium reserved for guest books, and a small brocade fainting couch that had a small table with a box of Kleenex snugged up next to it. Sighing, Suzanne decided it was time to be a little more proactive.

Gripping the pie tighter, Suzanne struck off to her left and peered through the open doorway into the smaller of the two chapels. The room was tastefully furnished in shades of dove gray and mauve. And it was empty, except for a nondescript sofa and a semicircle of black metal folding chairs that looked like a cluster of skinny crows.

"Ozzie?" Suzanne called out again. "I brought your pie." But there was no answer, save the ticking of the staid grandfather clock.

Suzanne re-crossed the entry hall. Maybe Ozzie was scurrying about in the other chapel. She touched fingertips to an ornate brass pull and slid open a heavy wooden pocket door. As she glanced in expectantly, a bronze coffin met her eyes. Lid propped up, resting on a wooden bier, the coffin was flanked by two pots of slightly drooping irises.

Oops, this room is ocupado.

Suzanne caught a quick glimpse of cream-colored satin brocade as well as the coffin's occupant lying in still repose. Letting out a quick breath, she quickly turned her gaze to a brass candle holder that held six white tapers. And couldn't shut the door fast enough.

Shifting uncomfortably, a little unnerved, Suzanne stared at the double doors that led to the back of the funeral home. The room where Ozzie did his sad business.

"Hey . . . Ozzie?" she called out again, drumming her fingers nervously on the underside of the tin pie plate.

No answer. Nada. And the insistent ticking of the grandfather clock was beginning to seriously grate on Suzanne's nerves. Glancing at the offending antique clock, she suddenly recalled fragments of a long-ago childhood story, whispered at night around a flickering campfire. Something about a grandfather clock that stopped dead the exact moment its creaky old owner drew his final, rattly breath.

"Silly," Suzanne murmured to herself. She wasn't a big believer in legends or signs or portents. Suzanne was a woman who believed in living fully and wholly in the present and not fretting unduly about what might be coming down the road. That didn't mean Suzanne hadn't noodled a five-year plan or even a ten-year plan, because she had. But that was for business. Mostly, in her personal life, she just tried to keep things on an even keel and obsess as little as possible. She found this approach helpful in retaining positive mental energy. It wasn't a bad way to keep crow's feet and wrinkles at bay, either.

Shifting the pie to her left hand, Suzanne smoothed the front of her blouse, then placed her palm flat against one of the double doors. They were swinging doors, of course, similar in design to the service doors restaurants installed between dining room and kitchen. Except, in this case, there was no eye-level window to peek through. Because who in their right mind wanted to see into the back of a funeral home, anyway?

Suzanne pushed lightly, felt the door move inward.

So not locked, she told herself. Which meant Ozzie was probably puttering around in back. And since there was a body out here, there probably wouldn't be one in back. At least she hoped there wasn't. Suzanne couldn't recall any recent obituaries in the *Bugle*. Could only think of the one last Thursday for Julius Carr.

And she'd just encountered *him*.

So . . . okay.

But as the door continued to swing inward, it clanked hard, hitting a rolling metal cart. Suzanne did a double take. The cart lay wheels up, half blocking the door. To either side of her, stacks of blue and white pharmaceutical boxes, no longer lined up nice and neat on their grid of shiny metal shelving, were tumbled haphazardly on gray linoleum. Suzanne could read the labels on the upended boxes: Hizone, Lynch, ESCO.

What just happened here? she wondered.

And suddenly heard a faint clink.

What was that? The snick of a metal door, the click of an instrument being set down?

Sure it was. So Ozzie was back here. Probably.

"Ozzie," Suzanne called, rounding a corner. "What the heck hap . . ."

Suzanne stopped dead in her tracks, her words segueing to a sputter, then a dying gasp. Her mouth opened reflexively, snapped shut, then opened again. But no sound issued forth.

Because Ozzie was back here, all right. Splayed out on an enormous metal table like some sort of medical experiment gone horribly wrong.

Suzanne's eyelids fluttered uncontrollably as she took in the ghastly scene. Plastic hoses kinked around Ozzie, his right arm stuck rigidly out to one side. And there, sticking into that arm, his very white, waxy arm, was a large needle attached to a length of tubing.

Suicide? The word exploded in Suzanne's brain like a thousand points of light. *Oh no, not Ozzie Driesden. He wouldn't do that, would he?*

Suzanne's stomach lurched unsteadily and the beginnings of bitter, hot bile rose in the back of her throat.

Struggling to force her mind to work, to reboot her brain's frozen hard drive, she thought to herself, *Got to get help.*

As that thought popped into her head like a bubble above a cartoon drawing, there was a sudden, sharp snap, like a freshly laundered towel jerking on a clothesline. A soft shuffle sounded behind Suzanne, then a cold, wet, foul-smelling rag was clamped viciously across her nose and mouth.

Throwing up her hands in protest, the pie flipped end over end and crashed to the floor. Struggling blindly, not thinking clearly now, Suzanne inhaled sharply and involuntarily breathed in the prickly chemical that soaked the rag. Her heart lurched painfully in her chest and her lungs burned like hot coals. Staggering drunkenly, Suzanne's spinning mind spat out a single word: *Camphor?*

Then her head was filled with the drone of a thousand

angry hornets and her knees began to buckle like a cheap card table.

No . . . chloroform, was Suzanne's last semi-lucid thought as blackness descended and she crumpled atop the ruined cherry pie.

"Breathe deeply," urged a voice from above her. Suzanne's eyes fluttered wildly for a few moments, then peeped open. And Suzanne found herself gazing up into the face of a kindly-looking EMT wearing a blue uniform with a red-and-white patch. He was young and good-looking, with an olive complexion and curly, dark hair.

When did EMTs get so young? Suzanne wondered to herself. *And when did I start thinking guys in their early thirties were young?*

That brought a semblance of a giggle mixed with a few hiccups.

"She's coming around," said Petra.

At hearing her friend's calming voice, Suzanne lifted her head. Not a great idea. Her brain was still spinning like a centrifuge even though her body was laid out flat on the floor, right where she'd fallen.

Cotton in my head, Suzanne thought, crazily. *And bright red cherry pie all over the floor.*

The EMT, whose name tag read J. Jellen, held a plastic mask to Suzanne's mouth and smiled encouragingly. "Breathe," he instructed.

Suzanne fought to bat the mask away.

"It's only oxygen," Jellen told her, calmly. "Help clear your head."

"Breathe the Os, honey," Petra pleaded, kneeling down next to her.

Suzanne breathed in deeply and, a few moments later, really did feel better. She relaxed, inhaled a few more Os, then raised a hand and pushed the mask aside. "What happened?" she asked Petra. "How did you get here?"

"When you didn't come back right away, I sent Sheriff Doogie over to check on you," explained Petra. "He'd been hanging around the park, snarfing down hot dogs and cookies. After he left, and when I saw the ambulance heading over there—Doogie must have found you and called for it right away—I came running. Like the proverbial cavalry." Petra put a hand to her ample chest. "Well, a cavalry that walks awful darn fast, anyway."

"Doogie's here?" asked Suzanne, struggling to sit up.

Petra nodded. "And a deputy." She peered anxiously at Suzanne. "How much do you remember, honey?"

It was starting to come back to her now. Suzanne touched a hand to her head and sighed deeply. "Oh man. Ozzie . . . ?"

Petra gave a solemn shake of her head.

"Dead?" asked Suzanne. Her mouth felt parched and dry.

"Afraid so," Petra whispered.

Suzanne pushed herself into a sitting position, gritted her teeth as her head spun wildly, then struggled to get her legs under her. The paramedic, Jellen, curved an arm around her waist and asked, "You sure you want to do this?"

Suzanne nodded and suddenly found herself being lifted with ease by the helpful paramedic. She continued to stare down at the floor for a long moment, noting the sticky smear of cherry pie and a flattened hunk of golden crust that seemed to carry the partial imprint of a shoe. Then she raised her eyes.

Ozzie was still lying there, of course. That harsh reality hadn't changed one iota. But now Sheriff Roy Doogie and his young deputy, Wilbur Halpern, were circling the metal table like coyotes surveying roadkill. Another fellow, George Draper, the Draper of Driesden and Draper, was standing there with them, making nervous, futile hand gestures. Obviously, Draper had been summoned posthaste.

"Killed himself," said the deputy. He shook his head even

as he hooked both fingers in his belt in a kind of postmortem show of disapproval.

Sheriff Doogie, a big bear of a man in rumpled khaki, turned toward George Draper, Ozzie's partner, now the sole owner of Driesden and Draper. "Had he been depressed?"

Draper, who was tall, gangly, slightly stooped, and looked like *he* might be suffering a mild bout of depression, gave a slightly furtive shrug. "Maybe. A little bit."

"What are you talking about?" Suzanne suddenly croaked as she staggered toward them. She was fighting mightily to get her feet and legs to coordinate with her brain. But walking a straight line wasn't easy.

Sheriff Roy Doogie shifted his bulk and bobbed his head at Suzanne. He was the duly elected sheriff of Logan County and had been in office for more than a dozen years. With his meaty face, cap of gray hair, and rattlesnake eyes, Doogie only looked slow-moving. Truth was, not much got past him.

"You feeling better now, Suzanne?" Doogie asked as she continued to wobble toward him. "You must've had quite a start, seeing poor Ozzie like this. No wonder you fainted dead away."

"I didn't faint," Suzanne protested. "I've never fainted in my life."

The young deputy let loose a slightly derisive snort. "Then how come you was sprawled on the floor?"

"If you give me a minute, instead of jumping to conclusions," snapped Suzanne, "I'll tell you."

"Tell us what?" asked Doogie. A frown and something else . . . curiosity? . . . had insinuated itself on his lined face.

"Someone attacked me!" Suzanne told him in a rush. "From behind. Clamped some kind of damp cloth over my mouth and . . . and . . . *drugged* me!" She touched the back of her palm to her head, trying to recall the exact sequence of events. But everything was still fuzzy, like a long-ago dream that could only be remembered in disjointed fragments.

"Huh?" said the deputy.

"What are you sayin'?" asked Doogie. His jowls sloshed vigorously as he stared at Suzanne, his eyes suddenly wide with surprise.

"I came back here to deliver Ozzie's pie," explained Suzanne, "and that's when I saw him. Just . . ." Suzanne grimaced as she glanced past Doogie. " . . . just lying there."

"Was he dead?" Sheriff Doogie asked.

"I don't know," said Suzanne. "Well, I *suppose* he was. I mean, he must have been. He was all white and waxy-looking, just like he is now." She felt hot tears prickle her eyes, but fought to keep them back. Men were funny about tears. Disdainful really. If she could keep the waterworks under control for the time being, her story would carry far more credibility. Suzanne tried to emphasize the chain of events with another hopefully cohesive statement: "Before I had time to react and really get a decent look, someone grabbed me from behind and slapped a rag across my face. Drugged me," she added again, for emphasis.

Sheriff Doogie seemed to be having trouble comprehending all this. "You mean they chloroformed you?"

"I don't know if that's the technical term," said Suzanne, starting to feel a little frustrated, "but yes. Someone chloroformed me. Like a friggin' bug dropped inside a Mason jar for biology class."

Doogie snatched his modified Smokey Bear hat from his head and slapped it against his knee. "Heck you say!" Doogie still seemed reluctant to buy into Suzanne's story.

"Sheriff Roy Doogie!" said Petra, in her sternest, steeliest voice, "you listen to Suzanne. She doesn't make up stories!"

Sheriff Doogie ushered them all into the small parlor, the unoccupied parlor, where they sat on lumpy couches and love seats and Suzanne told her story again. Slowly, filling in the details.

Doogie went over a few parts with her. "So when you

came in carrying the pie, the boxes were spilled all over." It was a statement, not a question.

"Yes," said Suzanne. "Like maybe there'd been a struggle."

"And then you saw Ozzie. With the . . ." Sheriff Doogie pointed an index finger at his own forearm. " . . . with the thing . . . the needle . . . stuck in his arm."

"Yes," Suzanne said again.

Doogie's lined face sagged. "Well, shit."

Suzanne glanced around the semicircle of somber faces. "He was murdered, wasn't he?" she said. But she really wasn't asking a question, either.

"We don't know that for sure," said Doogie, still hedging.

"Whoever attacked me had probably just murdered Ozzie," Suzanne said, forcefully this time.

Petra, who was perched next to Suzanne, gripped her forearm tightly.

"Wilbur," said Doogie, glancing at his deputy. "Go out to the truck and fetch my kit."

Wilbur rose hastily and left the room.

Petra stared directly at Doogie and said in an accusatory tone, "This could have easily been a double murder, Sheriff."

Doogie lifted both hands to belly level and made a calming gesture. "Now we don't know anything like that. But I'm going to go ahead and treat this as a crime scene . . . give it some serious investigation."

"You're going to call in the state crime lab?" asked George Draper. He hadn't said anything up to this point. Now he looked colossally unhappy.

"First things first," Doogie told Draper. "First thing I want to do is go back in there and take my own look-see. Is there anyone else besides you and Ozzie who worked back there?"

"Ozzie had a sort of lab assistant," said Draper. "A young

man he'd taken an interest in. Helped him, really. Fellow by the name of Bo Becker. I think Ozzie was hoping Bo might study for a degree as a diener."

"Get him in here," said Doogie.

When Sheriff Doogie, Deputy Halpern, and George Draper trooped back into the embalming room, Suzanne didn't hesitate to follow. Petra was a little more reluctant.

Doogie placed a black leather case on a rolling metal cart that normally held hemostats, dissecting scissors, and rib cutters.

As Doogie dug around inside his case, Suzanne asked, "Are you doing *CSI* stuff now?" She was feeling better. Not chipper, but definitely curious. And angry, too. After all, someone had tried to do her serious harm.

"Don't call it that," huffed Doogie. "Ever since that TV show, people put too much stock in all the whiz-bang assays and tests and electron microscope stuff. They don't realize it's good old legwork and deductive reasoning that really solves crimes."

"So what's your deductive reasoning on this?" Suzanne asked him.

"Just hold on," grunted Doogie. "First thing I want to do is take a careful look. You can learn a lot just through simple observation." He pulled a light from his case and untangled a long black cord.

"What's that?" asked Suzanne.

"UV black light," said Doogie. "These days, a county sheriff's got to be prepared for anything."

Suzanne had to agree. Kindred had been a sleepy small town for more years than she could remember. Now, like a bolt from the blue, they had a ripped-from-the-headlines type of murder on their hands.

"Kill the lights, will you?" Doogie instructed his deputy. The deputy, stumbling over his size-fourteen feet, hurried to comply.

Doogie flicked the switch on his SPEX Mini-CrimeScope 400, shone it on Ozzie's knees, then slowly ran it up the length of Ozzie's body. Everyone clustered behind Doogie, holding their breath. They weren't sure what Doogie was going to find, but they were watching his every motion with rapt attention.

"Anything?" asked the deputy. He sounded wistful, like he'd been purposely left out of the action.

Doogie continued to run the light across Ozzie's neck and up onto his face. Hesitating for a split second, Doogie ran the light in a circle, then his eyes widened and his jaw dropped onto his second chin. "Oh, horse pucky!" he exclaimed.

Don't Miss the Next
Scrapbooking Mystery

Fiber and Brimstone

It's a week before Halloween and Carmela is designing a giant puppet for the French Quarter's Monsters and Mayhem parade. But the murder of a Ponzi scheme partner sends her into investigation mode and takes her to the Ballet Dracula, a treasure hunt in a cemetery, and strange encounters with the mysterious Mr. Bones.

Watch for the Next
Cackleberry Club Mystery

Eggs Benedict Arnold

When Ozzie Driesden, Kindred's local mortician, ends up on his own slab, the ladies from the Cackleberry Club launch their own investigation. But as friends become suspects, one suspect turns traitor.

Don't Miss the New
Tea Shop Mystery

The Teaberry Strangler

A back alley candlelight tour ends in murder and sends Theodosia Browning, proprietor of Charleston's Indigo Tea Shop, seeking justice for a friend. But who stands to benefit from inheriting a map store, how are the ladies from Jardin Perfumerie involved, and why is a mysterious woman suddenly stalking her?

Find out more about the author
and her mysteries
at www.laurachilds.com.